twilight

STEPHENIE MEYER

Megan Tingley Books

LITTLE, BROWN AND COMPANY

New York   Boston

Little, Brown and Company

Hachette Book Group
237 Park Avenue, New York, NY 10017
Visit our Web site at www.lb-teens.com

Little, Brown and Company is a division of Hachette Book Group, Inc.
The Little, Brown name and logo are trademarks of Hachette Book Group, Inc.

First Media Tie-in Edition: October 2008
First published in hardcover in October 2005 by Little, Brown and Company

The characters and events portrayed in this book are fictitious. Any similarity to
real persons, living or dead, is coincidental and not intended by the author.

Library of Congress Cataloging-in-Publication Data

Meyer, Stephenie, 1973–
Twilight : a novel / by Stephenie Meyer. — 1st ed.
p. cm.
Summary: When seventeen-year-old Bella leaves Phoenix to live with her
father in Forks, Washington, she meets an exquisitely handsome boy at
school for whom she feels an overwhelming attraction and who she comes to
realize is not wholly human.

ISBN 978-0-316-03838-6
. [1. Vampires — Fiction. 2. High schools — Fiction. 3. Schools — Fiction. 4.
Washington (State) — Fiction.] I. Title.
PZ7.M57188Tw 2005
[Fic] — dc22   2004024730

10

RRD-C

Printed in the United States of America

For my big sister, Emily,
without whose enthusiasm this story might still be unfinished.

◄◄ ►►

CONTENTS

-+ +-

*B*ut of the tree of the knowledge of good and evil,
thou shalt not eat of it:
for in the day that thou eatest thereof
thou shalt surely die.

Genesis 2:17

PREFACE

I'D NEVER GIVEN MUCH THOUGHT TO HOW I WOULD die — though I'd had reason enough in the last few months — but even if I had, I would not have imagined it like this.

I stared without breathing across the long room, into the dark eyes of the hunter, and he looked pleasantly back at me.

Surely it was a good way to die, in the place of someone else, someone I loved. Noble, even. That ought to count for something.

I knew that if I'd never gone to Forks, I wouldn't be facing death now. But, terrified as I was, I couldn't bring myself to regret the decision. When life offers you a dream so far beyond any of your expectations, it's not reasonable to grieve when it comes to an end.

The hunter smiled in a friendly way as he sauntered forward to kill me.

1. FIRST SIGHT

MY MOTHER DROVE ME TO THE AIRPORT WITH THE windows rolled down. It was seventy-five degrees in Phoenix, the sky a perfect, cloudless blue. I was wearing my favorite shirt — sleeveless, white eyelet lace; I was wearing it as a farewell gesture. My carry-on item was a parka.

In the Olympic Peninsula of northwest Washington State, a small town named Forks exists under a near-constant cover of clouds. It rains on this inconsequential town more than any other place in the United States of America. It was from this town and its gloomy, omnipresent shade that my mother escaped with me when I was only a few months old. It was in this town that I'd been compelled to spend a month every summer until I was fourteen. That was the year I finally put my foot down; these past three summers, my dad, Charlie, vacationed with me in California for two weeks instead.

It was to Forks that I now exiled myself — an action that I took with great horror. I detested Forks.

I loved Phoenix. I loved the sun and the blistering heat. I loved the vigorous, sprawling city.

"Bella," my mom said to me — the last of a thousand times — before I got on the plane. "You don't have to do this."

My mom looks like me, except with short hair and laugh lines. I felt a spasm of panic as I stared at her wide, childlike eyes. How could I leave my loving, erratic, hare-brained mother to fend for herself? Of course she had Phil now, so the bills would probably get paid, there would be food in the refrigerator, gas in her car, and someone to call when she got lost, but still . . .

"I *want* to go," I lied. I'd always been a bad liar, but I'd been saying this lie so frequently lately that it sounded almost convincing now.

"Tell Charlie I said hi."

"I will."

"I'll see you soon," she insisted. "You can come home whenever you want — I'll come right back as soon as you need me."

But I could see the sacrifice in her eyes behind the promise.

"Don't worry about me," I urged. "It'll be great. I love you, Mom."

She hugged me tightly for a minute, and then I got on the plane, and she was gone.

It's a four-hour flight from Phoenix to Seattle, another hour in a small plane up to Port Angeles, and then an hour drive back down to Forks. Flying doesn't bother me; the hour in the car with Charlie, though, I was a little worried about.

Charlie had really been fairly nice about the whole thing. He seemed genuinely pleased that I was coming to live with him for the first time with any degree of permanence. He'd already gotten me registered for high school and was going to help me get a car.

But it was sure to be awkward with Charlie. Neither of us was what anyone would call verbose, and I didn't know what there was to say regardless. I knew he was more than a little confused by my decision — like my mother before me, I hadn't made a secret of my distaste for Forks.

When I landed in Port Angeles, it was raining. I didn't see it as an omen — just unavoidable. I'd already said my goodbyes to the sun.

Charlie was waiting for me with the cruiser. This I was expecting, too. Charlie is Police Chief Swan to the good people of Forks. My primary motivation behind buying a car, despite the scarcity of my funds, was that I refused to be driven around town in a car with red and blue lights on top. Nothing slows down traffic like a cop.

Charlie gave me an awkward, one-armed hug when I stumbled my way off the plane.

"It's good to see you, Bells," he said, smiling as he

automatically caught and steadied me. "You haven't changed much. How's Renée?"

"Mom's fine. It's good to see you, too, Dad." I wasn't allowed to call him Charlie to his face.

I had only a few bags. Most of my Arizona clothes were too permeable for Washington. My mom and I had pooled our resources to supplement my winter wardrobe, but it was still scanty. It all fit easily into the trunk of the cruiser.

"I found a good car for you, really cheap," he announced when we were strapped in.

"What kind of car?" I was suspicious of the way he said "good car for *you*" as opposed to just "good car."

"Well, it's a truck actually, a Chevy."

"Where did you find it?"

"Do you remember Billy Black down at La Push?" La Push is the tiny Indian reservation on the coast.

"No."

"He used to go fishing with us during the summer," Charlie prompted.

That would explain why I didn't remember him. I do a good job of blocking painful, unnecessary things from my memory.

"He's in a wheelchair now," Charlie continued when I didn't respond, "so he can't drive anymore, and he offered to sell me his truck cheap."

"What year is it?" I could see from his change of expression that this was the question he was hoping I wouldn't ask.

"Well, Billy's done a lot of work on the engine — it's only a few years old, really."

I hoped he didn't think so little of me as to believe I would give up that easily. "When did he buy it?"

"He bought it in 1984, I think."

"Did he buy it new?"

"Well, no. I think it was new in the early sixties — or late fifties at the earliest," he admitted sheepishly.

"Ch — Dad, I don't really know anything about cars. I wouldn't be able to fix it if anything went wrong, and I couldn't afford a mechanic. . . ."

"Really, Bella, the thing runs great. They don't build them like that anymore."

The thing, I thought to myself . . . it had possibilities — as a nickname, at the very least.

"How cheap is cheap?" After all, that was the part I couldn't compromise on.

"Well, honey, I kind of already bought it for you. As a homecoming gift." Charlie peeked sideways at me with a hopeful expression.

Wow. Free.

"You didn't need to do that, Dad. I was going to buy myself a car."

"I don't mind. I want you to be happy here." He was looking ahead at the road when he said this. Charlie wasn't comfortable with expressing his emotions out loud. I inherited that from him. So I was looking straight ahead as I responded.

"That's really nice, Dad. Thanks. I really appreciate it." No need to add that my being happy in Forks is an impossibility. He didn't need to suffer along with me. And I never looked a free truck in the mouth — or engine.

"Well, now, you're welcome," he mumbled, embarrassed by my thanks.

We exchanged a few more comments on the weather, which was wet, and that was pretty much it for conversation. We stared out the windows in silence.

It was beautiful, of course; I couldn't deny that. Everything was green: the trees, their trunks covered with moss, their branches hanging with a canopy of it, the ground covered with ferns. Even the air filtered down greenly through the leaves.

It was too green — an alien planet.

Eventually we made it to Charlie's. He still lived in the small, two-bedroom house that he'd bought with my mother in the early days of their marriage. Those were the only kind of days their marriage had — the early ones. There, parked on the street in front of the house that never changed, was my new — well, new to me — truck. It was a faded red color, with big, rounded fenders and a bulbous cab. To my intense surprise, I loved it. I didn't know if it would run, but I could see myself in it. Plus, it was one of those solid iron affairs that never gets damaged — the kind you see at the scene of an accident, paint unscratched, surrounded by the pieces of the foreign car it had destroyed.

"Wow, Dad, I love it! Thanks!" Now my horrific day tomorrow would be just that much less dreadful. I wouldn't be faced with the choice of either walking two miles in the rain to school or accepting a ride in the Chief's cruiser.

"I'm glad you like it," Charlie said gruffly, embarrassed again.

It took only one trip to get all my stuff upstairs. I got the west bedroom that faced out over the front yard. The room was familiar; it had belonged to me since I was born. The wooden floor, the light blue walls, the peaked ceiling, the yellowed lace curtains around the window — these were all a part of my childhood. The only changes Charlie had ever made were switching the crib for a bed and adding a desk as I grew. The desk now held a second-hand computer, with the phone line for the modem stapled along the floor to the nearest phone jack. This was a stipulation from my mother, so that we could stay in touch easily. The rocking chair from my baby days was still in the corner.

There was only one small bathroom at the top of the stairs, which I would have to share with Charlie. I was trying not to dwell too much on that fact.

One of the best things about Charlie is he doesn't hover. He left me alone to unpack and get settled, a feat that would have been altogether impossible for my mother. It was nice to be alone, not to have to smile and look pleased; a relief to stare dejectedly out the window at the sheeting rain and let just a few tears escape. I wasn't in the mood to go on a real crying jag. I would save that for bedtime, when I would have to think about the coming morning.

Forks High School had a frightening total of only three hundred and fifty-seven — now fifty-eight — students; there were more than seven hundred people in my junior class alone back home. All of the kids here had grown up together — their grandparents had been toddlers together.

I would be the new girl from the big city, a curiosity, a freak.

Maybe, if I looked like a girl from Phoenix should, I could work this to my advantage. But physically, I'd never fit in anywhere. I *should* be tan, sporty, blond — a volleyball player, or a cheerleader, perhaps — all the things that go with living in the valley of the sun.

Instead, I was ivory-skinned, without even the excuse of blue eyes or red hair, despite the constant sunshine. I had always been slender, but soft somehow, obviously not an athlete; I didn't have the necessary hand-eye coordination to play sports without humiliating myself — and harming both myself and anyone else who stood too close.

When I finished putting my clothes in the old pine dresser, I took my bag of bathroom necessities and went to the communal bathroom to clean myself up after the day of travel. I looked at my face in the mirror as I brushed through my tangled, damp hair. Maybe it was the light, but already I looked sallower, unhealthy. My skin could be pretty — it was very clear, almost translucent-looking — but it all depended on color. I had no color here.

Facing my pallid reflection in the mirror, I was forced to admit that I was lying to myself. It wasn't just physically that I'd never fit in. And if I couldn't find a niche in a school with three thousand people, what were my chances here?

I didn't relate well to people my age. Maybe the truth was that I didn't relate well to people, period. Even my mother, who I was closer to than anyone else on the planet, was never in harmony with me, never on exactly the same page. Sometimes I wondered if I was seeing the same things through my eyes that the rest of the world was seeing through theirs. Maybe there was a glitch in my brain.

But the cause didn't matter. All that mattered was the effect. And tomorrow would be just the beginning.

I didn't sleep well that night, even after I was done crying. The constant *whoosh*ing of the rain and wind across the roof wouldn't fade into the background. I pulled the faded old quilt over my head, and later added the pillow, too. But I couldn't fall asleep until after midnight, when the rain finally settled into a quieter drizzle.

Thick fog was all I could see out my window in the morning, and I could feel the claustrophobia creeping up on me. You could never see the sky here; it was like a cage.

Breakfast with Charlie was a quiet event. He wished me good luck at school. I thanked him, knowing his hope was wasted. Good luck tended to avoid me. Charlie left first, off to the police station that was his wife and family. After he left, I sat at the old square oak table in one of the three unmatching chairs and examined his small kitchen, with its dark paneled walls, bright yellow cabinets, and white linoleum floor. Nothing was changed. My mother had painted the cabinets eighteen years ago in an attempt to bring some sunshine into the house. Over the small fireplace in the adjoining handkerchief-sized family room was a row of pictures. First a wedding picture of Charlie and my mom in Las Vegas, then one of the three of us in the hospital after I was born, taken by a helpful nurse, followed by the procession of my school pictures up to last year's. Those were embarrassing to look at — I would have to see what I could do to get Charlie to put them somewhere else, at least while I was living here.

It was impossible, being in this house, not to realize that Charlie had never gotten over my mom. It made me uncomfortable.

I didn't want to be too early to school, but I couldn't stay in the house anymore. I donned my jacket — which had the feel of a biohazard suit — and headed out into the rain.

It was just drizzling still, not enough to soak me through immediately as I reached for the house key that was always hidden under the eaves by the door, and locked up. The sloshing of my new waterproof boots was unnerving. I missed the normal crunch of gravel as I walked. I couldn't pause and admire my truck again as I wanted; I was in a hurry to get out of the misty wet that swirled around my head and clung to my hair under my hood.

Inside the truck, it was nice and dry. Either Billy or Charlie had obviously cleaned it up, but the tan upholstered seats still smelled faintly of tobacco, gasoline, and peppermint. The engine started quickly, to my relief, but loudly, roaring to life and then idling at top volume. Well, a truck this old was bound to have a flaw. The antique radio worked, a plus that I hadn't expected.

Finding the school wasn't difficult, though I'd never been there before. The school was, like most other things, just off the highway. It was not obvious that it was a school; only the sign, which declared it to be the Forks High School, made me stop. It looked like a collection of matching houses, built with maroon-colored bricks. There were so many trees and shrubs I couldn't see its size at first. Where was the feel of the institution? I wondered nostalgically. Where were the chain-link fences, the metal detectors?

I parked in front of the first building, which had a small sign over the door reading FRONT OFFICE. No one else was parked there, so I was sure it was off limits, but I decided I would get directions inside instead of circling around in the rain like an idiot. I stepped unwillingly out of the toasty truck cab and walked down a little stone path lined with dark hedges. I took a deep breath before opening the door.

Inside, it was brightly lit, and warmer than I'd hoped. The office was small; a little waiting area with padded folding chairs, orange-flecked commercial carpet, notices and awards cluttering the walls, a big clock ticking loudly. Plants grew everywhere in large plastic pots, as if there wasn't enough greenery outside. The room was cut in half by a long counter, cluttered with wire baskets full of papers and brightly colored flyers taped to its front. There were three desks behind the counter, one of which was manned by a large, red-haired woman wearing glasses. She was wearing a purple t-shirt, which immediately made me feel overdressed.

The red-haired woman looked up. "Can I help you?"

"I'm Isabella Swan," I informed her, and saw the immediate awareness light her eyes. I was expected, a topic of gossip no doubt. Daughter of the Chief's flighty ex-wife, come home at last.

"Of course," she said. She dug through a precariously stacked pile of documents on her desk till she found the ones she was looking for. "I have your schedule right here, and a map of the school." She brought several sheets to the counter to show me.

She went through my classes for me, highlighting the best route to each on the map, and gave me a slip to have each teacher sign, which I was to bring back at the end of the day. She smiled at me and hoped, like Charlie, that I would like it here in Forks. I smiled back as convincingly as I could.

When I went back out to my truck, other students were starting to arrive. I drove around the school, following the line of traffic. I was glad to see that most of the cars were older like mine, nothing flashy. At home I'd lived in one of the few lower-income neighborhoods that were included in the Paradise Valley District. It was a common thing to see a new Mercedes or Porsche in the student lot. The nicest car here was a shiny Volvo, and it stood out. Still, I cut the engine as soon as I was in a spot, so that the thunderous volume wouldn't draw attention to me.

I looked at the map in the truck, trying to memorize it now; hopefully I wouldn't have to walk around with it stuck in front of my nose all day. I stuffed everything in my bag, slung the strap over my shoulder, and sucked in a huge breath. I can do this, I lied to myself feebly. No one was going to bite me. I finally exhaled and stepped out of the truck.

I kept my face pulled back into my hood as I walked to

the sidewalk, crowded with teenagers. My plain black jacket didn't stand out, I noticed with relief.

Once I got around the cafeteria, building three was easy to spot. A large black "3" was painted on a white square on the east corner. I felt my breathing gradually creeping toward hyperventilation as I approached the door. I tried holding my breath as I followed two unisex raincoats through the door.

The classroom was small. The people in front of me stopped just inside the door to hang up their coats on a long row of hooks. I copied them. They were two girls, one a porcelain-colored blonde, the other also pale, with light brown hair. At least my skin wouldn't be a stand-out here.

I took the slip up to the teacher, a tall, balding man whose desk had a nameplate identifying him as Mr. Mason. He gawked at me when he saw my name — not an encouraging response — and of course I flushed tomato red. But at least he sent me to an empty desk at the back without introducing me to the class. It was harder for my new classmates to stare at me in the back, but somehow, they managed. I kept my eyes down on the reading list the teacher had given me. It was fairly basic: Brontë, Shakespeare, Chaucer, Faulkner. I'd already read everything. That was comforting . . . and boring. I wondered if my mom would send me my folder of old essays, or if she would think that was cheating. I went through different arguments with her in my head while the teacher droned on.

When the bell rang, a nasal buzzing sound, a gangly

boy with skin problems and hair black as an oil slick leaned across the aisle to talk to me.

"You're Isabella Swan, aren't you?" He looked like the overly helpful, chess club type.

"Bella," I corrected. Everyone within a three-seat radius turned to look at me.

"Where's your next class?" he asked.

I had to check in my bag. "Um, Government, with Jefferson, in building six."

There was nowhere to look without meeting curious eyes.

"I'm headed toward building four, I could show you the way. . . ." Definitely over-helpful. "I'm Eric," he added.

I smiled tentatively. "Thanks."

We got our jackets and headed out into the rain, which had picked up. I could have sworn several people behind us were walking close enough to eavesdrop. I hoped I wasn't getting paranoid.

"So, this is a lot different than Phoenix, huh?" he asked.

"Very."

"It doesn't rain much there, does it?"

"Three or four times a year."

"Wow, what must that be like?" he wondered.

"Sunny," I told him.

"You don't look very tan."

"My mother is part albino."

He studied my face apprehensively, and I sighed. It looked like clouds and a sense of humor didn't mix. A few months of this and I'd forget how to use sarcasm.

We walked back around the cafeteria, to the south

buildings by the gym. Eric walked me right to the door, though it was clearly marked.

"Well, good luck," he said as I touched the handle. "Maybe we'll have some other classes together." He sounded hopeful.

I smiled at him vaguely and went inside.

The rest of the morning passed in about the same fashion. My Trigonometry teacher, Mr. Varner, who I would have hated anyway just because of the subject he taught, was the only one who made me stand in front of the class and introduce myself. I stammered, blushed, and tripped over my own boots on the way to my seat.

After two classes, I started to recognize several of the faces in each class. There was always someone braver than the others who would introduce themselves and ask me questions about how I was liking Forks. I tried to be diplomatic, but mostly I just lied a lot. At least I never needed the map.

One girl sat next to me in both Trig and Spanish, and she walked with me to the cafeteria for lunch. She was tiny, several inches shorter than my five feet four inches, but her wildly curly dark hair made up a lot of the difference between our heights. I couldn't remember her name, so I smiled and nodded as she prattled about teachers and classes. I didn't try to keep up.

We sat at the end of a full table with several of her friends, who she introduced to me. I forgot all their names as soon as she spoke them. They seemed impressed by her bravery in speaking to me. The boy from English, Eric, waved at me from across the room.

It was there, sitting in the lunchroom, trying to make conversation with seven curious strangers, that I first saw them.

They were sitting in the corner of the cafeteria, as far away from where I sat as possible in the long room. There were five of them. They weren't talking, and they weren't eating, though they each had a tray of untouched food in front of them. They weren't gawking at me, unlike most of the other students, so it was safe to stare at them without fear of meeting an excessively interested pair of eyes. But it was none of these things that caught, and held, my attention.

They didn't look anything alike. Of the three boys, one was big — muscled like a serious weight lifter, with dark, curly hair. Another was taller, leaner, but still muscular, and honey blond. The last was lanky, less bulky, with untidy, bronze-colored hair. He was more boyish than the others, who looked like they could be in college, or even teachers here rather than students.

The girls were opposites. The tall one was statuesque. She had a beautiful figure, the kind you saw on the cover of the *Sports Illustrated* swimsuit issue, the kind that made every girl around her take a hit on her self-esteem just by being in the same room. Her hair was golden, gently waving to the middle of her back. The short girl was pixielike, thin in the extreme, with small features. Her hair was a deep black, cropped short and pointing in every direction.

And yet, they were all exactly alike. Every one of them was chalky pale, the palest of all the students living in this sunless town. Paler than me, the albino. They all had very dark eyes despite the range in hair tones. They also had dark shadows under those eyes — purplish, bruise-like shadows. As if they were all suffering from a sleepless night, or almost done recovering from a broken nose. Though their noses, all their features, were straight, perfect, angular.

But all this is not why I couldn't look away.

I stared because their faces, so different, so similar, were all devastatingly, inhumanly beautiful. They were faces you never expected to see except perhaps on the airbrushed pages of a fashion magazine. Or painted by an old master as the face of an angel. It was hard to decide who was the most beautiful — maybe the perfect blond girl, or the bronze-haired boy.

They were all looking away — away from each other, away from the other students, away from anything in particular as far as I could tell. As I watched, the small girl rose with her tray — unopened soda, unbitten apple — and walked away with a quick, graceful lope that belonged on a runway. I watched, amazed at her lithe dancer's step, till she dumped her tray and glided through the back door, faster than I would have thought possible. My eyes darted back to the others, who sat unchanging.

"Who are *they*?" I asked the girl from my Spanish class, whose name I'd forgotten.

As she looked up to see who I meant — though already knowing, probably, from my tone — suddenly he looked at her, the thinner one, the boyish one, the youngest, perhaps. He looked at my neighbor for just a fraction of a second, and then his dark eyes flickered to mine.

He looked away quickly, more quickly than I could, though in a flush of embarrassment I dropped my eyes at once. In that brief flash of a glance, his face held nothing of interest — it was as if she had called his name, and he'd looked up in involuntary response, already having decided not to answer.

My neighbor giggled in embarrassment, looking at the table like I did.

"That's Edward and Emmett Cullen, and Rosalie and Jasper Hale. The one who left was Alice Cullen; they all live together with Dr. Cullen and his wife." She said this under her breath.

I glanced sideways at the beautiful boy, who was looking at his tray now, picking a bagel to pieces with long, pale fingers. His mouth was moving very quickly, his perfect lips barely opening. The other three still looked away, and yet I felt he was speaking quietly to them.

Strange, unpopular names, I thought. The kinds of names grandparents had. But maybe that was in vogue here — small town names? I finally remembered that my neighbor was called Jessica, a perfectly common name. There were two girls named Jessica in my History class back home.

"They are . . . very nice-looking." I struggled with the conspicuous understatement.

"Yes!" Jessica agreed with another giggle. "They're all *together* though — Emmett and Rosalie, and Jasper and Alice, I mean. And they *live* together." Her voice held all the shock and condemnation of the small town, I thought critically. But, if I was being honest, I had to admit that even in Phoenix, it would cause gossip.

"Which ones are the Cullens?" I asked. "They don't look related. . . ."

"Oh, they're not. Dr. Cullen is really young, in his twenties or early thirties. They're all adopted. The Hales *are* brother and sister, twins — the blondes — and they're foster children."

"They look a little old for foster children."

"They are now, Jasper and Rosalie are both eighteen, but they've been with Mrs. Cullen since they were eight. She's their aunt or something like that."

"That's really kind of nice — for them to take care of all those kids like that, when they're so young and everything."

"I guess so," Jessica admitted reluctantly, and I got the impression that she didn't like the doctor and his wife for some reason. With the glances she was throwing at their adopted children, I would presume the reason was jealousy. "I think that Mrs. Cullen can't have any kids, though," she added, as if that lessened their kindness.

Throughout all this conversation, my eyes flickered again and again to the table where the strange family sat. They continued to look at the walls and not eat.

"Have they always lived in Forks?" I asked. Surely I would have noticed them on one of my summers here.

"No," she said in a voice that implied it should be obvious, even to a new arrival like me. "They just moved down two years ago from somewhere in Alaska."

I felt a surge of pity, and relief. Pity because, as beautiful as they were, they were outsiders, clearly not accepted. Relief that I wasn't the only newcomer here, and certainly not the most interesting by any standard.

As I examined them, the youngest, one of the Cullens, looked up and met my gaze, this time with evident curiosity in his expression. As I looked swiftly away, it seemed to me that his glance held some kind of unmet expectation.

"Which one is the boy with the reddish brown hair?" I asked. I peeked at him from the corner of my eye, and he was still staring at me, but not gawking like the other students had today — he had a slightly frustrated expression. I looked down again.

"That's Edward. He's gorgeous, of course, but don't waste your time. He doesn't date. Apparently none of the girls here are good-looking enough for him." She sniffed, a clear case of sour grapes. I wondered when he'd turned her down.

I bit my lip to hide my smile. Then I glanced at him again. His face was turned away, but I thought his cheek appeared lifted, as if he were smiling, too.

After a few more minutes, the four of them left the table together. They all were noticeably graceful — even the big, brawny one. It was unsettling to watch. The one named Edward didn't look at me again.

I sat at the table with Jessica and her friends longer than I would have if I'd been sitting alone. I was anxious not to be late for class on my first day. One of my new acquaintances, who considerately reminded me that her name was Angela, had Biology II with me the next hour. We walked to class together in silence. She was shy, too.

When we entered the classroom, Angela went to sit at a black-topped lab table exactly like the ones I was used to. She already had a neighbor. In fact, all the tables were filled but one. Next to the center aisle, I recognized Edward Cullen by his unusual hair, sitting next to that single open seat.

As I walked down the aisle to introduce myself to the teacher and get my slip signed, I was watching him surreptitiously. Just as I passed, he suddenly went rigid in his seat. He stared at me again, meeting my eyes with the strangest expression on his face — it was hostile, furious. I looked away quickly, shocked, going red again. I stumbled over a book in the walkway and had to catch myself on the edge of a table. The girl sitting there giggled.

I'd noticed that his eyes were black — coal black.

Mr. Banner signed my slip and handed me a book with no nonsense about introductions. I could tell we were going to get along. Of course, he had no choice but to send me to the one open seat in the middle of the room. I kept my eyes down as I went to sit by *him,* bewildered by the antagonistic stare he'd given me.

I didn't look up as I set my book on the table and took my seat, but I saw his posture change from the corner of my eye. He was leaning away from me, sitting on the extreme edge of his chair and averting his face like he smelled something bad. Inconspicuously, I sniffed my hair. It smelled like strawberries, the scent of my favorite shampoo. It seemed an innocent enough odor. I let my hair fall over my right shoulder, making a dark curtain between us, and tried to pay attention to the teacher.

Unfortunately the lecture was on cellular anatomy, something I'd already studied. I took notes carefully anyway, always looking down.

I couldn't stop myself from peeking occasionally through the screen of my hair at the strange boy next to me. During the whole class, he never relaxed his stiff position on the edge of his chair, sitting as far from me as possible. I could see his hand on his left leg was clenched into a fist, tendons standing out under his pale skin. This, too, he never relaxed. He had the long sleeves of his white shirt pushed up to his elbows, and his forearm was surprisingly hard and muscular beneath his light skin. He wasn't nearly as slight as he'd looked next to his burly brother.

The class seemed to drag on longer than the others. Was it because the day was finally coming to a close, or because I was waiting for his tight fist to loosen? It never did; he continued to sit so still it looked like he wasn't breathing. What was wrong with him? Was this his normal behavior? I questioned my judgment on Jessica's bitterness at lunch today. Maybe she was not as resentful as I'd thought.

It couldn't have anything to do with me. He didn't know me from Eve.

I peeked up at him one more time, and regretted it. He was glaring down at me again, his black eyes full of revulsion. As I flinched away from him, shrinking against my chair, the phrase *if looks could kill* suddenly ran through my mind.

At that moment, the bell rang loudly, making me jump, and Edward Cullen was out of his seat. Fluidly he rose — he was much taller than I'd thought — his back to me, and he was out the door before anyone else was out of their seat.

I sat frozen in my seat, staring blankly after him. He was so mean. It wasn't fair. I began gathering up my things slowly, trying to block the anger that filled me, for fear my eyes would tear up. For some reason, my temper was hardwired to my tear ducts. I usually cried when I was angry, a humiliating tendency.

"Aren't you Isabella Swan?" a male voice asked.

I looked up to see a cute, baby-faced boy, his pale blond hair carefully gelled into orderly spikes, smiling at me in a friendly way. He obviously didn't think I smelled bad.

"Bella," I corrected him, with a smile.

"I'm Mike."

"Hi, Mike."

"Do you need any help finding your next class?"

"I'm headed to the gym, actually. I think I can find it."

"That's my next class, too." He seemed thrilled, though it wasn't that big of a coincidence in a school this small.

We walked to class together; he was a chatterer — he supplied most of the conversation, which made it easy for me. He'd lived in California till he was ten, so he knew how I felt about the sun. It turned out he was in my English class also. He was the nicest person I'd met today.

But as we were entering the gym, he asked, "So, did you stab Edward Cullen with a pencil or what? I've never seen him act like that."

I cringed. So I wasn't the only one who had noticed. And, apparently, that *wasn't* Edward Cullen's usual behavior. I decided to play dumb.

"Was that the boy I sat next to in Biology?" I asked artlessly.

"Yes," he said. "He looked like he was in pain or something."

"I don't know," I responded. "I never spoke to him."

"He's a weird guy." Mike lingered by me instead of heading to the dressing room. "If I were lucky enough to sit by you, I would have talked to you."

I smiled at him before walking through the girls' locker room door. He was friendly and clearly admiring. But it wasn't enough to ease my irritation.

The Gym teacher, Coach Clapp, found me a uniform but didn't make me dress down for today's class. At home, only two years of P.E. were required. Here, P.E. was mandatory all four years. Forks was literally my personal hell on Earth.

I watched four volleyball games running simultaneously. Remembering how many injuries I had sustained — and inflicted — playing volleyball, I felt faintly nauseated.

The final bell rang at last. I walked slowly to the office to return my paperwork. The rain had drifted away, but the wind was strong, and colder. I wrapped my arms around myself.

When I walked into the warm office, I almost turned around and walked back out.

Edward Cullen stood at the desk in front of me. I recognized again that tousled bronze hair. He didn't appear to notice the sound of my entrance. I stood pressed against the back wall, waiting for the receptionist to be free.

He was arguing with her in a low, attractive voice. I quickly picked up the gist of the argument. He was trying to trade from sixth-hour Biology to another time — any other time.

I just couldn't believe that this was about me. It had to be something else, something that happened before I entered the Biology room. The look on his face must have been about another aggravation entirely. It was impossible that this stranger could take such a sudden, intense dislike to me.

The door opened again, and the cold wind suddenly gusted through the room, rustling the papers on the desk, swirling my hair around my face. The girl who came in merely stepped to the desk, placed a note in the wire basket, and walked out again. But Edward Cullen's back stiffened, and he turned slowly to glare at me — his face was absurdly handsome — with piercing, hate-filled eyes. For an instant, I felt a thrill of genuine fear, raising the hair on my arms. The look only lasted a second, but it chilled me more than the freezing wind. He turned back to the receptionist.

"Never mind, then," he said hastily in a voice like velvet. "I can see that it's impossible. Thank you so much for your help." And he turned on his heel without another look at me, and disappeared out the door.

I went meekly to the desk, my face white for once instead of red, and handed her the signed slip.

"How did your first day go, dear?" the receptionist asked maternally.

"Fine," I lied, my voice weak. She didn't look convinced.

When I got to the truck, it was almost the last car in the lot. It seemed like a haven, already the closest thing to home I had in this damp green hole. I sat inside for a while, just staring out the windshield blankly. But soon I was cold enough to need the heater, so I turned the key and the engine roared to life. I headed back to Charlie's house, fighting tears the whole way there.

2. OPEN BOOK

THE NEXT DAY WAS BETTER . . . AND WORSE.

It was better because it wasn't raining yet, though the clouds were dense and opaque. It was easier because I knew what to expect of my day. Mike came to sit by me in English, and walked me to my next class, with Chess Club Eric glaring at him all the while; that was flattering. People didn't look at me quite as much as they had yesterday. I sat with a big group at lunch that included Mike, Eric, Jessica, and several other people whose names and faces I now remembered. I began to feel like I was treading water, instead of drowning in it.

It was worse because I was tired; I still couldn't sleep with the wind echoing around the house. It was worse because Mr. Varner called on me in Trig when my hand wasn't raised and I had the wrong answer. It was miserable because I had to play volleyball, and the one time I didn't cringe out of the way of the ball, I hit my teammate in the head with it. And it was worse because Edward Cullen wasn't in school at all.

All morning I was dreading lunch, fearing his bizarre glares. Part of me wanted to confront him and demand to know what his problem was. While I was lying sleepless in my bed, I even imagined what I would say. But I knew myself too well to think I would really have the guts to do it. I made the Cowardly Lion look like the terminator.

But when I walked into the cafeteria with Jessica — trying to keep my eyes from sweeping the place for him, and failing entirely — I saw that his four siblings of sorts were sitting together at the same table, and he was not with them.

Mike intercepted us and steered us to his table. Jessica seemed elated by the attention, and her friends quickly joined us. But as I tried to listen to their easy chatter, I was terribly uncomfortable, waiting nervously for the moment he would arrive. I hoped that he would simply ignore me when he came, and prove my suspicions false.

He didn't come, and as time passed I grew more and more tense.

I walked to Biology with more confidence when, by the end of lunch, he still hadn't showed. Mike, who was taking on the qualities of a golden retriever, walked faithfully by my side to class. I held my breath at the door, but

Edward Cullen wasn't there, either. I exhaled and went to my seat. Mike followed, talking about an upcoming trip to the beach. He lingered by my desk till the bell rang. Then he smiled at me wistfully and went to sit by a girl with braces and a bad perm. It looked like I was going to have to do something about Mike, and it wouldn't be easy. In a town like this, where everyone lived on top of everyone else, diplomacy was essential. I had never been enormously tactful; I had no practice dealing with overly friendly boys.

I was relieved that I had the desk to myself, that Edward was absent. I told myself that repeatedly. But I couldn't get rid of the nagging suspicion that I was the reason he wasn't there. It was ridiculous, and egotistical, to think that I could affect anyone that strongly. It was impossible. And yet I couldn't stop worrying that it was true.

When the school day was finally done, and the blush was fading out of my cheeks from the volleyball incident, I changed quickly back into my jeans and navy blue sweater. I hurried from the girls' locker room, pleased to find that I had successfully evaded my retriever friend for the moment. I walked swiftly out to the parking lot. It was crowded now with fleeing students. I got in my truck and dug through my bag to make sure I had what I needed.

Last night I'd discovered that Charlie couldn't cook much besides fried eggs and bacon. So I requested that I be assigned kitchen detail for the duration of my stay. He was willing enough to hand over the keys to the banquet hall. I also found out that he had no food in the house. So

I had my shopping list and the cash from the jar in the cupboard labeled FOOD MONEY, and I was on my way to the Thriftway.

I gunned my deafening engine to life, ignoring the heads that turned in my direction, and backed carefully into a place in the line of cars that were waiting to exit the parking lot. As I waited, trying to pretend that the earsplitting rumble was coming from someone else's car, I saw the two Cullens and the Hale twins getting into their car. It was the shiny new Volvo. Of course. I hadn't noticed their clothes before — I'd been too mesmerized by their faces. Now that I looked, it was obvious that they were all dressed exceptionally well; simply, but in clothes that subtly hinted at designer origins. With their remarkable good looks, the style with which they carried themselves, they could have worn dishrags and pulled it off. It seemed excessive for them to have both looks and money. But as far as I could tell, life worked that way most of the time. It didn't look as if it bought them any acceptance here.

No, I didn't fully believe that. The isolation must be their desire; I couldn't imagine any door that wouldn't be opened by that degree of beauty.

They looked at my noisy truck as I passed them, just like everyone else. I kept my eyes straight forward and was relieved when I finally was free of the school grounds.

The Thriftway was not far from the school, just a few streets south, off the highway. It was nice to be inside the supermarket; it felt normal. I did the shopping at home, and I fell into the pattern of the familiar task gladly. The store was big enough inside that I couldn't hear the tapping of the rain on the roof to remind me where I was.

When I got home, I unloaded all the groceries, stuffing them in wherever I could find an open space. I hoped Charlie wouldn't mind. I wrapped potatoes in foil and stuck them in the oven to bake, covered a steak in marinade and balanced it on top of a carton of eggs in the fridge.

When I was finished with that, I took my book bag upstairs. Before starting my homework, I changed into a pair of dry sweats, pulled my damp hair up into a ponytail, and checked my e-mail for the first time. I had three messages.

"Bella," my mom wrote . . .

Write me as soon as you get in. Tell me how your flight was. Is it raining? I miss you already. I'm almost finished packing for Florida, but I can't find my pink blouse. Do you know where I put it? Phil says hi. Mom.

I sighed and went to the next. It was sent eight hours after the first.

"Bella," she wrote . . .

Why haven't you e-mailed me yet? What are you waiting for? Mom.

The last was from this morning.

Isabella,
If I haven't heard from you by 5:30 p.m. today I'm calling Charlie.

I checked the clock. I still had an hour, but my mom
was well known for jumping the gun.

Mom,
Calm down. I'm writing right now. Don't do
anything rash.
    Bella.

I sent that, and began again.

Mom,
Everything is great. Of course it's raining.
I was waiting for something to write about.
School isn't bad, just a little repetitive.
I met some nice kids who sit by me at lunch.
    Your blouse is at the dry cleaners — you
were supposed to pick it up Friday.
    Charlie bought me a truck, can you be-
lieve it? I love it. It's old, but really
sturdy, which is good, you know, for me.
    I miss you, too. I'll write again soon,
but I'm not going to check my e-mail every
five minutes. Relax, breathe. I love you.
    Bella.

I had decided to read *Wuthering Heights* — the novel we
were currently studying in English — yet again for the

fun of it, and that's what I was doing when Charlie came home. I'd lost track of the time, and I hurried downstairs to take the potatoes out and put the steak in to broil.

"Bella?" my father called out when he heard me on the stairs.

Who else? I thought to myself.

"Hey, Dad, welcome home."

"Thanks." He hung up his gun belt and stepped out of his boots as I bustled about the kitchen. As far as I was aware, he'd never shot the gun on the job. But he kept it ready. When I came here as a child, he would always remove the bullets as soon as he walked in the door. I guess he considered me old enough now not to shoot myself by accident, and not depressed enough to shoot myself on purpose.

"What's for dinner?" he asked warily. My mother was an imaginative cook, and her experiments weren't always edible. I was surprised, and sad, that he seemed to remember that far back.

"Steak and potatoes," I answered, and he looked relieved.

He seemed to feel awkward standing in the kitchen doing nothing; he lumbered into the living room to watch TV while I worked. We were both more comfortable that way. I made a salad while the steaks cooked, and set the table.

I called him in when dinner was ready, and he sniffed appreciatively as he walked into the room.

"Smells good, Bell."

"Thanks."

We ate in silence for a few minutes. It wasn't uncomfortable. Neither of us was bothered by the quiet. In some ways, we were well suited for living together.

"So, how did you like school? Have you made any friends?" he asked as he was taking seconds.

"Well, I have a few classes with a girl named Jessica. I sit with her friends at lunch. And there's this boy, Mike, who's very friendly. Everybody seems pretty nice." With one outstanding exception.

"That must be Mike Newton. Nice kid — nice family. His dad owns the sporting goods store just outside of town. He makes a good living off all the backpackers who come through here."

"Do you know the Cullen family?" I asked hesitantly.

"Dr. Cullen's family? Sure. Dr. Cullen's a great man."

"They . . . the kids . . . are a little different. They don't seem to fit in very well at school."

Charlie surprised me by looking angry.

"People in this town," he muttered. "Dr. Cullen is a brilliant surgeon who could probably work in any hospital in the world, make ten times the salary he gets here," he continued, getting louder. "We're lucky to have him — lucky that his wife wanted to live in a small town. He's an asset to the community, and all of those kids are well behaved and polite. I had my doubts, when they first moved in, with all those adopted teenagers. I thought we might have some problems with them. But they're all very mature — I haven't had one speck of trouble from any of them. That's more than I can say for the children of some folks who have lived in this town for generations. And they stick together the way a family should — camping trips every other weekend. . . . Just because they're newcomers, people have to talk."

It was the longest speech I'd ever heard Charlie make. He must feel strongly about whatever people were saying.

I backpedaled. "They seemed nice enough to me. I just noticed they kept to themselves. They're all very attractive," I added, trying to be more complimentary.

"You should see the doctor," Charlie said, laughing. "It's a good thing he's happily married. A lot of the nurses at the hospital have a hard time concentrating on their work with him around."

We lapsed back into silence as we finished eating. He cleared the table while I started on the dishes. He went back to the TV, and after I finished washing the dishes by hand — no dishwasher — I went upstairs unwillingly to work on my math homework. I could feel a tradition in the making.

That night it was finally quiet. I fell asleep quickly, exhausted.

The rest of the week was uneventful. I got used to the routine of my classes. By Friday I was able to recognize, if not name, almost all the students at school. In Gym, the kids on my team learned not to pass me the ball and to step quickly in front of me if the other team tried to take advantage of my weakness. I happily stayed out of their way.

Edward Cullen didn't come back to school.

Every day, I watched anxiously until the rest of the

Cullens entered the cafeteria without him. Then I could relax and join in the lunchtime conversation. Mostly it centered around a trip to the La Push Ocean Park in two weeks that Mike was putting together. I was invited, and I had agreed to go, more out of politeness than desire. Beaches should be hot and dry.

By Friday I was perfectly comfortable entering my Biology class, no longer worried that Edward would be there. For all I knew, he had dropped out of school. I tried not to think about him, but I couldn't totally suppress the worry that I was responsible for his continued absence, ridiculous as it seemed.

My first weekend in Forks passed without incident. Charlie, unused to spending time in the usually empty house, worked most of the weekend. I cleaned the house, got ahead on my homework, and wrote my mom more bogusly cheerful e-mail. I did drive to the library Saturday, but it was so poorly stocked that I didn't bother to get a card; I would have to make a date to visit Olympia or Seattle soon and find a good bookstore. I wondered idly what kind of gas mileage the truck got . . . and shuddered at the thought.

The rain stayed soft over the weekend, quiet, so I was able to sleep well.

People greeted me in the parking lot Monday morning. I didn't know all their names, but I waved back and smiled at everyone. It was colder this morning, but happily not raining. In English, Mike took his accustomed seat by my side. We had a pop quiz on *Wuthering Heights*. It was straightforward, very easy.

All in all, I was feeling a lot more comfortable than I had thought I would feel by this point. More comfortable than I had ever expected to feel here.

When we walked out of class, the air was full of swirling bits of white. I could hear people shouting excitedly to each other. The wind bit at my cheeks, my nose.

"Wow," Mike said. "It's snowing."

I looked at the little cotton fluffs that were building up along the sidewalk and swirling erratically past my face.

"Ew." Snow. There went my good day.

He looked surprised. "Don't you like snow?"

"No. That means it's too cold for rain." Obviously. "Besides, I thought it was supposed to come down in flakes — you know, each one unique and all that. These just look like the ends of Q-tips."

"Haven't you ever seen snow fall before?" he asked incredulously.

"Sure I have." I paused. "On TV."

Mike laughed. And then a big, squishy ball of dripping snow smacked into the back of his head. We both turned to see where it came from. I had my suspicions about Eric, who was walking away, his back toward us — in the wrong direction for his next class. Mike apparently had the same notion. He bent over and began scraping together a pile of the white mush.

"I'll see you at lunch, okay?" I kept walking as I spoke. "Once people start throwing wet stuff, I go inside."

He just nodded, his eyes on Eric's retreating figure.

Throughout the morning, everyone chattered excitedly

about the snow; apparently it was the first snowfall of the new year. I kept my mouth shut. Sure, it was drier than rain — until it melted in your socks.

I walked alertly to the cafeteria with Jessica after Spanish. Mush balls were flying everywhere. I kept a binder in my hands, ready to use it as a shield if necessary. Jessica thought I was hilarious, but something in my expression kept her from lobbing a snowball at me herself.

Mike caught up to us as we walked in the doors, laughing, with ice melting the spikes in his hair. He and Jessica were talking animatedly about the snow fight as we got in line to buy food. I glanced toward that table in the corner out of habit. And then I froze where I stood. There were five people at the table.

Jessica pulled on my arm.

"Hello? Bella? What do you want?"

I looked down; my ears were hot. I had no reason to feel self-conscious, I reminded myself. I hadn't done anything wrong.

"What's with Bella?" Mike asked Jessica.

"Nothing," I answered. "I'll just get a soda today." I caught up to the end of the line.

"Aren't you hungry?" Jessica asked.

"Actually, I feel a little sick," I said, my eyes still on the floor.

I waited for them to get their food, and then followed them to a table, my eyes on my feet.

I sipped my soda slowly, my stomach churning. Twice Mike asked, with unnecessary concern, how I was feeling.

I told him it was nothing, but I was wondering if I *should* play it up and escape to the nurse's office for the next hour.

Ridiculous. I shouldn't have to run away.

I decided to permit myself one glance at the Cullen family's table. If he was glaring at me, I would skip Biology, like the coward I was.

I kept my head down and glanced up under my lashes. None of them were looking this way. I lifted my head a little.

They were laughing. Edward, Jasper, and Emmett all had their hair entirely saturated with melting snow. Alice and Rosalie were leaning away as Emmett shook his dripping hair toward them. They were enjoying the snowy day, just like everyone else — only they looked more like a scene from a movie than the rest of us.

But, aside from the laughter and playfulness, there was something different, and I couldn't quite pinpoint what that difference was. I examined Edward the most carefully. His skin was less pale, I decided — flushed from the snow fight maybe — the circles under his eyes much less noticeable. But there was something more. I pondered, staring, trying to isolate the change.

"Bella, what are you staring at?" Jessica intruded, her eyes following my stare.

At that precise moment, his eyes flashed over to meet mine.

I dropped my head, letting my hair fall to conceal my face. I was sure, though, in the instant our eyes met, that he didn't look harsh or unfriendly as he had the last time

I'd seen him. He looked merely curious again, unsatisfied in some way.

"Edward Cullen is staring at you," Jessica giggled in my ear.

"He doesn't look angry, does he?" I couldn't help asking.

"No," she said, sounding confused by my question. "Should he be?"

"I don't think he likes me," I confided. I still felt queasy. I put my head down on my arm.

"The Cullens don't like anybody . . . well, they don't notice anybody enough to like them. But he's still staring at you."

"Stop looking at him," I hissed.

She snickered, but she looked away. I raised my head enough to make sure that she did, contemplating violence if she resisted.

Mike interrupted us then — he was planning an epic battle of the blizzard in the parking lot after school and wanted us to join. Jessica agreed enthusiastically. The way she looked at Mike left little doubt that she would be up for anything he suggested. I kept silent. I would have to hide in the gym until the parking lot cleared.

For the rest of the lunch hour I very carefully kept my eyes at my own table. I decided to honor the bargain I'd made with myself. Since he didn't look angry, I would go to Biology. My stomach did frightened little flips at the thought of sitting next to him again.

I didn't really want to walk to class with Mike as

usual — he seemed to be a popular target for the snowball snipers — but when we went to the door, everyone besides me groaned in unison. It was raining, washing all traces of the snow away in clear, icy ribbons down the side of the walkway. I pulled my hood up, secretly pleased. I would be free to go straight home after Gym.

Mike kept up a string of complaints on the way to building four.

Once inside the classroom, I saw with relief that my table was still empty. Mr. Banner was walking around the room, distributing one microscope and box of slides to each table. Class didn't start for a few minutes, and the room buzzed with conversation. I kept my eyes away from the door, doodling idly on the cover of my notebook.

I heard very clearly when the chair next to me moved, but my eyes stayed carefully focused on the pattern I was drawing.

"Hello," said a quiet, musical voice.

I looked up, stunned that he was speaking to me. He was sitting as far away from me as the desk allowed, but his chair was angled toward me. His hair was dripping wet, disheveled — even so, he looked like he'd just finished shooting a commercial for hair gel. His dazzling face was friendly, open, a slight smile on his flawless lips. But his eyes were careful.

"My name is Edward Cullen," he continued. "I didn't have a chance to introduce myself last week. You must be Bella Swan."

My mind was spinning with confusion. Had I made up

the whole thing? He was perfectly polite now. I had to speak; he was waiting. But I couldn't think of anything conventional to say.

"H-how do you know my name?" I stammered.

He laughed a soft, enchanting laugh.

"Oh, I think everyone knows your name. The whole town's been waiting for you to arrive."

I grimaced. I knew it was something like that.

"No," I persisted stupidly. "I meant, why did you call me Bella?"

He seemed confused. "Do you prefer Isabella?"

"No, I like Bella," I said. "But I think Charlie — I mean my dad — must call me Isabella behind my back — that's what everyone here seems to know me as," I tried to explain, feeling like an utter moron.

"Oh." He let it drop. I looked away awkwardly.

Thankfully, Mr. Banner started class at that moment. I tried to concentrate as he explained the lab we would be doing today. The slides in the box were out of order. Working as lab partners, we had to separate the slides of onion root tip cells into the phases of mitosis they represented and label them accordingly. We weren't supposed to use our books. In twenty minutes, he would be coming around to see who had it right.

"Get started," he commanded.

"Ladies first, partner?" Edward asked. I looked up to see him smiling a crooked smile so beautiful that I could only stare at him like an idiot.

"Or I could start, if you wish." The smile faded; he was obviously wondering if I was mentally competent.

"No," I said, flushing. "I'll go ahead."

I was showing off, just a little. I'd already done this lab, and I knew what I was looking for. It should be easy. I snapped the first slide into place under the microscope and adjusted it quickly to the 40X objective. I studied the slide briefly.

My assessment was confident. "Prophase."

"Do you mind if I look?" he asked as I began to remove the slide. His hand caught mine, to stop me, as he asked. His fingers were ice-cold, like he'd been holding them in a snowdrift before class. But that wasn't why I jerked my hand away so quickly. When he touched me, it stung my hand as if an electric current had passed through us.

"I'm sorry," he muttered, pulling his hand back immediately. However, he continued to reach for the microscope. I watched him, still staggered, as he examined the slide for an even shorter time than I had.

"Prophase," he agreed, writing it neatly in the first space on our worksheet. He swiftly switched out the first slide for the second, and then glanced at it cursorily.

"Anaphase," he murmured, writing it down as he spoke.

I kept my voice indifferent. "May I?"

He smirked and pushed the microscope to me.

I looked through the eyepiece eagerly, only to be disappointed. Dang it, he was right.

"Slide three?" I held out my hand without looking at him.

He handed it to me; it seemed like he was being careful not to touch my skin again.

I took the most fleeting look I could manage.

"Interphase." I passed him the microscope before he could ask for it. He took a swift peek, and then wrote it down. I would have written it while he looked, but his clear, elegant script intimidated me. I didn't want to spoil the page with my clumsy scrawl.

We were finished before anyone else was close. I could see Mike and his partner comparing two slides again and again, and another group had their book open under the table.

Which left me with nothing to do but try to not look at him . . . unsuccessfully. I glanced up, and he was staring at me, that same inexplicable look of frustration in his eyes. Suddenly I identified that subtle difference in his face.

"Did you get contacts?" I blurted out unthinkingly.

He seemed puzzled by my unexpected question. "No."

"Oh," I mumbled. "I thought there was something different about your eyes."

He shrugged, and looked away.

In fact, I was sure there was something different. I vividly remembered the flat black color of his eyes the last time he'd glared at me — the color was striking against the background of his pale skin and his auburn hair. Today, his eyes were a completely different color: a strange ocher, darker than butterscotch, but with the same golden tone. I didn't understand how that could be, unless he was lying for some reason about the contacts. Or maybe Forks was making me crazy in the literal sense of the word.

I looked down. His hands were clenched into hard fists again.

Mr. Banner came to our table then, to see why we

weren't working. He looked over our shoulders to glance at the completed lab, and then stared more intently to check the answers.

"So, Edward, didn't you think Isabella should get a chance with the microscope?" Mr. Banner asked.

"Bella," Edward corrected automatically. "Actually, she identified three of the five."

Mr. Banner looked at me now; his expression was skeptical.

"Have you done this lab before?" he asked.

I smiled sheepishly. "Not with onion root."

"Whitefish blastula?"

"Yeah."

Mr. Banner nodded. "Were you in an advanced placement program in Phoenix?"

"Yes."

"Well," he said after a moment, "I guess it's good you two are lab partners." He mumbled something else as he walked away. After he left, I began doodling on my notebook again.

"It's too bad about the snow, isn't it?" Edward asked. I had the feeling that he was forcing himself to make small talk with me. Paranoia swept over me again. It was like he had heard my conversation with Jessica at lunch and was trying to prove me wrong.

"Not really," I answered honestly, instead of pretending to be normal like everyone else. I was still trying to dislodge the stupid feeling of suspicion, and I couldn't concentrate.

"You don't like the cold." It wasn't a question.

"Or the wet."

"Forks must be a difficult place for you to live," he mused.

"You have no idea," I muttered darkly.

He looked fascinated by what I said, for some reason I couldn't imagine. His face was such a distraction that I tried not to look at it any more than courtesy absolutely demanded.

"Why did you come here, then?"

No one had asked me that — not straight out like he did, demanding.

"It's . . . complicated."

"I think I can keep up," he pressed.

I paused for a long moment, and then made the mistake of meeting his gaze. His dark gold eyes confused me, and I answered without thinking.

"My mother got remarried," I said.

"That doesn't sound so complex," he disagreed, but he was suddenly sympathetic. "When did that happen?"

"Last September." My voice sounded sad, even to me.

"And you don't like him," Edward surmised, his tone still kind.

"No, Phil is fine. Too young, maybe, but nice enough."

"Why didn't you stay with them?"

I couldn't fathom his interest, but he continued to stare at me with penetrating eyes, as if my dull life's story was somehow vitally important.

"Phil travels a lot. He plays ball for a living." I half-smiled.

"Have I heard of him?" he asked, smiling in response.

"Probably not. He doesn't play *well*. Strictly minor league. He moves around a lot."

"And your mother sent you here so that she could travel with him." He said it as an assumption again, not a question.

My chin raised a fraction. "No, she did not send me here. I sent myself."

His eyebrows knit together. "I don't understand," he admitted, and he seemed unnecessarily frustrated by that fact.

I sighed. Why was I explaining this to him? He continued to stare at me with obvious curiosity.

"She stayed with me at first, but she missed him. It made her unhappy . . . so I decided it was time to spend some quality time with Charlie." My voice was glum by the time I finished.

"But now you're unhappy," he pointed out.

"And?" I challenged.

"That doesn't seem fair." He shrugged, but his eyes were still intense.

I laughed without humor. "Hasn't anyone ever told you? Life isn't fair."

"I believe I *have* heard that somewhere before," he agreed dryly.

"So that's all," I insisted, wondering why he was still staring at me that way.

His gaze became appraising. "You put on a good show," he said slowly. "But I'd be willing to bet that you're suffering more than you let anyone see."

I grimaced at him, resisting the impulse to stick out my tongue like a five-year-old, and looked away.

"Am I wrong?"

I tried to ignore him.

"I didn't think so," he murmured smugly.

"Why does it matter to *you*?" I asked, irritated. I kept my eyes away, watching the teacher make his rounds.

"That's a very good question," he muttered, so quietly that I wondered if he was talking to himself. However, after a few seconds of silence, I decided that was the only answer I was going to get.

I sighed, scowling at the blackboard.

"Am I annoying you?" he asked. He sounded amused.

I glanced at him without thinking . . . and told the truth again. "Not exactly. I'm more annoyed at myself. My face is so easy to read — my mother always calls me her open book." I frowned.

"On the contrary, I find you very difficult to read." Despite everything that I'd said and he'd guessed, he sounded like he meant it.

"You must be a good reader then," I replied.

"Usually." He smiled widely, flashing a set of perfect, ultrawhite teeth.

Mr. Banner called the class to order then, and I turned with relief to listen. I was in disbelief that I'd just explained my dreary life to this bizarre, beautiful boy who may or may not despise me. He'd seemed engrossed in our conversation, but now I could see, from the corner of my eye, that he was leaning away from me again, his hands gripping the edge of the table with unmistakable tension.

I tried to appear attentive as Mr. Banner illustrated, with transparencies on the overhead projector, what I had seen without difficulty through the microscope. But my thoughts were unmanageable.

When the bell finally rang, Edward rushed as swiftly and as gracefully from the room as he had last Monday. And, like last Monday, I stared after him in amazement.

Mike skipped quickly to my side and picked up my books for me. I imagined him with a wagging tail.

"That was awful," he groaned. "They all looked exactly the same. You're lucky you had Cullen for a partner."

"I didn't have any trouble with it," I said, stung by his assumption. I regretted the snub instantly. "I've done the lab before, though," I added before he could get his feelings hurt.

"Cullen seemed friendly enough today," he commented as we shrugged into our raincoats. He didn't seem pleased about it.

I tried to sound indifferent. "I wonder what was with him last Monday."

I couldn't concentrate on Mike's chatter as we walked to Gym, and P.E. didn't do much to hold my attention, either. Mike was on my team today. He chivalrously covered my position as well as his own, so my woolgathering was only interrupted when it was my turn to serve; my team ducked warily out of the way every time I was up.

The rain was just a mist as I walked to the parking lot, but I was happier when I was in the dry cab. I got the heater running, for once not caring about the mind-numbing roar of the engine. I unzipped my jacket, put the hood down, and fluffed my damp hair out so the heater could dry it on the way home.

I looked around me to make sure it was clear. That's when I noticed the still, white figure. Edward Cullen was leaning against the front door of the Volvo, three cars down from me, and staring intently in my direction. I swiftly looked away and threw the truck into reverse, almost hitting a rusty Toyota Corolla in my haste. Lucky for the Toyota, I stomped on the brake in time. It was just the sort of car that my truck would make scrap metal of. I took a deep breath, still looking out the other side of my car, and cautiously pulled out again, with greater success. I stared straight ahead as I passed the Volvo, but from a peripheral peek, I would swear I saw him laughing.

3. PHENOMENON

WHEN I OPENED MY EYES IN THE MORNING, SOMETHING was different.

It was the light. It was still the gray-green light of a cloudy day in the forest, but it was clearer somehow. I realized there was no fog veiling my window.

I jumped up to look outside, and then groaned in horror.

A fine layer of snow covered the yard, dusted the top of my truck, and whitened the road. But that wasn't the worst part. All the rain from yesterday had frozen solid — coating the needles on the trees in fantastic, gorgeous patterns, and making the driveway a deadly ice slick. I had enough trouble not falling down when the ground was dry; it might be safer for me to go back to bed now.

Charlie had left for work before I got downstairs. In a lot of ways, living with Charlie was like having my own place, and I found myself reveling in the aloneness instead of being lonely.

I threw down a quick bowl of cereal and some orange juice from the carton. I felt excited to go to school, and that scared me. I knew it wasn't the stimulating learning environment I was anticipating, or seeing my new set of friends. If I was being honest with myself, I knew I was eager to get to school because I would see Edward Cullen. And that was very, very stupid.

I should be avoiding him entirely after my brainless and embarrassing babbling yesterday. And I was suspicious of him; why should he lie about his eyes? I was still frightened of the hostility I sometimes felt emanating from him, and I was still tongue-tied whenever I pictured his perfect face. I was well aware that my league and his league were spheres that did not touch. So I shouldn't be at all anxious to see him today.

It took every ounce of my concentration to make it down the icy brick driveway alive. I almost lost my balance when I finally got to the truck, but I managed to cling to the side mirror and save myself. Clearly, today was going to be nightmarish.

Driving to school, I distracted myself from my fear of falling and my unwanted speculations about Edward Cullen by thinking about Mike and Eric, and the obvious difference in how teenage boys responded to me here. I was sure I looked exactly the same as I had in Phoenix. Maybe it was just that the boys back home had watched me pass slowly through all the awkward phases of adolescence and still thought of me that way. Perhaps it was because I was a novelty here, where novelties were few and far between. Possibly my crippling clumsiness was seen as endearing rather than pathetic, casting me as a damsel in distress. Whatever the reason, Mike's puppy dog behavior and Eric's apparent rivalry with him were disconcerting. I wasn't sure if I didn't prefer being ignored.

My truck seemed to have no problem with the black ice that covered the roads. I drove very slowly, though, not wanting to carve a path of destruction through Main Street.

When I got out of my truck at school, I saw why I'd had so little trouble. Something silver caught my eye, and I walked to the back of the truck — carefully holding the side for support — to examine my tires. There were thin chains crisscrossed in diamond shapes around them. Charlie had gotten up who knows how early to put snow chains on my truck. My throat suddenly felt tight. I wasn't used to being taken care of, and Charlie's unspoken concern caught me by surprise.

I was standing by the back corner of the truck, struggling to fight back the sudden wave of emotion the snow chains had brought on, when I heard an odd sound.

It was a high-pitched screech, and it was fast becoming painfully loud. I looked up, startled.

I saw several things simultaneously. Nothing was moving in slow motion, the way it does in the movies. Instead, the adrenaline rush seemed to make my brain work much faster, and I was able to absorb in clear detail several things at once.

Edward Cullen was standing four cars down from me, staring at me in horror. His face stood out from a sea of faces, all frozen in the same mask of shock. But of more immediate importance was the dark blue van that was skidding, tires locked and squealing against the brakes, spinning wildly across the ice of the parking lot. It was going to hit the back corner of my truck, and I was standing between them. I didn't even have time to close my eyes.

Just before I heard the shattering crunch of the van folding around the truck bed, something hit me, hard, but not from the direction I was expecting. My head cracked against the icy blacktop, and I felt something solid and cold pinning me to the ground. I was lying on the pavement behind the tan car I'd parked next to. But I didn't have a chance to notice anything else, because the van was still coming. It had curled gratingly around the end of the truck and, still spinning and sliding, was about to collide with me *again*.

A low oath made me aware that someone was with me, and the voice was impossible not to recognize. Two long, white hands shot out protectively in front of me, and the van shuddered to a stop a foot from my face, the large hands fitting providentially into a deep dent in the side of the van's body.

Then his hands moved so fast they blurred. One was suddenly gripping under the body of the van, and something was dragging me, swinging my legs around like a rag doll's, till they hit the tire of the tan car. A groaning metallic thud hurt my ears, and the van settled, glass popping, onto the asphalt — exactly where, a second ago, my legs had been.

It was absolutely silent for one long second before the screaming began. In the abrupt bedlam, I could hear more than one person shouting my name. But more clearly than all the yelling, I could hear Edward Cullen's low, frantic voice in my ear.

"Bella? Are you all right?"

"I'm fine." My voice sounded strange. I tried to sit up, and realized he was holding me against the side of his body in an iron grasp.

"Be careful," he warned as I struggled. "I think you hit your head pretty hard."

I became aware of a throbbing ache centered above my left ear.

"Ow," I said, surprised.

"That's what I thought." His voice, amazingly, sounded like he was suppressing laughter.

"How in the . . ." I trailed off, trying to clear my head, get my bearings. "How did you get over here so fast?"

"I was standing right next to you, Bella," he said, his tone serious again.

I turned to sit up, and this time he let me, releasing his hold around my waist and sliding as far from me as he could in the limited space. I looked at his concerned, innocent expression and was disoriented again by the force of his gold-colored eyes. What was I asking him?

And then they found us, a crowd of people with tears streaming down their faces, shouting at each other, shouting at us.

"Don't move," someone instructed.

"Get Tyler out of the van!" someone else shouted.

There was a flurry of activity around us. I tried to get up, but Edward's cold hand pushed my shoulder down.

"Just stay put for now."

"But it's cold," I complained. It surprised me when he chuckled under his breath. There was an edge to the sound.

"You were over there," I suddenly remembered, and his chuckle stopped short. "You were by your car."

His expression turned hard. "No, I wasn't."

"I saw you." All around us was chaos. I could hear the gruffer voices of adults arriving on the scene. But I obstinately held on to our argument; I was right, and he was going to admit it.

"Bella, I was standing with you, and I pulled you out of the way." He unleashed the full, devastating power of his eyes on me, as if trying to communicate something crucial.

"No." I set my jaw.

The gold in his eyes blazed. "Please, Bella."

"Why?" I demanded.

"Trust me," he pleaded, his soft voice overwhelming.

I could hear the sirens now. "Will you promise to explain everything to me later?"

"Fine," he snapped, abruptly exasperated.

"Fine," I repeated angrily.

It took six EMTs and two teachers — Mr. Varner and Coach Clapp — to shift the van far enough away from us to bring the stretchers in. Edward vehemently refused his, and I tried to do the same, but the traitor told them I'd hit my head and probably had a concussion. I almost died of humiliation when they put on the neck brace. It looked like the entire school was there, watching soberly as they loaded me in the back of the ambulance. Edward got to ride in the front. It was maddening.

To make matters worse, Chief Swan arrived before they could get me safely away.

"Bella!" he yelled in panic when he recognized me on the stretcher.

"I'm completely fine, Char — Dad," I sighed. "There's nothing wrong with me."

He turned to the closest EMT for a second opinion. I tuned him out to consider the jumble of inexplicable images churning chaotically in my head. When they'd lifted me away from the car, I had seen the deep dent in the tan car's bumper — a very distinct dent that fit the contours of Edward's shoulders . . . as if he had braced himself against the car with enough force to damage the metal frame. . . .

And then there was his family, looking on from the distance, with expressions that ranged from disapproval to fury but held no hint of concern for their brother's safety.

I tried to think of a logical solution that could explain what I had just seen — a solution that excluded the assumption that I was insane.

Naturally, the ambulance got a police escort to the county hospital. I felt ridiculous the whole time they were unloading me. What made it worse was that Edward simply glided through the hospital doors under his own power. I ground my teeth together.

They put me in the emergency room, a long room with a line of beds separated by pastel-patterned curtains. A nurse put a pressure cuff on my arm and a thermometer under my tongue. Since no one bothered pulling the curtain around to give me some privacy, I decided I wasn't obligated to wear the stupid-looking neck brace anymore. When the nurse walked away, I quickly unfastened the Velcro and threw it under the bed.

There was another flurry of hospital personnel, another stretcher brought to the bed next to me. I recognized Tyler Crowley from my Government class beneath the bloodstained bandages wrapped tightly around his head. Tyler looked a hundred times worse than I felt. But he was staring anxiously at me.

"Bella, I'm so sorry!"

"I'm fine, Tyler — you look awful, are you all right?" As we spoke, nurses began unwinding his soiled bandages, exposing a myriad of shallow slices all over his forehead and left cheek.

He ignored me. "I thought I was going to kill you! I was going too fast, and I hit the ice wrong. . . ." He winced as one nurse started dabbing at his face.

"Don't worry about it; you missed me."

"How did you get out of the way so fast? You were there, and then you were gone. . . ."

"Umm . . . Edward pulled me out of the way."

He looked confused. "Who?"

"Edward Cullen — he was standing next to me." I'd always been a terrible liar; I didn't sound convincing at all.

"Cullen? I didn't see him . . . wow, it was all so fast, I guess. Is he okay?"

"I think so. He's here somewhere, but they didn't make him use a stretcher."

I knew I wasn't crazy. What had happened? There was no way to explain away what I'd seen.

They wheeled me away then, to X-ray my head. I told them there was nothing wrong, and I was right. Not even a concussion. I asked if I could leave, but the nurse said I had to talk to a doctor first. So I was trapped in the ER, waiting, harassed by Tyler's constant apologies and promises to make it up to me. No matter how many times I tried to convince him I was fine, he continued to torment himself. Finally, I closed my eyes and ignored him. He kept up a remorseful mumbling.

"Is she sleeping?" a musical voice asked. My eyes flew open.

Edward was standing at the foot of my bed, smirking. I glared at him. It wasn't easy — it would have been more natural to ogle.

"Hey, Edward, I'm really sorry —" Tyler began.

Edward lifted a hand to stop him.

"No blood, no foul," he said, flashing his brilliant teeth. He moved to sit on the edge of Tyler's bed, facing me. He smirked again.

"So, what's the verdict?" he asked me.

"There's nothing wrong with me at all, but they won't let me go," I complained. "How come you aren't strapped to a gurney like the rest of us?"

"It's all about who you know," he answered. "But don't worry, I came to spring you."

Then a doctor walked around the corner, and my mouth fell open. He was young, he was blond . . . and he was handsomer than any movie star I'd ever seen. He was pale, though, and tired-looking, with circles under his eyes. From Charlie's description, this had to be Edward's father.

"So, Miss Swan," Dr. Cullen said in a remarkably appealing voice, "how are you feeling?"

"I'm fine," I said, for the last time, I hoped.

He walked to the lightboard on the wall over my head, and turned it on.

"Your X-rays look good," he said. "Does your head hurt? Edward said you hit it pretty hard."

"It's fine," I repeated with a sigh, throwing a quick scowl toward Edward.

The doctor's cool fingers probed lightly along my skull. He noticed when I winced.

"Tender?" he asked.

"Not really." I'd had worse.

I heard a chuckle, and looked over to see Edward's patronizing smile. My eyes narrowed.

"Well, your father is in the waiting room — you can go home with him now. But come back if you feel dizzy or have trouble with your eyesight at all."

"Can't I go back to school?" I asked, imagining Charlie trying to be attentive.

"Maybe you should take it easy today."

I glanced at Edward. "Does *he* get to go to school?"

"Someone has to spread the good news that we survived," Edward said smugly.

"Actually," Dr. Cullen corrected, "most of the school seems to be in the waiting room."

"Oh no," I moaned, covering my face with my hands.

Dr. Cullen raised his eyebrows. "Do you want to stay?"

"No, no!" I insisted, throwing my legs over the side of the bed and hopping down quickly. Too quickly — I staggered, and Dr. Cullen caught me. He looked concerned.

"I'm fine," I assured him again. No need to tell him my balance problems had nothing to do with hitting my head.

"Take some Tylenol for the pain," he suggested as he steadied me.

"It doesn't hurt that bad," I insisted.

"It sounds like you were extremely lucky," Dr. Cullen said, smiling as he signed my chart with a flourish.

"Lucky Edward happened to be standing next to me," I amended with a hard glance at the subject of my statement.

"Oh, well, yes," Dr. Cullen agreed, suddenly occupied with the papers in front of him. Then he looked away, at Tyler, and walked to the next bed. My intuition flickered; the doctor was in on it.

"I'm afraid that *you'll* have to stay with us just a little bit longer," he said to Tyler, and began checking his cuts.

As soon as the doctor's back was turned, I moved to Edward's side.

"Can I talk to you for a minute?" I hissed under my breath. He took a step back from me, his jaw suddenly clenched.

"Your father is waiting for you," he said through his teeth.

I glanced at Dr. Cullen and Tyler.

"I'd like to speak with you alone, if you don't mind," I pressed.

He glared, and then turned his back and strode down the long room. I nearly had to run to keep up. As soon as we turned the corner into a short hallway, he spun around to face me.

"What do you want?" he asked, sounding annoyed. His eyes were cold.

His unfriendliness intimidated me. My words came out with less severity than I'd intended. "You owe me an explanation," I reminded him.

"I saved your life — I don't owe you anything."

I flinched back from the resentment in his voice. "You promised."

"Bella, you hit your head, you don't know what you're talking about." His tone was cutting.

My temper flared now, and I glared defiantly at him. "There's nothing wrong with my head."

He glared back. "What do you want from me, Bella?"

"I want to know the truth," I said. "I want to know why I'm lying for you."

"What do you *think* happened?" he snapped.

It came out in a rush.

"All I know is that you weren't anywhere near me — Tyler didn't see you, either, so don't tell me I hit my head too hard. That van was going to crush us both — and it didn't, and your hands left dents in the side of it — and you left a dent in the other car, and you're not hurt at all — and the van should have smashed my legs, but you were holding it up. . . ." I could hear how crazy it sounded, and I couldn't continue. I was so mad I could feel the tears coming; I tried to force them back by grinding my teeth together.

He was staring at me incredulously. But his face was tense, defensive.

"You think I lifted a van off you?" His tone questioned my sanity, but it only made me more suspicious. It was like a perfectly delivered line by a skilled actor.

I merely nodded once, jaw tight.

"Nobody will believe that, you know." His voice held an edge of derision now.

"I'm not going to tell anybody." I said each word slowly, carefully controlling my anger.

Surprise flitted across his face. "Then why does it matter?"

"It matters to me," I insisted. "I don't like to lie — so there'd better be a good reason why I'm doing it."

"Can't you just thank me and get over it?"

"Thank you." I waited, fuming and expectant.

"You're not going to let it go, are you?"

"No."

"In that case . . . I hope you enjoy disappointment."

We scowled at each other in silence. I was the first to speak, trying to keep myself focused. I was in danger of being distracted by his livid, glorious face. It was like trying to stare down a destroying angel.

"Why did you even bother?" I asked frigidly.

He paused, and for a brief moment his stunning face was unexpectedly vulnerable.

"I don't know," he whispered.

And then he turned his back on me and walked away.

I was so angry, it took me a few minutes until I could move. When I could walk, I made my way slowly to the exit at the end of the hallway.

The waiting room was more unpleasant than I'd feared. It seemed like every face I knew in Forks was there, staring at me. Charlie rushed to my side; I put up my hands.

"There's nothing wrong with me," I assured him sullenly. I was still aggravated, not in the mood for chitchat.

"What did the doctor say?"

"Dr. Cullen saw me, and he said I was fine and I could go home." I sighed. Mike and Jessica and Eric were all there, beginning to converge on us. "Let's go," I urged.

Charlie put one arm behind my back, not quite touching me, and led me to the glass doors of the exit. I waved sheepishly at my friends, hoping to convey that they didn't need to worry anymore. It was a huge relief — the first time I'd ever felt that way — to get into the cruiser.

We drove in silence. I was so wrapped up in my thoughts that I barely knew Charlie was there. I was positive that Edward's defensive behavior in the hall was a confirmation of the bizarre things I still could hardly believe I'd witnessed.

When we got to the house, Charlie finally spoke.

"Um . . . you'll need to call Renée." He hung his head, guilty.

I was appalled. "You told Mom!"

"Sorry."

I slammed the cruiser's door a little harder than necessary on my way out.

My mom was in hysterics, of course. I had to tell her I felt fine at least thirty times before she would calm down. She begged me to come home — forgetting the fact that home was empty at the moment — but her pleas were easier to resist than I would have thought. I was consumed by the mystery Edward presented. And more than a little obsessed by Edward himself. Stupid, stupid, stupid. I wasn't as eager to escape Forks as I should be, as any normal, sane person would be.

I decided I might as well go to bed early that night. Charlie continued to watch me anxiously, and it was getting on my nerves. I stopped on my way to grab three Tylenol from the bathroom. They did help, and, as the pain eased, I drifted to sleep.

That was the first night I dreamed of Edward Cullen.

4. INVITATIONS

I**N MY DREAM IT WAS VERY DARK, AND WHAT DIM LIGHT** there was seemed to be radiating from Edward's skin. I couldn't see his face, just his back as he walked away from me, leaving me in the blackness. No matter how fast I ran, I couldn't catch up to him; no matter how loud I called, he never turned. Troubled, I woke in the middle of the night and couldn't sleep again for what seemed like a very long time. After that, he was in my dreams nearly every night, but always on the periphery, never within reach.

The month that followed the accident was uneasy, tense, and, at first, embarrassing.

To my dismay, I found myself the center of attention

for the rest of that week. Tyler Crowley was impossible, following me around, obsessed with making amends to me somehow. I tried to convince him what I wanted more than anything else was for him to forget all about it — especially since nothing had actually happened to me — but he remained insistent. He followed me between classes and sat at our now-crowded lunch table. Mike and Eric were even less friendly toward him than they were to each other, which made me worry that I'd gained another unwelcome fan.

No one seemed concerned about Edward, though I explained over and over that he was the hero — how he had pulled me out of the way and had nearly been crushed, too. I tried to be convincing. Jessica, Mike, Eric, and everyone else always commented that they hadn't even seen him there till the van was pulled away.

I wondered to myself why no one else had seen him standing so far away, before he was suddenly, impossibly saving my life. With chagrin, I realized the probable cause — no one else was as aware of Edward as I always was. No one else watched him the way I did. How pitiful.

Edward was never surrounded by crowds of curious bystanders eager for his firsthand account. People avoided him as usual. The Cullens and the Hales sat at the same table as always, not eating, talking only among themselves. None of them, especially Edward, glanced my way anymore.

When he sat next to me in class, as far from me as the table would allow, he seemed totally unaware of my presence. Only now and then, when his fists would suddenly ball up — skin stretched even whiter over the bones — did I wonder if he wasn't quite as oblivious as he appeared.

He wished he hadn't pulled me from the path of Tyler's van — there was no other conclusion I could come to.

I wanted very much to talk to him, and the day after the accident I tried. The last time I'd seen him, outside the ER, we'd both been so furious. I still was angry that he wouldn't trust me with the truth, even though I was keeping my part of the bargain flawlessly. But he had in fact saved my life, no matter how he'd done it. And, overnight, the heat of my anger faded into awed gratitude.

He was already seated when I got to Biology, looking straight ahead. I sat down, expecting him to turn toward me. He showed no sign that he realized I was there.

"Hello, Edward," I said pleasantly, to show him I was going to behave myself.

He turned his head a fraction toward me without meeting my gaze, nodded once, and then looked the other way.

And that was the last contact I'd had with him, though he was there, a foot away from me, every day. I watched him sometimes, unable to stop myself — from a distance, though, in the cafeteria or parking lot. I watched as his golden eyes grew perceptibly darker day by day. But in class I gave no more notice that he existed than he showed toward me. I was miserable. And the dreams continued.

Despite my outright lies, the tenor of my e-mails alerted Renée to my depression, and she called a few times, worried. I tried to convince her it was just the weather that had me down.

Mike, at least, was pleased by the obvious coolness between me and my lab partner. I could see he'd been worried that Edward's daring rescue might have impressed me, and he was relieved that it seemed to have the opposite effect. He grew more confident, sitting on the edge of my table to talk before Biology class started, ignoring Edward as completely as he ignored us.

The snow washed away for good after that one dangerously icy day. Mike was disappointed he'd never gotten to stage his snowball fight, but pleased that the beach trip would soon be possible. The rain continued heavily, though, and the weeks passed.

Jessica made me aware of another event looming on the horizon — she called the first Tuesday of March to ask my permission to invite Mike to the girls' choice spring dance in two weeks.

"Are you sure you don't mind . . . you weren't planning to ask him?" she persisted when I told her I didn't mind in the least.

"No, Jess, I'm not going," I assured her. Dancing was glaringly outside my range of abilities.

"It will be really fun." Her attempt to convince me was halfhearted. I suspected that Jessica enjoyed my inexplicable popularity more than my actual company.

"You have fun with Mike," I encouraged.

The next day, I was surprised that Jessica wasn't her usual gushing self in Trig and Spanish. She was silent as she walked by my side between classes, and I was afraid to ask her why. If Mike had turned her down, I was the last person she would want to tell.

My fears were strengthened during lunch when Jessica sat as far from Mike as possible, chatting animatedly with Eric. Mike was unusually quiet.

Mike was still quiet as he walked me to class, the uncomfortable look on his face a bad sign. But he didn't broach the subject until I was in my seat and he was perched on my desk. As always, I was electrically aware of Edward sitting close enough to touch, as distant as if he were merely an invention of my imagination.

"So," Mike said, looking at the floor, "Jessica asked me to the spring dance."

"That's great." I made my voice bright and enthusiastic. "You'll have a lot of fun with Jessica."

"Well . . ." He floundered as he examined my smile, clearly not happy with my response. "I told her I had to think about it."

"Why would you do that?" I let disapproval color my tone, though I was relieved he hadn't given her an absolute no.

His face was bright red as he looked down again. Pity shook my resolve.

"I was wondering if . . . well, if you might be planning to ask me."

I paused for a moment, hating the wave of guilt that swept through me. But I saw, from the corner of my eye, Edward's head tilt reflexively in my direction.

"Mike, I think you should tell her yes," I said.

"Did you already ask someone?" Did Edward notice how Mike's eyes flickered in his direction?

"No," I assured him. "I'm not going to the dance at all."

"Why not?" Mike demanded.

I didn't want to get into the safety hazards that dancing presented, so I quickly made new plans.

"I'm going to Seattle that Saturday," I explained. I needed to get out of town anyway — it was suddenly the perfect time to go.

"Can't you go some other weekend?"

"Sorry, no," I said. "So you shouldn't make Jess wait any longer — it's rude."

"Yeah, you're right," he mumbled, and turned, dejected, to walk back to his seat. I closed my eyes and pressed my fingers to my temples, trying to push the guilt and sympathy out of my head. Mr. Banner began talking. I sighed and opened my eyes.

And Edward was staring at me curiously, that same, familiar edge of frustration even more distinct now in his black eyes.

I stared back, surprised, expecting him to look quickly away. But instead he continued to gaze with probing intensity into my eyes. There was no question of me looking away. My hands started to shake.

"Mr. Cullen?" the teacher called, seeking the answer to a question that I hadn't heard.

"The Krebs Cycle," Edward answered, seeming reluctant as he turned to look at Mr. Banner.

I looked down at my book as soon as his eyes released me, trying to find my place. Cowardly as ever, I shifted my hair over my right shoulder to hide my face. I couldn't believe the rush of emotion pulsing through me — just because he'd happened to look at me for the first time in a half-dozen weeks. I couldn't allow him to have this level of influence over me. It was pathetic. More than pathetic, it was unhealthy.

I tried very hard not to be aware of him for the rest of the hour, and, since that was impossible, at least not to let him know that I was aware of him. When the bell rang at last, I turned my back to him to gather my things, expecting him to leave immediately as usual.

"Bella?" His voice shouldn't have been so familiar to me, as if I'd known the sound of it all my life rather than for just a few short weeks.

I turned slowly, unwillingly. I didn't want to feel what I knew I *would* feel when I looked at his too-perfect face. My expression was wary when I finally turned to him; his expression was unreadable. He didn't say anything.

"What? Are you speaking to me again?" I finally asked, an unintentional note of petulance in my voice.

His lips twitched, fighting a smile. "No, not really," he admitted.

I closed my eyes and inhaled slowly through my nose, aware that I was gritting my teeth. He waited.

"Then what do you want, Edward?" I asked, keeping my eyes closed; it was easier to talk to him coherently that way.

"I'm sorry." He sounded sincere. "I'm being very rude, I know. But it's better this way, really."

I opened my eyes. His face was very serious.

"I don't know what you mean," I said, my voice guarded.

"It's better if we're not friends," he explained. "Trust me."

My eyes narrowed. I'd heard *that* before.

"It's too bad you didn't figure that out earlier," I hissed through my teeth. "You could have saved yourself all this regret."

"Regret?" The word, and my tone, obviously caught him off guard. "Regret for what?"

"For not just letting that stupid van squish me."

He was astonished. He stared at me in disbelief.

When he finally spoke, he almost sounded mad. "You think I regret saving your life?"

"I *know* you do," I snapped.

"You don't know anything." He was definitely mad.

I turned my head sharply away from him, clenching my jaw against all the wild accusations I wanted to hurl at him. I gathered my books together, then stood and walked to the door. I meant to sweep dramatically out of the room, but of course I caught the toe of my boot on the doorjamb and dropped my books. I stood there for a moment, thinking about leaving them. Then I sighed and bent to pick them up. He was there; he'd already stacked them into a pile. He handed them to me, his face hard.

"Thank you," I said icily.

His eyes narrowed.

"You're welcome," he retorted.

I straightened up swiftly, turned away from him again, and stalked off to Gym without looking back.

Gym was brutal. We'd moved on to basketball. My team never passed me the ball, so that was good, but I fell down a lot. Sometimes I took people with me. Today I was worse than usual because my head was so filled with

Edward. I tried to concentrate on my feet, but he kept creeping back into my thoughts just when I really needed my balance.

It was a relief, as always, to leave. I almost ran to the truck; there were just so many people I wanted to avoid. The truck had suffered only minimal damage in the accident. I'd had to replace the taillights, and if I'd had a real paint job, I would have touched that up. Tyler's parents had to sell their van for parts.

I almost had a stroke when I rounded the corner and saw a tall, dark figure leaning against the side of my truck. Then I realized it was just Eric. I started walking again.

"Hey, Eric," I called.

"Hi, Bella."

"What's up?" I said as I was unlocking the door. I wasn't paying attention to the uncomfortable edge in his voice, so his next words took me by surprise.

"Uh, I was just wondering . . . if you would go to the spring dance with me?" His voice broke on the last word.

"I thought it was girls' choice," I said, too startled to be diplomatic.

"Well, yeah," he admitted, shamefaced.

I recovered my composure and tried to make my smile warm. "Thank you for asking me, but I'm going to be in Seattle that day."

"Oh," he said. "Well, maybe next time."

"Sure," I agreed, and then bit my lip. I wouldn't want him to take that too literally.

He slouched off, back toward the school. I heard a low chuckle.

Edward was walking past the front of my truck, looking straight forward, his lips pressed together. I yanked the door open and jumped inside, slamming it loudly behind me. I revved the engine deafeningly and reversed out into the aisle. Edward was in his car already, two spaces down, sliding out smoothly in front of me, cutting me off. He stopped there — to wait for his family; I could see the four of them walking this way, but still by the cafeteria. I considered taking out the rear of his shiny Volvo, but there were too many witnesses. I looked in my rearview mirror. A line was beginning to form. Directly behind me, Tyler Crowley was in his recently acquired used Sentra, waving. I was too aggravated to acknowledge him.

While I was sitting there, looking everywhere but at the car in front of me, I heard a knock on my passenger side window. I looked over; it was Tyler. I glanced back in my rearview mirror, confused. His car was still running, the door left open. I leaned across the cab to crank the window down. It was stiff. I got it halfway down, then gave up.

"I'm sorry, Tyler, I'm stuck behind Cullen." I was annoyed — obviously the holdup wasn't my fault.

"Oh, I know — I just wanted to ask you something while we're trapped here." He grinned.

This could not be happening.

"Will you ask me to the spring dance?" he continued.

"I'm not going to be in town, Tyler." My voice sounded a little sharp. I had to remember it wasn't his fault that Mike and Eric had already used up my quota of patience for the day.

"Yeah, Mike said that," he admitted.

"Then why —"

He shrugged. "I was hoping you were just letting him down easy."

Okay, it was completely his fault.

"Sorry, Tyler," I said, working to hide my irritation. "I really am going out of town."

"That's cool. We still have prom."

And before I could respond, he was walking back to his car. I could feel the shock on my face. I looked forward to see Alice, Rosalie, Emmett, and Jasper all sliding into the Volvo. In his rearview mirror, Edward's eyes were on me. He was unquestionably shaking with laughter, as if he'd heard every word Tyler had said. My foot itched toward the gas pedal . . . one little bump wouldn't hurt any of them, just that glossy silver paint job. I revved the engine.

But they were all in, and Edward was speeding away. I drove home slowly, carefully, muttering to myself the whole way.

When I got home, I decided to make chicken enchiladas for dinner. It was a long process, and it would keep me busy. While I was simmering the onions and chilies, the phone rang. I was almost afraid to answer it, but it might be Charlie or my mom.

It was Jessica, and she was jubilant; Mike had caught her after school to accept her invitation. I celebrated with her briefly while I stirred. She had to go, she wanted to call Angela and Lauren to tell them. I suggested — with casual innocence — that maybe Angela, the shy girl who had Biology with me, could ask Eric. And Lauren, a standoffish girl who had always ignored me at the lunch table, could ask Tyler; I'd heard he was still available. Jess thought that was a great idea. Now that she was sure of Mike, she actually sounded sincere when she said she wished I would go to the dance. I gave her my Seattle excuse.

After I hung up, I tried to concentrate on dinner — dicing the chicken especially; I didn't want to take another trip to the emergency room. But my head was spinning, trying to analyze every word Edward had spoken today. What did he mean, it was better if we weren't friends?

My stomach twisted as I realized what he must have meant. He must see how absorbed I was by him; he must not want to lead me on . . . so we couldn't even be friends . . . because he wasn't interested in me at all.

Of course he wasn't interested in me, I thought angrily, my eyes stinging — a delayed reaction to the onions. I wasn't *interesting*. And he was. Interesting . . . and brilliant . . . and mysterious . . . and perfect . . . and beautiful . . . and possibly able to lift full-sized vans with one hand.

Well, that was fine. I could leave him alone. I *would* leave him alone. I would get through my self-imposed sentence here in purgatory, and then hopefully some school in the Southwest, or possibly Hawaii, would offer me a scholarship. I focused my thoughts on sunny beaches and palm trees as I finished the enchiladas and put them in the oven.

Charlie seemed suspicious when he came home and smelled the green peppers. I couldn't blame him — the closest edible Mexican food was probably in southern

California. But he was a cop, even if just a small-town cop, so he was brave enough to take the first bite. He seemed to like it. It was fun to watch as he slowly began trusting me in the kitchen.

"Dad?" I asked when he was almost done.

"Yeah, Bella?"

"Um, I just wanted to let you know that I'm going to Seattle for the day a week from Saturday . . . if that's okay?" I didn't want to ask permission — it set a bad precedent — but I felt rude, so I tacked it on at the end.

"Why?" He sounded surprised, as if he were unable to imagine something that Forks couldn't offer.

"Well, I wanted to get few books — the library here is pretty limited — and maybe look at some clothes." I had more money than I was used to having, since, thanks to Charlie, I hadn't had to pay for a car. Not that the truck didn't cost me quite a bit in the gas department.

"That truck probably doesn't get very good gas mileage," he said, echoing my thoughts.

"I know, I'll stop in Montesano and Olympia — and Tacoma if I have to."

"Are you going all by yourself?" he asked, and I couldn't tell if he was suspicious I had a secret boyfriend or just worried about car trouble.

"Yes."

"Seattle is a big city — you could get lost," he fretted.

"Dad, Phoenix is five times the size of Seattle — and I can read a map, don't worry about it."

"Do you want me to come with you?"

I tried to be crafty as I hid my horror.

"That's all right, Dad, I'll probably just be in dressing rooms all day — very boring."

"Oh, okay." The thought of sitting in women's clothing stores for any period of time immediately put him off.

"Thanks." I smiled at him.

"Will you be back in time for the dance?"

Grrr. Only in a town this small would a *father* know when the high school dances were.

"No — I don't dance, Dad." He, of all people, should understand that — I didn't get my balance problems from my mother.

He did understand. "Oh, that's right," he realized.

The next morning, when I pulled into the parking lot, I deliberately parked as far as possible from the silver Volvo. I didn't want to put myself in the path of too much temptation and end up owing him a new car. Getting out of the cab, I fumbled with my key and it fell into a puddle at my feet. As I bent to get it, a white hand flashed out and grabbed it before I could. I jerked upright. Edward Cullen was right next to me, leaning casually against my truck.

"How do you *do* that?" I asked in amazed irritation.

"Do what?" He held my key out as he spoke. As I reached for it, he dropped it into my palm.

"Appear out of thin air."

"Bella, it's not my fault if you are exceptionally unobservant." His voice was quiet as usual — velvet, muted.

I scowled at his perfect face. His eyes were light again today, a deep, golden honey color. Then I had to look down, to reassemble my now-tangled thoughts.

"Why the traffic jam last night?" I demanded, still

looking away. "I thought you were supposed to be pretending I don't exist, not irritating me to death."

"That was for Tyler's sake, not mine. I had to give him his chance." He snickered.

"You . . ." I gasped. I couldn't think of a bad enough word. It felt like the heat of my anger should physically burn him, but he only seemed more amused.

"And I'm not pretending you don't exist," he continued.

"So you *are* trying to irritate me to death? Since Tyler's van didn't do the job?"

Anger flashed in his tawny eyes. His lips pressed into a hard line, all signs of humor gone.

"Bella, you are utterly absurd," he said, his low voice cold.

My palms tingled — I wanted so badly to hit something. I was surprised at myself. I was usually a nonviolent person. I turned my back and started to walk away.

"Wait," he called. I kept walking, sloshing angrily through the rain. But he was next to me, easily keeping pace.

"I'm sorry, that was rude," he said as we walked. I ignored him. "I'm not saying it isn't true," he continued, "but it was rude to say it, anyway."

"Why won't you leave me alone?" I grumbled.

"I wanted to ask you something, but you sidetracked me," he chuckled. He seemed to have recovered his good humor.

"Do you have a multiple personality disorder?" I asked severely.

"You're doing it again."

I sighed. "Fine then. What do you want to ask?"

"I was wondering if, a week from Saturday — you know, the day of the spring dance —"

"Are you trying to be *funny?*" I interrupted him, wheeling toward him. My face got drenched as I looked up at his expression.

His eyes were wickedly amused. "Will you please allow me to finish?"

I bit my lip and clasped my hands together, interlocking my fingers, so I couldn't do anything rash.

"I heard you say you were going to Seattle that day, and I was wondering if you wanted a ride."

That was unexpected.

"What?" I wasn't sure what he was getting at.

"Do you want a ride to Seattle?"

"With who?" I asked, mystified.

"Myself, obviously." He enunciated every syllable, as if he were talking to someone mentally handicapped.

I was still stunned. *"Why?"*

"Well, I was planning to go to Seattle in the next few weeks, and, to be honest, I'm not sure if your truck can make it."

"My truck works just fine, thank you very much for your concern." I started to walk again, but I was too surprised to maintain the same level of anger.

"But can your truck make it there on one tank of gas?" He matched my pace again.

"I don't see how that is any of your business." Stupid, shiny Volvo owner.

"The wasting of finite resources is everyone's business."

"Honestly, Edward." I felt a thrill go through me as I said his name, and I hated it. "I can't keep up with you. I thought you didn't want to be my friend."

"I said it would be better if we weren't friends, not that I didn't want to be."

"Oh, thanks, now that's *all* cleared up." Heavy sarcasm. I realized I had stopped walking again. We were under the shelter of the cafeteria roof now, so I could more easily look at his face. Which certainly didn't help my clarity of thought.

"It would be more . . . *prudent* for you not to be my friend," he explained. "But I'm tired of trying to stay away from you, Bella."

His eyes were gloriously intense as he uttered that last sentence, his voice smoldering. I couldn't remember how to breathe.

"Will you go with me to Seattle?" he asked, still intense.

I couldn't speak yet, so I just nodded.

He smiled briefly, and then his face became serious.

"You really *should* stay away from me," he warned. "I'll see you in class."

He turned abruptly and walked back the way we'd come.

5. BLOOD TYPE

I MADE MY WAY TO ENGLISH IN A DAZE. I DIDN'T EVEN realize when I first walked in that class had already started.

"Thank you for joining us, Miss Swan," Mr. Mason said in a disparaging tone.

I flushed and hurried to my seat.

It wasn't till class ended that I realized Mike wasn't sitting in his usual seat next to me. I felt a twinge of guilt. But he and Eric both met me at the door as usual, so I figured I wasn't totally unforgiven. Mike seemed to become more himself as we walked, gaining enthusiasm as he talked about the weather report for this weekend. The rain was supposed to take a minor break, and so maybe his beach trip would be possible. I tried to sound eager, to make up for disappointing him yesterday. It was hard; rain or no rain, it would still only be in the high forties, if we were lucky.

The rest of the morning passed in a blur. It was difficult to believe that I hadn't just imagined what Edward had said, and the way his eyes had looked. Maybe it was just a very convincing dream that I'd confused with reality. That seemed more probable than that I really appealed to him on any level.

So I was impatient and frightened as Jessica and I entered the cafeteria. I wanted to see his face, to see if he'd gone back to the cold, indifferent person I'd known for the last several weeks. Or if, by some miracle, I'd really heard what I thought I'd heard this morning. Jessica babbled on and on about her dance plans — Lauren and Angela had asked the other boys and they were all going together — completely unaware of my inattention.

Disappointment flooded through me as my eyes unerringly focused on his table. The other four were there, but he was absent. Had he gone home? I followed the still-babbling Jessica through the line, crushed. I'd lost my appetite — I bought nothing but a bottle of lemonade. I just wanted to go sit down and sulk.

"Edward Cullen is staring at you again," Jessica said, finally breaking through my abstraction with his name. "I wonder why he's sitting alone today."

My head snapped up. I followed her gaze to see Edward, smiling crookedly, staring at me from an empty table across the cafeteria from where he usually sat. Once he'd caught my eye, he raised one hand and motioned with his index finger for me to join him. As I stared in disbelief, he winked.

"Does he mean *you?*" Jessica asked with insulting astonishment in her voice.

"Maybe he needs help with his Biology homework," I muttered for her benefit. "Um, I'd better go see what he wants."

I could feel her staring after me as I walked away.

When I reached his table, I stood behind the chair across from him, unsure.

"Why don't you sit with me today?" he asked, smiling.

I sat down automatically, watching him with caution. He was still smiling. It was hard to believe that someone so beautiful could be real. I was afraid that he might disappear in a sudden puff of smoke, and I would wake up.

He seemed to be waiting for me to say something.

"This is different," I finally managed.

"Well . . ." He paused, and then the rest of the words followed in a rush. "I decided as long as I was going to hell, I might as well do it thoroughly."

I waited for him to say something that made sense. The seconds ticked by.

"You know I don't have any idea what you mean," I eventually pointed out.

"I know." He smiled again, and then he changed the subject. "I think your friends are angry with me for stealing you."

"They'll survive." I could feel their stares boring into my back.

"I may not give you back, though," he said with a wicked glint in his eyes.

I gulped.

He laughed. "You look worried."

"No," I said, but, ridiculously, my voice broke. "Surprised, actually . . . what brought all this on?"

"I told you — I got tired of trying to stay away from you. So I'm giving up." He was still smiling, but his ocher eyes were serious.

"Giving up?" I repeated in confusion.

"Yes — giving up trying to be good. I'm just going to do what I want now, and let the chips fall where they may." His smile faded as he explained, and a hard edge crept into his voice.

"You lost me again."

The breathtaking crooked smile reappeared.

"I always say too much when I'm talking to you — that's one of the problems."

"Don't worry — I don't understand any of it," I said wryly.

"I'm counting on that."

"So, in plain English, are we friends now?"

"Friends . . . ," he mused, dubious.

"Or not," I muttered.

He grinned. "Well, we can try, I suppose. But I'm warning you now that I'm not a good friend for you." Behind his smile, the warning was real.

"You say that a lot," I noted, trying to ignore the sudden trembling in my stomach and keep my voice even.

"Yes, because you're not listening to me. I'm still waiting for you to believe it. If you're smart, you'll avoid me."

"I think you've made your opinion on the subject of my intellect clear, too." My eyes narrowed.

He smiled apologetically.

"So, as long as I'm being . . . not smart, we'll try to be friends?" I struggled to sum up the confusing exchange.

"That sounds about right."

I looked down at my hands wrapped around the lemonade bottle, not sure what to do now.

"What are you thinking?" he asked curiously.

I looked up into his deep gold eyes, became befuddled, and, as usual, blurted out the truth.

"I'm trying to figure out what you are."

His jaw tightened, but he kept his smile in place with some effort.

"Are you having any luck with that?" he asked in an offhand tone.

"Not too much," I admitted.

He chuckled. "What are your theories?"

I blushed. I had been vacillating during the last month between Bruce Wayne and Peter Parker. There was no way I was going to own up to that.

"Won't you tell me?" he asked, tilting his head to one side with a shockingly tempting smile.

I shook my head. "Too embarrassing."

"That's *really* frustrating, you know," he complained.

"No," I disagreed quickly, my eyes narrowing, "I can't *imagine* why that would be frustrating at all — just because someone refuses to tell you what they're thinking, even if all the while they're making cryptic little remarks specifically designed to keep you up at night wondering what they could possibly mean . . . now, why would that be frustrating?"

He grimaced.

"Or better," I continued, the pent-up annoyance flowing freely now, "say that person also did a wide range of bizarre things — from saving your life under impossible circumstances one day to treating you like a pariah the next, and he never explained any of that, either, even after he promised. That, also, would be *very* non-frustrating."

"You've got a bit of a temper, don't you?"

"I don't like double standards."

We stared at each other, unsmiling.

He glanced over my shoulder, and then, unexpectedly, he snickered.

"What?"

"Your boyfriend seems to think I'm being unpleasant to you — he's debating whether or not to come break up our fight." He snickered again.

"I don't know who you're talking about," I said frostily. "But I'm sure you're wrong, anyway."

"I'm not. I told you, most people are easy to read."

"Except me, of course."

"Yes. Except for you." His mood shifted suddenly; his eyes turned brooding. "I wonder why that is."

I had to look away from the intensity of his stare. I concentrated on unscrewing the lid of my lemonade. I took a swig, staring at the table without seeing it.

"Aren't you hungry?" he asked, distracted.

"No." I didn't feel like mentioning that my stomach was already full — of butterflies. "You?" I looked at the empty table in front of him.

"No, I'm not hungry." I didn't understand his expression — it looked like he was enjoying some private joke.

"Can you do me a favor?" I asked after a second of hesitation.

He was suddenly wary. "That depends on what you want."

"It's not much," I assured him.

He waited, guarded but curious.

"I just wondered . . . if you could warn me beforehand the next time you decide to ignore me for my own good. Just so I'm prepared." I looked at the lemonade bottle as I spoke, tracing the circle of the opening with my pinkie finger.

"That sounds fair." He was pressing his lips together to keep from laughing when I looked up.

"Thanks."

"Then can I have one answer in return?" he demanded.

"One."

"Tell me *one* theory."

Whoops. "Not that one."

"You didn't qualify, you just promised one answer," he reminded me.

"And you've broken promises yourself," I reminded him back.

"Just one theory — I won't laugh."

"Yes, you will." I was positive about that.

He looked down, and then glanced up at me through his long black lashes, his ocher eyes scorching.

"Please?" he breathed, leaning toward me.

I blinked, my mind going blank. Holy crow, how did he *do* that?

"Er, what?" I asked, dazed.

"Please tell me just one little theory." His eyes still smoldered at me.

"Um, well, bitten by a radioactive spider?" Was he a hypnotist, too? Or was I just a hopeless pushover?

"That's not very creative," he scoffed.

"I'm sorry, that's all I've got," I said, miffed.

"You're not even close," he teased.

"No spiders?"

"Nope."

"And no radioactivity?"

"None."

"Dang," I sighed.

"Kryptonite doesn't bother me, either," he chuckled.

"You're not supposed to laugh, remember?"

He struggled to compose his face.

"I'll figure it out eventually," I warned him.

"I wish you wouldn't try." He was serious again.

"Because . . . ?"

"What if I'm not a superhero? What if I'm the bad guy?" He smiled playfully, but his eyes were impenetrable.

"Oh," I said, as several things he'd hinted fell suddenly into place. "I see."

"Do you?" His face was abruptly severe, as if he were afraid that he'd accidentally said too much.

"You're dangerous?" I guessed, my pulse quickening as I intuitively realized the truth of my own words. He *was* dangerous. He'd been trying to tell me that all along.

He just looked at me, eyes full of some emotion I couldn't comprehend.

"But not bad," I whispered, shaking my head. "No, I don't believe that you're bad."

"You're wrong." His voice was almost inaudible. He looked down, stealing my bottle lid and then spinning it on its side between his fingers. I stared at him, wondering why I didn't feel afraid. He meant what he was saying — that was obvious. But I just felt anxious, on edge . . . and, more than anything else, fascinated. The same way I always felt when I was near him.

The silence lasted until I noticed that the cafeteria was almost empty.

I jumped to my feet. "We're going to be late."

"I'm not going to class today," he said, twirling the lid so fast it was just a blur.

"Why not?"

"It's healthy to ditch class now and then." He smiled up at me, but his eyes were still troubled.

"Well, I'm going," I told him. I was far too big a coward to risk getting caught.

He turned his attention back to his makeshift top. "I'll see you later, then."

I hesitated, torn, but then the first bell sent me hurrying out the door — with a last glance confirming that he hadn't moved a centimeter.

As I half-ran to class, my head was spinning faster than the bottle cap. So few questions had been answered in comparison to how many new questions had been raised. At least the rain had stopped.

I was lucky; Mr. Banner wasn't in the room yet when I arrived. I settled quickly into my seat, aware that both Mike and Angela were staring at me. Mike looked resentful; Angela looked surprised, and slightly awed.

Mr. Banner came in the room then, calling the class to order. He was juggling a few small cardboard boxes in his arms. He put them down on Mike's table, telling him to start passing them around the class.

"Okay, guys, I want you all to take one piece from each box," he said as he produced a pair of rubber gloves from the pocket of his lab jacket and pulled them on. The sharp sound as the gloves snapped into place against his wrists seemed ominous to me. "The first should be an indicator card," he went on, grabbing a white card with four squares marked on it and displaying it. "The second is a four-pronged applicator —" he held up something that looked like a nearly toothless hair pick "— and the third is a sterile micro-lancet." He held up a small piece of blue plastic and split it open. The barb was invisible from this distance, but my stomach flipped.

"I'll be coming around with a dropper of water to prepare your cards, so please don't start until I get to you." He began at Mike's table again, carefully putting one drop of water in each of the four squares. "Then I want you to carefully prick your finger with the lancet. . . ." He grabbed Mike's hand and jabbed the spike into the tip of Mike's middle finger. Oh no. Clammy moisture broke out across my forehead.

"Put a small drop of blood on each of the prongs." He demonstrated, squeezing Mike's finger till the blood flowed. I swallowed convulsively, my stomach heaving.

"And then apply it to the card," he finished, holding up the dripping red card for us to see. I closed my eyes, trying to hear through the ringing in my ears.

"The Red Cross is having a blood drive in Port Angeles next weekend, so I thought you should all know your blood type." He sounded proud of himself. "Those of you who aren't eighteen yet will need a parent's permission — I have slips at my desk."

He continued through the room with his water drops. I put my cheek against the cool black tabletop and tried to hold on to my consciousness. All around me I could hear squeals, complaints, and giggles as my classmates skewered their fingers. I breathed slowly in and out through my mouth.

"Bella, are you all right?" Mr. Banner asked. His voice was close to my head, and it sounded alarmed.

"I already know my blood type, Mr. Banner," I said in a weak voice. I was afraid to raise my head.

"Are you feeling faint?"

"Yes, sir," I muttered, internally kicking myself for not ditching when I had the chance.

"Can someone take Bella to the nurse, please?" he called.

I didn't have to look up to know that it would be Mike who volunteered.

"Can you walk?" Mr. Banner asked.

"Yes," I whispered. Just let me get out of here, I thought. I'll crawl.

Mike seemed eager as he put his arm around my waist and pulled my arm over his shoulder. I leaned against him heavily on the way out of the classroom.

Mike towed me slowly across campus. When we were around the edge of the cafeteria, out of sight of building four in case Mr. Banner was watching, I stopped.

"Just let me sit for a minute, please?" I begged.

He helped me sit on the edge of the walk.

"And whatever you do, keep your hand in your pocket," I warned. I was still so dizzy. I slumped over on my side, putting my cheek against the freezing, damp cement of the sidewalk, closing my eyes. That seemed to help a little.

"Wow, you're green, Bella," Mike said nervously.

"Bella?" a different voice called from the distance.

No! Please let me be imagining that horribly familiar voice.

"What's wrong — is she hurt?" His voice was closer now, and he sounded upset. I wasn't imagining it. I squeezed my eyes shut, hoping to die. Or, at the very least, not to throw up.

Mike seemed stressed. "I think she's fainted. I don't know what happened, she didn't even stick her finger."

"Bella." Edward's voice was right beside me, relieved now. "Can you hear me?"

"No," I groaned. "Go away."

He chuckled.

"I was taking her to the nurse," Mike explained in a defensive tone, "but she wouldn't go any farther."

"I'll take her," Edward said. I could hear the smile still in his voice. "You can go back to class."

"No," Mike protested. "I'm supposed to do it."

Suddenly the sidewalk disappeared from beneath me. My eyes flew open in shock. Edward had scooped me up in his arms, as easily as if I weighed ten pounds instead of a hundred and ten.

"Put me down!" Please, please let me not vomit on him. He was walking before I was finished talking.

"Hey!" Mike called, already ten paces behind us.

Edward ignored him. "You look awful," he told me, grinning.

"Put me back on the sidewalk," I moaned. The rocking movement of his walk was not helping. He held me away from his body, gingerly, supporting all my weight with just his arms — it didn't seem to bother him.

"So you faint at the sight of blood?" he asked. This seemed to entertain him.

I didn't answer. I closed my eyes again and fought the nausea with all my strength, clamping my lips together.

"And not even your own blood," he continued, enjoying himself.

I don't know how he opened the door while carrying me, but it was suddenly warm, so I knew we were inside.

"Oh my," I heard a female voice gasp.

"She fainted in Biology," Edward explained.

I opened my eyes. I was in the office, and Edward was striding past the front counter toward the nurse's door. Ms. Cope, the redheaded front office receptionist, ran ahead of him to hold it open. The grandmotherly nurse looked up from a novel, astonished, as Edward swung me into the room and placed me gently on the crackly paper that covered the brown vinyl mattress on the one cot. Then he moved to stand against the wall as far across the narrow room as possible. His eyes were bright, excited.

"She's just a little faint," he reassured the startled nurse. "They're blood typing in Biology."

The nurse nodded sagely. "There's always one."

He muffled a snicker.

"Just lie down for a minute, honey; it'll pass."

"I know," I sighed. The nausea was already fading.

"Does this happen a lot?" she asked.

"Sometimes," I admitted. Edward coughed to hide another laugh.

"You can go back to class now," she told him.

"I'm supposed to stay with her." He said this with such assured authority that — even though she pursed her lips — the nurse didn't argue it further.

"I'll go get you some ice for your forehead, dear," she said to me, and then bustled out of the room.

"You were right," I moaned, letting my eyes close.

"I usually am — but about what in particular this time?"

"Ditching *is* healthy." I practiced breathing evenly.

"You scared me for a minute there," he admitted after a

pause. His tone made it sound like he was confessing a humiliating weakness. "I thought Newton was dragging your dead body off to bury it in the woods."

"Ha ha." I still had my eyes closed, but I was feeling more normal every minute.

"Honestly — I've seen corpses with better color. I was concerned that I might have to avenge your murder."

"Poor Mike. I'll bet he's mad."

"He absolutely loathes me," Edward said cheerfully.

"You can't know that," I argued, but then I wondered suddenly if he could.

"I saw his face — I could tell."

"How did you see me? I thought you were ditching." I was almost fine now, though the queasiness would probably pass faster if I'd eaten something for lunch. On the other hand, maybe it was lucky my stomach was empty.

"I was in my car, listening to a CD." Such a normal response — it surprised me.

I heard the door and opened my eyes to see the nurse with a cold compress in her hand.

"Here you go, dear." She laid it across my forehead. "You're looking better," she added.

"I think I'm fine," I said, sitting up. Just a little ringing in my ears, no spinning. The mint green walls stayed where they should.

I could see she was about to make me lie back down, but the door opened just then, and Ms. Cope stuck her head in.

"We've got another one," she warned.

I hopped down to free up the cot for the next invalid.

I handed the compress back to the nurse. "Here, I don't need this."

And then Mike staggered through the door, now supporting a sallow-looking Lee Stephens, another boy in our Biology class. Edward and I drew back against the wall to give them room.

"Oh no," Edward muttered. "Go out to the office, Bella."

I looked up at him, bewildered.

"Trust me — go."

I spun and caught the door before it closed, darting out of the infirmary. I could feel Edward right behind me.

"You actually listened to me." He was stunned.

"I smelled the blood," I said, wrinkling my nose. Lee wasn't sick from watching other people, like me.

"People can't smell blood," he contradicted.

"Well, I can — that's what makes me sick. It smells like rust . . . and salt."

He was staring at me with an unfathomable expression.

"What?" I asked.

"It's nothing."

Mike came through the door then, glancing from me to Edward. The look he gave Edward confirmed what Edward had said about loathing. He looked back at me, his eyes glum.

"*You* look better," he accused.

"Just keep your hand in your pocket," I warned him again.

"It's not bleeding anymore," he muttered. "Are you going back to class?"

"Are you kidding? I'd just have to turn around and come back."

"Yeah, I guess. . . . So are you going this weekend? To the beach?" While he spoke, he flashed another glare toward Edward, who was standing against the cluttered counter, motionless as a sculpture, staring off into space.

I tried to sound as friendly as possible. "Sure, I said I was in."

"We're meeting at my dad's store, at ten." His eyes flickered to Edward again, wondering if he was giving out too much information. His body language made it clear that it wasn't an open invitation.

"I'll be there," I promised.

"I'll see you in Gym, then," he said, moving uncertainly toward the door.

"See you," I replied. He looked at me once more, his round face slightly pouting, and then as he walked slowly through the door, his shoulders slumped. A swell of sympathy washed over me. I pondered seeing his disappointed face again . . . in Gym.

"Gym," I groaned.

"I can take care of that." I hadn't noticed Edward moving to my side, but he spoke now in my ear. "Go sit down and look pale," he muttered.

That wasn't a challenge; I was always pale, and my recent swoon had left a light sheen of sweat on my face. I sat in one of the creaky folding chairs and rested my head against the wall with my eyes closed. Fainting spells always exhausted me.

I heard Edward speaking softly at the counter.

"Ms. Cope?"

"Yes?" I hadn't heard her return to her desk.

"Bella has Gym next hour, and I don't think she feels well enough. Actually, I was thinking I should take her home now. Do you think you could excuse her from class?" His voice was like melting honey. I could imagine how much more overwhelming his eyes would be.

"Do you need to be excused, too, Edward?" Ms. Cope fluttered. Why couldn't I do that?

"No, I have Mrs. Goff, she won't mind."

"Okay, it's all taken care of. You feel better, Bella," she called to me. I nodded weakly, hamming it up just a bit.

"Can you walk, or do you want me to carry you again?" With his back to the receptionist, his expression became sarcastic.

"I'll walk."

I stood carefully, and I was still fine. He held the door for me, his smile polite but his eyes mocking. I walked out into the cold, fine mist that had just begun to fall. It felt nice — the first time I'd enjoyed the constant moisture falling out of the sky — as it washed my face clean of the sticky perspiration.

"Thanks," I said as he followed me out. "It's almost worth getting sick to miss Gym."

"Anytime." He was staring straight forward, squinting into the rain.

"So are you going? This Saturday, I mean?" I was hoping he would, though it seemed unlikely. I couldn't picture him loading up to carpool with the rest of the kids from school; he didn't belong in the same world. But just hoping that he might gave me the first twinge of enthusiasm I'd felt for the outing.

"Where are you all going, exactly?" He was still looking ahead, expressionless.

"Down to La Push, to First Beach." I studied his face, trying to read it. His eyes seemed to narrow infinitesimally.

He glanced down at me from the corner of his eye, smiling wryly. "I really don't think I was invited."

I sighed. "I just invited you."

"Let's you and I not push poor Mike any further this week. We don't want him to snap." His eyes danced; he was enjoying the idea more than he should.

"Mike-schmike," I muttered, preoccupied by the way he'd said "you and I." I liked it more than *I* should.

We were near the parking lot now. I veered left, toward my truck. Something caught my jacket, yanking me back.

"Where do you think you're going?" he asked, outraged. He was gripping a fistful of my jacket in one hand.

I was confused. "I'm going home."

"Didn't you hear me promise to take you safely home? Do you think I'm going to let you drive in your condition?" His voice was still indignant.

"What condition? And what about my truck?" I complained.

"I'll have Alice drop it off after school." He was towing me toward his car now, pulling me by my jacket. It was all I could do to keep from falling backward. He'd probably just drag me along anyway if I did.

"Let go!" I insisted. He ignored me. I staggered along sideways across the wet sidewalk until we reached the Volvo. Then he finally freed me — I stumbled against the passenger door.

"You are so *pushy*!" I grumbled.

"It's open," was all he responded. He got in the driver's side.

"I am perfectly capable of driving myself home!" I stood by the car, fuming. It was raining harder now, and I'd never put my hood up, so my hair was dripping down my back.

He lowered the automatic window and leaned toward me across the seat. "Get in, Bella."

I didn't answer. I was mentally calculating my chances of reaching the truck before he could catch me. I had to admit, they weren't good.

"I'll just drag you back," he threatened, guessing my plan.

I tried to maintain what dignity I could as I got into his car. I wasn't very successful — I looked like a half-drowned cat and my boots squeaked.

"This is completely unnecessary," I said stiffly.

He didn't answer. He fiddled with the controls, turning the heater up and the music down. As he pulled out of the parking lot, I was preparing to give him the silent treatment — my face in full pout mode — but then I recognized the music playing, and my curiosity got the better of my intentions.

"Clair de Lune?" I asked, surprised.

"You know Debussy?" He sounded surprised, too.

"Not well," I admitted. "My mother plays a lot of classical music around the house — I only know my favorites."

"It's one of my favorites, too." He stared out through the rain, lost in thought.

I listened to the music, relaxing against the light gray leather seat. It was impossible not to respond to the familiar, soothing melody. The rain blurred everything outside the window into gray and green smudges. I began to realize we were driving very fast; the car moved so steadily, so evenly, though, I didn't feel the speed. Only the town flashing by gave it away.

"What is your mother like?" he asked me suddenly.

I glanced over to see him studying me with curious eyes.

"She looks a lot like me, but she's prettier," I said. He raised his eyebrows. "I have too much Charlie in me. She's more outgoing than I am, and braver. She's irresponsible and slightly eccentric, and she's a very unpredictable cook. She's my best friend." I stopped. Talking about her was making me depressed.

"How old are you, Bella?" His voice sounded frustrated for some reason I couldn't imagine. He'd stopped the car, and I realized we were at Charlie's house already. The rain was so heavy that I could barely see the house at all. It was like the car was submerged under a river.

"I'm seventeen," I responded, a little confused.

"You don't seem seventeen."

His tone was reproachful; it made me laugh.

"What?" he asked, curious again.

"My mom always says I was born thirty-five years old and that I get more middle-aged every year." I laughed, and then sighed. "Well, someone has to be the adult." I paused for a second. "You don't seem much like a junior in high school yourself," I noted.

He made a face and changed the subject.

"So why did your mother marry Phil?"

I was surprised he would remember the name; I'd mentioned it just once, almost two months ago. It took me a moment to answer.

"My mother . . . she's very young for her age. I think Phil makes her feel even younger. At any rate, she's crazy about him." I shook my head. The attraction was a mystery to me.

"Do you approve?" he asked.

"Does it matter?" I countered. "I want her to be happy . . . and he is who she wants."

"That's very generous. . . . I wonder," he mused.

"What?"

"Would she extend the same courtesy to you, do you think? No matter who your choice was?" He was suddenly intent, his eyes searching mine.

"I-I think so," I stuttered. "But she's the parent, after all. It's a little bit different."

"No one too scary then," he teased.

I grinned in response. "What do you mean by scary? Multiple facial piercings and extensive tattoos?"

"That's one definition, I suppose."

"What's your definition?"

But he ignored my question and asked me another. "Do you think that *I* could be scary?" He raised one eyebrow, and the faint trace of a smile lightened his face.

I thought for a moment, wondering whether the truth or a lie would go over better. I decided to go with the truth. "Hmmm . . . I think you *could* be, if you wanted to."

"Are you frightened of me now?" The smile vanished, and his heavenly face was suddenly serious.

"No." But I answered too quickly. The smile returned.

"So, now are you going to tell me about your family?" I asked to distract him. "It's got to be a much more interesting story than mine."

He was instantly cautious. "What do you want to know?"

"The Cullens adopted you?" I verified.

"Yes."

I hesitated for a moment. "What happened to your parents?"

"They died many years ago." His tone was matter-of-fact.

"I'm sorry," I mumbled.

"I don't really remember them that clearly. Carlisle and Esme have been my parents for a long time now."

"And you love them." It wasn't a question. It was obvious in the way he spoke of them.

"Yes." He smiled. "I couldn't imagine two better people."

"You're very lucky."

"I know I am."

"And your brother and sister?"

He glanced at the clock on the dashboard.

"My brother and sister, and Jasper and Rosalie for that matter, are going to be quite upset if they have to stand in the rain waiting for me."

"Oh, sorry, I guess you have to go." I didn't want to get out of the car.

"And you probably want your truck back before Chief Swan gets home, so you don't have to tell him about the Biology incident." He grinned at me.

"I'm sure he's already heard. There are no secrets in Forks." I sighed.

He laughed, and there was an edge to his laughter.

"Have fun at the beach . . . good weather for sunbathing." He glanced out at the sheeting rain.

"Won't I see you tomorrow?"

"No. Emmett and I are starting the weekend early."

"What are you going to do?" A friend could ask that, right? I hoped the disappointment wasn't too apparent in my voice.

"We're going to be hiking in the Goat Rocks Wilderness, just south of Rainier."

I remembered Charlie had said the Cullens went camping frequently.

"Oh, well, have fun." I tried to sound enthusiastic. I don't think I fooled him, though. A smile was playing around the edges of his lips.

"Will you do something for me this weekend?" He turned to look me straight in the face, utilizing the full power of his burning gold eyes.

I nodded helplessly.

"Don't be offended, but you seem to be one of those people who just attract accidents like a magnet. So . . . try not to fall into the ocean or get run over or anything, all right?" He smiled crookedly.

The helplessness had faded as he spoke. I glared at him.

"I'll see what I can do," I snapped as I jumped out into the rain. I slammed the door behind me with excessive force.

He was still smiling as he drove away.

6. SCARY STORIES

As I sat in my room, trying to concentrate on the third act of *Macbeth,* I was really listening for my truck. I would have thought, even over the pounding rain, I could have heard the engine's roar. But when I went to peek out the curtain — again — it was suddenly there.

I wasn't looking forward to Friday, and it more than lived up to my non-expectations. Of course there were the fainting comments. Jessica especially seemed to get a kick out of that story. Luckily Mike had kept his mouth shut, and no one seemed to know about Edward's involvement. She did have a lot of questions about lunch, though.

"So what did Edward Cullen want yesterday?" Jessica asked in Trig.

"I don't know," I answered truthfully. "He never really got to the point."

"You looked kind of mad," she fished.

"Did I?" I kept my expression blank.

"You know, I've never seen him sit with anyone but his family before. That was weird."

"Weird," I agreed. She seemed annoyed; she flipped her dark curls impatiently — I guessed she'd been hoping to hear something that would make a good story for her to pass on.

The worst part about Friday was that, even though I knew he wasn't going to be there, I still hoped. When I walked into the cafeteria with Jessica and Mike, I couldn't keep from looking at his table, where Rosalie, Alice, and Jasper sat talking, heads close together. And I couldn't stop the gloom that engulfed me as I realized I didn't know how long I would have to wait before I saw him again.

At my usual table, everyone was full of our plans for the next day. Mike was animated again, putting a great deal of trust in the local weatherman who promised sun tomorrow. I'd have to see that before I believed it. But it was warmer today — almost sixty. Maybe the outing wouldn't be completely miserable.

I intercepted a few unfriendly glances from Lauren during lunch, which I didn't understand until we were all walking out of the room together. I was right behind her, just a foot from her slick, silver blond hair, and she was evidently unaware of that.

". . . don't know why *Bella*" — she sneered my name — "doesn't just sit with the Cullens from now on,"

I heard her muttering to Mike. I'd never noticed what an unpleasant, nasal voice she had, and I was surprised by the malice in it. I really didn't know her well at all, certainly not well enough for her to dislike me — or so I'd thought.

"She's my friend; she sits with us," Mike whispered back loyally, but also a bit territorially. I paused to let Jess and Angela pass me. I didn't want to hear any more.

That night at dinner, Charlie seemed enthusiastic about my trip to La Push in the morning. I think he felt guilty for leaving me home alone on the weekends, but he'd spent too many years building his habits to break them now. Of course he knew the names of all the kids going, and their parents, and their great-grandparents, too, probably. He seemed to approve. I wondered if he would approve of my plan to ride to Seattle with Edward Cullen. Not that I was going to tell him.

"Dad, do you know a place called Goat Rocks or something like that? I think it's south of Mount Rainier," I asked casually.

"Yeah — why?"

I shrugged. "Some kids were talking about camping there."

"It's not a very good place for camping." He sounded surprised. "Too many bears. Most people go there during the hunting season."

"Oh," I murmured. "Maybe I got the name wrong."

I meant to sleep in, but an unusual brightness woke me. I opened my eyes to see a clear yellow light streaming through my window. I couldn't believe it. I hurried to the window to check, and sure enough, there was the sun. It was in the wrong place in the sky, too low, and it didn't seem to be as close as it should be, but it was definitely the sun. Clouds ringed the horizon, but a large patch of blue was visible in the middle. I lingered by the window as long as I could, afraid that if I left the blue would disappear again.

The Newtons' Olympic Outfitters store was just north of town. I'd seen the store, but I'd never stopped there — not having much need for any supplies required for being outdoors over an extended period of time. In the parking lot I recognized Mike's Suburban and Tyler's Sentra. As I pulled up next to their vehicles, I could see the group standing around in front of the Suburban. Eric was there, along with two other boys I had class with; I was fairly sure their names were Ben and Conner. Jess was there, flanked by Angela and Lauren. Three other girls stood with them, including one I remembered falling over in Gym on Friday. That one gave me a dirty look as I got out of the truck, and whispered something to Lauren. Lauren shook out her cornsilk hair and eyed me scornfully.

So it was going to be one of *those* days.

At least Mike was happy to see me.

"You came!" he called, delighted. "And I said it would be sunny today, didn't I?"

"I told you I was coming," I reminded him.

"We're just waiting for Lee and Samantha . . . unless you invited someone," Mike added.

"Nope," I lied lightly, hoping I wouldn't get caught in the lie. But also wishing that a miracle would occur, and Edward would appear.

Mike looked satisfied.

"Will you ride in my car? It's that or Lee's mom's minivan."

"Sure."

He smiled blissfully. It was so easy to make Mike happy.

"You can have shotgun," he promised. I hid my chagrin. It wasn't as simple to make Mike and Jessica happy at the same time. I could see Jessica glowering at us now.

The numbers worked out in my favor, though. Lee brought two extra people, and suddenly every seat was necessary. I managed to wedge Jess in between Mike and me in the front seat of the Suburban. Mike could have been more graceful about it, but at least Jess seemed appeased.

It was only fifteen miles to La Push from Forks, with gorgeous, dense green forests edging the road most of the way and the wide Quillayute River snaking beneath it twice. I was glad I had the window seat. We'd rolled the windows down — the Suburban was a bit claustrophobic with nine people in it — and I tried to absorb as much sunlight as possible.

I'd been to the beaches around La Push many times during my Forks summers with Charlie, so the mile-long crescent of First Beach was familiar to me. It was still breathtaking. The water was dark gray, even in the sunlight, white-capped and heaving to the gray, rocky shore. Islands rose out of the steel harbor waters with sheer cliff sides, reaching to uneven summits, and crowned with austere, soaring firs. The beach had only a thin border of actual sand at the water's edge, after which it grew into millions of large, smooth stones that looked uniformly gray from a distance, but close up were every shade a stone could be: terra-cotta, sea green, lavender, blue gray, dull gold. The tide line was strewn with huge driftwood trees, bleached bone white in the salt waves, some piled together against the edge of the forest fringe, some lying solitary, just out of reach of the waves.

There was a brisk wind coming off the waves, cool and briny. Pelicans floated on the swells while seagulls and a lone eagle wheeled above them. The clouds still circled the sky, threatening to invade at any moment, but for now the sun shone bravely in its halo of blue sky.

We picked our way down to the beach, Mike leading the way to a ring of driftwood logs that had obviously been used for parties like ours before. There was a fire circle already in place, filled with black ashes. Eric and the boy I thought was named Ben gathered broken branches of driftwood from the drier piles against the forest edge, and soon had a teepee-shaped construction built atop the old cinders.

"Have you ever seen a driftwood fire?" Mike asked me. I was sitting on one of the bone-colored benches; the other girls clustered, gossiping excitedly, on either side of me. Mike kneeled by the fire, lighting one of the smaller sticks with a cigarette lighter.

"No," I said as he placed the blazing twig carefully against the teepee.

"You'll like this then — watch the colors." He lit another small branch and laid it alongside the first. The flames started to lick quickly up the dry wood.

"It's blue," I said in surprise.

"The salt does it. Pretty, isn't it?" He lit one more piece, placed it where the fire hadn't yet caught, and then came to sit by me. Thankfully, Jess was on his other side. She turned to him and claimed his attention. I watched the strange blue and green flames crackle toward the sky.

After a half hour of chatter, some of the boys wanted to hike to the nearby tidal pools. It was a dilemma. On the one hand, I loved the tide pools. They had fascinated me since I was a child; they were one of the only things I ever looked forward to when I had to come to Forks. On the other hand, I'd also fallen into them a lot. Not a big deal when you're seven and with your dad. It reminded me of Edward's request — that I not fall into the ocean.

Lauren was the one who made my decision for me. She didn't want to hike, and she was definitely wearing the wrong shoes for it. Most of the other girls besides Angela and Jessica decided to stay on the beach as well. I waited until Tyler and Eric had committed to remaining with them before I got up quietly to join the pro-hiking group. Mike gave me a huge smile when he saw that I was coming.

The hike wasn't too long, though I hated to lose the sky in the woods. The green light of the forest was strangely at odds with the adolescent laughter, too murky and ominous to be in harmony with the light banter around me. I had to watch each step I took very carefully, avoiding roots below and branches above, and I soon fell behind. Eventually I broke through the emerald confines of the forest and found the rocky shore again. It was low tide, and a tidal river flowed past us on its way to the sea. Along its pebbled banks, shallow pools that never completely drained were teeming with life.

I was very cautious not to lean too far over the little ocean ponds. The others were fearless, leaping over the rocks, perching precariously on the edges. I found a very stable-looking rock on the fringe of one of the largest pools and sat there cautiously, spellbound by the natural aquarium below me. The bouquets of brilliant anemones undulated ceaselessly in the invisible current, twisted shells scurried about the edges, obscuring the crabs within them, starfish stuck motionless to the rocks and each other, while one small black eel with white racing stripes wove through the bright green weeds, waiting for the sea to return. I was completely absorbed, except for one small part of my mind that wondered what Edward was doing now, and trying to imagine what he would be saying if he were here with me.

Finally the boys were hungry, and I got up stiffly to follow them back. I tried to keep up better this time through the woods, so naturally I fell a few times. I got some shallow scrapes on my palms, and the knees of my jeans were stained green, but it could have been worse.

When we got back to First Beach, the group we'd left behind had multiplied. As we got closer we could see the shining, straight black hair and copper skin of the newcomers, teenagers from the reservation come to socialize.

The food was already being passed around, and the boys hurried to claim a share while Eric introduced us as we each entered the driftwood circle. Angela and I were the last to arrive, and, as Eric said our names, I noticed a younger boy sitting on the stones near the fire glance up at me in interest. I sat down next to Angela, and Mike brought us sandwiches and an array of sodas to choose from, while a boy who looked to be the oldest of the visitors rattled off the names of the seven others with him. All I caught was that one of the girls was also named Jessica, and the boy who noticed me was named Jacob.

It was relaxing to sit with Angela; she was a restful kind of person to be around — she didn't feel the need to fill every silence with chatter. She left me free to think undisturbed while we ate. And I was thinking about how disjointedly time seemed to flow in Forks, passing in a blur at times, with single images standing out more clearly than others. And then, at other times, every second was significant, etched in my mind. I knew exactly what caused the difference, and it disturbed me.

During lunch the clouds started to advance, slinking across the blue sky, darting in front of the sun momentarily, casting long shadows across the beach, and blackening the waves. As they finished eating, people started to drift away in twos and threes. Some walked down to the edge of the waves, trying to skip rocks across the choppy surface. Others were gathering a second expedition to the tide pools. Mike — with Jessica shadowing him — headed up to the one shop in the village. Some of the local kids went with them; others went along on the hike. By the time they all had scattered, I was sitting alone on my driftwood log, with Lauren and Tyler occupying themselves by the CD player someone had thought to bring, and three teenagers from the reservation perched around the circle, including the boy named Jacob and the oldest boy who had acted as spokesperson.

A few minutes after Angela left with the hikers, Jacob sauntered over to take her place by my side. He looked fourteen, maybe fifteen, and had long, glossy black hair pulled back with a rubber band at the nape of his neck. His skin was beautiful, silky and russet-colored; his eyes were dark, set deep above the high planes of his cheekbones. He still had just a hint of childish roundness left around his chin. Altogether, a very pretty face. However, my positive opinion of his looks was damaged by the first words out of his mouth.

"You're Isabella Swan, aren't you?"

It was like the first day of school all over again.

"Bella," I sighed.

"I'm Jacob Black." He held his hand out in a friendly gesture. "You bought my dad's truck."

"Oh," I said, relieved, shaking his sleek hand. "You're Billy's son. I probably should remember you."

"No, I'm the youngest of the family — you would remember my older sisters."

"Rachel and Rebecca," I suddenly recalled. Charlie and Billy had thrown us together a lot during my visits, to keep us busy while they fished. We were all too shy to make much progress as friends. Of course, I'd kicked up enough tantrums to end the fishing trips by the time I was eleven.

"Are they here?" I examined the girls at the ocean's edge, wondering if I would recognize them now.

"No." Jacob shook his head. "Rachel got a scholarship to Washington State, and Rebecca married a Samoan surfer — she lives in Hawaii now."

"Married. Wow." I was stunned. The twins were only a little over a year older than I was.

"So how do you like the truck?" he asked.

"I love it. It runs great."

"Yeah, but it's really slow," he laughed. "I was so relived when Charlie bought it. My dad wouldn't let me work on building another car when we had a perfectly good vehicle right there."

"It's not that slow," I objected.

"Have you tried to go over sixty?"

"No," I admitted.

"Good. Don't." He grinned.

I couldn't help grinning back. "It does great in a collision," I offered in my truck's defense.

"I don't think a tank could take out that old monster," he agreed with another laugh.

"So you build cars?" I asked, impressed.

"When I have free time, and parts. You wouldn't happen to know where I could get my hands on a master cylinder for a 1986 Volkswagen Rabbit?" he added jokingly. He had a pleasant, husky voice.

"Sorry," I laughed, "I haven't seen any lately, but I'll keep my eyes open for you." As if I knew what that was. He was very easy to talk with.

He flashed a brilliant smile, looking at me appreciatively in a way I was learning to recognize. I wasn't the only one who noticed.

"You know Bella, Jacob?" Lauren asked — in what I imagined was an insolent tone — from across the fire.

"We've sort of known each other since I was born," he laughed, smiling at me again.

"How nice." She didn't sound like she thought it was nice at all, and her pale, fishy eyes narrowed.

"Bella," she called again, watching my face carefully, "I was just saying to Tyler that it was too bad none of the Cullens could come out today. Didn't anyone think to invite them?" Her expression of concern was unconvincing.

"You mean Dr. Carlisle Cullen's family?" the tall, older boy asked before I could respond, much to Lauren's irritation. He was really closer to a man than a boy, and his voice was very deep.

"Yes, do you know them?" she asked condescendingly, turning halfway toward him.

"The Cullens don't come here," he said in a tone that closed the subject, ignoring her question.

Tyler, trying to win back her attention, asked Lauren's opinion on a CD he held. She was distracted.

I stared at the deep-voiced boy, taken aback, but he was looking away toward the dark forest behind us. He'd said that the Cullens didn't come here, but his tone had implied something more — that they weren't allowed; they were prohibited. His manner left a strange impression on me, and I tried to ignore it without success.

Jacob interrupted my meditation. "So is Forks driving you insane yet?"

"Oh, I'd say that's an understatement." I grimaced. He grinned understandingly.

I was still turning over the brief comment on the Cullens, and I had a sudden inspiration. It was a stupid plan, but I didn't have any better ideas. I hoped that young Jacob was as yet inexperienced around girls, so that he wouldn't see through my sure-to-be-pitiful attempts at flirting.

"Do you want to walk down the beach with me?" I asked, trying to imitate that way Edward had of looking up from underneath his eyelashes. It couldn't have nearly the same effect, I was sure, but Jacob jumped up willingly enough.

As we walked north across the multihued stones toward the driftwood seawall, the clouds finally closed ranks across the sky, causing the sea to darken and the temperature to drop. I shoved my hands deep into the pockets of my jacket.

"So you're, what, sixteen?" I asked, trying not to look like an idiot as I fluttered my eyelids the way I'd seen girls do on TV.

"I just turned fifteen," he confessed, flattered.

"Really?" My face was full of false surprise. "I would have thought you were older."

"I'm tall for my age," he explained.

"Do you come up to Forks much?" I asked archly, as if I was hoping for a yes. I sounded idiotic to myself. I was afraid he would turn on me with disgust and accuse me of my fraud, but he still seemed flattered.

"Not too much," he admitted with a frown. "But when I get my car finished I can go up as much as I want — after I get my license," he amended.

"Who was that other boy Lauren was talking to? He seemed a little old to be hanging out with us." I purposefully lumped myself in with the youngsters, trying to make it clear that I preferred Jacob.

"That's Sam — he's nineteen," he informed me.

"What was that he was saying about the doctor's family?" I asked innocently.

"The Cullens? Oh, they're not supposed to come onto the reservation." He looked away, out toward James Island, as he confirmed what I'd thought I'd heard in Sam's voice.

"Why not?"

He glanced back at me, biting his lip. "Oops. I'm not supposed to say anything about that."

"Oh, I won't tell anyone, I'm just curious." I tried to make my smile alluring, wondering if I was laying it on too thick.

He smiled back, though, looking allured. Then he lifted one eyebrow and his voice was even huskier than before.

"Do you like scary stories?" he asked ominously.

"I *love* them," I enthused, making an effort to smolder at him.

Jacob strolled to a nearby driftwood tree that had its roots sticking out like the attenuated legs of a huge, pale spider. He perched lightly on one of the twisted roots while I sat beneath him on the body of the tree. He stared down at the rocks, a smile hovering around the edges of his broad lips. I could see he was going to try to make this good. I focused on keeping the vital interest I felt out of my eyes.

"Do you know any of our old stories, about where we came from — the Quileutes, I mean?" he began.

"Not really," I admitted.

"Well, there are lots of legends, some of them claiming to date back to the Flood — supposedly, the ancient Quileutes tied their canoes to the tops of the tallest trees on the mountain to survive like Noah and the ark." He smiled, to show me how little stock he put in the histories. "Another legend claims that we descended from wolves — and that the wolves are our brothers still. It's against tribal law to kill them.

"Then there are the stories about the *cold ones*." His voice dropped a little lower.

"The cold ones?" I asked, not faking my intrigue now.

"Yes. There are stories of the cold ones as old as the wolf legends, and some much more recent. According to legend, my own great-grandfather knew some of them. He was the one who made the treaty that kept them off our land." He rolled his eyes.

"Your great-grandfather?" I encouraged.

"He was a tribal elder, like my father. You see, the cold ones are the natural enemies of the wolf — well, not the wolf, really, but the wolves that turn into men, like our ancestors. You would call them werewolves."

"Werewolves have enemies?"

"Only one."

I stared at him earnestly, hoping to disguise my impatience as admiration.

"So you see," Jacob continued, "the cold ones are traditionally our enemies. But this pack that came to our territory during my great-grandfather's time was different. They didn't hunt the way others of their kind did — they weren't supposed to be dangerous to the tribe. So my great-grandfather made a truce with them. If they would promise to stay off our lands, we wouldn't expose them to the pale-faces." He winked at me.

"If they weren't dangerous, then why . . . ?" I tried to understand, struggling not to let him see how seriously I was considering his ghost story.

"There's always a risk for humans to be around the cold ones, even if they're civilized like this clan was. You never know when they might get too hungry to resist." He deliberately worked a thick edge of menace into his tone.

"What do you mean, 'civilized'?"

"They claimed that they didn't hunt humans. They supposedly were somehow able to prey on animals instead."

I tried to keep my voice casual. "So how does it fit in with the Cullens? Are they like the cold ones your great-grandfather met?"

"No." He paused dramatically. "They are the *same* ones."

He must have thought the expression on my face was fear inspired by his story. He smiled, pleased, and continued.

"There are more of them now, a new female and a new

male, but the rest are the same. In my great-grandfather's time they already knew of the leader, Carlisle. He'd been here and gone before *your* people had even arrived." He was fighting a smile.

"And what are they?" I finally asked. "What *are* the cold ones?"

He smiled darkly.

"Blood drinkers," he replied in a chilling voice. "Your people call them vampires."

I stared out at the rough surf after he answered, not sure what my face was exposing.

"You have goose bumps," he laughed delightedly.

"You're a good storyteller," I complimented him, still staring into the waves.

"Pretty crazy stuff, though, isn't it? No wonder my dad doesn't want us to talk about it to anyone."

I couldn't control my expression enough to look at him yet. "Don't worry, I won't give you away."

"I guess I just violated the treaty," he laughed.

"I'll take it to the grave," I promised, and then I shivered.

"Seriously, though, don't say anything to Charlie. He was pretty mad at my dad when he heard that some of us weren't going to the hospital since Dr. Cullen started working there."

"I won't, of course not."

"So do you think we're a bunch of superstitious natives or what?" he asked in a playful tone, but with a hint of worry. I still hadn't looked away from the ocean.

I turned and smiled at him as normally as I could.

"No. I think you're very good at telling scary stories, though. I still have goose bumps, see?" I held up my arm.

"Cool." He smiled.

And then the sound of the beach rocks clattering against each other warned us that someone was approaching. Our heads snapped up at the same time to see Mike and Jessica about fifty yards away, walking toward us.

"There you are, Bella," Mike called in relief, waving his arm over his head.

"Is that your boyfriend?" Jacob asked, alerted by the jealous edge in Mike's voice. I was surprised it was so obvious.

"No, definitely not," I whispered. I was tremendously grateful to Jacob, and eager to make him as happy as possible. I winked at him, carefully turning away from Mike to do so. He smiled, elated by my inept flirting.

"So when I get my license . . . ," he began.

"You should come see me in Forks. We could hang out sometime." I felt guilty as I said this, knowing that I'd used him. But I really did like Jacob. He was someone I could easily be friends with.

Mike had reached us now, with Jessica still a few paces back. I could see his eyes appraising Jacob, and looking satisfied at his obvious youth.

"Where have you been?" he asked, though the answer was right in front of him.

"Jacob was just telling me some local stories," I volunteered. "It was really interesting."

I smiled at Jacob warmly, and he grinned back.

"Well," Mike paused, carefully reassessing the situation

as he watched our camaraderie. "We're packing up — it looks like it's going to rain soon."

We all looked up at the glowering sky. It certainly did look like rain.

"Okay." I jumped up. "I'm coming."

"It was nice to see you *again,*" Jacob said, and I could tell he was taunting Mike just a bit.

"It really was. Next time Charlie comes down to see Billy, I'll come, too," I promised.

His grin stretched across his face. "That would be cool."

"And thanks," I added earnestly.

I pulled up my hood as we tramped across the rocks toward the parking lot. A few drops were beginning to fall, making black spots on the stones where they landed. When we got to the Suburban the others were already loading everything back in. I crawled into the backseat by Angela and Tyler, announcing that I'd already had my turn in the shotgun position. Angela just stared out the window at the escalating storm, and Lauren twisted around in the middle seat to occupy Tyler's attention, so I could simply lay my head back on the seat and close my eyes and try very hard not to think.

7. NIGHTMARE

I TOLD CHARLIE I HAD A LOT OF HOMEWORK TO DO, AND that I didn't want anything to eat. There was a basketball game on that he was excited about, though of course *I* had no idea what was special about it, so he wasn't aware of anything unusual in my face or tone.

Once in my room, I locked the door. I dug through my desk until I found my old headphones, and I plugged them into my little CD player. I picked up a CD that Phil had given to me for Christmas. It was one of his favorite bands, but they used a little too much bass and shrieking for my tastes. I popped it into place and lay down on my bed. I put on the headphones, hit Play, and turned up the volume until it hurt my ears. I closed my eyes, but the light still intruded, so I added a pillow over the top half of my face.

I concentrated very carefully on the music, trying to understand the lyrics, to unravel the complicated drum patterns. By the third time I'd listened through the CD, I knew all the words to the choruses, at least. I was surprised to find that I really did like the band after all, once I got past the blaring noise. I'd have to thank Phil again.

And it worked. The shattering beats made it impossible for me to think — which was the whole purpose of the exercise. I listened to the CD again and again, until I was singing along with all the songs, until, finally, I fell asleep.

I opened my eyes to a familiar place. Aware in some corner of my consciousness that I was dreaming, I recognized the green light of the forest. I could hear the waves crashing against the rocks somewhere nearby. And I knew that if I found the ocean, I'd be able to see the sun. I was trying to follow the sound, but then Jacob Black was there, tugging on my hand, pulling me back toward the blackest part of the forest.

"Jacob? What's wrong?" I asked. His face was frightened as he yanked with all his strength against my resistance; I didn't want to go into the dark.

"Run, Bella, you have to run!" he whispered, terrified.

"This way, Bella!" I recognized Mike's voice calling out of the gloomy heart of the trees, but I couldn't see him.

"Why?" I asked, still pulling against Jacob's grasp, desperate now to find the sun.

But Jacob let go of my hand and yelped, suddenly

shaking, falling to the dim forest floor. He twitched on the ground as I watched in horror.

"Jacob!" I screamed. But he was gone. In his place was a large red-brown wolf with black eyes. The wolf faced away from me, pointing toward the shore, the hair on the back of his shoulders bristling, low growls issuing from between his exposed fangs.

"Bella, run!" Mike cried out again from behind me. But I didn't turn. I was watching a light coming toward me from the beach.

And then Edward stepped out from the trees, his skin faintly glowing, his eyes black and dangerous. He held up one hand and beckoned me to come to him. The wolf growled at my feet.

I took a step forward, toward Edward. He smiled then, and his teeth were sharp, pointed.

"Trust me," he purred.

I took another step.

The wolf launched himself across the space between me and the vampire, fangs aiming for the jugular.

"No!" I screamed, wrenching upright out of my bed.

My sudden movement caused the headphones to pull the CD player off the bedside table, and it clattered to the wooden floor.

My light was still on, and I was sitting fully dressed on the bed, with my shoes on. I glanced, disoriented, at the clock on my dresser. It was five-thirty in the morning.

I groaned, fell back, and rolled over onto my face, kicking off my boots. I was too uncomfortable to get anywhere near sleep, though. I rolled back over and unbuttoned my jeans, yanking them off awkwardly as I tried to stay horizontal. I could feel the braid in my hair, an uncomfortable ridge along the back of my skull. I turned onto my side and ripped the rubber band out, quickly combing through the plaits with my fingers. I pulled the pillow back over my eyes.

It was all no use, of course. My subconscious had dredged up exactly the images I'd been trying so desperately to avoid. I was going to have to face them now.

I sat up, and my head spun for a minute as the blood flowed downward. First things first, I thought to myself, happy to put it off as long as possible. I grabbed my bathroom bag.

The shower didn't last nearly as long as I hoped it would, though. Even taking the time to blow-dry my hair, I was soon out of things to do in the bathroom. Wrapped in a towel, I crossed back to my room. I couldn't tell if Charlie was still asleep, or if he had already left. I went to look out my window, and the cruiser was gone. Fishing again.

I dressed slowly in my most comfy sweats and then made my bed — something I never did. I couldn't put it off any longer. I went to my desk and switched on my old computer.

I hated using the Internet here. My modem was sadly outdated, my free service substandard; just dialing up took so long that I decided to go get myself a bowl of cereal while I waited.

I ate slowly, chewing each bite with care. When I was done, I washed the bowl and spoon, dried them, and put them away. My feet dragged as I climbed the stairs. I went to my CD player first, picking it up off the floor and placing it precisely in the center of the table. I pulled out the headphones, and put them away in the desk drawer. Then I turned the same CD on, turning it down to the point where it was background noise.

With another sigh, I turned to my computer. Naturally, the screen was covered in pop-up ads. I sat in my hard folding chair and began closing all the little windows. Eventually I made it to my favorite search engine. I shot down a few more pop-ups and then typed in one word.

Vampire.

It took an infuriatingly long time, of course. When the results came up, there was a lot to sift through — everything from movies and TV shows to role-playing games, underground metal, and gothic cosmetic companies.

Then I found a promising site — Vampires A–Z. I waited impatiently for it to load, quickly clicking closed each ad that flashed across the screen. Finally the screen was finished — simple white background with black text, academic-looking. Two quotes greeted me on the home page:

Throughout the vast shadowy world of ghosts and demons there is no figure so terrible, no figure so dreaded and abhorred, yet dight with such fearful fascination, as the vampire, who is himself neither ghost nor demon, but yet who partakes the dark natures and possesses the mysterious and terrible qualities of both. — Rev. Montague Summers

If there is in this world a well-attested account, it is that of the vampires. Nothing is lacking: official reports, affidavits of well-known people, of

surgeons, of priests, of magistrates; the judicial proof is most complete.
And with all that, who is there who believes in vampires? — *Rousseau*

The rest of the site was an alphabetized listing of all the different myths of vampires held throughout the world. The first I clicked on, the *Danag,* was a Filipino vampire supposedly responsible for planting taro on the islands long ago. The myth continued that the *Danag* worked with humans for many years, but the partnership ended one day when a woman cut her finger and a *Danag* sucked her wound, enjoying the taste so much that it drained her body completely of blood.

I read carefully through the descriptions, looking for anything that sounded familiar, let alone plausible. It seemed that most vampire myths centered around beautiful women as demons and children as victims; they also seemed like constructs created to explain away the high mortality rates for young children, and to give men an excuse for infidelity. Many of the stories involved bodiless spirits and warnings against improper burials. There wasn't much that sounded like the movies I'd seen, and only a very few, like the Hebrew *Estrie* and the Polish *Upier,* who were even preoccupied with drinking blood.

Only three entries really caught my attention: the Romanian *Varacolaci,* a powerful undead being who could appear as a beautiful, pale-skinned human, the Slovak *Nelapsi,* a creature so strong and fast it could massacre an entire village in the single hour after midnight, and one other, the *Stregoni benefici.*

About this last there was only one brief sentence.

Stregoni benefici: An Italian vampire, said to be on the side of goodness, and a mortal enemy of all evil vampires.

It was a relief, that one small entry, the one myth among hundreds that claimed the existence of good vampires.

Overall, though, there was little that coincided with Jacob's stories or my own observations. I'd made a little catalogue in my mind as I'd read and carefully compared it with each myth. Speed, strength, beauty, pale skin, eyes that shift color; and then Jacob's criteria: blood drinkers, enemies of the werewolf, cold-skinned, and immortal. There were very few myths that matched even one factor.

And then another problem, one that I'd remembered from the small number of scary movies that I'd seen and was backed up by today's reading — vampires couldn't come out in the daytime, the sun would burn them to a cinder. They slept in coffins all day and came out only at night.

Aggravated, I snapped off the computer's main power switch, not waiting to shut things down properly. Through my irritation, I felt overwhelming embarrassment. It was all so stupid. I was sitting in my room, researching vampires. What was wrong with me? I decided that most of the blame belonged on the doorstep of the town of Forks — and the entire sodden Olympic Peninsula, for that matter.

I had to get out of the house, but there was nowhere I wanted to go that didn't involve a three-day drive. I pulled on my boots anyway, unclear where I was headed, and went downstairs. I shrugged into my raincoat without checking the weather and stomped out the door.

It was overcast, but not raining yet. I ignored my truck

and started east on foot, angling across Charlie's yard toward the ever-encroaching forest. It didn't take long till I was deep enough for the house and the road to be invisible, for the only sound to be the squish of the damp earth under my feet and the sudden cries of the jays.

There was a thin ribbon of a trail that led through the forest here, or I wouldn't risk wandering on my own like this. My sense of direction was hopeless; I could get lost in much less helpful surroundings. The trail wound deeper and deeper into the forest, mostly east as far as I could tell. It snaked around the Sitka spruces and the hemlocks, the yews and the maples. I only vaguely knew the names of the trees around me, and all I knew was due to Charlie pointing them out to me from the cruiser window in earlier days. There were many I didn't know, and others I couldn't be sure about because they were so covered in green parasites.

I followed the trail as long as my anger at myself pushed me forward. As that started to ebb, I slowed. A few drops of moisture trickled down from the canopy above me, but I couldn't be certain if it was beginning to rain or if it was simply pools left over from yesterday, held high in the leaves above me, slowly dripping their way back to the earth. A recently fallen tree — I knew it was recent because it wasn't entirely carpeted in moss — rested against the trunk of one of her sisters, creating a sheltered little bench just a few safe feet off the trail. I stepped over the ferns and sat carefully, making sure my jacket was between the damp seat and my clothes wherever they touched, and leaned my hooded head back against the living tree.

This was the wrong place to have come. I should have known, but where else was there to go? The forest was deep green and far too much like the scene in last night's dream to allow for peace of mind. Now that there was no longer the sound of my soggy footsteps, the silence was piercing. The birds were quiet, too, the drops increasing in frequency, so it must be raining above. The ferns stood higher than my head, now that I was seated, and I knew someone could walk by on the path, three feet away, and not see me.

Here in the trees it was much easier to believe the absurdities that embarrassed me indoors. Nothing had changed in this forest for thousands of years, and all the myths and legends of a hundred different lands seemed much more likely in this green haze than they had in my clear-cut bedroom.

I forced myself to focus on the two most vital questions I had to answer, but I did so unwillingly.

First, I had to decide if it was possible that what Jacob had said about the Cullens could be true.

Immediately my mind responded with a resounding negative. It was silly and morbid to entertain such ridiculous notions. But what, then? I asked myself. There was no rational explanation for how I was alive at this moment. I listed again in my head the things I'd observed myself: the impossible speed and strength, the eye color shifting from black to gold and back again, the inhuman beauty, the pale, frigid skin. And more — small things that registered slowly — how they never seemed to eat, the disturbing grace with which they moved. And the way *he* sometimes spoke, with unfamiliar cadences and phrases that better fit the style of a turn-of-the-century novel than that of a twenty-first-century classroom. He had skipped class the day we'd done blood typing. He hadn't said no to the beach trip till he heard where we were going. He seemed to know what everyone around him was thinking . . . except me. He had told me he was the villain, dangerous. . . .

Could the Cullens be vampires?

Well, they were *something*. Something outside the possibility of rational justification was taking place in front of my incredulous eyes. Whether it be Jacob's *cold ones* or my own superhero theory, Edward Cullen was not . . . human. He was something more.

So then — maybe. That would have to be my answer for now.

And then the most important question of all. What was I going to do if it was true?

If Edward was a vampire — I could hardly make myself think the words — then what should I do? Involving someone else was definitely out. I couldn't even believe myself; anyone I told would have me committed.

Only two options seemed practical. The first was to take his advice: to be smart, to avoid him as much as possible. To cancel our plans, to go back to ignoring him as far as I was able. To pretend there was an impenetrably thick glass wall between us in the one class where we were forced together. To tell him to leave me alone — and mean it this time.

I was gripped in a sudden agony of despair as I considered that alternative. My mind rejected the pain, quickly skipping on to the next option.

I could do nothing different. After all, if he was something . . . sinister, he'd done nothing to hurt me so far. In fact, I would be a dent in Tyler's fender if he hadn't acted so quickly. So quickly, I argued with myself, that it might have been sheer reflexes. But if it was a reflex to save lives, how bad could he be? I retorted. My head spun around in answerless circles.

There was one thing I was sure of, if I was sure of anything. The dark Edward in my dream last night was a reflection only of my fear of the word Jacob had spoken, and not Edward himself. Even so, when I'd screamed out in terror at the werewolf's lunge, it wasn't fear for the wolf that brought the cry of "no" to my lips. It was fear that *he* would be harmed — even as he called to me with sharp-edged fangs, I feared for *him*.

And I knew in that I had my answer. I didn't know if there ever was a choice, really. I was already in too deep. Now that I knew — *if* I knew — I could do nothing about my frightening secret. Because when I thought of him, of his voice, his hypnotic eyes, the magnetic force of his personality, I wanted nothing more than to be with him right now. Even if . . . but I couldn't think it. Not here, alone in the darkening forest. Not while the rain made it dim as twilight under the canopy and pattered like footsteps across the matted earthen floor. I shivered and rose quickly from my place of concealment, worried that somehow the path would have disappeared with the rain.

But it was there, safe and clear, winding its way out of the dripping green maze. I followed it hastily, my hood pulled close around my face, becoming surprised, as I nearly ran through the trees, at how far I had come. I started to wonder if I was heading out at all, or following the path farther into the confines of the forest. Before I could get too panicky, though, I began to glimpse some open spaces through the webbed branches. And then I could hear a car passing on the street, and I was free, Charlie's lawn stretched out in front of me, the house beckoning me, promising warmth and dry socks.

It was just noon when I got back inside. I went upstairs and got dressed for the day, jeans and a t-shirt, since I was staying indoors. It didn't take too much effort to concentrate on my task for the day, a paper on *Macbeth* that was due Wednesday. I settled into outlining a rough draft contentedly, more serene than I'd felt since . . . well, since Thursday afternoon, if I was being honest.

That had always been my way, though. Making decisions was the painful part for me, the part I agonized over. But once the decision was made, I simply followed through — usually with relief that the choice was made. Sometimes the relief was tainted by despair, like my decision to come to Forks. But it was still better than wrestling with the alternatives.

This decision was ridiculously easy to live with. Dangerously easy.

And so the day was quiet, productive — I finished my paper before eight. Charlie came home with a large catch, and I made a mental note to pick up a book of recipes for fish while I was in Seattle next week. The chills that flashed up my spine whenever I thought of that trip were no different than the ones I'd felt before I'd taken my walk with Jacob Black. They should be different, I thought. I should be afraid — I knew I should be, but I couldn't feel the right kind of fear.

I slept dreamlessly that night, exhausted from beginning my day so early, and sleeping so poorly the night before. I woke, for the second time since arriving in Forks, to the bright yellow light of a sunny day. I skipped to the window, stunned to see that there was hardly a cloud in the sky, and those there were just fleecy little white puffs that couldn't possibly be carrying any rain. I opened the window — surprised when it opened silently, without sticking, not having opened it in who knows how many years — and sucked in the relatively dry air. It was nearly warm and hardly windy at all. My blood was electric in my veins.

Charlie was finishing breakfast when I came downstairs, and he picked up on my mood immediately.

"Nice day out," he commented.

"Yes," I agreed with a grin.

He smiled back, his brown eyes crinkling around the edges. When Charlie smiled, it was easier to see why he and my mother had jumped too quickly into an early marriage. Most of the young romantic he'd been in those days had faded before I'd known him, as the curly brown hair — the same color, if not the same texture, as mine — had dwindled, slowly revealing more and more of the shiny skin of his forehead. But when he smiled I could see a little of the man who had run away with Renée when she was just two years older than I was now.

I ate breakfast cheerily, watching the dust moats stirring in the sunlight that streamed in the back window. Charlie called out a goodbye, and I heard the cruiser pull away from the house. I hesitated on my way out the door, hand on my rain jacket. It would be tempting fate to leave it home. With a sigh, I folded it over my arm and stepped out into the brightest light I'd seen in months.

By dint of much elbow grease, I was able to get both windows in the truck almost completely rolled down. I was one of the first ones to school; I hadn't even checked the clock in my hurry to get outside. I parked and headed toward the seldom-used picnic benches on the south side of the cafeteria. The benches were still a little damp, so I sat on my jacket, glad to have a use for it. My homework was done — the product of a slow social life — but there were a few Trig problems I wasn't sure I had right. I took out my book industriously, but halfway through rechecking the first problem I was daydreaming, watching the sunlight play on the red-barked trees. I sketched inattentively along the margins of my homework. After a few minutes, I suddenly realized I'd drawn five pairs of dark eyes staring out of the page at me. I scrubbed them out with the eraser.

"Bella!" I heard someone call, and it sounded like Mike.

I looked around to realize that the school had become populated while I'd been sitting there, absentminded. Everyone was in t-shirts, some even in shorts though the temperature couldn't be over sixty. Mike was coming toward me in khaki shorts and a striped Rugby shirt, waving.

"Hey, Mike," I called, waving back, unable to be half-hearted on a morning like this.

He came to sit by me, the tidy spikes of his hair shining golden in the light, his grin stretching across his face. He was so delighted to see me, I couldn't help but feel gratified.

"I never noticed before — your hair has red in it," he commented, catching between his fingers a strand that was fluttering in the light breeze.

"Only in the sun."

I became just a little uncomfortable as he tucked the lock behind my ear.

"Great day, isn't it?"

"My kind of day," I agreed.

"What did you do yesterday?" His tone was just a bit too proprietary.

"I mostly worked on my essay." I didn't add that I was finished with it — no need to sound smug.

He hit his forehead with the heel of his hand. "Oh yeah — that's due Thursday, right?"

"Um, Wednesday, I think."

"Wednesday?" He frowned. "That's not good. . . . What are you writing yours on?"

"Whether Shakespeare's treatment of the female characters is misogynistic."

He stared at me like I'd just spoken in pig Latin.

"I guess I'll have to get to work on that tonight," he said, deflated. "I was going to ask if you wanted to go out."

"Oh." I was taken off guard. Why couldn't I ever have a pleasant conversation with Mike anymore without it getting awkward?

"Well, we could go to dinner or something . . . and I could work on it later." He smiled at me hopefully.

"Mike . . ." I hated being put on the spot. "I don't think that would be the best idea."

His face fell. "Why?" he asked, his eyes guarded. My thoughts flickered to Edward, wondering if that's where his thoughts were as well.

"I think . . . and if you ever repeat what I'm saying right now I will cheerfully beat you to death," I threatened, "but I think that would hurt Jessica's feelings."

He was bewildered, obviously not thinking in *that* direction at all. "Jessica?"

"Really, Mike, are you *blind*?"

"Oh," he exhaled — clearly dazed. I took advantage of that to make my escape.

"It's time for class, and I can't be late again." I gathered my books up and stuffed them in my bag.

We walked in silence to building three, and his expression was distracted. I hoped whatever thoughts he was immersed in were leading him in the right direction.

When I saw Jessica in Trig, she was bubbling with enthusiasm. She, Angela, and Lauren were going to Port Angeles tonight to go dress shopping for the dance, and she wanted me to come, too, even though I didn't need one. I was indecisive. It would be nice to get out of town with some girlfriends, but Lauren would be there. And who knew what I could be doing tonight. . . . But that was definitely the wrong path to let my mind wander down. Of course I was happy about the sunlight. But that wasn't completely responsible for the euphoric mood I was in, not even close.

So I gave her a maybe, telling her I'd have to talk with Charlie first.

She talked of nothing but the dance on the way to Spanish, continuing as if without an interruption when class finally ended, five minutes late, and we were on our way to lunch. I was far too lost in my own frenzy of anticipation to notice much of what she said. I was painfully eager to see not just him but all the Cullens — to compare them with the new suspicions that plagued my mind. As I crossed the threshold of the cafeteria, I felt the first true tingle of fear slither down my spine and settle in my stomach. Would they be able to know what I was thinking? And then a different feeling jolted through me — would Edward be waiting to sit with me again?

As was my routine, I glanced first toward the Cullens' table. A shiver of panic trembled in my stomach as I realized it was empty. With dwindling hope, my eyes scoured the rest of the cafeteria, hoping to find him alone, waiting for me. The place was nearly filled — Spanish had made us late — but there was no sign of Edward or any of his family. Desolation hit me with crippling strength.

I shambled along behind Jessica, not bothering to pretend to listen anymore.

We were late enough that everyone was already at our table. I avoided the empty chair next to Mike in favor of one by Angela. I vaguely noticed that Mike held the chair out politely for Jessica, and that her face lit up in response.

Angela asked a few quiet questions about the *Macbeth* paper, which I answered as naturally as I could while spiraling downward in misery. She, too, invited me to go with them tonight, and I agreed now, grasping at anything to distract myself.

I realized I'd been holding on to a last shred of hope when I entered Biology, saw his empty seat, and felt a new wave of disappointment.

The rest of the day passed slowly, dismally. In Gym, we had a lecture on the rules of badminton, the next torture they had lined up for me. But at least it meant I got to sit and listen instead of stumbling around on the court. The best part was the coach didn't finish, so I got another day off tomorrow. Never mind that the day after they would arm me with a racket before unleashing me on the rest of the class.

I was glad to leave campus, so I would be free to pout and mope before I went out tonight with Jessica and company. But right after I walked in the door of Charlie's house, Jessica called to cancel our plans. I tried to be happy that Mike had asked her out to dinner — I really was relieved that he finally seemed to be catching on — but my enthusiasm sounded false in my own ears. She rescheduled our shopping trip for tomorrow night.

Which left me with little in the way of distractions. I had fish marinating for dinner, with a salad and bread left over from the night before, so there was nothing to do there. I spent a focused half hour on homework, but then I was through with that, too. I checked my e-mail, reading the backlog of letters from my mother, getting snippier as they progressed to the present. I sighed and typed a quick response.

```
Mom,
Sorry. I've been out. I went to the beach with
some friends. And I had to write a paper.
```

My excuses were fairly pathetic, so I gave up on that.

```
It's sunny outside today — I know, I'm shocked,
too — so I'm going to go outside and soak up
as much vitamin D as I can. I love you,
    Bella.
```

I decided to kill an hour with non-school-related reading. I had a small collection of books that came with me to Forks, the shabbiest volume being a compilation of the works of Jane Austen. I selected that one and headed to the backyard, grabbing a ragged old quilt from the linen cupboard at the top of the stairs on my way down.

Outside in Charlie's small, square yard, I folded the quilt in half and laid it out of the reach of the trees' shadows on the thick lawn that would always be slightly wet, no matter how long the sun shone. I lay on my stomach, crossing my ankles in the air, flipping through the different novels in the book, trying to decide which would occupy my mind the most thoroughly. My favorites were *Pride and Prejudice* and *Sense and Sensibility.* I'd read the first most recently, so I started into *Sense and Sensibility,* only to remember after I began chapter three that the hero of the story happened to be named *Edward.* Angrily, I turned to *Mansfield Park,* but the hero of that piece was named *Edmund,* and that was just too close. Weren't there any other names available in the late eighteenth century? I snapped the book shut, annoyed, and rolled over onto my back. I pushed my sleeves up as high as they would go, and closed my eyes. I would think of nothing but the warmth on my skin, I told myself severely. The breeze was still light, but it blew tendrils of my hair around my face, and that tickled a bit. I pulled all my hair over my head, letting it fan out on the quilt above me, and focused again on the heat that touched my eyelids, my cheekbones, my nose, my lips, my forearms, my neck, soaked through my light shirt. . . .

The next thing I was conscious of was the sound of Charlie's cruiser turning onto the bricks of the driveway. I sat up in surprise, realizing the light was gone, behind the trees, and I had fallen asleep. I looked around, muddled, with the sudden feeling that I wasn't alone.

"Charlie?" I asked. But I could hear his door slamming in front of the house.

I jumped up, foolishly edgy, gathering the now-damp quilt and my book. I ran inside to get some oil heating on the stove, realizing that dinner would be late. Charlie was hanging up his gun belt and stepping out of his boots when I came in.

"Sorry, Dad, dinner's not ready yet — I fell asleep outside." I stifled a yawn.

"Don't worry about it," he said. "I wanted to catch the score on the game, anyway."

I watched TV with Charlie after dinner, for something to do. There wasn't anything on I wanted to watch, but he knew I didn't like baseball, so he turned it to some mindless sitcom that neither of us enjoyed. He seemed happy, though, to be doing something together. And it felt good, despite my depression, to make him happy.

"Dad," I said during a commercial, "Jessica and Angela are going to look at dresses for the dance tomorrow night in Port Angeles, and they wanted me to help them choose . . . do you mind if I go with them?"

"Jessica Stanley?" he asked.

"And Angela Weber." I sighed as I gave him the details.

He was confused. "But you're not going to the dance, right?"

"No, Dad, but I'm helping *them* find dresses — you know, giving them constructive criticism." I wouldn't have to explain this to a woman.

"Well, okay." He seemed to realize that he was out of his depth with the girlie stuff. "It's a school night, though."

"We'll leave right after school, so we can get back early. You'll be okay for dinner, right?"

"Bells, I fed myself for seventeen years before you got here," he reminded me.

"I don't know how you survived," I muttered, then added more clearly, "I'll leave some things for cold-cut sandwiches in the fridge, okay? Right on top."

It was sunny again in the morning. I awakened with renewed hope that I grimly tried to suppress. I dressed for the warmer weather in a deep blue V-neck blouse — something I'd worn in the dead of winter in Phoenix.

I had planned my arrival at school so that I barely had time to make it to class. With a sinking heart, I circled the full lot looking for a space, while also searching for the silver Volvo that was clearly not there. I parked in the last row and hurried to English, arriving breathless, but subdued, before the final bell.

It was the same as yesterday — I just couldn't keep little sprouts of hope from budding in my mind, only to have them squashed painfully as I searched the lunchroom in vain and sat at my empty Biology table.

The Port Angeles scheme was back on again for tonight and made all the more attractive by the fact that Lauren had other obligations. I was anxious to get out of town so I could stop glancing over my shoulder, hoping to see him appearing out of the blue the way he always did. I vowed to myself that I would be in a good mood tonight and not ruin Angela's or Jessica's enjoyment in the dress hunting. Maybe I could do a little clothes shopping as well. I refused to think that I might be shopping alone in Seattle this weekend, no longer interested in the earlier arrangement. Surely he wouldn't cancel without at least telling me.

After school, Jessica followed me home in her old white Mercury so that I could ditch my books and truck. I brushed through my hair quickly when I was inside, feeling a slight lift of excitement as I contemplated getting out of Forks. I left a note for Charlie on the table, explaining again where to find dinner, switched my scruffy wallet from my school bag to a purse I rarely used, and ran out to join Jessica. We went to Angela's house next, and she was waiting for us. My excitement increased exponentially as we actually drove out of the town limits.

8. PORT ANGELES

Jess drove faster than the Chief, so we made it to Port Angeles by four. It had been a while since I'd had a girls' night out, and the estrogen rush was invigorating. We listened to whiny rock songs while Jessica jabbered on about the boys we hung out with. Jessica's dinner with Mike had gone very well, and she was hoping that by Saturday night they would have progressed to the first-kiss stage. I smiled to myself, pleased. Angela was passively happy to be going to the dance, but not really interested in Eric. Jess tried to get her to confess who her type was, but I interrupted with a question about dresses after a bit, to spare her. Angela threw a grateful glance my way.

Port Angeles was a beautiful little tourist trap, much

more polished and quaint than Forks. But Jessica and Angela knew it well, so they didn't plan to waste time on the picturesque boardwalk by the bay. Jess drove straight to the one big department store in town, which was a few streets in from the bay area's visitor-friendly face.

The dance was billed as semiformal, and we weren't exactly sure what that meant. Both Jessica and Angela seemed surprised and almost disbelieving when I told them I'd never been to a dance in Phoenix.

"Didn't you ever go with a boyfriend or something?" Jess asked dubiously as we walked through the front doors of the store.

"Really," I tried to convince her, not wanting to confess my dancing problems. "I've never had a boyfriend or anything close. I didn't go out much."

"Why not?" Jessica demanded.

"No one asked me," I answered honestly.

She looked skeptical. "People ask you out here," she reminded me, "and you tell them no." We were in the juniors' section now, scanning the racks for dress-up clothes.

"Well, except for Tyler," Angela amended quietly.

"Excuse me?" I gasped. "What did you say?"

"Tyler told everyone he's taking you to prom," Jessica informed me with suspicious eyes.

"He said *what*?" I sounded like I was choking.

"I told you it wasn't true," Angela murmured to Jessica.

I was silent, still lost in shock that was quickly turning to irritation. But we had found the dress racks, and now we had work to do.

"That's why Lauren doesn't like you," Jessica giggled while we pawed through the clothes.

I ground my teeth. "Do you think that if I ran him over with my truck he would stop feeling guilty about the accident? That he might give up on making amends and call it even?"

"Maybe," Jess snickered. "*If* that's why he's doing this."

The dress selection wasn't large, but both of them found a few things to try on. I sat on a low chair just inside the dressing room, by the three-way mirror, trying to control my fuming.

Jess was torn between two — one a long, strapless, basic black number, the other a knee-length electric blue with spaghetti straps. I encouraged her to go with the blue; why not play up the eyes? Angela chose a pale pink dress that draped around her tall frame nicely and brought out honey tints in her light brown hair. I complimented them both generously and helped by returning the rejects to their racks. The whole process was much shorter and easier than similar trips I'd taken with Renée at home. I guess there was something to be said for limited choices.

We headed over to shoes and accessories. While they tried things on I merely watched and critiqued, not in the mood to shop for myself, though I did need new shoes. The girls'-night high was wearing off in the wake of my annoyance at Tyler, leaving room for the gloom to move back in.

"Angela?" I began, hesitant, while she was trying on a pair of pink strappy heels — she was overjoyed to have a date tall enough that she could wear high heels at all.

Jessica had drifted to the jewelry counter and we were alone.

"Yes?" She held her leg out, twisting her ankle to get a better view of the shoe.

I chickened out. "I like those."

"I think I'll get them — though they'll never match anything but the one dress," she mused.

"Oh, go ahead — they're on sale," I encouraged. She smiled, putting the lid back on a box that contained more practical-looking off-white shoes.

I tried again. "Um, Angela . . ." She looked up curiously.

"Is it normal for the . . . Cullens" — I kept my eyes on the shoes — "to be out of school a lot?" I failed miserably in my attempt to sound nonchalant.

"Yes, when the weather is good they go backpacking all the time — even the doctor. They're all real outdoorsy," she told me quietly, examining her shoes, too. She didn't ask one question, let alone the hundreds that Jessica would have unleashed. I was beginning to really like Angela.

"Oh." I let the subject drop as Jessica returned to show us the rhinestone jewelry she'd found to match her silver shoes.

We planned to go to dinner at a little Italian restaurant on the boardwalk, but the dress shopping hadn't taken as long as we'd expected. Jess and Angela were going to take their clothes back to the car and then walk down to the bay. I told them I would meet them at the restaurant in an hour — I wanted to look for a bookstore. They were both willing to come with me, but I encouraged them to go have fun — they didn't know how preoccupied I could get when surrounded by books; it was something I preferred to do alone. They walked off to the car chattering happily, and I headed in the direction Jess pointed out.

I had no trouble finding the bookstore, but it wasn't what I was looking for. The windows were full of crystals, dream-catchers, and books about spiritual healing. I didn't even go inside. Through the glass I could see a fifty-year-old woman with long, gray hair worn straight down her back, clad in a dress right out of the sixties, smiling welcomingly from behind the counter. I decided that was one conversation I could skip. There had to be a normal bookstore in town.

I meandered through the streets, which were filling up with end-of-the-workday traffic, and hoped I was headed toward downtown. I wasn't paying as much attention as I should to where I was going; I was wrestling with despair. I was trying so hard not to think about him, and what Angela had said . . . and more than anything trying to beat down my hopes for Saturday, fearing a disappointment more painful than the rest, when I looked up to see someone's silver Volvo parked along the street and it all came crashing down on me. Stupid, unreliable vampire, I thought to myself.

I stomped along in a southerly direction, toward some glass-fronted shops that looked promising. But when I got to them, they were just a repair shop and a vacant space. I still had too much time to go looking for Jess and Angela yet, and I definitely needed to get my mood in hand before

I met back up with them. I ran my fingers through my hair a couple of times and took some deep breaths before I continued around the corner.

I started to realize, as I crossed another road, that I was going the wrong direction. The little foot traffic I had seen was going north, and it looked like the buildings here were mostly warehouses. I decided to turn east at the next corner, and then loop around after a few blocks and try my luck on a different street on my way back to the boardwalk.

A group of four men turned around the corner I was heading for, dressed too casually to be heading home from the office, but they were too grimy to be tourists. As they approached me, I realized they weren't too many years older than I was. They were joking loudly among themselves, laughing raucously and punching each other's arms. I scooted as far to the inside of the sidewalk as I could to give them room, walking swiftly, looking past them to the corner.

"Hey, there!" one of them called as they passed, and he had to be talking to me since no one else was around. I glanced up automatically. Two of them had paused, the other two were slowing. The closest, a heavyset, dark-haired man in his early twenties, seemed to be the one who had spoken. He was wearing a flannel shirt open over a dirty t-shirt, cut-off jeans, and sandals. He took half a step toward me.

"Hello," I mumbled, a knee-jerk reaction. Then I quickly looked away and walked faster toward the corner. I could hear them laughing at full volume behind me.

"Hey, wait!" one of them called after me again, but I kept my head down and rounded the corner with a sigh of relief. I could still hear them chortling behind me.

I found myself on a sidewalk leading past the backs of several somber-colored warehouses, each with large bay doors for unloading trucks, padlocked for the night. The south side of the street had no sidewalk, only a chain-link fence topped with barbed wire protecting some kind of engine parts storage yard. I'd wandered far past the part of Port Angeles that I, as a guest, was intended to see. It was getting dark, I realized, the clouds finally returning, piling up on the western horizon, creating an early sunset. The eastern sky was still clear, but graying, shot through with streaks of pink and orange. I'd left my jacket in the car, and a sudden shiver made me cross my arms tightly across my chest. A single van passed me, and then the road was empty.

The sky suddenly darkened further, and, as I looked over my shoulder to glare at the offending cloud, I realized with a shock that two men were walking quietly twenty feet behind me.

They were from the same group I'd passed at the corner, though neither was the dark one who'd spoken to me. I turned my head forward at once, quickening my pace. A chill that had nothing to do with the weather made me shiver again. My purse was on a shoulder strap and I had it slung across my body, the way you were supposed to wear it so it wouldn't get snatched. I knew exactly where my pepper spray was — still in my duffle bag under the bed, never unpacked. I didn't have much money with me, just a twenty and some ones, and I thought about "acciden-tally" dropping my bag and walking away. But a small, frightened voice in the back of my mind warned me that they might be something worse than thieves.

I listened intently to their quiet footsteps, which were much too quiet when compared to the boisterous noise they'd been making earlier, and it didn't sound like they were speeding up, or getting any closer to me. Breathe, I had to remind myself. You don't know they're following you. I continued to walk as quickly as I could without ac-tually running, focusing on the right-hand turn that was only a few yards away from me now. I could hear them, staying as far back as they'd been before. A blue car turned onto the street from the south and drove quickly past me. I thought of jumping out in front of it, but I hesitated, in-hibited, unsure that I was really being pursued, and then it was too late.

I reached the corner, but a swift glance revealed that it was only a blind drive to the back of another building. I was half-turned in anticipation; I had to hurriedly correct and dash across the narrow drive, back to the sidewalk. The street ended at the next corner, where there was a stop sign. I concentrated on the faint footsteps behind me, de-ciding whether or not to run. They sounded farther back, though, and I knew they could outrun me in any case. I was sure to trip and go sprawling if I tried to go any faster. The footfalls were definitely farther back. I risked a quick glance over my shoulder, and they were maybe forty feet back now, I saw with relief. But they were both staring at me.

It seemed to take forever for me to get to the corner. I kept my pace steady, the men behind me falling ever so slightly farther behind with every step. Maybe they realized they had scared me and were sorry. I saw two cars going north pass the intersection I was heading for, and I exhaled in relief. There would be more people around once I got off this deserted street. I skipped around the corner with a grateful sigh.

And skidded to a stop.

The street was lined on both sides by blank, doorless, windowless walls. I could see in the distance, two intersections down, streetlamps, cars, and more pedestrians, but they were all too far away. Because lounging against the western building, midway down the street, were the other two men from the group, both watching with excited smiles as I froze dead on the sidewalk. I realized then that I wasn't being followed.

I was being herded.

I paused for only a second, but it felt like a very long time. I turned then and darted to the other side of the road. I had a sinking feeling that it was a wasted attempt. The footsteps behind me were louder now.

"There you are!" The booming voice of the stocky, dark-haired man shattered the intense quiet and made me jump. In the gathering darkness, it seemed like he was looking past me.

"Yeah," a voice called loudly from behind me, making me jump again as I tried to hurry down the street. "We just took a little detour."

My steps had to slow now. I was closing the distance between myself and the lounging pair too quickly. I had a good loud scream, and I sucked in air, preparing to use it, but my throat was so dry I wasn't sure how much volume I could manage. With a quick movement I slipped my purse over my head, gripping the strap with one hand, ready to surrender it or use it as weapon as need demanded.

The thickset man shrugged away from the wall as I warily came to a stop, and walked slowly into the street.

"Stay away from me," I warned in a voice that was supposed to sound strong and fearless. But I was right about the dry throat — no volume.

"Don't be like that, sugar," he called, and the raucous laughter started again behind me.

I braced myself, feet apart, trying to remember through my panic what little self-defense I knew. Heel of the hand thrust upward, hopefully breaking the nose or shoving it into the brain. Finger through the eye socket — try to hook around and pop the eye out. And the standard knee to the groin, of course. That same pessimistic voice in my mind spoke up then, reminding me that I probably wouldn't have a chance against one of them, and there were four. Shut up! I commanded the voice before terror could incapacitate me. I wasn't going out without taking someone with me. I tried to swallow so I could build up a decent scream.

Headlights suddenly flew around the corner, the car almost hitting the stocky one, forcing him to jump back toward the sidewalk. I dove into the road — *this* car was

going to stop, or have to hit me. But the silver car unexpectedly fishtailed around, skidding to a stop with the
passenger door open just a few feet from me.

"Get in," a furious voice commanded.

It was amazing how instantaneously the choking fear
vanished, amazing how suddenly the feeling of security
washed over me — even before I was off the street — as
soon as I heard his voice. I jumped into the seat, slamming
the door shut behind me.

It was dark in the car, no light had come on with the
opening of the door, and I could barely see his face in the
glow from the dashboard. The tires squealed as he spun
around to face north, accelerating too quickly, swerving
toward the stunned men on the street. I caught a glimpse
of them diving for the sidewalk as we straightened out and
sped toward the harbor.

"Put on your seat belt," he commanded, and I realized
I was clutching the seat with both hands. I quickly
obeyed; the snap as the belt connected was loud in the
darkness. He took a sharp left, racing forward, blowing
through several stop signs without a pause.

But I felt utterly safe and, for the moment, totally un-
concerned about where we were going. I stared at his face
in profound relief, relief that went beyond my sudden de-
liverance. I studied his flawless features in the limited
light, waiting for my breath to return to normal, until it
occurred to me that his expression was murderously angry.

"Are you okay?" I asked, surprised at how hoarse my
voice sounded.

"No," he said curtly, and his tone was livid.

I sat in silence, watching his face while his blazing eyes stared straight ahead, until the car came to a sudden stop. I glanced around, but it was too dark to see anything beside the vague outline of dark trees crowding the roadside. We weren't in town anymore.

"Bella?" he asked, his voice tight, controlled.

"Yes?" My voice was still rough. I tried to clear my throat quietly.

"Are you all right?" He still didn't look at me, but the fury was plain on his face.

"Yes," I croaked softly.

"Distract me, please," he ordered.

"I'm sorry, what?"

He exhaled sharply.

"Just prattle about something unimportant until I calm down," he clarified, closing his eyes and pinching the bridge of his nose with his thumb and forefinger.

"Um." I wracked my brain for something trivial. "I'm going to run over Tyler Crowley tomorrow before school?"

He was still squeezing his eyes closed, but the corner of his mouth twitched.

"Why?"

"He's telling everyone that he's taking me to prom — either he's insane or he's still trying to make up for almost killing me last . . . well, you remember it, and he thinks *prom* is somehow the correct way to do this. So I figure if I endanger his life, then we're even, and he can't keep trying to make amends. I don't need enemies and maybe Lauren would back off if he left me alone. I might have to total his Sentra, though. If he doesn't have a ride he can't take anyone to prom . . . ," I babbled on.

"I heard about that." He sounded a bit more composed.

"*You* did?" I asked in disbelief, my previous irritation flaring. "If he's paralyzed from the neck down, he can't go to the prom, either," I muttered, refining my plan.

Edward sighed, and finally opened his eyes.

"Better?"

"Not really."

I waited, but he didn't speak again. He leaned his head back against the seat, staring at the ceiling of the car. His face was rigid.

"What's wrong?" My voice came out in a whisper.

"Sometimes I have a problem with my temper, Bella." He was whispering, too, and as he stared out the window, his eyes narrowed into slits. "But it *wouldn't* be helpful for me to turn around and hunt down those . . ." He didn't finish his sentence, looking away, struggling for a moment to control his anger again. "At least," he continued, "that's what I'm trying to convince myself."

"Oh." The word seemed inadequate, but I couldn't think of a better response.

We sat in silence again. I glanced at the clock on the dashboard. It was past six-thirty.

"Jessica and Angela will be worried," I murmured. "I was supposed to meet them."

He started the engine without another word, turning around smoothly and speeding back toward town. We were under the streetlights in no time at all, still going too fast, weaving with ease through the cars slowly cruising the boardwalk. He parallel-parked against the curb in a space I would have thought much too small for the Volvo, but he slid in effortlessly in one try. I looked out the window to see the lights of La Bella Italia, and Jess and Angela just leaving, pacing anxiously away from us.

"How did you know where . . . ?" I began, but then I just shook my head. I heard the door open and turned to see him getting out.

"What are you doing?" I asked.

"I'm taking you to dinner." He smiled slightly, but his eyes were hard. He stepped out of the car and slammed the door. I fumbled with my seat belt, and then hurried to get out of the car as well. He was waiting for me on the sidewalk.

He spoke before I could. "Go stop Jessica and Angela before I have to track them down, too. I don't think I could restrain myself if I ran into your other friends again."

I shivered at the threat in his voice.

"Jess! Angela!" I yelled after them, waving when they turned. They rushed back to me, the pronounced relief on both their faces simultaneously changing to surprise as they saw who I was standing next to. They hesitated a few feet from us.

"Where have you been?" Jessica's voice was suspicious.

"I got lost," I admitted sheepishly. "And then I ran into Edward." I gestured toward him.

"Would it be all right if I joined you?" he asked in his

silken, irresistible voice. I could see from their staggered expressions that he had never unleashed his talents on them before.

"Er . . . sure," Jessica breathed.

"Um, actually, Bella, we already ate while we were waiting — sorry," Angela confessed.

"That's fine — I'm not hungry." I shrugged.

"I think you should eat something." Edward's voice was low, but full of authority. He looked up at Jessica and spoke slightly louder. "Do you mind if I drive Bella home tonight? That way you won't have to wait while she eats."

"Uh, no problem, I guess . . ." She bit her lip, trying to figure out from my expression whether that was what I wanted. I winked at her. I wanted nothing more than to be alone with my perpetual savior. There were so many questions that I couldn't bombard him with till we were by ourselves.

"Okay." Angela was quicker than Jessica. "See you tomorrow, Bella . . . Edward." She grabbed Jessica's hand and pulled her toward the car, which I could see a little ways away, parked across First Street. As they got in, Jess turned and waved, her face eager with curiosity. I waved back, waiting for them to drive away before I turned to face him.

"Honestly, I'm not hungry," I insisted, looking up to scrutinize his face. His expression was unreadable.

"Humor me."

He walked to the door of the restaurant and held it open with an obstinate expression. Obviously, there would be no further discussion. I walked past him into the restaurant with a resigned sigh.

The restaurant wasn't crowded — it was the off-season in Port Angeles. The host was female, and I understood the look in her eyes as she assessed Edward. She welcomed him a little more warmly than necessary. I was surprised by how much that bothered me. She was several inches taller than I was, and unnaturally blond.

"A table for two?" His voice was alluring, whether he was aiming for that or not. I saw her eyes flicker to me and then away, satisfied by my obvious ordinariness, and by the cautious, no-contact space Edward kept between us. She led us to a table big enough for four in the center of the most crowded area of the dining floor.

I was about to sit, but Edward shook his head at me.

"Perhaps something more private?" he insisted quietly to the host. I wasn't sure, but it looked like he smoothly handed her a tip. I'd never seen anyone refuse a table except in old movies.

"Sure." She sounded as surprised as I was. She turned and led us around a partition to a small ring of booths — all of them empty. "How's this?"

"Perfect." He flashed his gleaming smile, dazing her momentarily.

"Um" — she shook her head, blinking — "your server will be right out." She walked away unsteadily.

"You really shouldn't do that to people," I criticized. "It's hardly fair."

"Do what?"

"Dazzle them like that — she's probably hyperventilating in the kitchen right now."

He seemed confused.

"Oh, come on," I said dubiously. "You *have* to know the effect you have on people."

He tilted his head to one side, and his eyes were curious. "I dazzle people?"

"You haven't noticed? Do you think everybody gets their way so easily?"

He ignored my questions. "Do I dazzle *you*?"

"Frequently," I admitted.

And then our server arrived, her face expectant. The hostess had definitely dished behind the scenes, and this new girl didn't look disappointed. She flipped a strand of short black hair behind one ear and smiled with unnecessary warmth.

"Hello. My name is Amber, and I'll be your server tonight. What can I get you to drink?" I didn't miss that she was speaking only to him.

He looked at me.

"I'll have a Coke." It sounded like a question.

"Two Cokes," he said.

"I'll be right back with that," she assured him with another unnecessary smile. But he didn't see it. He was watching me.

"What?" I asked when she left.

His eyes stayed fixed on my face. "How are you feeling?"

"I'm fine," I replied, surprised by his intensity.

"You don't feel dizzy, sick, cold . . . ?"

"Should I?"

He chuckled at my puzzled tone.

"Well, I'm actually waiting for you to go into shock." His face twisted up into that perfect crooked smile.

"I don't think that will happen," I said after I could breathe again. "I've always been very good at repressing unpleasant things."

"Just the same, I'll feel better when you have some sugar and food in you."

Right on cue, the waitress appeared with our drinks and a basket of breadsticks. She stood with her back to me as she placed them on the table.

"Are you ready to order?" she asked Edward.

"Bella?" he asked. She turned unwillingly toward me.

I picked the first thing I saw on the menu. "Um . . . I'll have the mushroom ravioli."

"And you?" She turned back to him with a smile.

"Nothing for me," he said. Of course not.

"Let me know if you change your mind." The coy smile was still in place, but he wasn't looking at her, and she left dissatisfied.

"Drink," he ordered.

I sipped at my soda obediently, and then drank more deeply, surprised by how thirsty I was. I realized I had finished the whole thing when he pushed his glass toward me.

"Thanks," I muttered, still thirsty. The cold from the icy soda was radiating through my chest, and I shivered.

"Are you cold?"

"It's just the Coke," I explained, shivering again.

"Don't you have a jacket?" His voice was disapproving.

"Yes." I looked at the empty bench next to me. "Oh — I left it in Jessica's car," I realized.

Edward was shrugging out of his jacket. I suddenly realized that I had never once noticed what he was wearing —

not just tonight, but ever. I just couldn't seem to look away from his face. I made myself look now, focusing. He was removing a light beige leather jacket now; underneath he wore an ivory turtleneck sweater. It fit him snugly, emphasizing how muscular his chest was.

He handed me the jacket, interrupting my ogling.

"Thanks," I said again, sliding my arms into his jacket. It was cold — the way my jacket felt when I first picked it up in the morning, hanging in the drafty hallway. I shivered again. It smelled amazing. I inhaled, trying to identify the delicious scent. It didn't smell like cologne. The sleeves were much too long; I shoved them back so I could free my hands.

"That color blue looks lovely with your skin," he said, watching me. I was surprised; I looked down, flushing, of course.

He pushed the bread basket toward me.

"Really, I'm not going into shock," I protested.

"You should be — a *normal* person would be. You don't even look shaken." He seemed unsettled. He stared into my eyes, and I saw how light his eyes were, lighter than I'd ever seen them, golden butterscotch.

"I feel very safe with you," I confessed, mesmerized into telling the truth again.

That displeased him; his alabaster brow furrowed. He shook his head, frowning.

"This is more complicated than I'd planned," he murmured to himself.

I picked up a breadstick and began nibbling on the

end, measuring his expression. I wondered when it would be okay to start questioning him.

"Usually you're in a better mood when your eyes are so light," I commented, trying to distract him from whatever thought had left him frowning and somber.

He stared at me, stunned. "What?"

"You're always crabbier when your eyes are black — I expect it then," I went on. "I have a theory about that."

His eyes narrowed. "More theories?"

"Mm-hm." I chewed on a small bite of the bread, trying to look indifferent.

"I hope you were more creative this time . . . or are you still stealing from comic books?" His faint smile was mocking; his eyes were still tight.

"Well, no, I didn't get it from a comic book, but I didn't come up with it on my own, either," I confessed.

"And?" he prompted.

But then the waitress strode around the partition with my food. I realized we'd been unconsciously leaning toward each other across the table, because we both straightened up as she approached. She set the dish in front of me — it looked pretty good — and turned quickly to Edward.

"Did you change your mind?" she asked. "Isn't there anything I can get you?" I may have been imagining the double meaning in her words.

"No, thank you, but some more soda would be nice." He gestured with a long white hand to the empty cups in front of me.

"Sure." She removed the empty glasses and walked away.

"You were saying?" he asked.

"I'll tell you about it in the car. If . . ." I paused.

"There are conditions?" He raised one eyebrow, his voice ominous.

"I do have a few questions, of course."

"Of course."

The waitress was back with two more Cokes. She sat them down without a word this time, and left again.

I took a sip.

"Well, go ahead," he pushed, his voice still hard.

I started with the most undemanding. Or so I thought. "Why are you in Port Angeles?"

He looked down, folding his large hands together slowly on the table. His eyes flickered up at me from under his lashes, the hint of a smirk on his face.

"Next."

"But that's the easiest one," I objected.

"Next," he repeated.

I looked down, frustrated. I unrolled my silverware, picked up my fork, and carefully speared a ravioli. I put it in my mouth slowly, still looking down, chewing while I thought. The mushrooms were good. I swallowed and took another sip of Coke before I looked up.

"Okay, then." I glared at him, and continued slowly. "Let's say, hypothetically of course, that . . . someone . . . could know what people are thinking, read minds, you know — with a few exceptions."

"Just *one* exception," he corrected, "hypothetically."

"All right, with one exception, then." I was thrilled that he was playing along, but I tried to seem casual.

"How does that work? What are the limitations? How would . . . that someone . . . find someone else at exactly the right time? How would he know she was in trouble?" I wondered if my convoluted questions even made sense.

"Hypothetically?" he asked.

"Sure."

"Well, if . . . that someone . . ."

"Let's call him 'Joe,'" I suggested.

He smiled wryly. "Joe, then. If Joe had been paying attention, the timing wouldn't have needed to be quite so exact." He shook his head, rolling his eyes. "Only *you* could get into trouble in a town this small. You would have devastated their crime rate statistics for a decade, you know."

"We were speaking of a hypothetical case," I reminded him frostily.

He laughed at me, his eyes warm.

"Yes, we were," he agreed. "Shall we call you 'Jane'?"

"How did you know?" I asked, unable to curb my intensity. I realized I was leaning toward him again.

He seemed to be wavering, torn by some internal dilemma. His eyes locked with mine, and I guessed he was making the decision right then whether or not to simply tell me the truth.

"You can trust me, you know," I murmured. I reached forward, without thinking, to touch his folded hands, but he slid them away minutely, and I pulled my hand back.

"I don't know if I have a choice anymore." His voice was almost a whisper. "I was wrong — you're much more observant than I gave you credit for."

"I thought you were always right."

"I used to be." He shook his head again. "I was wrong about you on one other thing, as well. You're not a magnet for accidents — that's not a broad enough classification. You are a magnet for *trouble.* If there is anything dangerous within a ten-mile radius, it will invariably find you."

"And you put yourself into that category?" I guessed.

His face turned cold, expressionless. "Unequivocally."

I stretched my hand across the table again — ignoring him when he pulled back slightly once more — to touch the back of his hand shyly with my fingertips. His skin was cold and hard, like a stone.

"Thank you." My voice was fervent with gratitude. "That's twice now."

His face softened. "Let's not try for three, agreed?"

I scowled, but nodded. He moved his hand out from under mine, placing both of his under the table. But he leaned toward me.

"I followed you to Port Angeles," he admitted, speaking in a rush. "I've never tried to keep a specific person alive before, and it's much more troublesome than I would have believed. But that's probably just because it's you. Ordinary people seem to make it through the day without so many catastrophes." He paused. I wondered if it should bother me that he was following me; instead I felt a strange surge of pleasure. He stared, maybe wondering why my lips were curving into an involuntary smile.

"Did you ever think that maybe my number was up the first time, with the van, and that you've been interfering with fate?" I speculated, distracting myself.

"That wasn't the first time," he said, and his voice was hard to hear. I stared at him in amazement, but he was looking down. "Your number was up the first time I met you."

I felt a spasm of fear at his words, and the abrupt memory of his violent black glare that first day . . . but the overwhelming sense of safety I felt in his presence stifled it. By the time he looked up to read my eyes, there was no trace of fear in them.

"You remember?" he asked, his angel's face grave.

"Yes." I was calm.

"And yet here you sit." There was a trace of disbelief in his voice; he raised one eyebrow.

"Yes, here I sit . . . because of you." I paused. "Because somehow you knew how to find me today . . . ?" I prompted.

He pressed his lips together, staring at me through narrowed eyes, deciding again. His eyes flashed down to my full plate, and then back to me.

"You eat, I'll talk," he bargained.

I quickly scooped up another ravioli and popped it in my mouth.

"It's harder than it should be — keeping track of you. Usually I can find someone very easily, once I've heard their mind before." He looked at me anxiously, and I realized I had frozen. I made myself swallow, then stabbed another ravioli and tossed it in.

"I was keeping tabs on Jessica, not carefully — like I said, only you could find trouble in Port Angeles — and at first I didn't notice when you took off on your own. Then, when I realized that you weren't with her anymore, I went looking for you at the bookstore I saw in her head. I could tell that you hadn't gone in, and that you'd gone south . . . and I knew you would have to turn around soon. So I was just waiting for you, randomly searching through the thoughts of people on the street — to see if anyone had noticed you so I would know where you were. I had no reason to be worried . . . but I was strangely anxious. . . ." He was lost in thought, staring past me, seeing things I couldn't imagine.

"I started to drive in circles, still . . . listening. The sun was finally setting, and I was about to get out and follow you on foot. And then —" He stopped, clenching his teeth together in sudden fury. He made an effort to calm himself.

"Then what?" I whispered. He continued to stare over my head.

"I heard what they were thinking," he growled, his upper lip curling slightly back over his teeth. "I saw your face in his mind." He suddenly leaned forward, one elbow appearing on the table, his hand covering his eyes. The movement was so swift it startled me.

"It was very . . . hard — you can't imagine how hard — for me to simply take you away, and leave them . . . alive." His voice was muffled by his arm. "I could have let you go with Jessica and Angela, but I was afraid if you left me alone, I would go looking for them," he admitted in a whisper.

I sat quietly, dazed, my thoughts incoherent. My hands were folded in my lap, and I was leaning weakly against the back of the seat. He still had his face in his hand, and he was as still as if he'd been carved from the stone his skin resembled.

Finally he looked up, his eyes seeking mine, full of his own questions.

"Are you ready to go home?" he asked.

"I'm ready to leave," I qualified, overly grateful that we had the hour-long ride home together. I wasn't ready to say goodbye to him.

The waitress appeared as if she'd been called. Or watching.

"How are we doing?" she asked Edward.

"We're ready for the check, thank you." His voice was quiet, rougher, still reflecting the strain of our conversation. It seemed to muddle her. He looked up, waiting.

"S-sure," she stuttered. "Here you go." She pulled a small leather folder from the front pocket of her black apron and handed it to him.

There was a bill in his hand already. He slipped it into the folder and handed it right back to her.

"No change." He smiled. Then he stood up, and I scrambled awkwardly to my feet.

She smiled invitingly at him again. "You have a nice evening."

He didn't look away from me as he thanked her. I suppressed a smile.

He walked close beside me to the door, still careful not to touch me. I remembered what Jessica had said about her relationship with Mike, how they were almost to the first-kiss stage. I sighed. Edward seemed to hear me, and he looked down curiously. I looked at the sidewalk, grateful that he didn't seem to be able to know what I was thinking.

He opened the passenger door, holding it for me as I stepped in, shutting it softly behind me. I watched him walk around the front of the car, amazed, yet again, by how graceful he was. I probably should have been used to that by now — but I wasn't. I had a feeling Edward wasn't the kind of person anyone got used to.

Once inside the car, he started the engine and turned the heater on high. It had gotten very cold, and I guessed the good weather was at an end. I was warm in his jacket, though, breathing in the scent of it when I thought he couldn't see.

Edward pulled out through the traffic, apparently without a glance, flipping around to head toward the freeway.

"Now," he said significantly, "it's your turn."

9. THEORY

"CAN I ASK JUST ONE MORE?" I PLEADED AS EDWARD accelerated much too quickly down the quiet street. He didn't seem to be paying any attention to the road.

He sighed.

"One," he agreed. His lips pressed together into a cautious line.

"Well . . . you said you knew I hadn't gone into the bookstore, and that I had gone south. I was just wondering how you knew that."

He looked away, deliberating.

"I thought we were past all the evasiveness," I grumbled.

He almost smiled.

"Fine, then. I followed your scent." He looked at the road, giving me time to compose my face. I couldn't think of an acceptable response to that, but I filed it carefully away for future study. I tried to refocus. I wasn't ready to let him be finished, now that he was finally explaining things.

"And then you didn't answer one of my first questions . . ." I stalled.

He looked at me with disapproval. "Which one?"

"How does it work — the mind-reading thing? Can you read anybody's mind, anywhere? How do you do it? Can the rest of your family . . . ?" I felt silly, asking for clarification on make-believe.

"That's more than one," he pointed out. I simply intertwined my fingers and gazed at him, waiting.

"No, it's just me. And I can't hear anyone, anywhere. I have to be fairly close. The more familiar someone's . . . 'voice' is, the farther away I can hear them. But still, no more than a few miles." He paused thoughtfully. "It's a little like being in a huge hall filled with people, everyone talking at once. It's just a hum — a buzzing of voices in the background. Until I focus on one voice, and then what they're thinking is clear.

"Most of the time I tune it all out — it can be very distracting. And then it's easier to seem *normal*" — he frowned as he said the word — "when I'm not accidentally answering someone's thoughts rather than their words."

"Why do you think you can't hear me?" I asked curiously.

He looked at me, his eyes enigmatic.

"I don't know," he murmured. "The only guess I have is that maybe your mind doesn't work the same way the rest of theirs do. Like your thoughts are on the AM frequency and I'm only getting FM." He grinned at me, suddenly amused.

"My mind doesn't work right? I'm a freak?" The words bothered me more than they should — probably because his speculation hit home. I'd always suspected as much, and it embarrassed me to have it confirmed.

"I hear voices in my mind and you're worried that *you're* the freak," he laughed. "Don't worry, it's just a theory. . . ." His face tightened. "Which brings us back to you."

I sighed. How to begin?

"Aren't we past all the evasions now?" he reminded me softly.

I looked away from his face for the first time, trying to find words. I happened to notice the speedometer.

"Holy crow!" I shouted. "Slow down!"

"What's wrong?" He was startled. But the car didn't decelerate.

"You're going a hundred miles an hour!" I was still shouting. I shot a panicky glance out the window, but it was too dark to see much. The road was only visible in the long patch of bluish brightness from the headlights. The forest along both sides of the road was like a black wall — as hard as a wall of steel if we veered off the road at this speed.

"Relax, Bella." He rolled his eyes, still not slowing.

"Are you trying to kill us?" I demanded.

"We're not going to crash."

I tried to modulate my voice. "Why are you in such a hurry?"

"I always drive like this." He turned to smile crookedly at me.

"Keep your eyes on the road!"

"I've never been in an accident, Bella — I've never even gotten a ticket." He grinned and tapped his forehead. "Built-in radar detector."

"Very funny." I fumed. "Charlie's a cop, remember? I was raised to abide by traffic laws. Besides, if you turn us into a Volvo pretzel around a tree trunk, you can probably just walk away."

"Probably," he agreed with a short, hard laugh. "But you can't." He sighed, and I watched with relief as the needle gradually drifted toward eighty. "Happy?"

"Almost."

"I hate driving slow," he muttered.

"This is slow?"

"Enough commentary on my driving," he snapped. "I'm still waiting for your latest theory."

I bit my lip. He looked down at me, his honey eyes unexpectedly gentle.

"I won't laugh," he promised.

"I'm more afraid that you'll be angry with me."

"Is it that bad?"

"Pretty much, yeah."

He waited. I was looking down at my hands, so I couldn't see his expression.

"Go ahead." His voice was calm.

"I don't know how to start," I admitted.

"Why don't you start at the beginning . . . you said you didn't come up with this on your own."

"No."

"What got you started — a book? A movie?" he probed.

"No — it was Saturday, at the beach." I risked a glance up at his face. He looked puzzled.

"I ran into an old family friend — Jacob Black," I continued. "His dad and Charlie have been friends since I was a baby."

He still looked confused.

"His dad is one of the Quileute elders." I watched him carefully. His confused expression froze in place. "We went for a walk —" I edited all my scheming out of the story "— and he was telling me some old legends — trying to scare me, I think. He told me one . . ." I hesitated.

"Go on," he said.

"About vampires." I realized I was whispering. I couldn't look at his face now. But I saw his knuckles tighten convulsively on the wheel.

"And you immediately thought of me?" Still calm.

"No. He . . . mentioned your family."

He was silent, staring at the road.

I was worried suddenly, worried about protecting Jacob.

"He just thought it was a silly superstition," I said quickly. "He didn't expect me to think anything of it." It didn't seem like enough; I had to confess. "It was my fault, I forced him to tell me."

"Why?"

"Lauren said something about you — she was trying to provoke me. And an older boy from the tribe said your family didn't come to the reservation, only it sounded like he meant something different. So I got Jacob alone and I tricked it out of him," I admitted, hanging my head.

He startled me by laughing. I glared up at him. He was laughing, but his eyes were fierce, staring ahead.

"Tricked him how?" he asked.

"I tried to flirt — it worked better than I thought it would." Disbelief colored my tone as I remembered.

"I'd like to have seen that." He chuckled darkly. "And you accused me of dazzling people — poor Jacob Black."

I blushed and looked out my window into the night.

"What did you do then?" he asked after a minute.

"I did some research on the Internet."

"And did that convince you?" His voice sounded barely interested. But his hands were clamped hard onto the steering wheel.

"No. Nothing fit. Most of it was kind of silly. And then . . ." I stopped.

"What?"

"I decided it didn't matter," I whispered.

"It didn't *matter*?" His tone made me look up — I had finally broken through his carefully composed mask. His face was incredulous, with just a hint of the anger I'd feared.

"No," I said softly. "It doesn't matter to me what you are."

A hard, mocking edge entered his voice. "You don't care if I'm a monster? If I'm not *human*?"

"No."

He was silent, staring straight ahead again. His face was bleak and cold.

"You're angry," I sighed. "I shouldn't have said anything."

"No," he said, but his tone was as hard as his face. "I'd rather know what you're thinking — even if what you're thinking is insane."

"So I'm wrong again?" I challenged.

"That's not what I was referring to. 'It doesn't matter'!" he quoted, gritting his teeth together.

"I'm right?" I gasped.

"Does it *matter*?"

I took a deep breath.

"Not really." I paused. "But I *am* curious." My voice, at least, was composed.

He was suddenly resigned. "What are you curious about?"

"How old are you?"

"Seventeen," he answered promptly.

"And how long have you been seventeen?"

His lips twitched as he stared at the road. "A while," he admitted at last.

"Okay." I smiled, pleased that he was still being honest with me. He stared down at me with watchful eyes, much as he had before, when he was worried I would go into shock. I smiled wider in encouragement, and he frowned.

"Don't laugh — but how can you come out during the daytime?"

He laughed anyway. "Myth."

"Burned by the sun?"

"Myth."

"Sleeping in coffins?"

"Myth." He hesitated for a moment, and a peculiar tone entered his voice. "I can't sleep."

It took me a minute to absorb that. "At all?"

"Never," he said, his voice nearly inaudible. He turned to look at me with a wistful expression. The golden eyes held mine, and I lost my train of thought. I stared at him until he looked away.

"You haven't asked me the most important question yet." His voice was hard now, and when he looked at me again his eyes were cold.

I blinked, still dazed. "Which one is that?"

"You aren't concerned about my diet?" he asked sarcastically.

"Oh," I murmured, "that."

"Yes, that." His voice was bleak. "Don't you want to know if I drink blood?"

I flinched. "Well, Jacob said something about that."

"What did Jacob say?" he asked flatly.

"He said you didn't . . . hunt people. He said your family wasn't supposed to be dangerous because you only hunted animals."

"He said we weren't dangerous?" His voice was deeply skeptical.

"Not exactly. He said you weren't *supposed* to be dangerous. But the Quileutes still didn't want you on their land, just in case."

He looked forward, but I couldn't tell if he was watching the road or not.

"So was he right? About not hunting people?" I tried to keep my voice as even as possible.

"The Quileutes have a long memory," he whispered.

I took it as a confirmation.

"Don't let that make you complacent, though," he warned me. "They're right to keep their distance from us. We are still dangerous."

"I don't understand."

"We try," he explained slowly. "We're usually very good at what we do. Sometimes we make mistakes. Me, for example, allowing myself to be alone with you."

"This is a mistake?" I heard the sadness in my voice, but I didn't know if he could as well.

"A very dangerous one," he murmured.

We were both silent then. I watched the headlights twist with the curves of the road. They moved too fast; it didn't look real, it looked like a video game. I was aware of the time slipping away so quickly, like the black road beneath us, and I was hideously afraid that I would never have another chance to be with him like this again — openly, the walls between us gone for once. His words hinted at an end, and I recoiled from the idea. I couldn't waste one minute I had with him.

"Tell me more," I asked desperately, not caring what he said, just so I could hear his voice again.

He looked at me quickly, startled by the change in my tone. "What more do you want to know?"

"Tell me why you hunt animals instead of people," I suggested, my voice still tinged with desperation. I realized my eyes were wet, and I fought against the grief that was trying to overpower me.

"I don't *want* to be a monster." His voice was very low.

"But animals aren't enough?"

He paused. "I can't be sure, of course, but I'd compare it to living on tofu and soy milk; we call ourselves vegetarians, our little inside joke. It doesn't completely satiate the hunger — or rather thirst. But it keeps us strong enough to resist. Most of the time." His tone turned ominous. "Sometimes it's more difficult than others."

"Is it very difficult for you now?" I asked.

He sighed. "Yes."

"But you're not hungry now," I said confidently — stating, not asking.

"Why do you think that?"

"Your eyes. I told you I had a theory. I've noticed that people — men in particular — are crabbier when they're hungry."

He chuckled. "You are observant, aren't you?"

I didn't answer; I just listened to the sound of his laugh, committing it to memory.

"Were you hunting this weekend, with Emmett?" I asked when it was quiet again.

"Yes." He paused for a second, as if deciding whether or not to say something. "I didn't want to leave, but it was necessary. It's a bit easier to be around you when I'm not thirsty."

"Why didn't you want to leave?"

"It makes me . . . anxious . . . to be away from you." His eyes were gentle but intense, and they seemed to be making my bones turn soft. "I wasn't joking when I asked you to try not to fall in the ocean or get run over last Thursday. I was distracted all weekend, worrying about you. And after what happened tonight, I'm surprised that you did make it through a whole weekend unscathed." He shook his head, and then seemed to remember something. "Well, not totally unscathed."

"What?"

"Your hands," he reminded me. I looked down at my palms, at the almost-healed scrapes across the heels of my hands. His eyes missed nothing.

"I fell," I sighed.

"That's what I thought." His lips curved up at the corners. "I suppose, being you, it could have been much worse — and that possibility tormented me the entire time I was away. It was a very long three days. I really got on Emmett's nerves." He smiled ruefully at me.

"Three days? Didn't you just get back today?"

"No, we got back Sunday."

"Then why weren't any of you in school?" I was frustrated, almost angry as I thought of how much disappointment I had suffered because of his absence.

"Well, you asked if the sun hurt me, and it doesn't. But I can't go out in the sunlight — at least, not where anyone can see."

"Why?"

"I'll show you sometime," he promised.

I thought about it for a moment.

"You might have called me," I decided.

He was puzzled. "But I knew you were safe."

"But *I* didn't know where *you* were. I —" I hesitated, dropping my eyes.

"What?" His velvety voice was compelling.

"I didn't like it. Not seeing you. It makes me anxious, too." I blushed to be saying this out loud.

He was quiet. I glanced up, apprehensive, and saw that his expression was pained.

"Ah," he groaned quietly. "This is wrong."

I couldn't understand his response. "What did I say?"

"Don't you see, Bella? It's one thing for me to make myself miserable, but a wholly other thing for you to be so involved." He turned his anguished eyes to the road, his words flowing almost too fast for me to understand. "I don't want to hear that you feel that way." His voice was low but urgent. His words cut me. "It's wrong. It's not safe. I'm dangerous, Bella — please, grasp that."

"No." I tried very hard not to look like a sulky child.

"I'm serious," he growled.

"So am I. I told you, it doesn't matter what you are. It's too late."

His voice whipped out, low and harsh. "Never say that."

I bit my lip and was glad he couldn't know how much that hurt. I stared out at the road. We must be close now. He was driving much too fast.

"What are you thinking?" he asked, his voice still raw. I just shook my head, not sure if I could speak. I could feel his gaze on my face, but I kept my eyes forward.

"Are you crying?" He sounded appalled. I hadn't realized the moisture in my eyes had brimmed over. I quickly rubbed my hand across my cheek, and sure enough, traitor tears were there, betraying me.

"No," I said, but my voice cracked.

I saw him reach toward me hesitantly with his right hand, but then he stopped and placed it slowly back on the steering wheel.

"I'm sorry." His voice burned with regret. I knew he wasn't just apologizing for the words that had upset me.

The darkness slipped by us in silence.

"Tell me something," he asked after another minute, and I could hear him struggle to use a lighter tone.

"Yes?"

"What were you thinking tonight, just before I came around the corner? I couldn't understand your expression — you didn't look that scared, you looked like you were concentrating very hard on something."

"I was trying to remember how to incapacitate an attacker — you know, self-defense. I was going to smash his nose into his brain." I thought of the dark-haired man with a surge of hate.

"You were going to fight them?" This upset him. "Didn't you think about running?"

"I fall down a lot when I run," I admitted.

"What about screaming for help?"

"I was getting to that part."

He shook his head. "You were right — I'm definitely fighting fate trying to keep you alive."

I sighed. We were slowing, passing into the boundaries of Forks. It had taken less than twenty minutes.

"Will I see you tomorrow?" I demanded.

"Yes — I have a paper due, too." He smiled. "I'll save you a seat at lunch."

It was silly, after everything we'd been through tonight,

how that little promise sent flutters through my stomach, and made me unable to speak.

We were in front of Charlie's house. The lights were on, my truck in its place, everything utterly normal. It was like waking from a dream. He stopped the car, but I didn't move.

"Do you *promise* to be there tomorrow?"

"I promise."

I considered that for a moment, then nodded. I pulled his jacket off, taking one last whiff.

"You can keep it — you don't have a jacket for tomorrow," he reminded me.

I handed it back to him. "I don't want to have to explain to Charlie."

"Oh, right." He grinned.

I hesitated, my hand on the door handle, trying to prolong the moment.

"Bella?" he asked in a different tone — serious, but hesitant.

"Yes?" I turned back to him too eagerly.

"Will you promise me something?"

"Yes," I said, and instantly regretted my unconditional agreement. What if he asked me to stay away from him? I couldn't keep that promise.

"Don't go into the woods alone."

I stared at him in blank confusion. "Why?"

He frowned, and his eyes were tight as he stared past me out the window.

"I'm not always the most dangerous thing out there. Let's leave it at that."

I shuddered slightly at the sudden bleakness in his voice, but I was relieved. This, at least, was an easy promise to honor. "Whatever you say."

"I'll see you tomorrow," he sighed, and I knew he wanted me to leave now.

"Tomorrow, then." I opened the door unwillingly.

"Bella?" I turned and he was leaning toward me, his pale, glorious face just inches from mine. My heart stopped beating.

"Sleep well," he said. His breath blew in my face, stunning me. It was the same exquisite scent that clung to his jacket, but in a more concentrated form. I blinked, thoroughly dazed. He leaned away.

I was unable to move until my brain had somewhat unscrambled itself. Then I stepped out of the car awkwardly, having to use the frame for support. I thought I heard him chuckle, but the sound was too quiet for me to be certain.

He waited till I had stumbled to the front door, and then I heard his engine quietly rev. I turned to watch the silver car disappear around the corner. I realized it was very cold.

I reached for the key mechanically, unlocked the door, and stepped inside.

Charlie called from the living room. "Bella?"

"Yeah, Dad, it's me." I walked in to see him. He was watching a baseball game.

"You're home early."

"Am I?" I was surprised.

"It's not even eight yet," he told me. "Did you girls have fun?"

"Yeah — it was lots of fun." My head was spinning as I tried to remember all the way back to the girls' night out I had planned. "They both found dresses."

"Are you all right?"

"I'm just tired. I did a lot of walking."

"Well, maybe you should go lie down." He sounded concerned. I wondered what my face looked like.

"I'm just going to call Jessica first."

"Weren't you just with her?" he asked, surprised.

"Yes — but I left my jacket in her car. I want to make sure she brings it tomorrow."

"Well, give her a chance to get home first."

"Right," I agreed.

I went to the kitchen and fell, exhausted, into a chair. I was really feeling dizzy now. I wondered if I was going to go into shock after all. Get a grip, I told myself.

The phone rang suddenly, startling me. I yanked it off the hook.

"Hello?" I asked breathlessly.

"Bella?"

"Hey, Jess, I was just going to call you."

"You made it home?" Her voice was relieved . . . and surprised.

"Yes. I left my jacket in your car — could you bring it to me tomorrow?"

"Sure. But tell me what happened!" she demanded.

"Um, tomorrow — in Trig, okay?"

She caught on quickly. "Oh, is your dad there?"

"Yes, that's right."

"Okay, I'll talk to you tomorrow, then. Bye!" I could hear the impatience in her voice.

"Bye, Jess."

I walked up the stairs slowly, a heavy stupor clouding my mind. I went through the motions of getting ready for bed without paying any attention to what I was doing. It wasn't until I was in the shower — the water too hot, burning my skin — that I realized I was freezing. I shuddered violently for several minutes before the steaming spray could finally relax my rigid muscles. Then I stood in the shower, too tired to move, until the hot water began to run out.

I stumbled out, wrapping myself securely in a towel, trying to hold the heat from the water in so the aching shivers wouldn't return. I dressed for bed swiftly and climbed under my quilt, curling into a ball, hugging myself to keep warm. A few small shudders trembled through me.

My mind still swirled dizzily, full of images I couldn't understand, and some I fought to repress. Nothing seemed clear at first, but as I fell gradually closer to unconsciousness, a few certainties became evident.

About three things I was absolutely positive. First, Edward was a vampire. Second, there was part of him — and I didn't know how potent that part might be — that thirsted for my blood. And third, I was unconditionally and irrevocably in love with him.

10. INTERROGATIONS

It was very hard, in the morning, to argue with the part of me that was sure last night was a dream. Logic wasn't on my side, or common sense. I clung to the parts I couldn't have imagined — like his smell. I was sure I could never have dreamed that up on my own.

It was foggy and dark outside my window, absolutely perfect. He had no reason not to be in school today. I dressed in my heavy clothes, remembering I didn't have a jacket. Further proof that my memory was real.

When I got downstairs, Charlie was gone again — I was running later than I'd realized. I swallowed a granola bar in three bites, chased it down with milk straight from the carton, and then hurried out the door. Hopefully the rain would hold off until I could find Jessica.

It was unusually foggy; the air was almost smoky with it. The mist was ice cold where it clung to the exposed skin on my face and neck. I couldn't wait to get the heat going in my truck. It was such a thick fog that I was a few feet down the driveway before I realized there was a car in it: a silver car. My heart thudded, stuttered, and then picked up again in double time.

I didn't see where he came from, but suddenly he was there, pulling the door open for me.

"Do you want to ride with me today?" he asked, amused by my expression as he caught me by surprise yet again. There was uncertainty in his voice. He was really giving me a choice — I was free to refuse, and part of him hoped for that. It was a vain hope.

"Yes, thank you," I said, trying to keep my voice calm. As I stepped into the warm car, I noticed his tan jacket was slung over the headrest of the passenger seat. The door closed behind me, and, sooner than should be possible, he was sitting next to me, starting the car.

"I brought the jacket for you. I didn't want you to get sick or something." His voice was guarded. I noticed that he wore no jacket himself, just a light gray knit V-neck shirt with long sleeves. Again, the fabric clung to his perfectly muscled chest. It was a colossal tribute to his face that it kept my eyes away from his body.

"I'm not quite that delicate," I said, but I pulled the jacket onto my lap, pushing my arms through the too-long sleeves, curious to see if the scent could possibly be as good as I remembered. It was better.

"Aren't you?" he contradicted in a voice so low I wasn't sure if he meant for me to hear.

We drove through the fog-shrouded streets, always too fast, feeling awkward. I was, at least. Last night all the walls were down . . . almost all. I didn't know if we were still being as candid today. It left me tongue-tied. I waited for him to speak.

He turned to smirk at me. "What, no twenty questions today?"

"Do my questions bother you?" I asked, relieved.

"Not as much as your reactions do." He looked like he was joking, but I couldn't be sure.

I frowned. "Do I react badly?"

"No, that's the problem. You take everything so coolly — it's unnatural. It makes me wonder what you're really thinking."

"I always tell you what I'm really thinking."

"You edit," he accused.

"Not very much."

"Enough to drive me insane."

"You don't want to hear it," I mumbled, almost whispered. As soon as the words were out, I regretted them. The pain in my voice was very faint; I could only hope he hadn't noticed it.

He didn't respond, and I wondered if I had ruined the mood. His face was unreadable as we drove into the school parking lot. Something occurred to me belatedly.

"Where's the rest of your family?" I asked — more than glad to be alone with him, but remembering that his car was usually full.

"They took Rosalie's car." He shrugged as he parked next to a glossy red convertible with the top up. "Ostentatious, isn't it?"

"Um, wow," I breathed. "If she has *that,* why does she ride with you?"

"Like I said, it's ostentatious. We *try* to blend in."

"You don't succeed." I laughed and shook my head as we got out of the car. I wasn't late anymore; his lunatic driving had gotten me to school in plenty of time. "So why did Rosalie drive today if it's more conspicuous?"

"Hadn't you noticed? I'm breaking *all* the rules now." He met me at the front of the car, staying very close to my side as we walked onto campus. I wanted to close that little distance, to reach out and touch him, but I was afraid he wouldn't like me to.

"Why do you have cars like that at all?" I wondered aloud. "If you're looking for privacy?"

"An indulgence," he admitted with an impish smile. "We all like to drive fast."

"Figures," I muttered under my breath.

Under the shelter of the cafeteria roof's overhang, Jessica was waiting, her eyes about to bug out of their sockets. Over her arm, bless her, was my jacket.

"Hey, Jessica," I said when we were a few feet away. "Thanks for remembering." She handed me my jacket without speaking.

"Good morning, Jessica," Edward said politely. It wasn't really his fault that his voice was so irresistible. Or what his eyes were capable of.

"Er . . . hi." She shifted her wide eyes to me, trying to gather her jumbled thoughts. "I guess I'll see you in Trig." She gave me a meaningful look, and I suppressed a sigh. What on earth was I going to tell her?

"Yeah, I'll see you then."

She walked away, pausing twice to peek back over her shoulder at us.

"What are you going to tell her?" Edward murmured.

"Hey, I thought you couldn't read my mind!" I hissed.

"I can't," he said, startled. Then understanding brightened his eyes. "However, I can read hers — she'll be waiting to ambush you in class."

I groaned as I pulled off his jacket and handed it to him, replacing it with my own. He folded it over his arm.

"So what are you going to tell her?"

"A little help?" I pleaded. "What does she want to know?"

He shook his head, grinning wickedly. "That's not fair."

"No, you not sharing what you know — now *that's* not fair."

He deliberated for a moment as we walked. We stopped outside the door to my first class.

"She wants to know if we're secretly dating. And she wants to know how you feel about me," he finally said.

"Yikes. What should I say?" I tried to keep my expression very innocent. People were passing us on their way to class, probably staring, but I was barely aware of them.

"Hmmm." He paused to catch a stray lock of hair that was escaping the twist on my neck and wound it back into place. My heart spluttered hyperactively. "I suppose you could say yes to the first . . . if you don't mind — it's easier than any other explanation."

"I don't mind," I said in a faint voice.

"And as for her other question . . . well, I'll be listening to hear the answer to that one myself." One side of his mouth pulled up into my favorite uneven smile. I couldn't catch my breath soon enough to respond to that remark. He turned and walked away.

"I'll see you at lunch," he called over his shoulder. Three people walking in the door stopped to stare at me.

I hurried into class, flushed and irritated. He was such a cheater. Now I was even more worried about what I was going to say to Jessica. I sat in my usual seat, slamming my bag down in aggravation.

"Morning, Bella," Mike said from the seat next to me. I looked up to see an odd, almost resigned look on his face. "How was Port Angeles?"

"It was . . ." There was no honest way to sum it up. "Great," I finished lamely. "Jessica got a really cute dress."

"Did she say anything about Monday night?" he asked, his eyes brightening. I smiled at the turn the conversation had taken.

"She said she had a really good time," I assured him.

"She did?" he said eagerly.

"Most definitely."

Mr. Mason called the class to order then, asking us to turn in our papers. English and then Government passed in a blur, while I worried about how to explain things to Jessica and agonized over whether Edward would really be listening to what I said through the medium of Jess's thoughts. How very inconvenient his little talent could be — when it wasn't saving my life.

The fog had almost dissolved by the end of the second hour, but the day was still dark with low, oppressing clouds. I smiled up at the sky.

Edward was right, of course. When I walked into Trig Jessica was sitting in the back row, nearly bouncing off her seat in agitation. I reluctantly went to sit by her, trying to convince myself it would be better to get it over with as soon as possible.

"Tell me everything!" she commanded before I was in the seat.

"What do you want to know?" I hedged.

"What happened last night?"

"He bought me dinner, and then he drove me home."

She glared at me, her expression stiff with skepticism. "How did you get home so fast?"

"He drives like a maniac. It was terrifying." I hoped he heard that.

"Was it like a date — did you tell him to meet you there?"

I hadn't thought of that. "No — I was *very* surprised to see him there."

Her lips puckered in disappointment at the transparent honesty in my voice.

"But he picked you up for school today?" she probed.

"Yes — that was a surprise, too. He noticed I didn't have a jacket last night," I explained.

"So are you going out again?"

"He offered to drive me to Seattle Saturday because he thinks my truck isn't up to it — does that count?"

"Yes." She nodded.

"Well, then, yes."

"W-o-w." She exaggerated the word into three syllables. "Edward Cullen."

"I know," I agreed. "Wow" didn't even cover it.

"Wait!" Her hands flew up, palms toward me like she was stopping traffic. "Has he kissed you?"

"No," I mumbled. "It's not like that."

She looked disappointed. I'm sure I did, too.

"Do you think Saturday . . . ?" She raised her eyebrows.

"I really doubt it." The discontent in my voice was poorly disguised.

"What did you talk about?" She pushed for more information in a whisper. Class had started but Mr. Varner wasn't paying close attention and we weren't the only ones still talking.

"I don't know, Jess, lots of stuff," I whispered back. "We talked about the English essay a little." A very, very little. I think he mentioned it in passing.

"Please, Bella," she begged. "Give me some details."

"Well . . . okay, I've got one. You should have seen the waitress flirting with him — it was over the top. But he didn't pay any attention to her at all." Let him make what he could of that.

"That's a good sign," she nodded. "Was she pretty?"

"Very — and probably nineteen or twenty."

"Even better. He must like you."

"I *think* so, but it's hard to tell. He's always so cryptic," I threw in for his benefit, sighing.

"I don't know how you're brave enough to be alone with him," she breathed.

"Why?" I was shocked, but she didn't understand my reaction.

"He's so . . . intimidating. I wouldn't know what to say to him." She made a face, probably remembering this morning or last night, when he'd turned the overwhelming force of his eyes on her.

"I do have some trouble with incoherency when I'm around him," I admitted.

"Oh well. He *is* unbelievably gorgeous." Jessica shrugged as if this excused any flaws. Which, in her book, it probably did.

"There's a lot more to him than that."

"Really? Like what?"

I wished I had let it go. Almost as much as I was hoping he'd been kidding about listening in.

"I can't explain it right . . . but he's even more unbelievable *behind* the face." The vampire who wanted to be good — who ran around saving people's lives so he wouldn't be a monster . . . I stared toward the front of the room.

"Is that *possible*?" She giggled.

I ignored her, trying to look like I was paying attention to Mr. Varner.

"So you like him, then?" She wasn't about to give up.

"Yes," I said curtly.

"I mean, do you *really* like him?" she urged.

"Yes," I said again, blushing. I hoped that detail wouldn't register in her thoughts.

She'd had enough with the single syllable answers. "How *much* do you like him?"

"Too much," I whispered back. "More than he likes me. But I don't see how I can help that." I sighed, one blush blending into the next.

Then, thankfully, Mr. Varner called on Jessica for an answer.

She didn't get a chance to start on the subject again during class, and as soon as the bell rang, I took evasive action.

"In English, Mike asked me if you said anything about Monday night," I told her.

"You're kidding! What did you say?!" she gasped, completely sidetracked.

"I told him you said you had a lot of fun — he looked pleased."

"Tell me exactly what he said, and your exact answer!"

We spent the rest of the walk dissecting sentence structures and most of Spanish on a minute description of Mike's facial expressions. I wouldn't have helped draw it out for as long as I did if I wasn't worried about the subject returning to me.

And then the bell rang for lunch. As I jumped up out of my seat, shoving my books roughly in my bag, my uplifted expression must have tipped Jessica off.

"You're not sitting with us today, are you?" she guessed.

"I don't *think* so." I couldn't be sure that he wouldn't disappear inconveniently again.

But outside the door to our Spanish class, leaning against the wall — looking more like a Greek god than anyone had a right to — Edward was waiting for me. Jessica took one look, rolled her eyes, and departed.

"See you later, Bella." Her voice was thick with implications. I might have to turn off the ringer on the phone.

"Hello." His voice was amused and irritated at the same time. He had been listening, it was obvious.

"Hi."

I couldn't think of anything else to say, and he didn't speak — biding his time, I presumed — so it was a quiet walk to the cafeteria. Walking with Edward through the crowded lunchtime rush was a lot like my first day here; everyone stared.

He led the way into the line, still not speaking, though his eyes returned to my face every few seconds, their expression speculative. It seemed to me that irritation was winning out over amusement as the dominant emotion in his face. I fidgeted nervously with the zipper on my jacket.

He stepped up to the counter and filled a tray with food.

"What are you doing?" I objected. "You're not getting all that for me?"

He shook his head, stepping forward to buy the food.

"Half is for me, of course."

I raised one eyebrow.

He led the way to the same place we'd sat that one time before. From the other end of the long table, a group of seniors gazed at us in amazement as we sat across from each other. Edward seemed oblivious.

"Take whatever you want," he said, pushing the tray toward me.

"I'm curious," I said as I picked up an apple, turning it around in my hands, "what would you do if someone dared you to eat food?"

"You're always curious." He grimaced, shaking his head. He glared at me, holding my eyes as he lifted the slice of pizza off the tray, and deliberately bit off a mouthful, chewed quickly, and then swallowed. I watched, eyes wide.

"If someone dared you to eat dirt, you could, couldn't you?" he asked condescendingly.

I wrinkled my nose. "I did once . . . on a dare," I admitted. "It wasn't so bad."

He laughed. "I suppose I'm not surprised." Something over my shoulder seemed to catch his attention.

"Jessica's analyzing everything I do — she'll break it down for you later." He pushed the rest of the pizza toward me. The mention of Jessica brought a hint of his former irritation back to his features.

I put down the apple and took a bite of the pizza, looking away, knowing he was about to start.

"So the waitress was pretty, was she?" he asked casually.

"You really didn't notice?"

"No. I wasn't paying attention. I had a lot on my mind."

"Poor girl." I could afford to be generous now.

"Something you said to Jessica . . . well, it bothers me." He refused to be distracted. His voice was husky, and he glanced up from under his lashes with troubled eyes.

"I'm not surprised you heard something you didn't like. You know what they say about eavesdroppers," I reminded him.

"I warned you I would be listening."

"And I warned you that you didn't want to know everything I was thinking."

"You did," he agreed, but his voice was still rough. "You aren't precisely right, though. I do want to know what you're thinking — everything. I just wish . . . that you wouldn't be thinking some things."

I scowled. "That's quite a distinction."

"But that's not really the point at the moment."

"Then what is?" We were inclined toward each other across the table now. He had his large white hands folded under his chin; I leaned forward, my right hand cupped around my neck. I had to remind myself that we were in a crowded lunchroom, with probably many curious eyes on us. It was too easy to get wrapped up in our own private, tense little bubble.

"Do you truly believe that you care more for me than I do for you?" he murmured, leaning closer to me as he spoke, his dark golden eyes piercing.

I tried to remember how to exhale. I had to look away before it came back to me.

"You're doing it again," I muttered.

His eyes opened wide with surprise. "What?"

"Dazzling me," I admitted, trying to concentrate as I looked back at him.

"Oh." He frowned.

"It's not your fault," I sighed. "You can't help it."

"Are you going to answer the question?"

I looked down. "Yes."

"Yes, you are going to answer, or yes, you really think that?" He was irritated again.

"Yes, I really think that." I kept my eyes down on the table, my eyes tracing the pattern of the faux wood grains printed on the laminate. The silence dragged on. I stubbornly refused to be the first to break it this time, fighting hard against the temptation to peek at his expression.

Finally he spoke, voice velvet soft. "You're wrong."

I glanced up to see that his eyes were gentle.

"You can't know that," I disagreed in a whisper. I shook my head in doubt, though my heart throbbed at his words and I wanted so badly to believe them.

"What makes you think so?" His liquid topaz eyes were penetrating — trying futilely, I assumed, to lift the truth straight from my mind.

I stared back, struggling to think clearly in spite of his face, to find some way to explain. As I searched for the words, I could see him getting impatient; frustrated by my silence, he started to scowl. I lifted my hand from my neck, and held up one finger.

"Let me think," I insisted. His expression cleared, now that he was satisfied that I was planning to answer. I dropped my hand to the table, moving my left hand so that my palms were pressed together. I stared at my hands, twisting and untwisting my fingers, as I finally spoke.

"Well, aside from the obvious, sometimes . . ." I hesitated. "I can't be sure — *I* don't know how to read minds — but sometimes it seems like you're trying to say goodbye when you're saying something else." That was the best I could sum up the sensation of anguish that his words triggered in me at times.

"Perceptive," he whispered. And there was the anguish again, surfacing as he confirmed my fear. "That's exactly why you're wrong, though," he began to explain, but then his eyes narrowed. "What do you mean, 'the obvious'?"

"Well, look at me," I said, unnecessarily as he was already staring. "I'm absolutely ordinary — well, except for bad things like all the near-death experiences and being so clumsy that I'm almost disabled. And look at you." I waved my hand toward him and all his bewildering perfection.

His brow creased angrily for a moment, then smoothed as his eyes took on a knowing look. "You don't see yourself very clearly, you know. I'll admit you're dead-on about the bad things," he chuckled blackly, "but you didn't hear what every human male in this school was thinking on your first day."

I blinked, astonished. "I don't believe it . . . ," I mumbled to myself.

"Trust me just this once — you are the opposite of ordinary."

My embarrassment was much stronger than my pleasure at the look that came into his eyes when he said this. I quickly reminded him of my original argument.

"But I'm not saying goodbye," I pointed out.

"Don't you see? That's what proves me right. I care the most, because if I can do it" — he shook his head, seeming to struggle with the thought — "if leaving is the right thing to do, then I'll hurt myself to keep from hurting you, to keep you safe."

I glared. "And you don't think I would do the same?"

"You'd never have to make the choice."

Abruptly, his unpredictable mood shifted again; a mischievous, devastating smile rearranged his features. "Of course, keeping you safe is beginning to feel like a full-time occupation that requires my constant presence."

"No one has tried to do away with me today," I reminded him, grateful for the lighter subject. I didn't want him to talk about goodbyes anymore. If I had to, I supposed I could purposefully put myself in danger to keep him close. . . . I banished that thought before his quick eyes read it on my face. That idea would definitely get me in trouble.

"Yet," he added.

"Yet," I agreed; I would have argued, but now I wanted him to be expecting disasters.

"I have another question for you." His face was still casual.

"Shoot."

"Do you really need to go to Seattle this Saturday, or was that just an excuse to get out of saying no to all your admirers?"

I made a face at the memory. "You know, I haven't forgiven you for the Tyler thing yet," I warned him. "It's your fault that he's deluded himself into thinking I'm going to prom with him."

"Oh, he would have found a chance to ask you without me — I just really wanted to watch your face," he chuckled. I would have been angrier if his laughter wasn't so fascinating. "If I'd asked you, would you have turned *me* down?" he asked, still laughing to himself.

"Probably not," I admitted. "But I would have canceled later — faked an illness or a sprained ankle."

He was puzzled. "Why would you do that?"

I shook my head sadly. "You've never seen me in Gym, I guess, but I would have thought you would understand."

"Are you referring to the fact that you can't walk across a flat, stable surface without finding something to trip over?"

"Obviously."

"That wouldn't be a problem." He was very confident. "It's all in the leading." He could see that I was about to protest, and he cut me off. "But you never told me — are you resolved on going to Seattle, or do you mind if we do something different?"

As long as the "we" part was in, I didn't care about anything else.

"I'm open to alternatives," I allowed. "But I do have a favor to ask."

He looked wary, as he always did when I asked an open-ended question. "What?"

"Can I drive?"

He frowned. "Why?"

"Well, mostly because when I told Charlie I was going to Seattle, he specifically asked if I was going alone and, at the time, I was. If he asked again, I probably wouldn't lie, but I don't think he *will* ask again, and leaving my truck at home would just bring up the subject unnecessarily. And also, because your driving frightens me."

He rolled his eyes. "Of all the things about me that could frighten you, you worry about my driving." He shook his head in disgust, but then his eyes were serious again. "Won't you want to tell your father that you're spending the day with me?" There was an undercurrent to his question that I didn't understand.

"With Charlie, less is always more." I was definite about that. "Where are we going, anyway?"

"The weather will be nice, so I'll be staying out of the public eye . . . and you can stay with me, if you'd like to." Again, he was leaving the choice up to me.

"And you'll show me what you meant, about the sun?" I asked, excited by the idea of unraveling another of the unknowns.

"Yes." He smiled, and then paused. "But if you don't want to be . . . alone with me, I'd still rather you didn't go to Seattle by yourself. I shudder to think of the trouble you could find in a city that size."

I was miffed. "Phoenix is three times bigger than Seattle — just in population. In physical size —"

"But apparently," he interrupted me, "your number wasn't up in Phoenix. So I'd rather you stayed near me." His eyes did that unfair smoldering thing again.

I couldn't argue, with the eyes or the motivation, and it was a moot point anyway. "As it happens, I don't mind being alone with you."

"I know," he sighed, brooding. "You should tell Charlie, though."

"Why in the world would I do that?"

His eyes were suddenly fierce. "To give me some small incentive to bring you back."

I gulped. But, after a moment of thought, I was sure. "I think I'll take my chances."

He exhaled angrily, and looked away.

"Let's talk about something else," I suggested.

"What do you want to talk about?" he asked. He was still annoyed.

I glanced around us, making sure we were well out of anyone's hearing. As I cast my eyes around the room, I caught the eyes of his sister, Alice, staring at me. The others were looking at Edward. I looked away swiftly, back to him, and I asked the first thing that came to mind.

"Why did you go to that Goat Rocks place last week-end . . . to hunt? Charlie said it wasn't a good place to hike, because of bears."

He stared at me as if I was missing something very obvious.

"Bears?" I gasped, and he smirked. "You know, bears are not in season," I added sternly, to hide my shock.

"If you read carefully, the laws only cover hunting with weapons," he informed me.

He watched my face with enjoyment as that slowly sank in.

"Bears?" I repeated with difficulty.

"Grizzly is Emmett's favorite." His voice was still off-hand, but his eyes were scrutinizing my reaction. I tried to pull myself together.

"Hmmm," I said, taking another bite of pizza as an excuse to look down. I chewed slowly, and then took a long drink of Coke without looking up.

"So," I said after a moment, finally meeting his now-anxious gaze. "What's your favorite?"

He raised an eyebrow and the corners of his mouth turned down in disapproval. "Mountain lion."

"Ah," I said in a politely disinterested tone, looking for my soda again.

"Of course," he said, and his tone mirrored mine, "we have to be careful not to impact the environment with injudicious hunting. We try to focus on areas with an over-population of predators — ranging as far away as we need. There's always plenty of deer and elk here, and they'll do, but where's the fun in that?" He smiled teasingly.

"Where indeed," I murmured around another bite of pizza.

"Early spring is Emmett's favorite bear season — they're just coming out of hibernation, so they're more irritable." He smiled at some remembered joke.

"Nothing more fun than an irritated grizzly bear," I agreed, nodding.

He snickered, shaking his head. "Tell me what you're really thinking, please."

"I'm trying to picture it — but I can't," I admitted. "How do you hunt a bear without weapons?"

"Oh, we have weapons." He flashed his bright teeth in a brief, threatening smile. I fought back a shiver before it could expose me. "Just not the kind they consider when writing hunting laws. If you've ever seen a bear attack on television, you should be able to visualize Emmett hunting."

I couldn't stop the next shiver that flashed down my spine. I peeked across the cafeteria toward Emmett, grateful that he wasn't looking my way. The thick bands of muscle that wrapped his arms and torso were somehow even more menacing now.

Edward followed my gaze and chuckled. I stared at him, unnerved.

"Are you like a bear, too?" I asked in a low voice.

"More like the lion, or so they tell me," he said lightly. "Perhaps our preferences are indicative."

I tried to smile. "Perhaps," I repeated. But my mind was filled with opposing images that I couldn't merge together. "Is that something I might get to see?"

"Absolutely not!" His face turned even whiter than usual, and his eyes were suddenly furious. I leaned back, stunned and — though I'd never admit it to him — frightened by his reaction. He leaned back as well, folding his arms across his chest.

"Too scary for me?" I asked when I could control my voice again.

"If that were it, I would take you out tonight," he said, his voice cutting. "You *need* a healthy dose of fear. Nothing could be more beneficial for you."

"Then why?" I pressed, trying to ignore his angry expression.

He glared at me for a long minute.

"Later," he finally said. He was on his feet in one lithe movement. "We're going to be late."

I glanced around, startled to see that he was right and the cafeteria was nearly vacant. When I was with him, the time and the place were such a muddled blur that I completely lost track of both. I jumped up, grabbing my bag from the back of my chair.

"Later, then," I agreed. I wouldn't forget.

11. COMPLICATIONS

Everyone watched us as we walked together to our lab table. I noticed that he no longer angled the chair to sit as far from me as the desk would allow. Instead, he sat quite close beside me, our arms almost touching.

Mr. Banner backed into the room then — what superb timing the man had — pulling a tall metal frame on wheels that held a heavy-looking, outdated TV and VCR. A movie day — the lift in the class atmosphere was almost tangible.

Mr. Banner shoved the tape into the reluctant VCR and walked to the wall to turn off the lights.

And then, as the room went black, I was suddenly hyperaware that Edward was sitting less than an inch from me. I was stunned by the unexpected electricity that flowed through me, amazed that it was possible to be *more* aware of him than I already was. A crazy impulse to reach over and touch him, to stroke his perfect face just once in the darkness, nearly overwhelmed me. I crossed my arms tightly across my chest, my hands balling into fists. I was losing my mind.

The opening credits began, lighting the room by a token amount. My eyes, of their own accord, flickered to him. I smiled sheepishly as I realized his posture was identical to mine, fists clenched under his arms, right down to the eyes, peering sideways at me. He grinned back, his eyes somehow managing to smolder, even in the dark. I looked away before I could start hyperventilating. It was absolutely ridiculous that I should feel dizzy.

The hour seemed very long. I couldn't concentrate on the movie — I didn't even know what subject it was on. I tried unsuccessfully to relax, but the electric current that seemed to be originating from somewhere in his body never slackened. Occasionally I would permit myself a quick glance in his direction, but he never seemed to relax, either. The overpowering craving to touch him also refused to fade, and I crushed my fists safely against my ribs until my fingers were aching with the effort.

I breathed a sigh of relief when Mr. Banner flicked the lights back on at the end of class, and stretched my arms out in front of me, flexing my stiff fingers. Edward chuckled beside me.

"Well, that was interesting," he murmured. His voice was dark and his eyes were cautious.

"Umm," was all I was able to respond.

"Shall we?" he asked, rising fluidly.

I almost groaned. Time for Gym. I stood with care, worried my balance might have been affected by the strange new intensity between us.

He walked me to my next class in silence and paused at the door; I turned to say goodbye. His face startled me — his expression was torn, almost pained, and so fiercely beautiful that the ache to touch him flared as strong as before. My goodbye stuck in my throat.

He raised his hand, hesitant, conflict raging in his eyes, and then swiftly brushed the length of my cheekbone with his fingertips. His skin was as icy as ever, but the trail his fingers left on my skin was alarmingly warm — like I'd been burned, but didn't feel the pain of it yet.

He turned without a word and strode quickly away from me.

I walked into the gym, lightheaded and wobbly. I drifted to the locker room, changing in a trancelike state, only vaguely aware that there were other people surrounding me. Reality didn't fully set in until I was handed a racket. It wasn't heavy, yet it felt very unsafe in my hand. I could see a few of the other kids in class eyeing me furtively. Coach Clapp ordered us to pair up into teams.

Mercifully, some vestiges of Mike's chivalry still survived; he came to stand beside me.

"Do you want to be a team?"

"Thanks, Mike — you don't have to do this, you know." I grimaced apologetically.

"Don't worry, I'll keep out of your way." He grinned. Sometimes it was so easy to like Mike.

It didn't go smoothly. I somehow managed to hit myself in the head with my racket and clip Mike's shoulder on the same swing. I spent the rest of the hour in the back corner of the court, the racket held safely behind my back. Despite being handicapped by me, Mike was pretty good; he won three games out of four singlehandedly. He gave me an unearned high five when the coach finally blew the whistle ending class.

"So," he said as we walked off the court.

"So what?"

"You and Cullen, huh?" he asked, his tone rebellious. My previous feeling of affection disappeared.

"That's none of your business, Mike," I warned, internally cursing Jessica straight to the fiery pits of Hades.

"I don't like it," he muttered anyway.

"You don't have to," I snapped.

"He looks at you like . . . like you're something to eat," he continued, ignoring me.

I choked back the hysteria that threatened to explode, but a small giggle managed to get out despite my efforts. He glowered at me. I waved and fled to the locker room.

I dressed quickly, something stronger than butterflies battering recklessly against the walls of my stomach, my argument with Mike already a distant memory. I was wondering if Edward would be waiting, or if I should meet him at his car. What if his family was there? I felt a wave of real terror. Did they know that I knew? Was I supposed to know that they knew that I knew, or not?

By the time I walked out of the gym, I had just about decided to walk straight home without even looking toward the parking lot. But my worries were unnecessary. Edward was waiting, leaning casually against the side of the gym, his breathtaking face untroubled now. As I walked to his side, I felt a peculiar sense of release.

"Hi," I breathed, smiling hugely.

"Hello." His answering smile was brilliant. "How was Gym?"

My face fell a tiny bit. "Fine," I lied.

"Really?" He was unconvinced. His eyes shifted their focus slightly, looking over my shoulder and narrowing. I glanced behind me to see Mike's back as he walked away.

"What?" I demanded.

His eyes slid back to mine, still tight. "Newton's getting on my nerves."

"You weren't listening again?" I was horror-struck. All traces of my sudden good humor vanished.

"How's your head?" he asked innocently.

"You're unbelievable!" I turned, stomping away in the general direction of the parking lot, though I hadn't ruled out walking at this point.

He kept up with me easily.

"You were the one who mentioned how I'd never seen you in Gym — it made me curious." He didn't sound repentant, so I ignored him.

We walked in silence — a furious, embarrassed silence on my part — to his car. But I had to stop a few steps away — a crowd of people, all boys, were surrounding it.

Then I realized they weren't surrounding the Volvo, they were actually circled around Rosalie's red convertible, unmistakable lust in their eyes. None of them even looked up as Edward slid between them to open his door. I climbed quickly in the passenger side, also unnoticed.

"Ostentatious," he muttered.

"What kind of car is that?" I asked.

"An M3."

"I don't speak *Car and Driver.*"

"It's a BMW." He rolled his eyes, not looking at me, trying to back out without running over the car enthusiasts.

I nodded — I'd heard of that one.

"Are you still angry?" he asked as he carefully maneuvered his way out.

"Definitely."

He sighed. "Will you forgive me if I apologize?"

"Maybe . . . if you mean it. *And* if you promise not to do it again," I insisted.

His eyes were suddenly shrewd. "How about if I mean it, *and* I agree to let you drive Saturday?" he countered my conditions.

I considered, and decided it was probably the best offer I would get. "Deal," I agreed.

"Then I'm very sorry I upset you." His eyes burned with sincerity for a protracted moment — playing havoc with the rhythm of my heart — and then turned playful. "And I'll be on your doorstep bright and early Saturday morning."

"Um, it doesn't help with the Charlie situation if an unexplained Volvo is left in the driveway."

His smile was condescending now. "I wasn't intending to bring a car."

"How —"

He cut me off. "Don't worry about it. I'll be there, no car."

I let it go. I had a more pressing question.

"Is it later yet?" I asked significantly.

He frowned. "I suppose it is later."

I kept my expression polite as I waited.

He stopped the car. I looked up, surprised — of course we were already at Charlie's house, parked behind the truck. It was easier to ride with him if I only looked when it was over. When I looked back at him, he was staring at me, measuring with his eyes.

"And you still want to know why you can't see me hunt?" He seemed solemn, but I thought I saw a trace of humor deep in his eyes.

"Well," I clarified, "I was mostly wondering about your reaction."

"Did I frighten you?" Yes, there was definitely humor there.

"No," I lied. He didn't buy it.

"I apologize for scaring you," he persisted with a slight smile, but then all evidence of teasing disappeared. "It was just the very thought of you being there . . . while we hunted." His jaw tightened.

"That would be bad?"

He spoke from between clenched teeth. "Extremely."

"Because . . . ?"

He took a deep breath and stared through the windshield at the thick, rolling clouds that seemed to press down, almost within reach.

"When we hunt," he spoke slowly, unwillingly, "we give ourselves over to our senses . . . govern less with our minds. Especially our sense of smell. If you were anywhere near me when I lost control that way . . ." He shook his head, still gazing morosely at the heavy clouds.

I kept my expression firmly under control, expecting the swift flash of his eyes to judge my reaction that soon followed. My face gave nothing away.

But our eyes held, and the silence deepened — and changed. Flickers of the electricity I'd felt this afternoon began to charge the atmosphere as he gazed unrelentingly into my eyes. It wasn't until my head started to swim that I realized I wasn't breathing. When I drew in a jagged breath, breaking the stillness, he closed his eyes.

"Bella, I think you should go inside now." His low voice was rough, his eyes on the clouds again.

I opened the door, and the arctic draft that burst into the car helped clear my head. Afraid I might stumble in my woozy state, I stepped carefully out of the car and shut the door behind me without looking back. The whir of the automatic window unrolling made me turn.

"Oh, Bella?" he called after me, his voice more even. He leaned toward the open window with a faint smile on his lips.

"Yes?"

"Tomorrow it's my turn."

"Your turn to what?"

He smiled wider, flashing his gleaming teeth. "Ask the questions."

And then he was gone, the car speeding down the street and disappearing around the corner before I could even collect my thoughts. I smiled as I walked to the house. It was clear he was planning to see me tomorrow, if nothing else.

That night Edward starred in my dreams, as usual. However, the climate of my unconsciousness had changed. It thrilled with the same electricity that had charged the afternoon, and I tossed and turned restlessly, waking often. It was only in the early hours of the morning that I finally sank into an exhausted, dreamless sleep.

When I woke I was still tired, but edgy as well. I pulled on my brown turtleneck and the inescapable jeans, sighing as I daydreamed of spaghetti straps and shorts. Breakfast was the usual, quiet event I expected. Charlie fried eggs for himself; I had my bowl of cereal. I wondered if he had forgotten about this Saturday. He answered my unspoken question as he stood up to take his plate to the sink.

"About this Saturday . . . ," he began, walking across the kitchen and turning on the faucet.

I cringed. "Yes, Dad?"

"Are you still set on going to Seattle?" he asked.

"That was the plan." I grimaced, wishing he hadn't brought it up so I wouldn't have to compose careful half-truths.

He squeezed some dish soap onto his plate and swirled it around with the brush. "And you're sure you can't make it back in time for the dance?"

"I'm not going to the dance, Dad." I glared.

"Didn't anyone ask you?" he asked, trying to hide his concern by focusing on rinsing the plate.

I sidestepped the minefield. "It's a girl's choice."

"Oh." He frowned as he dried his plate.

I sympathized with him. It must be a hard thing, to be a father; living in fear that your daughter would meet a boy she liked, but also having to worry if she didn't. How ghastly it would be, I thought, shuddering, if Charlie had even the slightest inkling of exactly what I *did* like.

Charlie left then, with a goodbye wave, and I went upstairs to brush my teeth and gather my books. When I heard the cruiser pull away, I could only wait a few seconds before I had to peek out of my window. The silver car was already there, waiting in Charlie's spot on the driveway. I bounded down the stairs and out the front door, wondering how long this bizarre routine would continue. I never wanted it to end.

He waited in the car, not appearing to watch as I shut the door behind me without bothering to lock the deadbolt. I walked to the car, pausing shyly before opening the door and stepping in. He was smiling, relaxed — and, as usual, perfect and beautiful to an excruciating degree.

"Good morning." His voice was silky. "How are you today?" His eyes roamed over my face, as if his question was something more than simple courtesy.

"Good, thank you." I was always good — much more than good — when I was near him.

His gaze lingered on the circles under my eyes. "You look tired."

"I couldn't sleep," I confessed, automatically swinging my hair around my shoulder to provide some measure of cover.

"Neither could I," he teased as he started the engine. I was becoming used to the quiet purr. I was sure the roar of my truck would scare me, whenever I got to drive it again.

I laughed. "I guess that's right. I suppose I slept just a little bit more than you did."

"I'd wager you did."

"So what did you do last night?" I asked.

He chuckled. "Not a chance. It's my day to ask questions."

"Oh, that's right. What do you want to know?" My forehead creased. I couldn't imagine anything about me that could be in any way interesting to him.

"What's your favorite color?" he asked, his face grave.

I rolled my eyes. "It changes from day to day."

"What's your favorite color today?" He was still solemn.

"Probably brown." I tended to dress according to my mood.

He snorted, dropping his serious expression. "Brown?" he asked skeptically.

"Sure. Brown is warm. I *miss* brown. Everything that's supposed to be brown — tree trunks, rocks, dirt — is all covered up with squashy green stuff here," I complained.

He seemed fascinated by my little rant. He considered for a moment, staring into my eyes.

"You're right," he decided, serious again. "Brown is warm." He reached over, swiftly, but somehow still hesitantly, to sweep my hair back behind my shoulder.

We were at the school by now. He turned back to me as he pulled into a parking space.

"What music is in your CD player right now?" he asked, his face as somber as if he'd asked for a murder confession.

I realized I'd never removed the CD Phil had given me. When I said the name of the band, he smiled crookedly, a peculiar expression in his eyes. He flipped open a compartment under his car's CD player, pulled out one of thirty or so CDs that were jammed into the small space, and handed it to me.

"Debussy to this?" He raised an eyebrow.

It was the same CD. I examined the familiar cover art, keeping my eyes down.

It continued like that for the rest of the day. While he walked me to English, when he met me after Spanish, all through the lunch hour, he questioned me relentlessly about every insignificant detail of my existence. Movies I'd liked and hated, the few places I'd been and the many places I wanted to go, and books — endlessly books.

I couldn't remember the last time I'd talked so much. More often than not, I felt self-conscious, certain I must be boring him. But the absolute absorption of his face, and his never-ending stream of questions, compelled me to continue. Mostly his questions were easy, only a very few triggering my easy blushes. But when I did flush, it brought on a whole new round of questions.

Such as the time he asked my favorite gemstone, and I blurted out topaz before thinking. He'd been flinging questions at me with such speed that I felt like I was taking one of those psychiatric tests where you answer with the first word that comes to mind. I was sure he would have continued down whatever mental list he was following, except for the blush. My face reddened because, until very recently, my favorite gemstone was garnet. It was impossible, while staring back into his topaz eyes, not to remember the reason for the switch. And, naturally, he wouldn't rest until I'd admitted why I was embarrassed.

"Tell me," he finally commanded after persuasion failed — failed only because I kept my eyes safely away from his face.

"It's the color of your eyes today," I sighed, surrendering, staring down at my hands as I fiddled with a piece of my hair. "I suppose if you asked me in two weeks I'd say onyx." I'd given more information than necessary in my unwilling honesty, and I worried it would provoke the strange anger that flared whenever I slipped and revealed too clearly how obsessed I was.

But his pause was very short.

"What kinds of flowers do you prefer?" he fired off.

I sighed in relief, and continued with the psycho-analysis.

Biology was a complication again. Edward had continued with his quizzing up until Mr. Banner entered the room, dragging the audiovisual frame again. As the teacher approached the light switch, I noticed Edward slide his chair slightly farther away from mine. It didn't help. As soon as the room was dark, there was the same electric spark, the same restless craving to stretch my hand across the short space and touch his cold skin, as yesterday.

I leaned forward on the table, resting my chin on my folded arms, my hidden fingers gripping the table's edge as I fought to ignore the irrational longing that unsettled me. I didn't look at him, afraid that if he was looking at me, it would only make self-control that much harder. I sincerely tried to watch the movie, but at the end of the hour I had no idea what I'd just seen. I sighed in relief again when Mr. Banner turned the lights on, finally glancing at Edward; he was looking at me, his eyes ambivalent.

He rose in silence and then stood still, waiting for me. We walked toward the gym in silence, like yesterday. And, also like yesterday, he touched my face wordlessly — this time with the back of his cool hand, stroking once from my temple to my jaw — before he turned and walked away.

Gym passed quickly as I watched Mike's one-man badminton show. He didn't speak to me today, either in response to my vacant expression or because he was still angry about our squabble yesterday. Somewhere, in a corner of my mind, I felt bad about that. But I couldn't concentrate on him.

I hurried to change afterward, ill at ease, knowing the faster I moved, the sooner I would be with Edward. The pressure made me more clumsy than usual, but eventually I made it out the door, feeling the same release when I saw him standing there, a wide smile automatically spreading across my face. He smiled in reaction before launching into more cross-examination.

His questions were different now, though, not as easily answered. He wanted to know what I missed about home, insisting on descriptions of anything he wasn't familiar with. We sat in front of Charlie's house for hours, as the sky darkened and rain plummeted around us in a sudden deluge.

I tried to describe impossible things like the scent of creosote — bitter, slightly resinous, but still pleasant — the high, keening sound of the cicadas in July, the feathery barrenness of the trees, the very size of the sky, extending white-blue from horizon to horizon, barely interrupted by the low mountains covered with purple volcanic rock. The hardest thing to explain was why it was so beautiful to me — to justify a beauty that didn't depend on the sparse, spiny vegetation that often looked half dead, a beauty that had more to do with the exposed shape of the land, with the shallow bowls of valleys between the craggy hills, and the way they held on to the sun. I found myself using my hands as I tried to describe it to him.

His quiet, probing questions kept me talking freely, forgetting, in the dim light of the storm, to be embarrassed for monopolizing the conversation. Finally, when I had finished detailing my cluttered room at home, he paused instead of responding with another question.

"Are you finished?" I asked in relief.

"Not even close — but your father will be home soon."

"Charlie!" I suddenly recalled his existence, and sighed. I looked out at the rain-darkened sky, but it gave nothing away. "How late is it?" I wondered out loud as I glanced at the clock. I was surprised by the time — Charlie would be driving home now.

"It's twilight," Edward murmured, looking at the western horizon, obscured as it was with clouds. His voice was thoughtful, as if his mind were somewhere far away. I stared at him as he gazed unseeingly out the windshield.

I was still staring when his eyes suddenly shifted back to mine.

"It's the safest time of day for us," he said, answering the unspoken question in my eyes. "The easiest time. But also the saddest, in a way . . . the end of another day, the return of the night. Darkness is so predictable, don't you think?" He smiled wistfully.

"I like the night. Without the dark, we'd never see the stars." I frowned. "Not that you see them here much."

He laughed, and the mood abruptly lightened.

"Charlie will be here in a few minutes. So, unless you want to tell him that you'll be with me Saturday . . ." He raised one eyebrow.

"Thanks, but no thanks." I gathered my books, realizing I was stiff from sitting still so long. "So is it my turn tomorrow, then?"

"Certainly not!" His face was teasingly outraged. "I told you I wasn't done, didn't I?"

"What more is there?"

"You'll find out tomorrow." He reached across to open my door for me, and his sudden proximity sent my heart into frenzied palpitations.

But his hand froze on the handle.

"Not good," he muttered.

"What is it?" I was surprised to see that his jaw was clenched, his eyes disturbed.

He glanced at me for a brief second. "Another complication," he said glumly.

He flung the door open in one swift movement, and then moved, almost cringed, swiftly away from me.

The flash of headlights through the rain caught my attention as a dark car pulled up to the curb just a few feet away, facing us.

"Charlie's around the corner," he warned, staring through the downpour at the other vehicle.

I hopped out at once, despite my confusion and curiosity. The rain was louder as it glanced off my jacket.

I tried to make out the shapes in the front seat of the other car, but it was too dark. I could see Edward illuminated in the glare of the new car's headlights; he was still staring ahead, his gaze locked on something or someone I couldn't see. His expression was a strange mix of frustration and defiance.

Then he revved the engine, and the tires squealed against the wet pavement. The Volvo was out of sight in seconds.

"Hey, Bella," called a familiar, husky voice from the driver's side of the little black car.

"Jacob?" I asked, squinting through the rain. Just then, Charlie's cruiser swung around the corner, his lights shining on the occupants of the car in front of me.

Jacob was already climbing out, his wide grin visible even through the darkness. In the passenger seat was a much older man, a heavyset man with a memorable face — a face that overflowed, the cheeks resting against his shoulders, with creases running through the russet skin like an old leather jacket. And the surprisingly familiar eyes, black eyes that seemed at the same time both too young and too ancient for the broad face they were set in. Jacob's father, Billy Black. I knew him immediately, though in the more than five years since I'd seen him last I'd managed to forget his name when Charlie had spoken of him my first day here. He was staring at me, scrutinizing my face, so I smiled tentatively at him. His eyes were wide, as if in shock or fear, his nostrils flared. My smile faded.

Another complication, Edward had said.

Billy still stared at me with intense, anxious eyes. I groaned internally. Had Billy recognized Edward so easily? Could he really believe the impossible legends his son had scoffed at?

The answer was clear in Billy's eyes. Yes. Yes, he could.

12. BALANCING

"BILLY!" CHARLIE CALLED AS SOON AS HE GOT OUT OF the car.

I turned toward the house, beckoning to Jacob as I ducked under the porch. I heard Charlie greeting them loudly behind me.

"I'm going to pretend I didn't see you behind the wheel, Jake," he said disapprovingly.

"We get permits early on the rez," Jacob said while I unlocked the door and flicked on the porch light.

"Sure you do," Charlie laughed.

"I have to get around somehow." I recognized Billy's resonant voice easily, despite the years. The sound of it made me feel suddenly younger, a child.

I went inside, leaving the door open behind me and turning on lights before I hung up my jacket. Then I stood in the door, watching anxiously as Charlie and Jacob helped Billy out of the car and into his wheelchair.

I backed out of the way as the three of them hurried in, shaking off the rain.

"This is a surprise," Charlie was saying.

"It's been too long," Billy answered. "I hope it's not a bad time." His dark eyes flashed up to me again, their expression unreadable.

"No, it's great. I hope you can stay for the game."

Jacob grinned. "I think that's the plan — our TV broke last week."

Billy made a face at his son. "And, of course, Jacob was anxious to see Bella again," he added. Jacob scowled and ducked his head while I fought back a surge of remorse. Maybe I'd been too convincing on the beach.

"Are you hungry?" I asked, turning toward the kitchen. I was eager to escape Billy's searching gaze.

"Naw, we ate just before we came," Jacob answered.

"How about you, Charlie?" I called over my shoulder as I fled around the corner.

"Sure," he replied, his voice moving in the direction of the front room and the TV. I could hear Billy's chair follow.

The grilled cheese sandwiches were in the frying pan and I was slicing up a tomato when I sensed someone behind me.

"So, how are things?" Jacob asked.

"Pretty good." I smiled. His enthusiasm was hard to resist. "How about you? Did you finish your car?"

"No." He frowned. "I still need parts. We borrowed that one." He pointed with his thumb in the direction of the front yard.

"Sorry. I haven't seen any . . . what was it you were looking for?"

"Master cylinder." He grinned. "Is something wrong with the truck?" he added suddenly.

"No."

"Oh. I just wondered because you weren't driving it."

I stared down at the pan, pulling up the edge of a sandwich to check the bottom side. "I got a ride with a friend."

"Nice ride." Jacob's voice was admiring. "I didn't recognize the driver, though. I thought I knew most of the kids around here."

I nodded noncommittally, keeping my eyes down as I flipped sandwiches.

"My dad seemed to know him from somewhere."

"Jacob, could you hand me some plates? They're in the cupboard over the sink."

"Sure."

He got the plates in silence. I hoped he would let it drop now.

"So who was it?" he asked, setting two plates on the counter next to me.

I sighed in defeat. "Edward Cullen."

To my surprise, he laughed. I glanced up at him. He looked a little embarrassed.

"Guess that explains it, then," he said. "I wondered why my dad was acting so strange."

"That's right." I faked an innocent expression. "He doesn't like the Cullens."

"Superstitious old man," Jacob muttered under his breath.

"You don't think he'd say anything to Charlie?" I couldn't help asking, the words coming out in a low rush.

Jacob stared at me for a moment, and I couldn't read the expression in his dark eyes. "I doubt it," he finally answered. "I think Charlie chewed him out pretty good last time. They haven't spoken much since — tonight is sort of a reunion, I think. I don't think he'd bring it up again."

"Oh," I said, trying to sound indifferent.

I stayed in the front room after I carried the food out to Charlie, pretending to watch the game while Jacob chattered at me. I was really listening to the men's conversation, watching for any sign that Billy was about to rat me out, trying to think of ways to stop him if he began.

It was a long night. I had a lot of homework that was going undone, but I was afraid to leave Billy alone with Charlie. Finally, the game ended.

"Are you and your friends coming back to the beach soon?" Jacob asked as he pushed his father over the lip of the threshold.

"I'm not sure," I hedged.

"That was fun, Charlie," Billy said.

"Come up for the next game," Charlie encouraged.

"Sure, sure," Billy said. "We'll be here. Have a good night." His eyes shifted to mine, and his smile disappeared. "You take care, Bella," he added seriously.

"Thanks," I muttered, looking away.

I headed for the stairs while Charlie waved from the doorway.

"Wait, Bella," he said.

I cringed. Had Billy gotten something in before I'd joined them in the living room?

But Charlie was relaxed, still grinning from the unexpected visit.

"I didn't get a chance to talk to you tonight. How was your day?"

"Good." I hesitated with one foot on the first stair, searching for details I could safely share. "My badminton team won all four games."

"Wow, I didn't know you could play badminton."

"Well, actually I can't, but my partner is really good," I admitted.

"Who is it?" he asked with token interest.

"Um . . . Mike Newton," I told him reluctantly.

"Oh yeah — you said you were friends with the Newton kid." He perked up. "Nice family." He mused for a minute. "Why didn't you ask him to the dance this weekend?"

"Dad!" I groaned. "He's kind of dating my friend Jessica. Besides, you know I can't dance."

"Oh yeah," he muttered. Then he smiled at me apologetically. "So I guess it's good you'll be gone Saturday . . . I've made plans to go fishing with the guys from the station. The weather's supposed to be real warm. But if you wanted to put your trip off till someone could go with you, I'd stay home. I know I leave you here alone too much."

"Dad, you're doing a great job." I smiled, hoping my relief didn't show. "I've never minded being alone — I'm too much like you." I winked at him, and he smiled his crinkly-eyed smile.

I slept better that night, too tired to dream again. When I woke to the pearl gray morning, my mood was blissful. The tense evening with Billy and Jacob seemed harmless enough now; I decided to forget it completely. I caught myself whistling while I was pulling the front part of my hair back into a barrette, and later again as I skipped down the stairs. Charlie noticed.

"You're cheerful this morning," he commented over breakfast.

I shrugged. "It's Friday."

I hurried so I would be ready to go the second Charlie left. I had my bag ready, shoes on, teeth brushed, but even though I rushed to the door as soon as I was sure Charlie would be out of sight, Edward was faster. He was waiting in his shiny car, windows down, engine off.

I didn't hesitate this time, climbing in the passenger side quickly, the sooner to see his face. He grinned his crooked smile at me, stopping my breath and my heart. I couldn't imagine how an angel could be any more glorious. There was nothing about him that could be improved upon.

"How did you sleep?" he asked. I wondered if he had any idea how appealing his voice was.

"Fine. How was your night?"

"Pleasant." His smile was amused; I felt like I was missing an inside joke.

"Can I ask what you did?" I asked.

"No." He grinned. "Today is still *mine*."

He wanted to know about people today: more about Renée, her hobbies, what we'd done in our free time together. And then the one grandmother I'd known, my few school friends — embarrassing me when he asked about boys I'd dated. I was relieved that I'd never really dated anyone, so that particular conversation couldn't last long. He seemed as surprised as Jessica and Angela by my lack of romantic history.

"So you never met anyone you wanted?" he asked in a serious tone that made me wonder what he was thinking about.

I was grudgingly honest. "Not in Phoenix."

His lips pressed together into a hard line.

We were in the cafeteria at this point. The day had sped by in the blur that was rapidly becoming routine. I took advantage of his brief pause to take a bite of my bagel.

"I should have let you drive yourself today," he announced, apropos of nothing, while I chewed.

"Why?" I demanded.

"I'm leaving with Alice after lunch."

"Oh." I blinked, bewildered and disappointed. "That's okay, it's not that far of a walk."

He frowned at me impatiently. "I'm not going to make you walk home. We'll go get your truck and leave it here for you."

"I don't have my key with me," I sighed. "I really don't mind walking." What I minded was losing my time with him.

He shook his head. "Your truck will be here, and the key will be in the ignition — unless you're afraid someone might steal it." He laughed at the thought.

"All right," I agreed, pursing my lips. I was pretty sure my key was in the pocket of a pair of jeans I wore Wednesday, under a pile of clothes in the laundry room. Even if he broke into my house, or whatever he was planning, he'd never find it. He seemed to feel the challenge in my consent. He smirked, overconfident.

"So where are you going?" I asked as casually as I could manage.

"Hunting," he answered grimly. "If I'm going to be alone with you tomorrow, I'm going to take whatever precautions I can." His face grew morose . . . and pleading. "You can always cancel, you know."

I looked down, afraid of the persuasive power of his eyes. I refused to be convinced to fear him, no matter how real the danger might be. *It doesn't matter,* I repeated in my head.

"No," I whispered, glancing back at his face. "I can't."

"Perhaps you're right," he murmured bleakly. His eyes seemed to darken in color as I watched.

I changed the subject. "What time will I see you tomorrow?" I asked, already depressed by the thought of him leaving now.

"That depends . . . it's a Saturday, don't you want to sleep in?" he offered.

"No," I answered too fast. He restrained a smile.

"The same time as usual, then," he decided. "Will Charlie be there?"

"No, he's fishing tomorrow." I beamed at the memory of how conveniently things had worked out.

His voice turned sharp. "And if you don't come home, what will he think?"

"I have no idea," I answered coolly. "He knows I've been meaning to do the laundry. Maybe he'll think I fell in the washer."

He scowled at me and I scowled back. His anger was much more impressive than mine.

"What are you hunting tonight?" I asked when I was sure I had lost the glowering contest.

"Whatever we find in the park. We aren't going far." He seemed bemused by my casual reference to his secret realities.

"Why are you going with Alice?" I wondered.

"Alice is the most . . . supportive." He frowned as he spoke.

"And the others?" I asked timidly. "What are they?"

His brow puckered for a brief moment. "Incredulous, for the most part."

I peeked quickly behind me at his family. They sat staring off in different directions, exactly the same as the first time I'd seen them. Only now they were four; their beautiful, bronze-haired brother sat across from me, his golden eyes troubled.

"They don't like me," I guessed.

"That's not it," he disagreed, but his eyes were too innocent. "They don't understand why I can't leave you alone."

I grimaced. "Neither do I, for that matter."

Edward shook his head slowly, rolling his eyes toward the ceiling before he met my gaze again. "I told you — you don't see yourself clearly at all. You're not like anyone I've ever known. You fascinate me."

I glared at him, sure he was teasing now.

He smiled as he deciphered my expression. "Having the advantages I do," he murmured, touching his forehead discreetly, "I have a better than average grasp of human nature. People are predictable. But you . . . you never do what I expect. You always take me by surprise."

I looked away, my eyes wandering back to his family, embarrassed and dissatisfied. His words made me feel like a science experiment. I wanted to laugh at myself for expecting anything else.

"That part is easy enough to explain," he continued. I felt his eyes on my face but I couldn't look at him yet, afraid he might read the chagrin in my eyes. "But there's more . . . and it's not so easy to put into words —"

I was still staring at the Cullens while he spoke. Suddenly Rosalie, his blond and breathtaking sister, turned to look at me. No, not to look — to glare, with dark, cold eyes. I wanted to look away, but her gaze held me until Edward broke off mid-sentence and made an angry noise under his breath. It was almost a hiss.

Rosalie turned her head, and I was relieved to be free. I looked back at Edward — and I knew he could see the confusion and fear that widened my eyes.

His face was tight as he explained. "I'm sorry about

that. She's just worried. You see . . . it's dangerous for more than just me if, after spending so much time with you so publicly . . ." He looked down.

"If?"

"If this ends . . . badly." He dropped his head into his hands, as he had that night in Port Angeles. His anguish was plain; I yearned to comfort him, but I was at a loss to know how. My hand reached toward him involuntarily; quickly, though, I dropped it to the table, fearing that my touch would only make things worse. I realized slowly that his words should frighten me. I waited for that fear to come, but all I could seem to feel was an ache for his pain.

And frustration — frustration that Rosalie had interrupted whatever he was about to say. I didn't know how to bring it up again. He still had his head in his hands.

I tried to speak in a normal voice. "And you have to leave now?"

"Yes." He raised his face; it was serious for a moment, and then his mood shifted and he smiled. "It's probably for the best. We still have fifteen minutes of that wretched movie left to endure in Biology — I don't think I could take any more."

I started. Alice — her short, inky hair in a halo of spiky disarray around her exquisite, elfin face — was suddenly standing behind his shoulder. Her slight frame was willowy, graceful even in absolute stillness.

He greeted her without looking away from me. "Alice."

"Edward," she answered, her high soprano voice almost as attractive as his.

"Alice, Bella — Bella, Alice," he introduced us, gesturing casually with his hand, a wry smile on his face.

"Hello, Bella." Her brilliant obsidian eyes were unreadable, but her smile was friendly. "It's nice to finally meet you."

Edward flashed a dark look at her.

"Hi, Alice," I murmured shyly.

"Are you ready?" she asked him.

His voice was aloof. "Nearly. I'll meet you at the car."

She left without another word; her walk was so fluid, so sinuous that I felt a sharp pang of jealousy.

"Should I say 'have fun,' or is that the wrong sentiment?" I asked, turning back to him.

"No, 'have fun' works as well as anything." He grinned.

"Have fun, then." I worked to sound wholehearted. Of course I didn't fool him.

"I'll try." He still grinned. "And you try to be safe, please."

"Safe in Forks — what a challenge."

"For you it *is* a challenge." His jaw hardened. "Promise."

"I promise to try to be safe," I recited. "I'll do the laundry tonight — that ought to be fraught with peril."

"Don't fall in," he mocked.

"I'll do my best."

He stood then, and I rose, too.

"I'll see you tomorrow," I sighed.

"It seems like a long time to you, doesn't it?" he mused.

I nodded glumly.

"I'll be there in the morning," he promised, smiling his

crooked smile. He reached across the table to touch my face, lightly brushing along my cheekbone again. Then he turned and walked away. I stared after him until he was gone.

I was sorely tempted to ditch the rest of the day, at the very least Gym, but a warning instinct stopped me. I knew that if I disappeared now, Mike and others would assume I was with Edward. And Edward was worried about the time we'd spent together publicly . . . if things went wrong. I refused to dwell on the last thought, concentrating instead on making things safer for him.

I intuitively knew — and sensed he did, too — that tomorrow would be pivotal. Our relationship couldn't continue to balance, as it did, on the point of a knife. We would fall off one edge or the other, depending entirely upon his decision, or his instincts. My decision was made, made before I'd ever consciously chosen, and I was committed to seeing it through. Because there was nothing more terrifying to me, more excruciating, than the thought of turning away from him. It was an impossibility.

I went to class, feeling dutiful. I couldn't honestly say what happened in Biology; my mind was too preoccupied with thoughts of tomorrow. In Gym, Mike was speaking to me again; he wished me a good time in Seattle. I carefully explained that I'd canceled my trip, worried about my truck.

"Are you going to the dance with Cullen?" he asked, suddenly sulky.

"No, I'm not going to the dance at all."

"What are you doing, then?" he asked, too interested.

My natural urge was to tell him to butt out. Instead, I lied brightly.

"Laundry, and then I have to study for the Trig test or I'm going to fail."

"Is Cullen helping you study?"

"*Edward,*" I emphasized, "is not going to help me study. He's gone away somewhere for the weekend." The lies came more naturally than usual, I noted with surprise.

"Oh." He perked up. "You know, you could come to the dance with our group anyway — that would be cool. We'd all dance with you," he promised.

The mental image of Jessica's face made my tone sharper than necessary.

"I'm *not* going to the dance, Mike, okay?"

"Fine." He sulked again. "I was just offering."

When the school day had finally ended, I walked to the parking lot without enthusiasm. I did not especially want to walk home, but I couldn't see how he would have retrieved my truck. Then again, I was starting to believe that nothing was impossible for him. The latter instinct proved correct — my truck sat in the same space he'd parked his Volvo in this morning. I shook my head, incredulous, as I opened the unlocked door and saw the key in the ignition.

There was a piece of white paper folded on my seat. I got in and closed the door before I unfolded it. Two words were written in his elegant script.

Be safe.

The sound of the truck roaring to life frightened me. I laughed at myself.

When I got home, the handle of the door was locked, the dead bolt unlocked, just as I'd left it this morning. Inside, I went straight to the laundry room. It looked just the same as I'd left it, too. I dug for my jeans and, after finding them, checked the pockets. Empty. Maybe I'd hung my key up after all, I thought, shaking my head.

Following the same instinct that had prompted me to lie to Mike, I called Jessica on the pretense of wishing her luck at the dance. When she offered the same wish for my day with Edward, I told her about the cancellation. She was more disappointed than really necessary for a third-party observer to be. I said goodbye quickly after that.

Charlie was absentminded at dinner, worried over something at work, I guessed, or maybe a basketball game, or maybe he was just really enjoying the lasagna — it was hard to tell with Charlie.

"You know, Dad . . . ," I began, breaking into his reverie.

"What's that, Bell?"

"I think you're right about Seattle. I think I'll wait until Jessica or someone else can go with me."

"Oh," he said, surprised. "Oh, okay. So, do you want me to stay home?"

"No, Dad, don't change your plans. I've got a million things to do . . . homework, laundry . . . I need to go to the library and the grocery store. I'll be in and out all day . . . you go and have fun."

"Are you sure?"

"Absolutely, Dad. Besides, the freezer is getting dangerously low on fish — we're down to a two, maybe three years' supply."

"You're sure easy to live with, Bella." He smiled.

"I could say the same thing about you," I said, laughing. The sound of my laughter was off, but he didn't seem to notice. I felt so guilty for deceiving him that I almost took Edward's advice and told him where I would be. Almost.

After dinner, I folded clothes and moved another load through the dryer. Unfortunately it was the kind of job that only keeps hands busy. My mind definitely had too much free time, and it was getting out of control. I fluctuated between anticipation so intense that it was very nearly pain, and an insidious fear that picked at my resolve. I had to keep reminding myself that I'd made my choice, and I wasn't going back on it. I pulled his note out of my pocket much more often than necessary to absorb the two small words he'd written. He wants me to be safe, I told myself again and again. I would just hold on to the faith that, in the end, that desire would win out over the others. And what was my other choice — to cut him out of my life? Intolerable. Besides, since I'd come to Forks, it really seemed like my life was *about* him.

But a tiny voice in the back of my mind worried, wondering if it would hurt *very* much . . . if it ended badly.

I was relieved when it was late enough to be acceptable for bedtime. I knew I was far too stressed to sleep, so I did something I'd never done before. I deliberately took unnecessary cold medicine — the kind that knocked me out for a good eight hours. I normally wouldn't condone that type of behavior in myself, but tomorrow would be complicated enough without me being loopy from sleep deprivation on top of everything else. While I waited for the drugs to kick in, I dried my clean hair till it was impeccably straight, and fussed over what I would wear tomorrow.

With everything ready for the morning, I finally lay in my bed. I felt hyper; I couldn't stop twitching. I got up and rifled through my shoebox of CDs until I found a collection of Chopin's nocturnes. I put that on very quietly and then lay down again, concentrating on relaxing individual parts of my body. Somewhere in the middle of that exercise, the cold pills took effect, and I gladly sank into unconsciousness.

I woke early, having slept soundly and dreamlessly thanks to my gratuitous drug use. Though I was well rested, I slipped right back into the same hectic frenzy from the night before. I dressed in a rush, smoothing my collar against my neck, fidgeting with the tan sweater till it hung right over my jeans. I sneaked a swift look out the window to see that Charlie was already gone. A thin, cottony layer of clouds veiled the sky. They didn't look very lasting.

I ate breakfast without tasting the food, hurrying to clean up when I was done. I peeked out the window again, but nothing had changed. I had just finished brushing my teeth and was heading back downstairs when a quiet knock sent my heart thudding against my rib cage.

I flew to the door; I had a little trouble with the simple dead bolt, but I yanked the door open at last, and there he was. All the agitation dissolved as soon as I looked at his face, calm taking its place. I breathed a sigh of relief — yesterday's fears seemed very foolish with him here.

He wasn't smiling at first — his face was somber. But then his expression lightened as he looked me over, and he laughed.

"Good morning," he chuckled.

"What's wrong?" I glanced down to make sure I hadn't forgotten anything important, like shoes, or pants.

"We match." He laughed again. I realized he had a long, light tan sweater on, with a white collar showing underneath, and blue jeans. I laughed with him, hiding a secret twinge of regret — why did he have to look like a runway model when I couldn't?

I locked the door behind me while he walked to the truck. He waited by the passenger door with a martyred expression that was easy to understand.

"We made a deal," I reminded him smugly, climbing into the driver's seat, and reaching over to unlock his door.

"Where to?" I asked.

"Put your seat belt on — I'm nervous already."

I gave him a dirty look as I complied.

"Where to?" I repeated with a sigh.

"Take the one-oh-one north," he ordered.

It was surprisingly difficult to concentrate on the road while feeling his gaze on my face. I compensated by driving more carefully than usual through the still-sleeping town.

"Were you planning to make it out of Forks before nightfall?"

"This truck is old enough to be your car's grandfather — have some respect," I retorted.

We were soon out of the town limits, despite his negativity. Thick underbrush and green-swathed trunks replaced the lawns and houses.

"Turn right on the one-ten," he instructed just as I was about to ask. I obeyed silently.

"Now we drive until the pavement ends."

I could hear a smile in his voice, but I was too afraid of driving off the road and proving him right to look over and be sure.

"And what's there, at the pavement's end?" I wondered.

"A trail."

"We're hiking?" Thank goodness I'd worn tennis shoes.

"Is that a problem?" He sounded as if he'd expected as much.

"No." I tried to make the lie sound confident. But if he thought my truck was slow . . .

"Don't worry, it's only five miles or so, and we're in no hurry."

Five miles. I didn't answer, so that he wouldn't hear my voice crack in panic. Five miles of treacherous roots and loose stones, trying to twist my ankles or otherwise incapacitate me. This was going to be humiliating.

We drove in silence for a while as I contemplated the coming horror.

"What are you thinking?" he asked impatiently after a few moments.

I lied again. "Just wondering where we're going."

"It's a place I like to go when the weather is nice." We

both glanced out the windows at the thinning clouds after he spoke.

"Charlie said it would be warm today."

"And did you tell Charlie what you were up to?" he asked.

"Nope."

"But Jessica thinks we're going to Seattle together?" He seemed cheered by the idea.

"No, I told her you canceled on me — which is true."

"No one knows you're with me?" Angrily, now.

"That depends . . . I assume you told Alice?"

"That's very helpful, Bella," he snapped.

I pretended I didn't hear that.

"Are you so depressed by Forks that it's made you suicidal?" he demanded when I ignored him.

"You said it might cause trouble for you . . . us being together publicly," I reminded him.

"So you're worried about the trouble it might cause *me* — if *you* don't come *home*?" His voice was still angry, and bitingly sarcastic.

I nodded, keeping my eyes on the road.

He muttered something under his breath, speaking so quickly that I couldn't understand.

We were silent for the rest of the drive. I could feel the waves of infuriated disapproval rolling off of him, and I could think of nothing to say.

And then the road ended, constricting to a thin foot trail with a small wooden marker. I parked on the narrow shoulder and stepped out, afraid because he was angry with me and I didn't have driving as an excuse not to look at him. It was warm now, warmer than it had been in Forks since the day I'd arrived, almost muggy under the clouds. I pulled off my sweater and knotted it around my waist, glad that I'd worn the light, sleeveless shirt — especially if I had five miles of hiking ahead of me.

I heard his door slam, and looked over to see that he'd removed his sweater, too. He was facing away from me, into the unbroken forest beside my truck.

"This way," he said, glancing over his shoulder at me, eyes still annoyed. He started into the dark forest.

"The trail?" Panic was clear in my voice as I hurried around the truck to catch up to him.

"I said there was a trail at the end of the road, not that we were taking it."

"No trail?" I asked desperately.

"I won't let you get lost." He turned then, with a mocking smile, and I stifled a gasp. His white shirt was sleeveless, and he wore it unbuttoned, so that the smooth white skin of his throat flowed uninterrupted over the marble contours of his chest, his perfect musculature no longer merely hinted at behind concealing clothes. He was too perfect, I realized with a piercing stab of despair. There was no way this godlike creature could be meant for me.

He stared at me, bewildered by my tortured expression.

"Do you want to go home?" he said quietly, a different pain than mine saturating his voice.

"No." I walked forward till I was close beside him, anxious not to waste one second of whatever time I might have with him.

"What's wrong?" he asked, his voice gentle.

"I'm not a good hiker," I answered dully. "You'll have to be very patient."

"I can be patient — if I make a great effort." He smiled, holding my glance, trying to lift me out of my sudden, unexplained dejection.

I tried to smile back, but the smile was unconvincing. He scrutinized my face.

"I'll take you home," he promised. I couldn't tell if the promise was unconditional, or restricted to an immediate departure. I knew he thought it was fear that upset me, and I was grateful again that I was the one person whose mind he couldn't hear.

"If you want me to hack five miles through the jungle before sundown, you'd better start leading the way," I said acidly. He frowned at me, struggling to understand my tone and expression.

He gave up after a moment and led the way into the forest.

It wasn't as hard as I had feared. The way was mostly flat, and he held the damp ferns and webs of moss aside for me. When his straight path took us over fallen trees or boulders, he would help me, lifting me by the elbow, and then releasing me instantly when I was clear. His cold touch on my skin never failed to make my heart thud erratically. Twice, when that happened, I caught a look on his face that made me sure he could somehow hear it.

I tried to keep my eyes away from his perfection as much as possible, but I slipped often. Each time, his beauty pierced me through with sadness.

For the most part, we walked in silence. Occasionally

he would ask a random question that he hadn't gotten to in the past two days of interrogation. He asked about my birthdays, my grade school teachers, my childhood pets — and I had to admit that after killing three fish in a row, I'd given up on the whole institution. He laughed at that, louder than I was used to — bell-like echoes bouncing back to us from the empty woods.

The hike took me most of the morning, but he never showed any sign of impatience. The forest spread out around us in a boundless labyrinth of ancient trees, and I began to be nervous that we would never find our way out again. He was perfectly at ease, comfortable in the green maze, never seeming to feel any doubt about our direction.

After several hours, the light that filtered through the canopy transformed, the murky olive tone shifting to a brighter jade. The day had turned sunny, just as he'd foretold. For the first time since we'd entered the woods, I felt a thrill of excitement — which quickly turned to impatience.

"Are we there yet?" I teased, pretending to scowl.

"Nearly." He smiled at the change in my mood. "Do you see the brightness ahead?"

I peered into the thick forest. "Um, should I?"

He smirked. "Maybe it's a bit soon for *your* eyes."

"Time to visit the optometrist," I muttered. His smirk grew more pronounced.

But then, after another hundred yards, I could definitely see a lightening in the trees ahead, a glow that was yellow instead of green. I picked up the pace, my eagerness growing with every step. He let me lead now, following noiselessly.

I reached the edge of the pool of light and stepped through the last fringe of ferns into the loveliest place I had ever seen. The meadow was small, perfectly round, and filled with wildflowers — violet, yellow, and soft white. Somewhere nearby, I could hear the bubbling music of a stream. The sun was directly overhead, filling the circle with a haze of buttery sunshine. I walked slowly, awestruck, through the soft grass, swaying flowers, and warm, gilded air. I halfway turned, wanting to share this with him, but he wasn't behind me where I thought he'd be. I spun around, searching for him with sudden alarm. Finally I spotted him, still under the dense shade of the canopy at the edge of the hollow, watching me with cautious eyes. Only then did I remember what the beauty of the meadow had driven from my mind — the enigma of Edward and the sun, which he'd promised to illustrate for me today.

I took a step back toward him, my eyes alight with curiosity. His eyes were wary, reluctant. I smiled encouragingly and beckoned to him with my hand, taking another step back to him. He held up a hand in warning, and I hesitated, rocking back onto my heels.

Edward seemed to take a deep breath, and then he stepped out into the bright glow of the midday sun.

13. CONFESSIONS

EDWARD IN THE SUNLIGHT WAS SHOCKING. I COULDN'T
get used to it, though I'd been staring at him all afternoon. His skin, white despite the faint flush from yesterday's hunting trip, literally sparkled, like thousands of tiny
diamonds were embedded in the surface. He lay perfectly
still in the grass, his shirt open over his sculpted, incan-
descent chest, his scintillating arms bare. His glistening,
pale lavender lids were shut, though of course he didn't
sleep. A perfect statue, carved in some unknown stone,
smooth like marble, glittering like crystal.

Now and then, his lips would move, so fast it looked
like they were trembling. But, when I asked, he told me
he was singing to himself; it was too low for me to hear.

I enjoyed the sun, too, though the air wasn't quite dry enough for my taste. I would have liked to lie back, as he did, and let the sun warm my face. But I stayed curled up, my chin resting on my knees, unwilling to take my eyes off him. The wind was gentle; it tangled my hair and ruffled the grass that swayed around his motionless form.

The meadow, so spectacular to me at first, paled next to his magnificence.

Hesitantly, always afraid, even now, that he would disappear like a mirage, too beautiful to be real . . . hesitantly, I reached out one finger and stroked the back of his shimmering hand, where it lay within my reach. I marveled again at the perfect texture, satin smooth, cool as stone. When I looked up again, his eyes were open, watching me. Butterscotch today, lighter, warmer after hunting. His quick smile turned up the corners of his flawless lips.

"I don't scare you?" he asked playfully, but I could hear the real curiosity in his soft voice.

"No more than usual."

He smiled wider; his teeth flashed in the sun.

I inched closer, stretched out my whole hand now to trace the contours of his forearm with my fingertips. I saw that my fingers trembled, and knew it wouldn't escape his notice.

"Do you mind?" I asked, for he had closed his eyes again.

"No," he said without opening his eyes. "You can't imagine how that feels." He sighed.

I lightly trailed my hand over the perfect muscles of his arm, followed the faint pattern of bluish veins inside the crease at his elbow. With my other hand, I reached to turn his hand over. Realizing what I wished, he flipped his palm up in one of those blindingly fast, disconcerting movements of his. It startled me; my fingers froze on his arm for a brief second.

"Sorry," he murmured. I looked up in time to see his golden eyes close again. "It's too easy to be myself with you."

I lifted his hand, turning it this way and that as I watched the sun glitter on his palm. I held it closer to my face, trying to see the hidden facets in his skin.

"Tell me what you're thinking," he whispered. I looked to see his eyes watching me, suddenly intent. "It's still so strange for me, not knowing."

"You know, the rest of us feel that way all the time."

"It's a hard life." Did I imagine the hint of regret in his tone? "But you didn't tell me."

"I *was* wishing I could know what you were thinking . . ." I hesitated.

"And?"

"I was wishing that I could believe that you were real. And I was wishing that I wasn't afraid."

"I don't want you to be afraid." His voice was just a soft murmur. I heard what he couldn't truthfully say, that I didn't need to be afraid, that there was nothing to fear.

"Well, that's not exactly the fear I meant, though that's certainly something to think about."

So quickly that I missed his movement, he was half sitting, propped up on his right arm, his left palm still in my hands. His angel's face was only a few inches from mine. I might have — should have — flinched away from his unexpected closeness, but I was unable to move. His golden eyes mesmerized me.

"What are you afraid of, then?" he whispered intently.

But I couldn't answer. As I had just that once before, I smelled his cool breath in my face. Sweet, delicious, the scent made my mouth water. It was unlike anything else. Instinctively, unthinkingly, I leaned closer, inhaling.

And he was gone, his hand ripped from mine. In the time it took my eyes to focus, he was twenty feet away, standing at the edge of the small meadow, in the deep shade of a huge fir tree. He stared at me, his eyes dark in the shadows, his expression unreadable.

I could feel the hurt and shock on my face. My empty hands stung.

"I'm . . . sorry . . . Edward," I whispered. I knew he could hear.

"Give me a moment," he called, just loud enough for my less sensitive ears. I sat very still.

After ten incredibly long seconds, he walked back, slowly for him. He stopped, still several feet away, and sank gracefully to the ground, crossing his legs. His eyes never left mine. He took two deep breaths, and then smiled in apology.

"I am so very sorry." He hesitated. "Would you understand what I meant if I said I was only human?"

I nodded once, not quite able to smile at his joke. Adrenaline pulsed through my veins as the realization of danger slowly sank in. He could smell that from where he sat. His smile turned mocking.

"I'm the world's best predator, aren't I? Everything

about me invites you in — my voice, my face, even my *smell*. As if I need any of that!" Unexpectedly, he was on his feet, bounding away, instantly out of sight, only to appear beneath the same tree as before, having circled the meadow in half a second.

"As if you could outrun me," he laughed bitterly.

He reached up with one hand and, with a deafening crack, effortlessly ripped a two-foot-thick branch from the trunk of the spruce. He balanced it in that hand for a moment, and then threw it with blinding speed, shattering it against another huge tree, which shook and trembled at the blow.

And he was in front of me again, standing two feet away, still as a stone.

"As if you could fight me off," he said gently.

I sat without moving, more frightened of him than I had ever been. I'd never seen him so completely freed of that carefully cultivated façade. He'd never been less human . . . or more beautiful. Face ashen, eyes wide, I sat like a bird locked in the eyes of a snake.

His lovely eyes seem to glow with rash excitement. Then, as the seconds passed, they dimmed. His expression slowly folded into a mask of ancient sadness.

"Don't be afraid," he murmured, his velvet voice unintentionally seductive. "I promise . . ." He hesitated. "I *swear* not to hurt you." He seemed more concerned with convincing himself than me.

"Don't be afraid," he whispered again as he stepped closer, with exaggerated slowness. He sat sinuously, with deliberately unhurried movements, till our faces were on the same level, just a foot apart.

"Please forgive me," he said formally. "I *can* control myself. You caught me off guard. But I'm on my best behavior now."

He waited, but I still couldn't speak.

"I'm not thirsty today, honestly." He winked.

At that I had to laugh, though the sound was shaky and breathless.

"Are you all right?" he asked tenderly, reaching out slowly, carefully, to place his marble hand back in mine.

I looked at his smooth, cold hand, and then at his eyes. They were soft, repentant. I looked back at his hand, and then deliberately returned to tracing the lines in his hand with my fingertip. I looked up and smiled timidly.

His answering smile was dazzling.

"So where were we, before I behaved so rudely?" he asked in the gentle cadences of an earlier century.

"I honestly can't remember."

He smiled, but his face was ashamed. "I think we were talking about why you were afraid, besides the obvious reason."

"Oh, right."

"Well?"

I looked down at his hand and doodled aimlessly across his smooth, iridescent palm. The seconds ticked by.

"How easily frustrated I am," he sighed. I looked into his eyes, abruptly grasping that this was every bit as new to him as it was to me. As many years of unfathomable experience as he had, this was hard for him, too. I took courage from that thought.

"I was afraid . . . because, for, well, obvious reasons, I can't *stay* with you. And I'm afraid that I'd like to stay with you, much more than I should." I looked down at his hands as I spoke. It was difficult for me to say this aloud.

"Yes," he agreed slowly. "That is something to be afraid of, indeed. Wanting to be with me. That's really not in your best interest."

I frowned.

"I should have left long ago," he sighed. "I should leave now. But I don't know if I can."

"I don't want you to leave," I mumbled pathetically, staring down again.

"Which is exactly why I should. But don't worry. I'm essentially a selfish creature. I crave your company too much to do what I should."

"I'm glad."

"Don't be!" He withdrew his hand, more gently this time; his voice was harsher than usual. Harsh for him, still more beautiful than any human voice. It was hard to keep up — his sudden mood changes left me always a step behind, dazed.

"It's not only your company I crave! Never forget *that.* Never forget I am more dangerous to you than I am to anyone else." He stopped, and I looked to see him gazing unseeingly into the forest.

I thought for a moment.

"I don't think I understand exactly what you mean — by that last part anyway," I said.

He looked back at me and smiled, his mood shifting yet again.

"How do I explain?" he mused. "And without frightening you again . . . hmmmm." Without seeming to think about it, he placed his hand back in mine; I held it tightly in both of mine. He looked at our hands.

"That's amazingly pleasant, the warmth." He sighed.

A moment passed as he assembled his thoughts.

"You know how everyone enjoys different flavors?" he began. "Some people love chocolate ice cream, others prefer strawberry?"

I nodded.

"Sorry about the food analogy — I couldn't think of another way to explain."

I smiled. He smiled ruefully back.

"You see, every person smells different, has a different essence. If you locked an alcoholic in a room full of stale beer, he'd gladly drink it. But he could resist, if he wished to, if he were a recovering alcoholic. Now let's say you placed in that room a glass of hundred-year-old brandy, the rarest, finest cognac — and filled the room with its warm aroma — how do you think he would fare then?"

We sat silently, looking into each other's eyes — trying to read each other's thoughts.

He broke the silence first.

"Maybe that's not the right comparison. Maybe it would be too easy to turn down the brandy. Perhaps I should have made our alcoholic a heroin addict instead."

"So what you're saying is, I'm your brand of heroin?" I teased, trying to lighten the mood.

He smiled swiftly, seeming to appreciate my effort. "Yes, you are *exactly* my brand of heroin."

"Does that happen often?" I asked.

He looked across the treetops, thinking through his response.

"I spoke to my brothers about it." He still stared into the distance. "To Jasper, every one of you is much the same. He's the most recent to join our family. It's a struggle for him to abstain at all. He hasn't had time to grow sensitive to the differences in smell, in flavor." He glanced swiftly at me, his expression apologetic.

"Sorry," he said.

"I don't mind. Please don't worry about offending me, or frightening me, or whichever. That's the way you think. I can understand, or I can try to at least. Just explain however you can."

He took a deep breath and gazed at the sky again.

"So Jasper wasn't sure if he'd ever come across someone who was as" — he hesitated, looking for the right word — "*appealing* as you are to me. Which makes me think not. Emmett has been on the wagon longer, so to speak, and he understood what I meant. He says twice, for him, once stronger than the other."

"And for you?"

"Never."

The word hung there for a moment in the warm breeze.

"What did Emmett do?" I asked to break the silence.

It was the wrong question to ask. His face grew dark, his hand clenched into a fist inside mine. He looked away. I waited, but he wasn't going to answer.

"I guess I know," I finally said.

He lifted his eyes; his expression was wistful, pleading. "Even the strongest of us fall off the wagon, don't we?"

"What are you asking? My permission?" My voice was sharper than I'd intended. I tried to make my tone kinder — I could guess what his honesty must cost him. "I mean, is there no hope, then?" How calmly I could discuss my own death!

"No, no!" He was instantly contrite. "Of course there's hope! I mean, of course I won't . . ." He left the sentence hanging. His eyes burned into mine. "It's different for us. Emmett . . . these were strangers he happened across. It was a long time ago, and he wasn't as . . . practiced, as careful, as he is now."

He fell silent and watched me intently as I thought it through.

"So if we'd met . . . oh, in a dark alley or something . . ." I trailed off.

"It took everything I had not to jump up in the middle of that class full of children and —" He stopped abruptly, looking away. "When you walked past me, I could have ruined everything Carlisle has built for us, right then and there. If I hadn't been denying my thirst for the last, well, too many years, I wouldn't have been able to stop myself." He paused, scowling at the trees.

He glanced at me grimly, both of us remembering. "You must have thought I was possessed."

"I couldn't understand why. How you could hate me so quickly . . ."

"To me, it was like you were some kind of demon, summoned straight from my own personal hell to ruin me.

The fragrance coming off your skin . . . I thought it would make me deranged that first day. In that one hour, I thought of a hundred different ways to lure you from the room with me, to get you alone. And I fought them each back, thinking of my family, what I could do to them. I had to run out, to get away before I could speak the words that would make you follow. . . ."

He looked up then at my staggered expression as I tried to absorb his bitter memories. His golden eyes scorched from under his lashes, hypnotic and deadly.

"You would have come," he promised.

I tried to speak calmly. "Without a doubt."

He frowned down at my hands, releasing me from the force of his stare. "And then, as I tried to rearrange my schedule in a pointless attempt to avoid you, you were there — in that close, warm little room, the scent was maddening. I so very nearly took you then. There was only one other frail human there — so easily dealt with."

I shivered in the warm sun, seeing my memories anew through his eyes, only now grasping the danger. Poor Ms. Cope; I shivered again at how close I'd come to being inadvertently responsible for her death.

"But I resisted. I don't know how. I forced myself *not* to wait for you, *not* to follow you from the school. It was easier outside, when I couldn't smell you anymore, to think clearly, to make the right decision. I left the others near home — I was too ashamed to tell them how weak I was, they only knew something was very wrong — and then I went straight to Carlisle, at the hospital, to tell him I was leaving."

I stared in surprise.

"I traded cars with him — he had a full tank of gas and I didn't want to stop. I didn't dare to go home, to face Esme. She wouldn't have let me go without a scene. She would have tried to convince me that it wasn't necessary . . .

"By the next morning I was in Alaska." He sounded ashamed, as if admitting a great cowardice. "I spent two days there, with some old acquaintances . . . but I was homesick. I hated knowing I'd upset Esme, and the rest of them, my adopted family. In the pure air of the mountains it was hard to believe you were so irresistible. I convinced myself it was weak to run away. I'd dealt with temptation before, not of this magnitude, not even close, but I was strong. Who were you, an insignificant little girl" — he grinned suddenly — "to chase me from the place I wanted to be? So I came back. . . ." He stared off into space.

I couldn't speak.

"I took precautions, hunting, feeding more than usual before seeing you again. I was sure that I was strong enough to treat you like any other human. I was arrogant about it.

"It was unquestionably a complication that I couldn't simply read your thoughts to know what your reaction was to me. I wasn't used to having to go to such circuitous measures, listening to your words in Jessica's mind . . . her mind isn't very original, and it was annoying to have to stoop to that. And then I couldn't know if you really meant what you said. It was all extremely irritating." He frowned at the memory.

"I wanted you to forget my behavior that first day, if

possible, so I tried to talk with you like I would with any person. I was eager actually, hoping to decipher some of your thoughts. But you were too interesting, I found myself caught up in your expressions . . . and every now and then you would stir the air with your hand or your hair, and the scent would stun me again. . . .

"Of course, then you were nearly crushed to death in front of my eyes. Later I thought of a perfectly good excuse for why I acted at that moment — because if I hadn't saved you, if your blood had been spilled there in front of me, I don't think I could have stopped myself from exposing us for what we are. But I only thought of that excuse later. At the time, all I could think was, 'Not her.'"

He closed his eyes, lost in his agonized confession. I listened, more eager than rational. Common sense told me I should be terrified. Instead, I was relieved to finally understand. And I was filled with compassion for his suffering, even now, as he confessed his craving to take my life.

I finally was able to speak, though my voice was faint. "In the hospital?"

His eyes flashed up to mine. "I was appalled. I couldn't believe I had put us in danger after all, put myself in your power — you of all people. As if I needed another motive to kill you." We both flinched as that word slipped out. "But it had the opposite effect," he continued quickly. "I fought with Rosalie, Emmett, and Jasper when they suggested that now was the time . . . the worst fight we've ever had. Carlisle sided with me, and Alice." He grimaced when he said her name. I couldn't imagine why. "Esme told me to do whatever I had to in order to stay." He shook his head indulgently.

"All that next day I eavesdropped on the minds of everyone you spoke to, shocked that you kept your word. I didn't understand you at all. But I knew that I couldn't become more involved with you. I did my very best to stay as far from you as possible. And every day the perfume of your skin, your breath, your hair . . . it hit me as hard as the very first day."

He met my eyes again, and they were surprisingly tender.

"And for all that," he continued, "I'd have fared better if I *had* exposed us all at that first moment, than if now, here — with no witnesses and nothing to stop me — I were to hurt you."

I was human enough to have to ask. "Why?"

"Isabella." He pronounced my full name carefully, then playfully ruffled my hair with his free hand. A shock ran through my body at his casual touch. "Bella, I couldn't live with myself if I ever hurt you. You don't know how it's tortured me." He looked down, ashamed again. "The thought of you, still, white, cold . . . to never see you blush scarlet again, to never see that flash of intuition in your eyes when you see through my pretenses . . . it would be unendurable." He lifted his glorious, agonized eyes to mine. "You are the most important thing to me now. The most important thing to me ever."

My head was spinning at the rapid change in direction our conversation had taken. From the cheerful topic of my impending demise, we were suddenly declaring ourselves. He waited, and even though I looked down to study our hands between us, I knew his golden eyes were on me.

"You already know how I feel, of course," I finally said. "I'm here . . . which, roughly translated, means I would rather die than stay away from you." I frowned. "I'm an idiot."

"You *are* an idiot," he agreed with a laugh. Our eyes met, and I laughed, too. We laughed together at the idiocy and sheer impossibility of such a moment.

"And so the lion fell in love with the lamb . . . ," he murmured. I looked away, hiding my eyes as I thrilled to the word.

"What a stupid lamb," I sighed.

"What a sick, masochistic lion." He stared into the shadowy forest for a long moment, and I wondered where his thoughts had taken him.

"Why . . . ?" I began, and then paused, not sure how to continue.

He looked at me and smiled; sunlight glinted off his face, his teeth.

"Yes?"

"Tell me why you ran from me before."

His smile faded. "You know why."

"No, I mean, *exactly* what did I do wrong? I'll have to be on my guard, you see, so I better start learning what I shouldn't do. This, for example" — I stroked the back of his hand — "seems to be all right."

He smiled again. "You didn't do anything wrong, Bella. It was my fault."

"But I want to help, if I can, to not make this harder for you."

"Well . . ." He contemplated for a moment. "It was just how close you were. Most humans instinctively shy away from us, are repelled by our alienness. . . . I wasn't expecting you to come so close. And the smell of your *throat*." He stopped short, looking to see if he'd upset me.

"Okay, then," I said flippantly, trying to alleviate the suddenly tense atmosphere. I tucked my chin. "No throat exposure."

It worked; he laughed. "No, really, it was more the surprise than anything else."

He raised his free hand and placed it gently on the side of my neck. I sat very still, the chill of his touch a natural warning — a warning telling me to be terrified. But there was no feeling of fear in me. There were, however, other feelings. . . .

"You see," he said. "Perfectly fine."

My blood was racing, and I wished I could slow it, sensing that this must make everything so much more difficult — the thudding of my pulse in my veins. Surely he could hear it.

"The blush on your cheeks is lovely," he murmured. He gently freed his other hand. My hands fell limply into my lap. Softly he brushed my cheek, then held my face between his marble hands.

"Be very still," he whispered, as if I wasn't already frozen.

Slowly, never moving his eyes from mine, he leaned toward me. Then abruptly, but very gently, he rested his cold cheek against the hollow at the base of my throat. I was quite unable to move, even if I'd wanted to. I listened to the sound of his even breathing, watching the sun and wind play in his bronze hair, more human than any other part of him.

With deliberate slowness, his hands slid down the sides of my neck. I shivered, and I heard him catch his breath. But his hands didn't pause as they softly moved to my shoulders, and then stopped.

His face drifted to the side, his nose skimming across my collarbone. He came to rest with the side of his face pressed tenderly against my chest.

Listening to my heart.

"Ah," he sighed.

I don't know how long we sat without moving. It could have been hours. Eventually the throb of my pulse quieted, but he didn't move or speak again as he held me. I knew at any moment it could be too much, and my life could end — so quickly that I might not even notice. And I couldn't make myself be afraid. I couldn't think of anything, except that he was touching me.

And then, too soon, he released me.

His eyes were peaceful.

"It won't be so hard again," he said with satisfaction.

"Was that very hard for you?"

"Not nearly as bad as I imagined it would be. And you?"

"No, it wasn't bad . . . for me."

He smiled at my inflection. "You know what I mean."

I smiled.

"Here." He took my hand and placed it against his cheek. "Do you feel how warm it is?"

And it was almost warm, his usually icy skin. But I barely noticed, for I was touching his face, something I'd dreamed of constantly since the first day I'd seen him.

"Don't move," I whispered.

No one could be still like Edward. He closed his eyes and became as immobile as stone, a carving under my hand.

I moved even more slowly than he had, careful not to make one unexpected move. I caressed his cheek, delicately stroked his eyelid, the purple shadow in the hollow under his eye. I traced the shape of his perfect nose, and then, so carefully, his flawless lips. His lips parted under my hand, and I could feel his cool breath on my fingertips. I wanted to lean in, to inhale the scent of him. So I dropped my hand and leaned away, not wanting to push him too far.

He opened his eyes, and they were hungry. Not in a way to make me fear, but rather to tighten the muscles in the pit of my stomach and send my pulse hammering through my veins again.

"I wish," he whispered, "I wish you could feel the . . . complexity . . . the confusion . . . I feel. That you could understand."

He raised his hand to my hair, then carefully brushed it across my face.

"Tell me," I breathed.

"I don't think I can. I've told you, on the one hand, the hunger — the thirst — that, deplorable creature that I am, I feel for you. And I think you can understand that, to an extent. Though" — he half-smiled — "as you are not addicted to any illegal substances, you probably can't empathize completely.

"But . . ." His fingers touched my lips lightly, making me shiver again. "There are other hungers. Hungers I don't even understand, that are foreign to me."

"I may understand *that* better than you think."

"I'm not used to feeling so human. Is it always like this?"

"For me?" I paused. "No, never. Never before this."

He held my hands between his. They felt so feeble in his iron strength.

"I don't know how to be close to you," he admitted. "I don't know if I can."

I leaned forward very slowly, cautioning him with my eyes. I placed my cheek against his stone chest. I could hear his breath, and nothing else.

"This is enough," I sighed, closing my eyes.

In a very human gesture, he put his arms around me and pressed his face against my hair.

"You're better at this than you give yourself credit for," I noted.

"I have human instincts — they may be buried deep, but they're there."

We sat like that for another immeasurable moment; I wondered if he could be as unwilling to move as I was. But I could see the light was fading, the shadows of the forest beginning to touch us, and I sighed.

"You have to go."

"I thought you couldn't read my mind."

"It's getting clearer." I could hear a smile in his voice. He took my shoulders and I looked into his face.

"Can I show you something?" he asked, sudden excitement flaring in his eyes.

"Show me what?"

"I'll show you how *I* travel in the forest." He saw my expression. "Don't worry, you'll be very safe, and we'll get to your truck much faster." His mouth twitched up into that crooked smile so beautiful my heart nearly stopped.

"Will you turn into a bat?" I asked warily.

He laughed, louder than I'd ever heard. "Like I haven't heard *that* one before!"

"Right, I'm sure you get that all the time."

"Come on, little coward, climb on my back."

I waited to see if he was kidding, but, apparently, he meant it. He smiled as he read my hesitation, and reached for me. My heart reacted; even though he couldn't hear my thoughts, my pulse always gave me away. He then proceeded to sling me onto his back, with very little effort on my part, besides, when in place, clamping my legs and arms so tightly around him that it would choke a normal person. It was like clinging to a stone.

"I'm a bit heavier than your average backpack," I warned.

"Hah!" he snorted. I could almost hear his eyes rolling. I'd never seen him in such high spirits before.

He startled me, suddenly grabbing my hand, pressing my palm to his face, and inhaling deeply.

"Easier all the time," he muttered.

And then he was running.

If I'd ever feared death before in his presence, it was nothing compared to how I felt now.

He streaked through the dark, thick underbrush of the forest like a bullet, like a ghost. There was no sound, no evidence that his feet touched the earth. His breathing never changed, never indicated any effort. But the trees flew by at deadly speeds, always missing us by inches.

I was too terrified to close my eyes, though the cool forest air whipped against my face and burned them. I felt as if I were stupidly sticking my head out the window of an airplane in flight. And, for the first time in my life, I felt the dizzy faintness of motion sickness.

Then it was over. We'd hiked hours this morning to reach Edward's meadow, and now, in a matter of minutes, we were back to the truck.

"Exhilarating, isn't it?" His voice was high, excited.

He stood motionless, waiting for me to climb down. I tried, but my muscles wouldn't respond. My arms and legs stayed locked around him while my head spun uncomfortably.

"Bella?" he asked, anxious now.

"I think I need to lie down," I gasped.

"Oh, sorry." He waited for me, but I still couldn't move.

"I think I need help," I admitted.

He laughed quietly, and gently unloosened my stranglehold on his neck. There was no resisting the iron strength of his hands. Then he pulled me around to face him, cradling me in his arms like a small child. He held me for a moment, then carefully placed me on the springy ferns.

"How do you feel?" he asked.

I couldn't be sure how I felt when my head was spinning so crazily. "Dizzy, I think."

"Put your head between your knees."

I tried that, and it helped a little. I breathed in and out slowly, keeping my head very still. I felt him sitting beside me. The moments passed, and eventually I found that I could raise my head. There was a hollow ringing sound in my ears.

"I guess that wasn't the best idea," he mused.

I tried to be positive, but my voice was weak. "No, it was very interesting."

"Hah! You're as white as a ghost — no, you're as white as *me*!"

"I think I should have closed my eyes."

"Remember that next time."

"Next time!" I groaned.

He laughed, his mood still radiant.

"Show-off," I muttered.

"Open your eyes, Bella," he said quietly.

And he was right there, his face so close to mine. His beauty stunned my mind — it was too much, an excess I couldn't grow accustomed to.

"I was thinking, while I was running . . ." He paused.

"About not hitting the trees, I hope."

"Silly Bella," he chuckled. "Running is second nature to me, it's not something I have to think about."

"Show-off," I muttered again.

He smiled.

"No," he continued, "I was thinking there was something I wanted to try." And he took my face in his hands again.

I couldn't breathe.

He hesitated — not in the normal way, the human way.

Not the way a man might hesitate before he kissed a woman, to gauge her reaction, to see how he would be received. Perhaps he would hesitate to prolong the moment, that ideal moment of anticipation, sometimes better than the kiss itself.

Edward hesitated to test himself, to see if this was safe, to make sure he was still in control of his need.

And then his cold, marble lips pressed very softly against mine.

What neither of us was prepared for was my response.

Blood boiled under my skin, burned in my lips. My breath came in a wild gasp. My fingers knotted in his hair, clutching him to me. My lips parted as I breathed in his heady scent.

Immediately I felt him turn to unresponsive stone beneath my lips. His hands gently, but with irresistible force, pushed my face back. I opened my eyes and saw his guarded expression.

"Oops," I breathed.

"That's an understatement."

His eyes were wild, his jaw clenched in acute restraint, yet he didn't lapse from his perfect articulation. He held my face just inches from his. He dazzled my eyes.

"Should I . . . ?" I tried to disengage myself, to give him some room.

His hands refused to let me move so much as an inch.

"No, it's tolerable. Wait for a moment, please." His voice was polite, controlled.

I kept my eyes on his, watched as the excitement in them faded and gentled.

Then he smiled a surprisingly impish grin.

"There," he said, obviously pleased with himself.

"Tolerable?" I asked.

He laughed aloud. "I'm stronger than I thought. It's nice to know."

"I wish I could say the same. I'm sorry."

"You *are* only human, after all."

"Thanks so much," I said, my voice acerbic.

He was on his feet in one of his lithe, almost invisibly quick movements. He held out his hand to me, an unexpected gesture. I was so used to our standard of careful non-contact. I took his icy hand, needing the support more than I thought. My balance had not yet returned.

"Are you still faint from the run? Or was it my kissing expertise?" How lighthearted, how human he seemed as he laughed now, his seraphic face untroubled. He was a different Edward than the one I had known. And I felt all the more besotted by him. It would cause me physical pain to be separated from him now.

"I can't be sure, I'm still woozy," I managed to respond. "I think it's some of both, though."

"Maybe you should let me drive."

"Are you insane?" I protested.

"I can drive better than you on your best day," he teased. "You have much slower reflexes."

"I'm sure that's true, but I don't think my nerves, or my truck, could take it."

"Some trust, please, Bella."

My hand was in my pocket, curled tightly around the key. I pursed my lips, deliberated, then shook my head with a tight grin.

"Nope. Not a chance."

He raised his eyebrows in disbelief.

I started to step around him, heading for the driver's side. He might have let me pass if I hadn't wobbled slightly. Then again, he might not have. His arm created an inescapable snare around my waist.

"Bella, I've already expended a great deal of personal effort at this point to keep you alive. I'm not about to let you behind the wheel of a vehicle when you can't even walk straight. Besides, friends don't let friends drive drunk," he quoted with a chuckle. I could smell the unbearably sweet fragrance coming off his chest.

"Drunk?" I objected.

"You're intoxicated by my very presence." He was grinning that playful smirk again.

"I can't argue with that," I sighed. There was no way around it; I couldn't resist him in anything. I held the key high and dropped it, watching his hand flash like lightning to catch it soundlessly. "Take it easy — my truck is a senior citizen."

"Very sensible," he approved.

"And are you not affected at all?" I asked, irked. "By my presence?"

Again his mobile features transformed, his expression became soft, warm. He didn't answer at first; he simply bent his face to mine, and brushed his lips slowly along my jaw, from my ear to my chin, back and forth. I trembled.

"Regardless," he finally murmured, "I have better reflexes."

14. MIND OVER MATTER

HE COULD DRIVE WELL, WHEN HE KEPT THE SPEED reasonable, I had to admit. Like so many things, it seemed to be effortless to him. He barely looked at the road, yet the tires never deviated so much as a centimeter from the center of the lane. He drove one-handed, holding my hand on the seat. Sometimes he gazed into the setting sun, sometimes he glanced at me — my face, my hair blowing out the open window, our hands twined together.

He had turned the radio to an oldies station, and he sang along with a song I'd never heard. He knew every line.

"You like fifties music?" I asked.

"Music in the fifties was good. Much better than the

sixties, or the seventies, ugh!" He shuddered. "The eighties were bearable."

"Are you ever going to tell me how old you are?" I asked, tentative, not wanting to upset his buoyant humor.

"Does it matter much?" His smile, to my relief, remained unclouded.

"No, but I still wonder . . ." I grimaced. "There's nothing like an unsolved mystery to keep you up at night."

"I wonder if it will upset you," he reflected to himself. He gazed into the sun; the minutes passed.

"Try me," I finally said.

He sighed, and then looked into my eyes, seeming to forget the road completely for a time. Whatever he saw there must have encouraged him. He looked into the sun — the light of the setting orb glittered off his skin in ruby-tinged sparkles — and spoke.

"I was born in Chicago in 1901." He paused and glanced at me from the corner of his eyes. My face was carefully unsurprised, patient for the rest. He smiled a tiny smile and continued. "Carlisle found me in a hospital in the summer of 1918. I was seventeen, and dying of the Spanish influenza."

He heard my intake of breath, though it was barely audible to my own ears. He looked down into my eyes again.

"I don't remember it well — it was a very long time ago, and human memories fade." He was lost in his thoughts for a short time before he went on. "I do remember how it felt, when Carlisle saved me. It's not an easy thing, not something you could forget."

"Your parents?"

"They had already died from the disease. I was alone. That was why he chose me. In all the chaos of the epidemic, no one would ever realize I was gone."

"How did he . . . save you?"

A few seconds passed before he answered. He seemed to choose his words carefully.

"It was difficult. Not many of us have the restraint necessary to accomplish it. But Carlisle has always been the most humane, the most compassionate of us. . . . I don't think you could find his equal throughout all of history." He paused. "For me, it was merely very, very painful."

I could tell from the set of his lips, he would say no more on this subject. I suppressed my curiosity, though it was far from idle. There were many things I needed to think through on this particular issue, things that were only beginning to occur to me. No doubt his quick mind had already comprehended every aspect that eluded me.

His soft voice interrupted my thoughts. "He acted from loneliness. That's usually the reason behind the choice. I was the first in Carlisle's family, though he found Esme soon after. She fell from a cliff. They brought her straight to the hospital morgue, though, somehow, her heart was still beating."

"So you must be dying, then, to become . . ." We never said the word, and I couldn't frame it now.

"No, that's just Carlisle. He would never do that to someone who had another choice." The respect in his voice was profound whenever he spoke of his father figure. "It is easier he says, though," he continued, "if the blood is weak." He looked at the now-dark road, and I could feel the subject closing again.

"And Emmett and Rosalie?"

"Carlisle brought Rosalie to our family next. I didn't realize till much later that he was hoping she would be to me what Esme was to him — he was careful with his thoughts around me." He rolled his eyes. "But she was never more than a sister. It was only two years later that she found Emmett. She was hunting — we were in Appalachia at the time — and found a bear about to finish him off. She carried him back to Carlisle, more than a hundred miles, afraid she wouldn't be able to do it herself. I'm only beginning to guess how difficult that journey was for her." He threw a pointed glance in my direction, and raised our hands, still folded together, to brush my cheek with the back of his hand.

"But she made it," I encouraged, looking away from the unbearable beauty of his eyes.

"Yes," he murmured. "She saw something in his face that made her strong enough. And they've been together ever since. Sometimes they live separately from us, as a married couple. But the younger we pretend to be, the longer we can stay in any given place. Forks seemed perfect, so we all enrolled in high school." He laughed. "I suppose we'll have to go to their wedding in a few years, *again*."

"Alice and Jasper?"

"Alice and Jasper are two very rare creatures. They both developed a conscience, as we refer to it, with no outside guidance. Jasper belonged to another . . . family, a *very* different kind of family. He became depressed, and he wandered on his own. Alice found him. Like me, she has certain gifts above and beyond the norm for our kind."

"Really?" I interrupted, fascinated. "But you said you were the only one who could hear people's thoughts."

"That's true. She knows other things. She *sees* things — things that might happen, things that are coming. But it's very subjective. The future isn't set in stone. Things change."

His jaw set when he said that, and his eyes darted to my face and away so quickly that I wasn't sure if I only imagined it.

"What kinds of things does she see?"

"She saw Jasper and knew that he was looking for her before he knew it himself. She saw Carlisle and our family, and they came together to find us. She's most sensitive to non-humans. She always sees, for example, when another group of our kind is coming near. And any threat they may pose."

"Are there a lot of . . . your kind?" I was surprised. How many of them could walk among us undetected?

"No, not many. But most won't settle in any one place. Only those like us, who've given up hunting you people" — a sly glance in my direction — "can live together with humans for any length of time. We've only found one other family like ours, in a small village in Alaska. We lived together for a time, but there were so many of us that we became too noticeable. Those of us who live . . . differently tend to band together."

"And the others?"

"Nomads, for the most part. We've all lived that way at

times. It gets tedious, like anything else. But we run across the others now and then, because most of us prefer the North."

"Why is that?"

We were parked in front of my house now, and he'd turned off the truck. It was very quiet and dark; there was no moon. The porch light was off so I knew my father wasn't home yet.

"Did you have your eyes open this afternoon?" he teased. "Do you think I could walk down the street in the sunlight without causing traffic accidents? There's a reason why we chose the Olympic Peninsula, one of the most sunless places in the world. It's nice to be able to go outside in the day. You wouldn't believe how tired you can get of nighttime in eighty-odd years."

"So that's where the legends came from?"

"Probably."

"And Alice came from another family, like Jasper?"

"No, and that *is* a mystery. Alice doesn't remember her human life at all. And she doesn't know who created her. She awoke alone. Whoever made her walked away, and none of us understand why, or how, he could. If she hadn't had that other sense, if she hadn't seen Jasper and Carlisle and known that she would someday become one of us, she probably would have turned into a total savage."

There was so much to think through, so much I still wanted to ask. But, to my great embarrassment, my stomach growled. I'd been so intrigued, I hadn't even noticed I was hungry. I realized now that I was ravenous.

"I'm sorry, I'm keeping you from dinner."

"I'm fine, really."

"I've never spent much time around anyone who eats food. I forget."

"I want to stay with you." It was easier to say in the darkness, knowing as I spoke how my voice would betray me, my hopeless addiction to him.

"Can't I come in?" he asked.

"Would you like to?" I couldn't picture it, this godlike creature sitting in my father's shabby kitchen chair.

"Yes, if it's all right." I heard the door close quietly, and almost simultaneously he was outside my door, opening it for me.

"Very human," I complimented him.

"It's definitely resurfacing."

He walked beside me in the night, so quietly I had to peek at him constantly to be sure he was still there. In the darkness he looked much more normal. Still pale, still dreamlike in his beauty, but no longer the fantastic sparkling creature of our sunlit afternoon.

He reached the door ahead of me and opened it for me. I paused halfway through the frame.

"The door was unlocked?"

"No, I used the key from under the eave."

I stepped inside, flicked on the porch light, and turned to look at him with my eyebrows raised. I was sure I'd never used that key in front of him.

"I was curious about you."

"You spied on me?" But somehow I couldn't infuse my voice with the proper outrage. I was flattered.

He was unrepentant. "What else is there to do at night?"

I let it go for the moment and went down the hall to the kitchen. He was there before me, needing no guide. He sat in the very chair I'd tried to picture him in. His beauty lit up the kitchen. It was a moment before I could look away.

I concentrated on getting my dinner, taking last night's lasagna from the fridge, placing a square on a plate, heating it in the microwave. It revolved, filling the kitchen with the smell of tomatoes and oregano. I didn't take my eyes from the plate of food as I spoke.

"How often?" I asked casually.

"Hmmm?" He sounded as if I had pulled him from some other train of thought.

I still didn't turn around. "How often did you come here?"

"I come here almost every night."

I whirled, stunned. "Why?"

"You're interesting when you sleep." He spoke matter-of-factly. "You talk."

"No!" I gasped, heat flooding my face all the way to my hairline. I gripped the kitchen counter for support. I knew I talked in my sleep, of course; my mother teased me about it. I hadn't thought it was something I needed to worry about here, though.

His expression shifted instantly to chagrin. "Are you very angry with me?"

"That depends!" I felt and sounded like I'd had the breath knocked out of me.

He waited.

"On?" he urged.

"What you heard!" I wailed.

Instantly, silently, he was at my side, taking my hands carefully in his.

"Don't be upset!" he pleaded. He dropped his face to the level of my eyes, holding my gaze. I was embarrassed. I tried to look away.

"You miss your mother," he whispered. "You worry about her. And when it rains, the sound makes you restless. You used to talk about home a lot, but it's less often now. Once you said, 'It's too *green.*'" He laughed softly, hoping, I could see, not to offend me further.

"Anything else?" I demanded.

He knew what I was getting at. "You did say my name," he admitted.

I sighed in defeat. "A lot?"

"How much do you mean by 'a lot,' exactly?"

"Oh no!" I hung my head.

He pulled me against his chest, softly, naturally.

"Don't be self-conscious," he whispered in my ear. "If I could dream at all, it would be about you. And I'm not ashamed of it."

Then we both heard the sound of tires on the brick driveway, saw the headlights flash through the front windows, down the hall to us. I stiffened in his arms.

"Should your father know I'm here?" he asked.

"I'm not sure . . ." I tried to think it through quickly.

"Another time then . . ."

And I was alone.

"Edward!" I hissed.

I heard a ghostly chuckle, then nothing else.

My father's key turned in the door.

"Bella?" he called. It had bothered me before; who else would it be? Suddenly he didn't seem so far off base.

"In here." I hoped he couldn't hear the hysterical edge to my voice. I grabbed my dinner from the microwave and sat at the table as he walked in. His footsteps sounded so noisy after my day with Edward.

"Can you get me some of that? I'm bushed." He stepped on the heels of his boots to take them off, holding the back of Edward's chair for support.

I took my food with me, scarfing it down as I got his dinner. It burned my tongue. I filled two glasses with milk while his lasagna was heating, and gulped mine to put out the fire. As I set the glass down, I noticed the milk trembling and realized my hand was shaking. Charlie sat in the chair, and the contrast between him and its former occupant was comical.

"Thanks," he said as I placed his food on the table.

"How was your day?" I asked. The words were rushed; I was dying to escape to my room.

"Good. The fish were biting . . . how about you? Did you get everything done that you wanted to?"

"Not really — it was too nice out to stay indoors." I took another big bite.

"It was a nice day," he agreed. What an understatement, I thought to myself.

Finished with the last bite of lasagna, I lifted my glass and chugged the remains of my milk.

Charlie surprised me by being observant. "In a hurry?"

"Yeah, I'm tired. I'm going to bed early."

"You look kinda keyed up," he noted. Why, oh why, did this have to be his night to pay attention?

"Do I?" was all I could manage in response. I quickly scrubbed my dishes clean in the sink, and placed them upside down on a dish towel to dry.

"It's Saturday," he mused.

I didn't respond.

"No plans tonight?" he asked suddenly.

"No, Dad, I just want to get some sleep."

"None of the boys in town your type, eh?" He was suspicious, but trying to play it cool.

"No, none of the boys have caught my eye yet." I was careful not to over-emphasize the word *boys* in my quest to be truthful with Charlie.

"I thought maybe that Mike Newton . . . you said he was friendly."

"He's *just* a friend, Dad."

"Well, you're too good for them all, anyway. Wait till you get to college to start looking." Every father's dream, that his daughter will be out of the house before the hormones kick in.

"Sounds like a good idea to me," I agreed as I headed up the stairs.

"'Night, honey," he called after me. No doubt he would be listening carefully all evening, waiting for me to try to sneak out.

"See you in the morning, Dad." See you creeping into my room tonight at midnight to check on me.

I worked to make my tread sound slow and tired as I walked up the stairs to my room. I shut the door loud enough for him to hear, and then sprinted on my tiptoes to the window. I threw it open and leaned out into the night. My eyes scanned the darkness, the impenetrable shadows of the trees.

"Edward?" I whispered, feeling completely idiotic.

The quiet, laughing response came from behind me. "Yes?"

I whirled, one hand flying to my throat in surprise.

He lay, smiling hugely, across my bed, his hands behind his head, his feet dangling off the end, the picture of ease.

"Oh!" I breathed, sinking unsteadily to the floor.

"I'm sorry." He pressed his lips together, trying to hide his amusement.

"Just give me a minute to restart my heart."

He sat up slowly, so as not to startle me again. Then he leaned forward and reached out with his long arms to pick me up, gripping the tops of my arms like I was a toddler. He sat me on the bed beside him.

"Why don't you sit with me," he suggested, putting a cold hand on mine. "How's the heart?"

"You tell me — I'm sure you hear it better than I do."

I felt his quiet laughter shake the bed.

We sat there for a moment in silence, both listening to my heartbeat slow. I thought about having Edward in my room, with my father in the house.

"Can I have a minute to be human?" I asked.

"Certainly." He gestured with one hand that I should proceed.

"Stay," I said, trying to look severe.

"Yes, ma'am." And he made a show of becoming a statue on the edge of my bed.

I hopped up, grabbing my pajamas from off the floor, my bag of toiletries off the desk. I left the light off and slipped out, closing the door.

I could hear the sound from the TV rising up the stairs. I banged the bathroom door loudly, so Charlie wouldn't come up to bother me.

I meant to hurry. I brushed my teeth fiercely, trying to be thorough *and* speedy, removing all traces of lasagna. But the hot water of the shower couldn't be rushed. It unknotted the muscles in my back, calmed my pulse. The familiar smell of my shampoo made me feel like I might be the same person I had been this morning. I tried not to think of Edward, sitting in my room, waiting, because then I had to start all over with the calming process. Finally, I couldn't delay anymore. I shut off the water, toweling hastily, rushing again. I pulled on my holey t-shirt and gray sweatpants. Too late to regret not packing the Victoria's Secret silk pajamas my mother got me two birthdays ago, which still had the tags on them in a drawer somewhere back home.

I rubbed the towel through my hair again, and then yanked the brush through it quickly. I threw the towel in the hamper, flung my brush and toothpaste into my bag. Then I dashed down the stairs so Charlie could see that I was in my pajamas, with wet hair.

"'Night, Dad."

"'Night, Bella." He did look startled by my appearance. Maybe that would keep him from checking on me tonight.

I took the stairs two at a time, trying to be quiet, and flew into my room, closing the door tightly behind me.

Edward hadn't moved a fraction of an inch, a carving of Adonis perched on my faded quilt. I smiled, and his lips twitched, the statue coming to life.

His eyes appraised me, taking in the damp hair, the tattered shirt. He raised one eyebrow. "Nice."

I grimaced.

"No, it looks good on you."

"Thanks," I whispered. I went back to his side, sitting cross-legged beside him. I looked at the lines in the wooden floor.

"What was all that for?"

"Charlie thinks I'm sneaking out."

"Oh." He contemplated that. "Why?" As if he couldn't know Charlie's mind much more clearly than I could guess.

"Apparently, I look a little overexcited."

He lifted my chin, examining my face.

"You look very warm, actually."

He bent his face slowly to mine, laying his cool cheek against my skin. I held perfectly still.

"Mmmmmm . . . ," he breathed.

It was very difficult, while he was touching me, to frame a coherent question. It took me a minute of scattered concentration to begin.

"It seems to be . . . much easier for you, now, to be close to me."

"Does it seem that way to you?" he murmured, his nose gliding to the corner of my jaw. I felt his hand, lighter than a moth's wing, brushing my damp hair back, so that his lips could touch the hollow beneath my ear.

"Much, much easier," I said, trying to exhale.

"Hmm."

"So I was wondering . . . ," I began again, but his fingers were slowly tracing my collarbone, and I lost my train of thought.

"Yes?" he breathed.

"Why is that," my voice shook, embarrassing me, "do you think?"

I felt the tremor of his breath on my neck as he laughed. "Mind over matter."

I pulled back; as I moved, he froze — and I could no longer hear the sound of his breathing.

We stared cautiously at each other for a moment, and then, as his clenched jaw gradually relaxed, his expression became puzzled.

"Did I do something wrong?"

"No — the opposite. You're driving me crazy," I explained.

He considered that briefly, and when he spoke, he sounded pleased. "Really?" A triumphant smile slowly lit his face.

"Would you like a round of applause?" I asked sarcastically.

He grinned.

"I'm just pleasantly surprised," he clarified. "In the last hundred years or so," his voice was teasing, "I never imagined anything like this. I didn't believe I would ever find someone I wanted to be with . . . in another way than my brothers and sisters. And then to find, even though it's all new to me, that I'm good at it . . . at being with you . . ."

"You're good at everything," I pointed out.

He shrugged, allowing that, and we both laughed in whispers.

"But how can it be so easy now?" I pressed. "This afternoon . . ."

"It's not *easy*," he sighed. "But this afternoon, I was still . . . undecided. I am sorry about that, it was unforgivable for me to behave so."

"Not unforgivable," I disagreed.

"Thank you." He smiled. "You see," he continued, looking down now, "I wasn't sure if I was strong enough. . . ." He picked up one of my hands and pressed it lightly to his face. "And while there was still that possibility that I might be . . . overcome" — he breathed in the scent at my wrist — "I was . . . susceptible. Until I made up my mind that I *was* strong enough, that there was no possibility at all that I would . . . that I ever could . . ."

I'd never seen him struggle so hard for words. It was so . . . human.

"So there's no possibility now?"

"Mind over matter," he repeated, smiling, his teeth bright even in the darkness.

"Wow, that was easy," I said.

He threw back his head and laughed, quietly as a whisper, but still exuberantly.

"Easy for *you*!" he amended, touching my nose with his fingertip.

And then his face was abruptly serious.

"I'm trying," he whispered, his voice pained. "If it gets to be . . . too much, I'm fairly sure I'll be able to leave."

I scowled. I didn't like the talk of leaving.

"And it will be harder tomorrow," he continued. "I've had the scent of you in my head all day, and I've grown amazingly desensitized. If I'm away from you for any length of time, I'll have to start over again. Not quite from scratch, though, I think."

"Don't go away, then," I responded, unable to hide the longing in my voice.

"That suits me," he replied, his face relaxing into a gentle smile. "Bring on the shackles — I'm your prisoner." But his long hands formed manacles around *my* wrists as he spoke. He laughed his quiet, musical laugh. He'd laughed more tonight than I'd ever heard in all the time I'd spent with him.

"You seem more . . . optimistic than usual," I observed. "I haven't seen you like this before."

"Isn't it supposed to be like this?" He smiled. "The glory of first love, and all that. It's incredible, isn't it, the difference between reading about something, seeing it in the pictures, and experiencing it?"

"Very different," I agreed. "More forceful than I'd imagined."

"For example" — his words flowed swiftly now, I had to concentrate to catch it all — "the emotion of jealousy. I've read about it a hundred thousand times, seen actors portray it in a thousand different plays and movies. I believed I understood that one pretty clearly. But it shocked me. . . ." He grimaced. "Do you remember the day that Mike asked you to the dance?"

I nodded, though I remembered that day for a different reason. "The day you started talking to me again."

"I was surprised by the flare of resentment, almost fury, that I felt — I didn't recognize what it was at first. I was even more aggravated than usual that I couldn't know what you were thinking, why you refused him. Was it simply for your friend's sake? Was there someone else? I knew I had no right to care either way. I *tried* not to care.

"And then the line started forming," he chuckled. I scowled in the darkness.

"I waited, unreasonably anxious to hear what you would say to them, to watch your expressions. I couldn't deny the relief I felt, watching the annoyance on your face. But I couldn't be sure.

"That was the first night I came here. I wrestled all night, while watching you sleep, with the chasm between what I knew was *right,* moral, ethical, and what I *wanted.* I knew that if I continued to ignore you as I should, or if I left for a few years, till you were gone, that someday you would say yes to Mike, or someone like him. It made me angry.

"And then," he whispered, "as you were sleeping, you said my name. You spoke so clearly, at first I thought you'd woken. But you rolled over restlessly and mumbled my name once more, and sighed. The feeling that coursed through me then was unnerving, staggering. And I knew I couldn't ignore you any longer." He was silent for a moment, probably listening to the suddenly uneven pounding of my heart.

"But jealousy . . . it's a strange thing. So much more powerful than I would have thought. And irrational! Just now, when Charlie asked you about that vile Mike Newton . . ." He shook his head angrily.

"I should have known you'd be listening," I groaned.

"Of course."

"*That* made you feel jealous, though, really?"

"I'm new at this; you're resurrecting the human in me, and everything feels stronger because it's fresh."

"But honestly," I teased, "for that to bother you, after I have to hear that Rosalie — Rosalie, the incarnation of pure beauty, *Rosalie* — was meant for you. Emmett or no Emmett, how can I compete with that?"

"There's no competition." His teeth gleamed. He drew my trapped hands around his back, holding me to his chest. I kept as still as I could, even breathing with caution.

"I *know* there's no competition," I mumbled into his cold skin. "That's the problem."

"Of course Rosalie *is* beautiful in her way, but even if she wasn't like a sister to me, even if Emmett didn't belong with her, she could never have one tenth, no, one hundredth of the attraction you hold for me." He was serious now, thoughtful. "For almost ninety years I've walked among my kind, and yours . . . all the time thinking I was complete in myself, not realizing what I was seeking. And not finding anything, because you weren't alive yet."

"It hardly seems fair," I whispered, my face still resting

on his chest, listening to his breath come and go. "I haven't had to wait at all. Why should I get off so easily?"

"You're right," he agreed with amusement. "I should make this harder for you, definitely." He freed one of his hands, released my wrist, only to gather it carefully into his other hand. He stroked my wet hair softly, from the top of my head to my waist. "You only have to risk your life every second you spend with me, that's surely not much. You only have to turn your back on nature, on humanity . . . what's that worth?"

"Very little — I don't feel deprived of anything."

"Not yet." And his voice was abruptly full of ancient grief.

I tried to pull back, to look in his face, but his hand locked my wrists in an unbreakable hold.

"What —" I started to ask, when his body became alert. I froze, but he suddenly released my hands, and disappeared. I narrowly avoided falling on my face.

"Lie down!" he hissed. I couldn't tell where he spoke from in the darkness.

I rolled under my quilt, balling up on my side, the way I usually slept. I heard the door crack open, as Charlie peeked in to make sure I was where I was supposed to be. I breathed evenly, exaggerating the movement.

A long minute passed. I listened, not sure if I'd heard the door close. Then Edward's cool arm was around me, under the covers, his lips at my ear.

"You are a terrible actress — I'd say that career path is out for you."

"Darn it," I muttered. My heart was crashing in my chest.

He hummed a melody I didn't recognize; it sounded like a lullaby.

He paused. "Should I sing you to sleep?"

"Right," I laughed. "Like I could sleep with you here!"

"You do it all the time," he reminded me.

"But I didn't *know* you were here," I replied icily.

"So if you don't want to sleep . . . ," he suggested, ignoring my tone. My breath caught.

"If I don't want to sleep . . . ?"

He chuckled. "What do you want to do then?"

I couldn't answer at first.

"I'm not sure," I finally said.

"Tell me when you decide."

I could feel his cool breath on my neck, feel his nose sliding along my jaw, inhaling.

"I thought you were desensitized."

"Just because I'm resisting the wine doesn't mean I can't appreciate the bouquet," he whispered. "You have a very floral smell, like lavender . . . or freesia," he noted. "It's mouthwatering."

"Yeah, it's an off day when I don't get *somebody* telling me how edible I smell."

He chuckled, and then sighed.

"I've decided what I want to do," I told him. "I want to hear more about you."

"Ask me anything."

I sifted through my questions for the most vital. "Why do you do it?" I said. "I still don't understand how you can work so hard to resist what you . . . *are*. Please don't misunderstand, of course I'm glad that you do. I just don't see why you would bother in the first place."

He hesitated before answering. "That's a good question, and you are not the first one to ask it. The others — the majority of our kind who are quite content with our lot — they, too, wonder at how we live. But you see, just because we've been . . . dealt a certain hand . . . it doesn't mean that we can't choose to rise above — to conquer the boundaries of a destiny that none of us wanted. To try to retain whatever essential humanity we can."

I lay unmoving, locked in awed silence.

"Did you fall asleep?" he whispered after a few minutes.

"No."

"Is that all you were curious about?"

I rolled my eyes. "Not quite."

"What else do you want to know?"

"Why can you read minds — why only you? And Alice, seeing the future . . . why does that happen?"

I felt him shrug in the darkness. "We don't really know. Carlisle has a theory . . . he believes that we all bring something of our strongest human traits with us into the next life, where they are intensified — like our minds, and our senses. He thinks that I must have already been very sensitive to the thoughts of those around me. And that Alice had some precognition, wherever she was."

"What did he bring into the next life, and the others?"

"Carlisle brought his compassion. Esme brought her ability to love passionately. Emmett brought his strength, Rosalie her . . . tenacity. Or you could call it pigheadedness," he chuckled. "Jasper is very interesting. He was quite charismatic in his first life, able to influence those around him to see things his way. Now he is able to manipulate the emotions of those around him — calm down a room of angry people, for example, or excite a lethargic crowd, conversely. It's a very subtle gift."

I considered the impossibilities he described, trying to take it in. He waited patiently while I thought.

"So where did it all start? I mean, Carlisle changed you, and then someone must have changed him, and so on. . . ."

"Well, where did you come from? Evolution? Creation? Couldn't we have evolved in the same way as other species, predator and prey? Or, if you don't believe that all this world could have just happened on its own, which is hard for me to accept myself, is it so hard to believe that the same force that created the delicate angelfish with the shark, the baby seal and the killer whale, could create both our kinds together?"

"Let me get this straight — I'm the baby seal, right?"

"Right." He laughed, and something touched my hair — his lips?

I wanted to turn toward him, to see if it was really his lips against my hair. But I had to be good; I didn't want to make this any harder for him than it already was.

"Are you ready to sleep?" he asked, interrupting the short silence. "Or do you have any more questions?"

"Only a million or two."

"We have tomorrow, and the next day, and the next . . . ," he reminded me. I smiled, euphoric at the thought.

"Are you sure you won't vanish in the morning?" I wanted this to be certain. "You are mythical, after all."

"I won't leave you." His voice had the seal of a promise in it.

"One more, then, tonight . . ." And I blushed. The darkness was no help — I'm sure he could feel the sudden warmth under my skin.

"What is it?"

"No, forget it. I changed my mind."

"Bella, you can ask me anything."

I didn't answer, and he groaned.

"I keep thinking it will get less frustrating, not hearing your thoughts. But it just gets worse and *worse.*"

"I'm glad you can't read my thoughts. It's bad enough that you eavesdrop on my sleep-talking."

"Please?" His voice was so persuasive, so impossible to resist.

I shook my head.

"If you don't tell me, I'll just assume it's something much worse than it is," he threatened darkly. "Please?" Again, that pleading voice.

"Well," I began, glad that he couldn't see my face.

"Yes?"

"You said that Rosalie and Emmett will get married soon. . . . Is that . . . marriage . . . the same as it is for humans?"

He laughed in earnest now, understanding. "Is *that* what you're getting at?"

I fidgeted, unable to answer.

"Yes, I suppose it is much the same," he said. "I told

you, most of those human desires are there, just hidden behind more powerful desires."

"Oh," was all I could say.

"Was there a purpose behind your curiosity?"

"Well, I did wonder . . . about you and me . . . someday . . ."

He was instantly serious, I could tell by the sudden stillness of his body. I froze, too, reacting automatically.

"I don't think that . . . that . . . would be possible for us."

"Because it would be too hard for you, if I were that . . . close?"

"That's certainly a problem. But that's not what I was thinking of. It's just that you are so soft, so fragile. I have to mind my actions every moment that we're together so that I don't hurt you. I could kill you quite easily, Bella, simply by accident." His voice had become just a soft murmur. He moved his icy palm to rest it against my cheek. "If I was too hasty . . . if for one second I wasn't paying enough attention, I could reach out, meaning to touch your face, and crush your skull by mistake. You don't realize how incredibly *breakable* you are. I can never, never afford to lose any kind of control when I'm with you."

He waited for me to respond, growing anxious when I didn't. "Are you scared?" he asked.

I waited for a minute to answer, so the words would be true. "No. I'm fine."

He seemed to deliberate for a moment. "I'm curious

now, though," he said, his voice light again. "Have *you* ever . . . ?" He trailed off suggestively.

"Of course not." I flushed. "I told you I've never felt like this about anyone before, not even close."

"I know. It's just that I know other people's thoughts. I know love and lust don't always keep the same company."

"They do for me. Now, anyway, that they exist for me at all," I sighed.

"That's nice. We have that one thing in common, at least." He sounded satisfied.

"Your human instincts . . . ," I began. He waited. "Well, do you find me attractive, in *that* way, at all?"

He laughed and lightly rumpled my nearly dry hair.

"I may not be a human, but I am a man," he assured me.

I yawned involuntarily.

"I've answered your questions, now you should sleep," he insisted.

"I'm not sure if I can."

"Do you want me to leave?"

"No!" I said too loudly.

He laughed, and then began to hum that same, unfamiliar lullaby; the voice of an archangel, soft in my ear.

More tired than I realized, exhausted from the long day of mental and emotional stress like I'd never felt before, I drifted to sleep in his cold arms.

15. THE CULLENS

THE MUTED LIGHT OF YET ANOTHER CLOUDY DAY eventually woke me. I lay with my arm across my eyes, groggy and dazed. Something, a dream trying to be remembered, struggled to break into my consciousness. I moaned and rolled on my side, hoping more sleep would come. And then the previous day flooded back into my awareness.

"Oh!" I sat up so fast it made my head spin.

"Your hair looks like a haystack . . . but I like it." His unruffled voice came from the rocking chair in the corner.

"Edward! You stayed!" I rejoiced, and thoughtlessly threw myself across the room and into his lap. In the instant that my thoughts caught up with my actions, I froze, shocked by my own uncontrolled enthusiasm. I stared up at him, afraid that I had crossed the wrong line.

But he laughed.

"Of course," he answered, startled, but seeming pleased by my reaction. His hands rubbed my back.

I laid my head cautiously against his shoulder, breathing in the smell of his skin.

"I was sure it was a dream."

"You're not that creative," he scoffed.

"Charlie!" I remembered, thoughtlessly jumping up again and heading to the door.

"He left an hour ago — after reattaching your battery cables, I might add. I have to admit I was disappointed. Is that really all it would take to stop you, if you were determined to go?"

I deliberated where I stood, wanting to return to him badly, but afraid I might have morning breath.

"You're not usually this confused in the morning," he noted. He held his arms open for me to return. A nearly irresistible invitation.

"I need another human minute," I admitted.

"I'll wait."

I skipped to the bathroom, my emotions unrecognizable. I didn't know myself, inside or out. The face in the mirror was practically a stranger — eyes too bright, hectic spots of red across my cheekbones. After I brushed my teeth, I worked to straighten out the tangled chaos that was my hair. I splashed my face with cold water, and tried to breathe normally, with no noticeable success. I half-ran back to my room.

It seemed like a miracle that he was there, his arms still waiting for me. He reached out to me, and my heart thumped unsteadily.

"Welcome back," he murmured, taking me into his arms.

He rocked me for a while in silence, until I noticed that his clothes were changed, his hair smooth.

"You left?" I accused, touching the collar of his fresh shirt.

"I could hardly leave in the clothes I came in — what would the neighbors think?"

I pouted.

"You were very deeply asleep; I didn't miss anything." His eyes gleamed. "The talking came earlier."

I groaned. "What did you hear?"

His gold eyes grew very soft. "You said you loved me."

"You knew that already," I reminded him, ducking my head.

"It was nice to hear, just the same."

I hid my face against his shoulder.

"I love you," I whispered.

"You are my life now," he answered simply.

There was nothing more to say for the moment. He rocked us back and forth as the room grew lighter.

"Breakfast time," he said eventually, casually — to prove, I'm sure, that he remembered all my human frailties.

So I clutched my throat with both hands and stared at him with wide eyes. Shock crossed his face.

"Kidding!" I snickered. "And you said I couldn't act!"

He frowned in disgust. "That wasn't funny."

"It was very funny, and you know it." But I examined his gold eyes carefully, to make sure that I was forgiven. Apparently, I was.

"Shall I rephrase?" he asked. "Breakfast time for the human."

"Oh, okay."

He threw me over his stone shoulder, gently, but with a swiftness that left me breathless. I protested as he carried me easily down the stairs, but he ignored me. He sat me right side up on a chair.

The kitchen was bright, happy, seeming to absorb my mood.

"What's for breakfast?" I asked pleasantly.

That threw him for a minute.

"Er, I'm not sure. What would you like?" His marble brow puckered.

I grinned, hopping up.

"That's all right, I fend for myself pretty well. Watch me hunt."

I found a bowl and a box of cereal. I could feel his eyes on me as I poured the milk and grabbed a spoon. I sat my food on the table, and then paused.

"Can I get you anything?" I asked, not wanting to be rude.

He rolled his eyes. "Just eat, Bella."

I sat at the table, watching him as I took a bite. He was gazing at me, studying my every movement. It made me self-conscious. I cleared my mouth to speak, to distract him.

"What's on the agenda for today?" I asked.

"Hmmm . . ." I watched him frame his answer carefully. "What would you say to meeting my family?"

I gulped.

"Are you afraid now?" He sounded hopeful.

"Yes," I admitted; how could I deny it — he could see my eyes.

"Don't worry." He smirked. "I'll protect you."

"I'm not afraid of *them*," I explained. "I'm afraid they won't . . . like me. Won't they be, well, surprised that you would bring someone . . . like me . . . home to meet them? Do they know that I know about them?"

"Oh, they already know everything. They'd taken bets yesterday, you know" — he smiled, but his voice was harsh — "on whether I'd bring you back, though why anyone would bet against Alice, I can't imagine. At any rate, we don't have secrets in the family. It's not really feasible, what with my mind reading and Alice seeing the future and all that."

"And Jasper making you feel all warm and fuzzy about spilling your guts, don't forget that."

"You paid attention," he smiled approvingly.

"I've been known to do that every now and then." I grimaced. "So did Alice see me coming?"

His reaction was strange. "Something like that," he said uncomfortably, turning away so I couldn't see his eyes. I stared at him curiously.

"Is that any good?" he asked, turning back to me abruptly and eyeing my breakfast with a teasing look on his face. "Honestly, it doesn't look very appetizing."

"Well, it's no irritable grizzly . . . ," I murmured,

ignoring him when he glowered. I was still wondering why he responded that way when I mentioned Alice. I hurried through my cereal, speculating.

He stood in the middle of the kitchen, the statue of Adonis again, staring abstractedly out the back windows.

Then his eyes were back on me, and he smiled his heartbreaking smile.

"And you should introduce me to your father, too, I think."

"He already knows you," I reminded him.

"As your boyfriend, I mean."

I stared at him with suspicion. "Why?"

"Isn't that customary?" he asked innocently.

"I don't know," I admitted. My dating history gave me few reference points to work with. Not that any normal rules of dating applied here. "That's not necessary, you know. I don't expect you to . . . I mean, you don't have to pretend for me."

His smile was patient. "I'm not pretending."

I pushed the remains of my cereal around the edges of the bowl, biting my lip.

"Are you going to tell Charlie I'm your boyfriend or not?" he demanded.

"Is that what you are?" I suppressed my internal cringing at the thought of Edward and Charlie and the word *boyfriend* all in the same room at the same time.

"It's a loose interpretation of the word 'boy,' I'll admit."

"I was under the impression that you were something more, actually," I confessed, looking at the table.

"Well, I don't know if we need to give him all the gory

details." He reached across the table to lift my chin with a cold, gentle finger. "But he will need some explanation for why I'm around here so much. I don't want Chief Swan getting a restraining order put on me."

"Will you be?" I asked, suddenly anxious. "Will you really be here?"

"As long as you want me," he assured me.

"I'll always want you," I warned him. "Forever."

He walked slowly around the table, and, pausing a few feet away, he reached out to touch his fingertips to my cheek. His expression was unfathomable.

"Does that make you sad?" I asked.

He didn't answer. He stared into my eyes for an immeasurable period of time.

"Are you finished?" he finally asked.

I jumped up. "Yes."

"Get dressed — I'll wait here."

It was hard to decide what to wear. I doubted there were any etiquette books detailing how to dress when your vampire sweetheart takes you home to meet his vampire family. It was a relief to think the word to myself. I knew I shied away from it intentionally.

I ended up in my only skirt — long, khaki-colored, still casual. I put on the dark blue blouse he'd once complimented. A quick glance in the mirror told me my hair was entirely impossible, so I pulled it back into a ponytail.

"Okay." I bounced down the stairs. "I'm decent."

He was waiting at the foot of the stairs, closer than I'd

thought, and I bounded right into him. He steadied me, holding me a careful distance away for a few seconds before suddenly pulling me closer.

"Wrong again," he murmured in my ear. "You are utterly indecent — no one should look so tempting, it's not fair."

"Tempting how?" I asked. "I can change . . ."

He sighed, shaking his head. "You are *so* absurd." He pressed his cool lips delicately to my forehead, and the room spun. The smell of his breath made it impossible to think.

"Shall I explain how you are tempting me?" he said. It was clearly a rhetorical question. His fingers traced slowly down my spine, his breath coming more quickly against my skin. My hands were limp on his chest, and I felt light-headed again. He tilted his head slowly and touched his cool lips to mine for the second time, very carefully, parting them slightly.

And then I collapsed.

"Bella?" His voice was alarmed as he caught me and held me up.

"You . . . made . . . me . . . faint," I accused him dizzily.

"What am I going to do with you?" he groaned in exasperation. "Yesterday I kiss you, and you attack me! Today you pass out on me!"

I laughed weakly, letting his arms support me while my head spun.

"So much for being good at everything," he sighed.

"That's the problem." I was still dizzy. "You're *too* good. Far, far too good."

"Do you feel sick?" he asked; he'd seen me like this before.

"No — that wasn't the same kind of fainting at all. I don't know what happened." I shook my head apologetically. "I think I forgot to breathe."

"I can't take you anywhere like this."

"I'm fine," I insisted. "Your family is going to think I'm insane anyway, what's the difference?"

He measured my expression for a moment. "I'm very partial to that color with your skin," he offered unexpectedly. I flushed with pleasure, and looked away.

"Look, I'm trying really hard not to think about what I'm about to do, so can we go already?" I asked.

"And you're worried, not because you're headed to meet a houseful of vampires, but because you think those vampires won't approve of you, correct?"

"That's right," I answered immediately, hiding my surprise at his casual use of the word.

He shook his head. "You're incredible."

I realized, as he drove my truck out of the main part of town, that I had no idea where he lived. We passed over the bridge at the Calawah River, the road winding northward, the houses flashing past us growing farther apart, getting bigger. And then we were past the other houses altogether, driving through misty forest. I was trying to decide whether to ask or be patient, when he turned abruptly onto an unpaved road. It was unmarked, barely visible among the ferns. The forest encroached on both sides, leaving the road ahead only discernible for a few meters as it twisted, serpentlike, around the ancient trees.

And then, after a few miles, there was some thinning of the woods, and we were suddenly in a small meadow, or was it actually a lawn? The gloom of the forest didn't relent, though, for there were six primordial cedars that shaded an entire acre with their vast sweep of branches. The trees held their protecting shadow right up to the walls of the house that rose among them, making obsolete the deep porch that wrapped around the first story.

I don't know what I had expected, but it definitely wasn't this. The house was timeless, graceful, and probably a hundred years old. It was painted a soft, faded white, three stories tall, rectangular and well proportioned. The windows and doors were either part of the original structure or a perfect restoration. My truck was the only car in sight. I could hear the river close by, hidden in the obscurity of the forest.

"Wow."

"You like it?" He smiled.

"It . . . has a certain charm."

He pulled the end of my ponytail and chuckled.

"Ready?" he asked, opening my door.

"Not even a little bit — let's go." I tried to laugh, but it seemed to get stuck in my throat. I smoothed my hair nervously.

"You look lovely." He took my hand easily, without thinking about it.

We walked through the deep shade up to the porch. I

knew he could feel my tension; his thumb rubbed soothing circles into the back of my hand.

He opened the door for me.

The inside was even more surprising, less predictable,
than the exterior. It was very bright, very open, and very
large. This must have originally been several rooms, but the
walls had been removed from most of the first floor to create
one wide space. The back, south-facing wall had been entirely replaced with glass, and, beyond the shade of the
cedars, the lawn stretched bare to the wide river. A massive
curving staircase dominated the west side of the room. The
walls, the high-beamed ceiling, the wooden floors, and the
thick carpets were all varying shades of white.

Waiting to greet us, standing just to the left of the
door, on a raised portion of the floor by a spectacular grand
piano, were Edward's parents.

I'd seen Dr. Cullen before, of course, yet I couldn't help
but be struck again by his youth, his outrageous perfection. At his side was Esme, I assumed, the only one of the
family I'd never seen before. She had the same pale, beautiful features as the rest of them. Something about her
heart-shaped face, her billows of soft, caramel-colored
hair, reminded me of the ingenues of the silent-movie era.
She was small, slender, yet less angular, more rounded
than the others. They were both dressed casually, in light
colors that matched the inside of the house. They smiled
in welcome, but made no move to approach us. Trying not
to frighten me, I guessed.

"Carlisle, Esme," Edward's voice broke the short silence, "this is Bella."

"You're very welcome, Bella." Carlisle's step was measured, careful as he approached me. He raised his hand tentatively, and I stepped forward to shake hands with him.

"It's nice to see you again, Dr. Cullen."

"Please, call me Carlisle."

"Carlisle." I grinned at him, my sudden confidence surprising me. I could feel Edward's relief at my side.

Esme smiled and stepped forward as well, reaching for my hand. Her cold, stone grasp was just as I expected.

"It's very nice to know you," she said sincerely.

"Thank you. I'm glad to meet you, too." And I was. It was like meeting a fairy tale — Snow White, in the flesh.

"Where are Alice and Jasper?" Edward asked, but no one answered, as they had just appeared at the top of the wide staircase.

"Hey, Edward!" Alice called enthusiastically. She ran down the stairs, a streak of black hair and white skin, coming to a sudden and graceful stop in front of me. Carlisle and Esme shot warning glances at her, but I liked it. It was natural — for her, anyway.

"Hi, Bella!" Alice said, and she bounced forward to kiss my cheek. If Carlisle and Esme had looked cautious before, they now looked staggered. There was shock in my eyes, too, but I was also very pleased that she seemed to approve of me so entirely. I was startled to feel Edward stiffen at my side. I glanced at his face, but his expression was unreadable.

"You do smell nice, I never noticed before," she commented, to my extreme embarrassment.

No one else seemed to know quite what to say, and then Jasper was there — tall and leonine. A feeling of ease spread through me, and I was suddenly comfortable despite where I was. Edward stared at Jasper, raising one eyebrow, and I remembered what Jasper could do.

"Hello, Bella," Jasper said. He kept his distance, not offering to shake my hand. But it was impossible to feel awkward near him.

"Hello, Jasper." I smiled at him shyly, and then at the others. "It's nice to meet you all — you have a very beautiful home," I added conventionally.

"Thank you," Esme said. "We're so glad that you came." She spoke with feeling, and I realized that she thought I was brave.

I also realized that Rosalie and Emmett were nowhere to be seen, and I remembered Edward's too-innocent denial when I'd asked him if the others didn't like me.

Carlisle's expression distracted me from this train of thought; he was gazing meaningfully at Edward with an intense expression. Out of the corner of my eye, I saw Edward nod once.

I looked away, trying to be polite. My eyes wandered again to the beautiful instrument on the platform by the door. I suddenly remembered my childhood fantasy that, should I ever win a lottery, I would buy a grand piano for my mother. She wasn't really good — she only played for herself on our secondhand upright — but I loved to watch her play. She was happy, absorbed — she seemed like a new, mysterious being to me then, someone outside the "mom" persona I took for granted. She'd put me through lessons, of course, but like most kids, I whined until she let me quit.

Esme noticed my preoccupation.

"Do you play?" she asked, inclining her head toward the piano.

I shook my head. "Not at all. But it's so beautiful. Is it yours?"

"No," she laughed. "Edward didn't tell you he was musical?"

"No." I glared at his suddenly innocent expression with narrowed eyes. "I should have known, I guess."

Esme raised her delicate eyebrows in confusion.

"Edward can do everything, right?" I explained.

Jasper snickered and Esme gave Edward a reproving look.

"I hope you haven't been showing off — it's rude," she scolded.

"Just a bit," he laughed freely. Her face softened at the sound, and they shared a brief look that I didn't understand, though Esme's face seemed almost smug.

"He's been too modest, actually," I corrected.

"Well, play for her," Esme encouraged.

"You just said showing off was rude," he objected.

"There are exceptions to every rule," she replied.

"I'd like to hear you play," I volunteered.

"It's settled then." Esme pushed him toward the piano. He pulled me along, sitting me on the bench beside him.

He gave me a long, exasperated look before he turned to the keys.

And then his fingers flowed swiftly across the ivory, and the room was filled with a composition so complex, so luxuriant, it was impossible to believe only one set of hands played. I felt my chin drop, my mouth open in astonishment, and heard low chuckles behind me at my reaction.

Edward looked at me casually, the music still surging around us without a break, and winked. "Do you like it?"

"You wrote this?" I gasped, understanding.

He nodded. "It's Esme's favorite."

I closed my eyes, shaking my head.

"What's wrong?"

"I'm feeling extremely insignificant."

The music slowed, transforming into something softer, and to my surprise I detected the melody of his lullaby weaving through the profusion of notes.

"You inspired this one," he said softly. The music grew unbearably sweet.

I couldn't speak.

"They like you, you know," he said conversationally. "Esme especially."

I glanced behind me, but the huge room was empty now. "Where did they go?"

"Very subtly giving us some privacy, I suppose."

I sighed. "*They* like me. But Rosalie and Emmett . . ." I trailed off, not sure how to express my doubts.

He frowned. "Don't worry about Rosalie," he said, his eyes wide and persuasive. "She'll come around."

I pursed my lips skeptically. "Emmett?"

"Well, he thinks *I'm* a lunatic, it's true, but he doesn't

have a problem with you. He's trying to reason with Rosalie."

"What is it that upsets her?" I wasn't sure if I wanted to know the answer.

He sighed deeply. "Rosalie struggles the most with . . . with what we are. It's hard for her to have someone on the outside know the truth. And she's a little jealous."

"*Rosalie* is jealous of *me*?" I asked incredulously. I tried to imagine a universe in which someone as breathtaking as Rosalie would have any possible reason to feel jealous of someone like me.

"You're human." He shrugged. "She wishes that she were, too."

"Oh," I muttered, still stunned. "Even Jasper, though . . ."

"That's really my fault," he said. "I told you he was the most recent to try our way of life. I warned him to keep his distance."

I thought about the reason for that, and shuddered.

"Esme and Carlisle . . . ?" I continued quickly, to keep him from noticing.

"Are happy to see me happy. Actually, Esme wouldn't care if you had a third eye and webbed feet. All this time she's been worried about me, afraid that there was some-thing missing from my essential makeup, that I was too young when Carlisle changed me. . . . She's ecstatic. Every time I touch you, she just about chokes with satisfaction."

"Alice seems very . . . enthusiastic."

"Alice has her own way of looking at things," he said through tight lips.

"And you're not going to explain that, are you?"

A moment of wordless communication passed between us. He realized that I knew he was keeping something from me. I realized that he wasn't going to give anything away. Not now.

"So what was Carlisle telling you before?"

His eyebrows pulled together. "You noticed that, did you?"

I shrugged. "Of course."

He looked at me thoughtfully for a few seconds before answering. "He wanted to tell me some news — he didn't know if it was something I would share with you."

"Will you?"

"I have to, because I'm going to be a little . . . overbearingly protective over the next few days — or weeks — and I wouldn't want you to think I'm naturally a tyrant."

"What's wrong?"

"Nothing's wrong, exactly. Alice just sees some visitors coming soon. They know we're here, and they're curious."

"Visitors?"

"Yes . . . well, they aren't like us, of course — in their hunting habits, I mean. They probably won't come into town at all, but I'm certainly not going to let you out of my sight till they're gone."

I shivered.

"Finally, a rational response!" he murmured. "I was beginning to think you had no sense of self-preservation at all."

I let that one pass, looking away, my eyes wandering again around the spacious room.

He followed my gaze. "Not what you expected, is it?" he asked, his voice smug.

"No," I admitted.

"No coffins, no piled skulls in the corners; I don't even think we have cobwebs . . . what a disappointment this must be for you," he continued slyly.

I ignored his teasing. "It's so light . . . so open."

He was more serious when he answered. "It's the one place we never have to hide."

The song he was still playing, my song, drifted to an end, the final chords shifting to a more melancholy key. The last note hovered poignantly in the silence.

"Thank you," I murmured. I realized there were tears in my eyes. I dabbed at them, embarrassed.

He touched the corner of my eye, trapping one I missed. He lifted his finger, examining the drop of moisture broodingly. Then, so quickly I couldn't be positive that he really did, he put his finger to his mouth to taste it.

I looked at him questioningly, and he gazed back for a long moment before he finally smiled.

"Do you want to see the rest of the house?"

"No coffins?" I verified, the sarcasm in my voice not entirely masking the slight but genuine anxiety I felt.

He laughed, taking my hand, leading me away from the piano.

"No coffins," he promised.

We walked up the massive staircase, my hand trailing along the satin-smooth rail. The long hall at the top of the stairs was paneled with a honey-colored wood, the same as the floorboards.

"Rosalie and Emmett's room . . . Carlisle's office . . . Alice's room . . ." He gestured as he led me past the doors.

He would have continued, but I stopped dead at the end of the hall, staring incredulously at the ornament hanging on the wall above my head. Edward chuckled at my bewildered expression.

"You can laugh," he said. "It *is* sort of ironic."

I didn't laugh. My hand raised automatically, one finger extended as if to touch the large wooden cross, its dark patina contrasting with the lighter tone of the wall. I didn't touch it, though I was curious if the aged wood would feel as silky as it looked.

"It must be very old," I guessed.

He shrugged. "Early sixteen-thirties, more or less."

I looked away from the cross to stare at him.

"Why do you keep this here?" I wondered.

"Nostalgia. It belonged to Carlisle's father."

"He collected antiques?" I suggested doubtfully.

"No. He carved this himself. It hung on the wall above the pulpit in the vicarage where he preached."

I wasn't sure if my face betrayed my shock, but I returned to gazing at the simple, ancient cross, just in case. I quickly did the mental math; the cross was over three hundred and seventy years old. The silence stretched on as I struggled to wrap my mind around the concept of so many years.

"Are you all right?" He sounded worried.

"How old is Carlisle?" I asked quietly, ignoring his question, still staring up.

"He just celebrated his three hundred and sixty-second

birthday," Edward said. I looked back at him, a million questions in my eyes.

He watched me carefully as he spoke.

"Carlisle was born in London, in the sixteen-forties, he believes. Time wasn't marked as accurately then, for the common people anyway. It was just before Cromwell's rule, though."

I kept my face composed, aware of his scrutiny as I listened. It was easier if I didn't try to believe.

"He was the only son of an Anglican pastor. His mother died giving birth to him. His father was an intolerant man. As the Protestants came into power, he was enthusiastic in his persecution of Roman Catholics and other religions. He also believed very strongly in the reality of evil. He led hunts for witches, werewolves . . . and vampires." I grew very still at the word. I'm sure he noticed, but he went on without pausing.

"They burned a lot of innocent people — of course the real creatures that he sought were not so easy to catch.

"When the pastor grew old, he placed his obedient son in charge of the raids. At first Carlisle was a disappointment; he was not quick to accuse, to see demons where they did not exist. But he was persistent, and more clever than his father. He actually discovered a coven of true vampires that lived hidden in the sewers of the city, only coming out by night to hunt. In those days, when monsters were not just myths and legends, that was the way many lived.

"The people gathered their pitchforks and torches, of course" — his brief laugh was darker now — "and waited where Carlisle had seen the monsters exit into the street. Eventually one emerged."

His voice was very quiet; I strained to catch the words.

"He must have been ancient, and weak with hunger. Carlisle heard him call out in Latin to the others when he caught the scent of the mob. He ran through the streets, and Carlisle — he was twenty-three and very fast — was in the lead of the pursuit. The creature could have easily outrun them, but Carlisle thinks he was too hungry, so he turned and attacked. He fell on Carlisle first, but the others were close behind, and he turned to defend himself. He killed two men, and made off with a third, leaving Carlisle bleeding in the street."

He paused. I could sense he was editing something, keeping something from me.

"Carlisle knew what his father would do. The bodies would be burned — anything infected by the monster must be destroyed. Carlisle acted instinctively to save his own life. He crawled away from the alley while the mob followed the fiend and his victim. He hid in a cellar, buried himself in rotting potatoes for three days. It's a miracle he was able to keep silent, to stay undiscovered.

"It was over then, and he realized what he had become."

I'm not sure what my face was revealing, but he suddenly broke off.

"How are you feeling?" he asked.

"I'm fine," I assured him. And, though I bit my lip

in hesitation, he must have seen the curiosity burning in my eyes.

He smiled. "I expect you have a few more questions for me."

"A few."

His smile widened over his brilliant teeth. He started back down the hall, pulling me along by the hand. "Come on, then," he encouraged. "I'll show you."

16. CARLISLE

HE LED ME BACK TO THE ROOM THAT HE'D POINTED OUT as Carlisle's office. He paused outside the door for an instant.

"Come in," Carlisle's voice invited.

Edward opened the door to a high-ceilinged room with tall, west-facing windows. The walls were paneled again, in a darker wood — where they were visible. Most of the wall space was taken up by towering bookshelves that reached high above my head and held more books than I'd ever seen outside a library.

Carlisle sat behind a huge mahogany desk in a leather chair. He was just placing a bookmark in the pages of the thick volume he held. The room was how I'd always imagined a college dean's would look — only Carlisle looked too young to fit the part.

"What can I do for you?" he asked us pleasantly, rising from his seat.

"I wanted to show Bella some of our history," Edward said. "Well, your history, actually."

"We didn't mean to disturb you," I apologized.

"Not at all. Where are you going to start?"

"The Waggoner," Edward replied, placing one hand lightly on my shoulder and spinning me around to look back toward the door we'd just come through. Every time he touched me, in even the most casual way, my heart had an audible reaction. It was more embarrassing with Carlisle there.

The wall we faced now was different from the others. Instead of bookshelves, this wall was crowded with framed pictures of all sizes, some in vibrant colors, others dull monochromes. I searched for some logic, some binding motif the collection had in common, but I found nothing in my hasty examination.

Edward pulled me toward the far left side, standing me in front of a small square oil painting in a plain wooden frame. This one did not stand out among the bigger and brighter pieces; painted in varying tones of sepia, it depicted a miniature city full of steeply slanted roofs, with thin spires atop a few scattered towers. A wide river filled the foreground, crossed by a bridge covered with structures that looked like tiny cathedrals.

"London in the sixteen-fifties," Edward said.

"The London of my youth," Carlisle added, from a few

feet behind us. I flinched; I hadn't heard him approach. Edward squeezed my hand.

"Will *you* tell the story?" Edward asked. I twisted a little to see Carlisle's reaction.

He met my glance and smiled. "I would," he replied. "But I'm actually running a bit late. The hospital called this morning — Dr. Snow is taking a sick day. Besides, you know the stories as well as I do," he added, grinning at Edward now.

It was a strange combination to absorb — the everyday concerns of the town doctor stuck in the middle of a discussion of his early days in seventeenth-century London.

It was also unsettling to know that he spoke aloud only for my benefit.

After another warm smile for me, Carlisle left the room.

I stared at the little picture of Carlisle's hometown for a long moment.

"What happened then?" I finally asked, staring up at Edward, who was watching me. "When he realized what had happened to him?"

He glanced back to the paintings, and I looked to see which image caught his interest now. It was a larger landscape in dull fall colors — an empty, shadowed meadow in a forest, with a craggy peak in the distance.

"When he knew what he had become," Edward said quietly, "he rebelled against it. He tried to destroy himself. But that's not easily done."

"How?" I didn't mean to say it aloud, but the word broke through my shock.

"He jumped from great heights," Edward told me, his

voice impassive. "He tried to drown himself in the ocean . . . but he was young to the new life, and very strong. It is amazing that he was able to resist . . . feeding . . . while he was still so new. The instinct is more powerful then, it takes over everything. But he was so repelled by himself that he had the strength to try to kill himself with starvation."

"Is that possible?" My voice was faint.

"No, there are very few ways we can be killed."

I opened my mouth to ask, but he spoke before I could.

"So he grew very hungry, and eventually weak. He strayed as far as he could from the human populace, recognizing that his willpower was weakening, too. For months he wandered by night, seeking the loneliest places, loathing himself.

"One night, a herd of deer passed his hiding place. He was so wild with thirst that he attacked without a thought. His strength returned and he realized there was an alternative to being the vile monster he feared. Had he not eaten venison in his former life? Over the next months his new philosophy was born. He could exist without being a demon. He found himself again.

"He began to make better use of his time. He'd always been intelligent, eager to learn. Now he had unlimited time before him. He studied by night, planned by day. He swam to France and —"

"He *swam* to France?"

"People swim the Channel all the time, Bella," he reminded me patiently.

"That's true, I guess. It just sounded funny in that context. Go on."

"Swimming is easy for us —"

"Everything is easy for *you,*" I griped.

He waited, his expression amused.

"I won't interrupt again, I promise."

He chuckled darkly, and finished his sentence. "Because, technically, we don't need to breathe."

"You —"

"No, no, you promised." He laughed, putting his cold finger lightly to my lips. "Do you want to hear the story or not?"

"You can't spring something like that on me, and then expect me not to say anything," I mumbled against his finger.

He lifted his hand, moving it to rest against my neck. The speed of my heart reacted to that, but I persisted.

"You don't have to *breathe?*" I demanded.

"No, it's not necessary. Just a habit." He shrugged.

"How long can you go . . . without *breathing?*"

"Indefinitely, I suppose; I don't know. It gets a bit uncomfortable — being without a sense of smell."

"A bit uncomfortable," I echoed.

I wasn't paying attention to my own expression, but something in it made him grow somber. His hand dropped to his side and he stood very still, his eyes intent on my face. The silence lengthened. His features were immobile as stone.

"What is it?" I whispered, touching his frozen face.

His face softened under my hand, and he sighed. "I keep waiting for it to happen."

"For what to happen?"

"I know that at some point, something I tell you or something you see is going to be too much. And then you'll run away from me, screaming as you go." He smiled half a smile, but his eyes were serious. "I won't stop you. I want this to happen, because I want you to be safe. And yet, I want to be with you. The two desires are impossible to reconcile. . . ." He trailed off, staring at my face. Waiting.

"I'm not running anywhere," I promised.

"We'll see," he said, smiling again.

I frowned at him. "So, go on — Carlisle was swimming to France."

He paused, getting back into his story. Reflexively, his eyes flickered to another picture — the most colorful of them all, the most ornately framed, and the largest; it was twice as wide as the door it hung next to. The canvas overflowed with bright figures in swirling robes, writhing around long pillars and off marbled balconies. I couldn't tell if it represented Greek mythology, or if the characters floating in the clouds above were meant to be biblical.

"Carlisle swam to France, and continued on through Europe, to the universities there. By night he studied music, science, medicine — and found his calling, his penance, in that, in saving human lives." His expression became awed, almost reverent. "I can't adequately describe the struggle; it took Carlisle two centuries of torturous effort to perfect his self-control. Now he is all but immune to the scent of human blood, and he is able to do the work he loves without agony. He finds a great deal of peace there, at the hospital. . . ." Edward stared off into space for a long moment. Suddenly he seemed to recall his purpose. He tapped his finger against the huge painting in front of us.

"He was studying in Italy when he discovered the others there. They were much more civilized and educated than the wraiths of the London sewers."

He touched a comparatively sedate quartet of figures painted on the highest balcony, looking down calmly on the mayhem below them. I examined the grouping carefully and realized, with a startled laugh, that I recognized the golden-haired man.

"Solimena was greatly inspired by Carlisle's friends. He often painted them as gods," Edward chuckled. "Aro, Marcus, Caius," he said, indicating the other three, two black-haired, one snowy-white. "Nighttime patrons of the arts."

"What happened to them?" I wondered aloud, my fingertip hovering a centimeter from the figures on the canvas.

"They're still there." He shrugged. "As they have been for who knows how many millennia. Carlisle stayed with them only for a short time, just a few decades. He greatly admired their civility, their refinement, but they persisted in trying to cure his aversion to 'his natural food source,' as they called it. They tried to persuade him, and he tried to persuade them, to no avail. At that point, Carlisle decided to try the New World. He dreamed of finding others like himself. He was very lonely, you see.

"He didn't find anyone for a long time. But, as monsters became the stuff of fairy tales, he found he could interact with unsuspecting humans as if he were one of them. He began practicing medicine. But the companionship he craved evaded him; he couldn't risk familiarity.

"When the influenza epidemic hit, he was working nights in a hospital in Chicago. He'd been turning over an idea in his mind for several years, and he had almost decided to act — since he couldn't find a companion, he would create one. He wasn't absolutely sure how his own transformation had occurred, so he was hesitant. And he was loath to steal anyone's life the way his had been stolen. It was in that frame of mind that he found me. There was no hope for me; I was left in a ward with the dying. He had nursed my parents, and knew I was alone. He decided to try . . ."

His voice, nearly a whisper now, trailed off. He stared unseeingly through the west windows. I wondered which images filled his mind now, Carlisle's memories or his own. I waited quietly.

When he turned back to me, a gentle angel's smile lit his expression.

"And so we've come full circle," he concluded.

"Have you always stayed with Carlisle, then?" I wondered.

"Almost always." He put his hand lightly on my waist

and pulled me with him as he walked through the door. I stared back at the wall of pictures, wondering if I would ever get to hear the other stories.

Edward didn't say any more as we walked down the hall, so I asked, "Almost?"

He sighed, seeming reluctant to answer. "Well, I had a typical bout of rebellious adolescence — about ten years after I was . . . born . . . created, whatever you want to call it. I wasn't sold on his life of abstinence, and I resented him for curbing my appetite. So I went off on my own for a time."

"Really?" I was intrigued, rather than frightened, as I perhaps should have been.

He could tell. I vaguely realized that we were headed up the next flight of stairs, but I wasn't paying much attention to my surroundings.

"That doesn't repulse you?"

"No."

"Why not?"

"I guess . . . it sounds reasonable."

He barked a laugh, more loudly than before. We were at the top of the stairs now, in another paneled hallway.

"From the time of my new birth," he murmured, "I had the advantage of knowing what everyone around me was thinking, both human and non-human alike. That's why it took me ten years to defy Carlisle — I could read his perfect sincerity, understand exactly why he lived the way he did.

"It took me only a few years to return to Carlisle and recommit to his vision. I thought I would be exempt from the . . . depression . . . that accompanies a conscience. Because I knew the thoughts of my prey, I could pass over the innocent and pursue only the evil. If I followed a murderer down a dark alley where he stalked a young girl — if I saved her, then surely I wasn't so terrible."

I shivered, imagining only too clearly what he described — the alley at night, the frightened girl, the dark man behind her. And Edward, Edward as he hunted, terrible and glorious as a young god, unstoppable. Would she have been grateful, that girl, or more frightened than before?

"But as time went on, I began to see the monster in my eyes. I couldn't escape the debt of so much human life taken, no matter how justified. And I went back to Carlisle and Esme. They welcomed me back like the prodigal. It was more than I deserved."

We'd come to a stop in front of the last door in the hall.

"My room," he informed me, opening it and pulling me through.

His room faced south, with a wall-sized window like the great room below. The whole back side of the house must be glass. His view looked down on the winding Sol Duc River, across the untouched forest to the Olympic Mountain range. The mountains were much closer than I would have believed.

The western wall was completely covered with shelf after shelf of CDs. His room was better stocked than a music store. In the corner was a sophisticated-looking sound system, the kind I was afraid to touch because I'd be sure to break something. There was no bed, only a wide and inviting black leather sofa. The floor was covered with a thick golden carpet, and the walls were hung with heavy fabric in a slightly darker shade.

"Good acoustics?" I guessed.

He chuckled and nodded.

He picked up a remote and turned the stereo on. It was quiet, but the soft jazz number sounded like the band was in the room with us. I went to look at his mind-boggling music collection.

"How do you have these organized?" I asked, unable to find any rhyme or reason to the titles.

He wasn't paying attention.

"Ummm, by year, and then by personal preference within that frame," he said absently.

I turned, and he was looking at me with a peculiar expression in his eyes.

"What?"

"I was prepared to feel . . . relieved. Having you know about everything, not needing to keep secrets from you. But I didn't expect to feel more than that. I *like* it. It makes me . . . happy." He shrugged, smiling slightly.

"I'm glad," I said, smiling back. I'd worried that he might regret telling me these things. It was good to know that wasn't the case.

But then, as his eyes dissected my expression, his smile faded and his forehead creased.

"You're still waiting for the running and the screaming, aren't you?" I guessed.

A faint smile touched his lips, and he nodded.

"I hate to burst your bubble, but you're really not as scary as you think you are. I don't find you scary at all, actually," I lied casually.

He stopped, raising his eyebrows in blatant disbelief. Then he flashed a wide, wicked smile.

"You *really* shouldn't have said that," he chuckled.

He growled, a low sound in the back of his throat; his lips curled back over his perfect teeth. His body shifted suddenly, half-crouched, tensed like a lion about to pounce.

I backed away from him, glaring.

"You wouldn't."

I didn't see him leap at me — it was much too fast. I only found myself suddenly airborne, and then we crashed onto the sofa, knocking it into the wall. All the while, his arms formed an iron cage of protection around me — I was barely jostled. But I still was gasping as I tried to right myself.

He wasn't having that. He curled me into a ball against his chest, holding me more securely than iron chains. I glared at him in alarm, but he seemed well in control, his jaw relaxed as he grinned, his eyes bright only with humor.

"You were saying?" he growled playfully.

"That you are a very, very terrifying monster," I said, my sarcasm marred a bit by my breathless voice.

"Much better," he approved.

"Um." I struggled. "Can I get up now?"

He just laughed.

"Can we come in?" a soft voice sounded from the hall.

I struggled to free myself, but Edward merely readjusted

me so that I was somewhat more conventionally seated on his lap. I could see it was Alice, then, and Jasper behind her in the doorway. My cheeks burned, but Edward seemed at ease.

"Go ahead." Edward was still chuckling quietly.

Alice seemed to find nothing unusual in our embrace; she walked — almost danced, her movements were so graceful — to the center of the room, where she folded herself sinuously onto the floor. Jasper, however, paused at the door, his expression a trifle shocked. He stared at Edward's face, and I wondered if he was tasting the atmosphere with his unusual sensitivity.

"It sounded like you were having Bella for lunch, and we came to see if you would share," Alice announced.

I stiffened for an instant, until I realized Edward was grinning — whether at her comment or my response, I couldn't tell.

"Sorry, I don't believe I have enough to spare," he replied, his arms holding me recklessly close.

"Actually," Jasper said, smiling despite himself as he walked into the room, "Alice says there's going to be a real storm tonight, and Emmett wants to play ball. Are you game?"

The words were all common enough, but the context confused me. I gathered that Alice was a bit more reliable than the weatherman, though.

Edward's eyes lit up, but he hesitated.

"Of course you should bring Bella," Alice chirped. I thought I saw Jasper throw a quick glance at her.

"Do you want to go?" Edward asked me, excited, his expression vivid.

"Sure." I couldn't disappoint such a face. "Um, where are we going?"

"We have to wait for thunder to play ball — you'll see why," he promised.

"Will I need an umbrella?"

They all three laughed aloud.

"Will she?" Jasper asked Alice.

"No." She was positive. "The storm will hit over town. It should be dry enough in the clearing."

"Good, then." The enthusiasm in Jasper's voice was catching, naturally. I found myself eager, rather than scared stiff.

"Let's go see if Carlisle will come." Alice bounded up and to the door in a fashion that would break any ballerina's heart.

"Like you don't know," Jasper teased, and they were swiftly on their way. Jasper managed to inconspicuously close the door behind them.

"What will we be playing?" I demanded.

"*You* will be watching," Edward clarified. "We will be playing baseball."

I rolled my eyes. "Vampires like baseball?"

"It's the American pastime," he said with mock solemnity.

17. THE GAME

It was just beginning to drizzle when Edward turned onto my street. Up until that moment, I'd had no doubt that he'd be staying with me while I spent a few interim hours in the real world.

And then I saw the black car, a weathered Ford, parked in Charlie's driveway — and heard Edward mutter something unintelligible in a low, harsh voice.

Leaning away from the rain under the shallow front porch, Jacob Black stood behind his father's wheelchair. Billy's face was impassive as stone as Edward parked my truck against the curb. Jacob stared down, his expression mortified.

Edward's low voice was furious. "This is crossing the line."

"He came to warn Charlie?" I guessed, more horrified than angry.

Edward just nodded, answering Billy's gaze through the rain with narrowed eyes.

I felt weak with relief that Charlie wasn't home yet.

"Let me deal with this," I suggested. Edward's black glare made me anxious.

To my surprise, he agreed. "That's probably best. Be careful, though. The child has no idea."

I bridled a little at the word *child*. "Jacob is not that much younger than I am," I reminded him.

He looked at me then, his anger abruptly fading. "Oh, I know," he assured me with a grin.

I sighed and put my hand on the door handle.

"Get them inside," he instructed, "so I can leave. I'll be back around dusk."

"Do you want my truck?" I offered, meanwhile wondering how I would explain its absence to Charlie.

He rolled his eyes. "I could *walk* home faster than this truck moves."

"You don't have to leave," I said wistfully.

He smiled at my glum expression. "Actually, I do. After you get rid of them" — he threw a dark glance in the Blacks' direction — "you still have to prepare Charlie to meet your new boyfriend." He grinned widely, showing all of his teeth.

I groaned. "Thanks a lot."

He smiled the crooked smile that I loved. "I'll be back soon," he promised. His eyes flickered back to the porch, and then he leaned in to swiftly kiss me just under the edge of my jaw. My heart lurched frantically, and I, too, glanced toward the porch. Billy's face was no longer impassive, and his hands clutched at the armrests of his chair.

"Soon," I stressed as I opened the door and stepped out into the rain.

I could feel his eyes on my back as I half-ran through the light sprinkle toward the porch.

"Hey, Billy. Hi, Jacob." I greeted them as cheerfully as I could manage. "Charlie's gone for the day — I hope you haven't been waiting long."

"Not long," Billy said in a subdued tone. His black eyes were piercing. "I just wanted to bring this up." He indicated a brown paper sack resting in his lap.

"Thanks," I said, though I had no idea what it could be. "Why don't you come in for a minute and dry off?"

I pretended to be oblivious to his intense scrutiny as I unlocked the door, and waved them in ahead of me.

"Here, let me take that," I offered, turning to shut the door. I allowed myself one last glance at Edward. He was waiting, perfectly still, his eyes solemn.

"You'll want to put it in the fridge," Billy noted as he handed me the package. "It's some of Harry Clearwater's homemade fish fry — Charlie's favorite. The fridge keeps it drier." He shrugged.

"Thanks," I repeated, but with feeling this time. "I was

running out of new ways to fix fish, and he's bound to bring home more tonight."

"Fishing again?" Billy asked with a subtle gleam in his eye. "Down at the usual spot? Maybe I'll run by and see him."

"No," I quickly lied, my face going hard. "He was headed someplace new . . . but I have no idea where."

He took in my changed expression, and it made him thoughtful.

"Jake," he said, still appraising me. "Why don't you go get that new picture of Rebecca out of the car? I'll leave that for Charlie, too."

"Where is it?" Jacob asked, his voice morose. I glanced at him, but he was staring at the floor, his eyebrows pulling together.

"I think I saw it in the trunk," Billy said. "You may have to dig for it."

Jacob slouched back out into the rain.

Billy and I faced each other in silence. After a few seconds, the quiet started to feel awkward, so I turned and headed to the kitchen. I could hear his wet wheels squeak against the linoleum as he followed.

I shoved the bag onto the crowded top shelf of the fridge, and spun around to confront him. His deeply lined face was unreadable.

"Charlie won't be back for a long time." My voice was almost rude.

He nodded in agreement, but said nothing.

"Thanks again for the fish fry," I hinted.

He continued nodding. I sighed and folded my arms across my chest.

He seemed to sense that I had given up on small talk. "Bella," he said, and then he hesitated.

I waited.

"Bella," he said again, "Charlie is one of my best friends."

"Yes."

He spoke each word carefully in his rumbling voice. "I noticed you've been spending time with one of the Cullens."

"Yes," I repeated curtly.

His eyes narrowed. "Maybe it's none of my business, but I don't think that is such a good idea."

"You're right," I agreed. "It *is* none of your business."

He raised his graying eyebrows at my tone. "You probably don't know this, but the Cullen family has an unpleasant reputation on the reservation."

"Actually, I did know that," I informed him in a hard voice. This surprised him. "But that reputation couldn't be deserved, could it? Because the Cullens never set foot on the reservation, do they?" I could see that my less than subtle reminder of the agreement that both bound and protected his tribe pulled him up short.

"That's true," he acceded, his eyes guarded. "You seem . . . well informed about the Cullens. More informed than I expected."

I stared him down. "Maybe even better informed than you are."

He pursed his thick lips as he considered that. "Maybe,"

he allowed, but his eyes were shrewd. "Is Charlie as well informed?"

He had found the weak chink in my armor.

"Charlie likes the Cullens a lot," I hedged. He clearly understood my evasion. His expression was unhappy, but unsurprised.

"It's not my business," he said. "But it may be Charlie's."

"Though it would be my business, again, whether or not I think that it's Charlie's business, right?"

I wondered if he even understood my confused question as I struggled not to say anything compromising. But he seemed to. He thought about it while the rain picked up against the roof, the only sound breaking the silence.

"Yes," he finally surrendered. "I guess that's your business, too."

I sighed with relief. "Thanks, Billy."

"Just think about what you're doing, Bella," he urged.

"Okay," I agreed quickly.

He frowned. "What I meant to say was, don't do what you're doing."

I looked into his eyes, filled with nothing but concern for me, and there was nothing I could say.

Just then the front door banged loudly, and I jumped at the sound.

"There's no picture anywhere in that car." Jacob's complaining voice reached us before he did. The shoulders of his shirt were stained with the rain, his hair dripping, when he rounded the corner.

"Hmm," Billy grunted, suddenly detached, spinning his chair around to face his son. "I guess I left it at home."

Jacob rolled his eyes dramatically. "Great."

"Well, Bella, tell Charlie" — Billy paused before continuing — "that we stopped by, I mean."

"I will," I muttered.

Jacob was surprised. "Are we leaving already?"

"Charlie's gonna be out late," Billy explained as he rolled himself past Jacob.

"Oh." Jacob looked disappointed. "Well, I guess I'll see you later, then, Bella."

"Sure," I agreed.

"Take care," Billy warned me. I didn't answer.

Jacob helped his father out the door. I waved briefly, glancing swiftly toward my now-empty truck, and then shut the door before they were gone.

I stood in the hallway for a minute, listening to the sound of their car as it backed out and drove away. I stayed where I was, waiting for the irritation and anxiety to subside. When the tension eventually faded a bit, I headed upstairs to change out of my dressy clothes.

I tried on a couple of different tops, not sure what to expect tonight. As I concentrated on what was coming, what had just passed became insignificant. Now that I was removed from Jasper's and Edward's influence, I began to make up for not being terrified before. I gave up quickly on choosing an outfit — throwing on an old flannel shirt and jeans — knowing I would be in my raincoat all night anyway.

The phone rang and I sprinted downstairs to get it. There was only one voice I wanted to hear; anything else would be a disappointment. But I knew that if *he* wanted to talk to me, he'd probably just materialize in my room.

"Hello?" I asked, breathless.

"Bella? It's me," Jessica said.

"Oh, hey, Jess." I scrambled for a moment to come back down to reality. It felt like months rather than days since I'd spoken to Jess. "How was the dance?"

"It was so much fun!" Jessica gushed. Needing no more invitation than that, she launched into a minute-by-minute account of the previous night. I *mmm*'d and *ahh*'d at the right places, but it wasn't easy to concentrate. Jessica, Mike, the dance, the school — they all seemed strangely irrelevant at the moment. My eyes kept flashing to the window, trying to judge the degree of light behind the heavy clouds.

"Did you hear what I said, Bella?" Jess asked, irritated.

"I'm sorry, what?"

"I said, Mike kissed me! Can you believe it?"

"That's wonderful, Jess," I said.

"So what did *you* do yesterday?" Jessica challenged, still sounding bothered by my lack of attention. Or maybe she was upset because I hadn't asked for details.

"Nothing, really. I just hung around outside to enjoy the sun."

I heard Charlie's car in the garage.

"Did you ever hear anything more from Edward Cullen?"

The front door slammed and I could hear Charlie banging around under the stairs, putting his tackle away.

"Um." I hesitated, not sure what my story was anymore.

"Hi there, kiddo!" Charlie called as he walked into the kitchen. I waved at him.

Jess heard his voice. "Oh, your dad's there. Never mind — we'll talk tomorrow. See you in Trig."

"See ya, Jess." I hung up the phone.

"Hey, Dad," I said. He was scrubbing his hands in the sink. "Where's the fish?"

"I put it out in the freezer."

"I'll go grab a few pieces before they freeze — Billy dropped off some of Harry Clearwater's fish fry this afternoon." I worked to sound enthusiastic.

"He did?" Charlie's eyes lit up. "That's my favorite."

Charlie cleaned up while I got dinner ready. It didn't take long till we were sitting at the table, eating in silence. Charlie was enjoying his food. I was wondering desperately how to fulfill my assignment, struggling to think of a way to broach the subject.

"What did you do with yourself today?" he asked, snapping me out of my reverie.

"Well, this afternoon I just hung out around the house. . . ." Only the very recent part of this afternoon, actually. I tried to keep my voice upbeat, but my stomach was hollow. "And this morning I was over at the Cullens'."

Charlie dropped his fork.

"Dr. Cullen's place?" he asked in astonishment.

I pretended not to notice his reaction. "Yeah."

"What were you doing there?" He hadn't picked his fork back up.

"Well, I sort of have a date with Edward Cullen

tonight, and he wanted to introduce me to his parents . . . Dad?"

It appeared that Charlie was having an aneurysm.

"Dad, are you all right?"

"You are going out with Edward Cullen?" he thundered.

Uh-oh. "I thought you liked the Cullens."

"He's too old for you," he ranted.

"We're both juniors," I corrected, though he was more right than he dreamed.

"Wait . . ." He paused. "Which one is Edwin?"

"*Edward* is the youngest, the one with the reddish brown hair." The beautiful one, the godlike one . . .

"Oh, well, that's" — he struggled — "better, I guess. I don't like the look of that big one. I'm sure he's a nice boy and all, but he looks too . . . mature for you. Is this Edwin your boyfriend?"

"It's Edward, Dad."

"Is he?"

"Sort of, I guess."

"You said last night that you weren't interested in any of the boys in town." But he picked up his fork again, so I could see the worst was over.

"Well, Edward doesn't live in town, Dad."

He gave me a disparaging look as he chewed.

"And, anyways," I continued, "it's kind of at an early stage, you know. Don't embarrass me with all the boy-friend talk, okay?"

"When is he coming over?"

"He'll be here in a few minutes."

"Where is he taking you?"

I groaned loudly. "I hope you're getting the Spanish Inquisition out of your system now. We're going to play baseball with his family."

His face puckered, and then he finally chuckled. "*You're* playing baseball?"

"Well, I'll probably watch most of the time."

"You must really like this guy," he observed suspiciously.

I sighed and rolled my eyes for his benefit.

I heard the roar of an engine pull up in front of the house. I jumped up and started cleaning my dishes.

"Leave the dishes, I can do them tonight. You baby me too much."

The doorbell rang, and Charlie stalked off to answer it. I was half a step behind him.

I hadn't realized how hard it was pouring outside. Edward stood in the halo of the porch light, looking like a male model in an advertisement for raincoats.

"Come on in, Edward."

I breathed a sigh of relief when Charlie got his name right.

"Thanks, Chief Swan," Edward said in a respectful voice.

"Go ahead and call me Charlie. Here, I'll take your jacket."

"Thanks, sir."

"Have a seat there, Edward."

I grimaced.

Edward sat down fluidly in the only chair, forcing me to sit next to Chief Swan on the sofa. I quickly shot him a dirty look. He winked behind Charlie's back.

"So I hear you're getting my girl to watch baseball." Only in Washington would the fact that it was raining buckets have no bearing at all on the playing of outdoor sports.

"Yes, sir, that's the plan." He didn't look surprised that I'd told my father the truth. He might have been listening, though.

"Well, more power to you, I guess."

Charlie laughed, and Edward joined in.

"Okay." I stood up. "Enough humor at my expense. Let's go." I walked back to the hall and pulled on my jacket. They followed.

"Not too late, Bell."

"Don't worry, Charlie, I'll have her home early," Edward promised.

"You take care of my girl, all right?"

I groaned, but they ignored me.

"She'll be safe with me, I promise, sir."

Charlie couldn't doubt Edward's sincerity, it rang in every word.

I stalked out. They both laughed, and Edward followed me.

I stopped dead on the porch. There, behind my truck, was a monster Jeep. Its tires were higher than my waist. There were metal guards over the headlights and taillights, and four large spotlights attached to the crash bar. The hardtop was shiny red.

Charlie let out a low whistle.

"Wear your seat belts," he choked out.

Edward followed me around to my side and opened the

door. I gauged the distance to the seat and prepared to jump for it. He sighed, and then lifted me in with one hand. I hoped Charlie didn't notice.

As he went around to the driver's side, at a normal, human pace, I tried to put on my seat belt. But there were too many buckles.

"What's all this?" I asked when he opened the door.

"It's an off-roading harness."

"Uh-oh."

I tried to find the right places for all the buckles to fit, but it wasn't going too quickly. He sighed again and reached over to help me. I was glad that the rain was too heavy to see Charlie clearly on the porch. That meant he couldn't see how Edward's hands lingered at my neck, brushed along my collarbones. I gave up trying to help him and focused on not hyperventilating.

Edward turned the key and the engine roared to life. We pulled away from the house.

"This is a . . . um . . . *big* Jeep you have."

"It's Emmett's. I didn't think you'd want to run the whole way."

"Where do you keep this thing?"

"We remodeled one of the outbuildings into a garage."

"Aren't you going to put on your seat belt?"

He threw me a disbelieving look.

Then something sunk in.

"Run the *whole* way? As in, we're still going to run part of the way?" My voice edged up a few octaves.

He grinned tightly. "You're not going to run."

"*I'm* going to be sick."

"Keep your eyes closed, you'll be fine."

I bit my lip, fighting the panic.

He leaned over to kiss the top of my head, and then groaned. I looked at him, puzzled.

"You smell so good in the rain," he explained.

"In a good way, or in a bad way?" I asked cautiously.

He sighed. "Both, always both."

I don't know how he found his way in the gloom and downpour, but he somehow found a side road that was less of a road and more of a mountain path. For a long while conversation was impossible, because I was bouncing up and down on the seat like a jackhammer. He seemed to enjoy the ride, though, smiling hugely the whole way.

And then we came to the end of the road; the trees formed green walls on three sides of the Jeep. The rain was a mere drizzle, slowing every second, the sky brighter through the clouds.

"Sorry, Bella, we have to go on foot from here."

"You know what? I'll just wait here."

"What happened to all your courage? You were extraordinary this morning."

"I haven't forgotten the last time yet." Could it have been only yesterday?

He was around to my side of the car in a blur. He started unbuckling me.

"I'll get those, you go on ahead," I protested.

"Hmmm . . . ," he mused as he quickly finished. "It seems I'm going to have to tamper with your memory."

Before I could react, he pulled me from the Jeep and set my feet on the ground. It was barely misting now; Alice was going to be right.

"Tamper with my memory?" I asked nervously.

"Something like that." He was watching me intently, carefully, but there was humor deep in his eyes. He placed his hands against the Jeep on either side of my head and leaned forward, forcing me to press back against the door. He leaned in even closer, his face inches from mine. I had no room to escape.

"Now," he breathed, and just his smell disturbed my thought processes, "what exactly are you worrying about?"

"Well, um, hitting a tree —" I gulped "— and dying. And then getting sick."

He fought back a smile. Then he bent his head down and touched his cold lips softly to the hollow at the base of my throat.

"Are you still worried now?" he murmured against my skin.

"Yes." I struggled to concentrate. "About hitting trees and getting sick."

His nose drew a line up the skin of my throat to the point of my chin. His cold breath tickled my skin.

"And now?" His lips whispered against my jaw.

"Trees," I gasped. "Motion sickness."

He lifted his face to kiss my eyelids. "Bella, you don't really think I would hit a tree, do you?"

"No, but *I* might." There was no confidence in my voice. He smelled an easy victory.

He kissed slowly down my cheek, stopping just at the corner of my mouth.

"Would I let a tree hurt you?" His lips barely brushed against my trembling lower lip.

"No," I breathed. I knew there was a second part to my brilliant defense, but I couldn't quite call it back.

"You see," he said, his lips moving against mine. "There's nothing to be afraid of, is there?"

"No," I sighed, giving up.

Then he took my face in his hands almost roughly, and kissed me in earnest, his unyielding lips moving against mine.

There really was no excuse for my behavior. Obviously I knew better by now. And yet I couldn't seem to stop from reacting exactly as I had the first time. Instead of keeping safely motionless, my arms reached up to twine tightly around his neck, and I was suddenly welded to his stone figure. I sighed, and my lips parted.

He staggered back, breaking my grip effortlessly.

"Damn it, Bella!" he broke off, gasping. "You'll be the death of me, I swear you will."

I leaned over, bracing my hands against my knees for support.

"You're indestructible," I mumbled, trying to catch my breath.

"I might have believed that before I met *you*. Now let's get out of here before I do something really stupid," he growled.

He threw me across his back as he had before, and I

could see the extra effort it took for him to be as gentle as he was. I locked my legs around his waist and secured my arms in a choke hold around his neck.

"Don't forget to close your eyes," he warned severely.

I quickly tucked my face into his shoulder blade, under my own arm, and squeezed my eyes shut.

And I could hardly tell we were moving. I could feel him gliding along beneath me, but he could have been strolling down the sidewalk, the movement was so smooth. I was tempted to peek, just to see if he was really flying through the forest like before, but I resisted. It wasn't worth that awful dizziness. I contented myself with listening to his breath come and go evenly.

I wasn't quite sure we had stopped until he reached back and touched my hair.

"It's over, Bella."

I dared to open my eyes, and, sure enough, we were at a standstill. I stiffly unlocked my stranglehold on his body and slipped to the ground, landing on my backside.

"Oh!" I huffed as I hit the wet ground.

He stared at me incredulously, evidently not sure whether he was still too mad to find me funny. But my bewildered expression pushed him over the edge, and he broke into a roar of laughter.

I picked myself up, ignoring him as I brushed the mud and bracken off the back of my jacket. That only made him laugh harder. Annoyed, I began to stride off into the forest.

I felt his arm around my waist.

"Where are you going, Bella?"

"To watch a baseball game. You don't seem to be interested in playing anymore, but I'm sure the others will have fun without you."

"You're going the wrong way."

I turned around without looking at him, and stalked off in the opposite direction. He caught me again.

"Don't be mad, I couldn't help myself. You should have seen your face." He chuckled before he could stop himself.

"Oh, you're the only one who's allowed to get mad?" I asked, raising my eyebrows.

"I wasn't mad at you."

"'Bella, you'll be the death of me'?" I quoted sourly.

"*That* was simply a statement of fact."

I tried to turn away from him again, but he held me fast.

"You were mad," I insisted.

"Yes."

"But you just said —"

"That I wasn't mad at *you*. Can't you see that, Bella?" He was suddenly intense, all trace of teasing gone. "Don't you understand?"

"See what?" I demanded, confused by his sudden mood swing as much as his words.

"I'm never angry with you — how could I be? Brave, trusting . . . warm as you are."

"Then why?" I whispered, remembering the black moods that pulled him away from me, that I'd always interpreted as well-justified frustration — frustration at my weakness, my slowness, my unruly human reactions. . . .

He put his hands carefully on both sides of my face. "I infuriate myself," he said gently. "The way I can't seem to keep from putting you in danger. My very existence puts you at risk. Sometimes I truly hate myself. I should be stronger, I should be able to —"

I placed my hand over his mouth. "Don't."

He took my hand, moving it from his lips, but holding it to his face.

"I love you," he said. "It's a poor excuse for what I'm doing, but it's still true."

It was the first time he'd said he loved me — in so many words. He might not realize it, but I certainly did.

"Now, please try to behave yourself," he continued, and he bent to softly brush his lips against mine.

I held properly still. Then I sighed.

"You promised Chief Swan that you would have me home early, remember? We'd better get going."

"Yes, ma'am."

He smiled wistfully and released all of me but one hand. He led me a few feet through the tall, wet ferns and draping moss, around a massive hemlock tree, and we were there, on the edge of an enormous open field in the lap of the Olympic peaks. It was twice the size of any baseball stadium.

I could see the others all there; Esme, Emmett, and Rosalie, sitting on a bare outcropping of rock, were the closest to us, maybe a hundred yards away. Much farther out I could see Jasper and Alice, at least a quarter of a mile apart, appearing to throw something back and forth, but I never saw any ball. It looked like Carlisle was marking bases, but could they really be that far apart?

When we came into view, the three on the rocks rose.

Esme started toward us. Emmett followed after a long look at Rosalie's back; Rosalie had risen gracefully and strode off toward the field without a glance in our direction. My stomach quivered uneasily in response.

"Was that you we heard, Edward?" Esme asked as she approached.

"It sounded like a bear choking," Emmett clarified.

I smiled hesitantly at Esme. "That was him."

"Bella was being unintentionally funny," Edward explained, quickly settling the score.

Alice had left her position and was running, or dancing, toward us. She hurtled to a fluid stop at our feet. "It's time," she announced.

As soon as she spoke, a deep rumble of thunder shook the forest beyond us, and then crashed westward toward town.

"Eerie, isn't it?" Emmett said with easy familiarity, winking at me.

"Let's go." Alice reached for Emmett's hand and they darted toward the oversized field; she ran like a gazelle. He was nearly as graceful and just as fast — yet Emmett could never be compared to a gazelle.

"Are you ready for some ball?" Edward asked, his eyes eager, bright.

I tried to sound appropriately enthusiastic. "Go team!"

He snickered and, after mussing my hair, bounded off after the other two. His run was more aggressive, a cheetah rather than a gazelle, and he quickly overtook them. The grace and power took my breath away.

"Shall we go down?" Esme asked in her soft, melodic

voice, and I realized I was staring openmouthed after him. I quickly reassembled my expression and nodded. Esme kept a few feet between us, and I wondered if she was still being careful not to frighten me. She matched her stride to mine without seeming impatient at the pace.

"You don't play with them?" I asked shyly.

"No, I prefer to referee — I like keeping them honest," she explained.

"Do they like to cheat, then?"

"Oh yes — you should hear the arguments they get into! Actually, I hope you don't, you would think they were raised by a pack of wolves."

"You sound like my mom," I laughed, surprised.

She laughed, too. "Well, I do think of them as my children in most ways. I never could get over my mothering instincts — did Edward tell you I had lost a child?"

"No," I murmured, stunned, scrambling to understand what lifetime she was remembering.

"Yes, my first and only baby. He died just a few days after he was born, the poor tiny thing," she sighed. "It broke my heart — that's why I jumped off the cliff, you know," she added matter-of-factly.

"Edward just said you f-fell," I stammered.

"Always the gentleman." She smiled. "Edward was the first of my new sons. I've always thought of him that way, even though he's older than I, in one way at least." She smiled at me warmly. "That's why I'm so happy that he's found you, dear." The endearment sounded very natural on her lips. "He's been the odd man out for far too long; it's hurt me to see him alone."

"You don't mind, then?" I asked, hesitant again. "That I'm . . . all wrong for him?"

"No." She was thoughtful. "You're what he wants. It will work out, somehow," she said, though her forehead creased with worry. Another peal of thunder began.

Esme stopped then; apparently, we'd reached the edge of the field. It looked as if they had formed teams. Edward was far out in left field, Carlisle stood between the first and second bases, and Alice held the ball, positioned on the spot that must be the pitcher's mound.

Emmett was swinging an aluminum bat; it whistled almost untraceably through the air. I waited for him to approach home plate, but then I realized, as he took his stance, that he was already there — farther from the pitcher's mound than I would have thought possible. Jasper stood several feet behind him, catching for the other team. Of course, none of them had gloves.

"All right," Esme called in a clear voice, which I knew even Edward would hear, as far out as he was. "Batter up."

Alice stood straight, deceptively motionless. Her style seemed to be stealth rather than an intimidating windup. She held the ball in both hands at her waist, and then, like the strike of a cobra, her right hand flicked out and the ball smacked into Jasper's hand.

"Was that a strike?" I whispered to Esme.

"If they don't hit it, it's a strike," she told me.

Jasper hurled the ball back to Alice's waiting hand. She permitted herself a brief grin. And then her hand spun out again.

This time the bat somehow made it around in time to

smash into the invisible ball. The crack of impact was shattering, thunderous; it echoed off the mountains — I immediately understood the necessity of the thunderstorm.

The ball shot like a meteor above the field, flying deep into the surrounding forest.

"Home run," I murmured.

"Wait," Esme cautioned, listening intently, one hand raised. Emmett was a blur around the bases, Carlisle shadowing him. I realized Edward was missing.

"Out!" Esme cried in a clear voice. I stared in disbelief as Edward sprang from the fringe of the trees, ball in his upraised hand, his wide grin visible even to me.

"Emmett hits the hardest," Esme explained, "but Edward runs the fastest."

The inning continued before my incredulous eyes. It was impossible to keep up with the speed at which the ball flew, the rate at which their bodies raced around the field.

I learned the other reason they waited for a thunderstorm to play when Jasper, trying to avoid Edward's infallible fielding, hit a ground ball toward Carlisle. Carlisle ran into the ball, and then raced Jasper to first base. When they collided, the sound was like the crash of two massive falling boulders. I jumped up in concern, but they were somehow unscathed.

"Safe," Esme called in a calm voice.

Emmett's team was up by one — Rosalie managed to flit around the bases after tagging up on one of Emmett's long flies — when Edward caught the third out. He sprinted to my side, sparkling with excitement.

"What do you think?" he asked.

"One thing's for sure, I'll never be able to sit through dull old Major League Baseball again."

"And it sounds like you did so much of that before," he laughed.

"I am a little disappointed," I teased.

"Why?" he asked, puzzled.

"Well, it would be nice if I could find just one thing you didn't do better than everyone else on the planet."

He flashed his special crooked smile, leaving me breathless.

"I'm up," he said, heading for the plate.

He played intelligently, keeping the ball low, out of the reach of Rosalie's always-ready hand in the outfield, gaining two bases like lightning before Emmett could get the ball back in play. Carlisle knocked one so far out of the field — with a boom that hurt my ears — that he and Edward both made it in. Alice slapped them dainty high fives.

The score constantly changed as the game continued, and they razzed each other like any street ballplayers as they took turns with the lead. Occasionally Esme would call them to order. The thunder rumbled on, but we stayed dry, as Alice had predicted.

Carlisle was up to bat, Edward catching, when Alice suddenly gasped. My eyes were on Edward, as usual, and I saw his head snap up to look at her. Their eyes met and something flowed between them in an instant. He was at my side before the others could ask Alice what was wrong.

"Alice?" Esme's voice was tense.

"I didn't see — I couldn't tell," she whispered.

All the others were gathered by this time.

"What is it, Alice?" Carlisle asked with the calm voice of authority.

"They were traveling much quicker than I thought. I can see I had the perspective wrong before," she murmured.

Jasper leaned over her, his posture protective. "What changed?" he asked.

"They heard us playing, and it changed their path," she said, contrite, as if she felt responsible for whatever had frightened her.

Seven pairs of quick eyes flashed to my face and away.

"How soon?" Carlisle said, turning toward Edward.

A look of intense concentration crossed his face.

"Less than five minutes. They're running — they want to play." He scowled.

"Can you make it?" Carlisle asked him, his eyes flicking toward me again.

"No, not carrying —" He cut short. "Besides, the last thing we need is for them to catch the scent and start hunting."

"How many?" Emmett asked Alice.

"Three," she answered tersely.

"Three!" he scoffed. "Let them come." The steel bands of muscle flexed along his massive arms.

For a split second that seemed much longer than it really was, Carlisle deliberated. Only Emmett seemed unperturbed; the rest stared at Carlisle's face with anxious eyes.

"Let's just continue the game," Carlisle finally decided. His voice was cool and level. "Alice said they were simply curious."

All this was said in a flurry of words that lasted only a few seconds. I had listened carefully and caught most of it, though I couldn't hear what Esme now asked Edward with a silent vibration of her lips. I only saw the slight shake of his head and the look of relief on her face.

"You catch, Esme," he said. "I'll call it now." And he planted himself in front of me.

The others returned to the field, warily sweeping the dark forest with their sharp eyes. Alice and Esme seemed to orient themselves around where I stood.

"Take your hair down," Edward said in a low, even voice.

I obediently slid the rubber band out of my hair and shook it out around me.

I stated the obvious. "The others are coming now."

"Yes, stay very still, keep quiet, and don't move from my side, please." He hid the stress in his voice well, but I could hear it. He pulled my long hair forward, around my face.

"That won't help," Alice said softly. "I could smell her across the field."

"I know." A hint of frustration colored his tone.

Carlisle stood at the plate, and the others joined the game halfheartedly.

"What did Esme ask you?" I whispered.

He hesitated for a second before he answered. "Whether they were thirsty," he muttered unwillingly.

The seconds ticked by; the game progressed with apathy now. No one dared to hit harder than a bunt, and Emmett, Rosalie, and Jasper hovered in the infield. Now and again, despite the fear that numbed my brain, I was aware of Rosalie's eyes on me. They were expressionless, but something about the way she held her mouth made me think she was angry.

Edward paid no attention to the game at all, eyes and mind ranging the forest.

"I'm sorry, Bella," he muttered fiercely. "It was stupid, irresponsible, to expose you like this. I'm so sorry."

I heard his breath stop, and his eyes zeroed in on right field. He took a half step, angling himself between me and what was coming.

Carlisle, Emmett, and the others turned in the same direction, hearing sounds of passage much too faint for my ears.

18. THE HUNT

THEY EMERGED ONE BY ONE FROM THE FOREST EDGE, ranging a dozen meters apart. The first male into the clearing fell back immediately, allowing the other male to take the front, orienting himself around the tall, dark-haired man in a manner that clearly displayed who led the pack. The third was a woman; from this distance, all I could see of her was that her hair was a startling shade of red.

They closed ranks before they continued cautiously toward Edward's family, exhibiting the natural respect of a troop of predators as it encounters a larger, unfamiliar group of its own kind.

As they approached, I could see how different they were from the Cullens. Their walk was catlike, a gait that seemed constantly on the edge of shifting into a crouch. They dressed in the ordinary gear of backpackers: jeans and casual button-down shirts in heavy, weatherproof fabrics. The clothes were frayed, though, with wear, and they were barefoot. Both men had cropped hair, but the woman's brilliant orange hair was filled with leaves and debris from the woods.

Their sharp eyes carefully took in the more polished, urbane stance of Carlisle, who, flanked by Emmett and Jasper, stepped guardedly forward to meet them. Without any seeming communication between them, they each straightened into a more casual, erect bearing.

The man in front was easily the most beautiful, his skin olive-toned beneath the typical pallor, his hair a glossy black. He was of a medium build, hard-muscled, of course, but nothing next to Emmett's brawn. He smiled an easy smile, exposing a flash of gleaming white teeth.

The woman was wilder, her eyes shifting restlessly between the men facing her, and the loose grouping around me, her chaotic hair quivering in the slight breeze. Her posture was distinctly feline. The second male hovered unobtrusively behind them, slighter than the leader, his light brown hair and regular features both nondescript. His eyes, though completely still, somehow seemed the most vigilant.

Their eyes were different, too. Not the gold or black I had come to expect, but a deep burgundy color that was disturbing and sinister.

The dark-haired man, still smiling, stepped toward Carlisle.

"We thought we heard a game," he said in a relaxed voice with the slightest of French accents. "I'm Laurent, these are Victoria and James." He gestured to the vampires beside him.

"I'm Carlisle. This is my family, Emmett and Jasper, Rosalie, Esme and Alice, Edward and Bella." He pointed us out in groups, deliberately not calling attention to individuals. I felt a shock when he said my name.

"Do you have room for a few more players?" Laurent asked sociably.

Carlisle matched Laurent's friendly tone. "Actually, we were just finishing up. But we'd certainly be interested another time. Are you planning to stay in the area for long?"

"We're headed north, in fact, but we were curious to see who was in the neighborhood. We haven't run into any company in a long time."

"No, this region is usually empty except for us and the occasional visitor, like yourselves."

The tense atmosphere had slowly subsided into a casual conversation; I guessed that Jasper was using his peculiar gift to control the situation.

"What's your hunting range?" Laurent casually inquired.

Carlisle ignored the assumption behind the inquiry. "The Olympic Range here, up and down the Coast Ranges on occasion. We keep a permanent residence nearby. There's another permanent settlement like ours up near Denali."

Laurent rocked back on his heels slightly.

"Permanent? How do you manage that?" There was honest curiosity in his voice.

"Why don't you come back to our home with us and we can talk comfortably?" Carlisle invited. "It's a rather long story."

James and Victoria exchanged a surprised look at the mention of the word "home," but Laurent controlled his expression better.

"That sounds very interesting, and welcome." His smile was genial. "We've been on the hunt all the way down from Ontario, and we haven't had the chance to clean up in a while." His eyes moved appreciatively over Carlisle's refined appearance.

"Please don't take offense, but we'd appreciate it if you'd refrain from hunting in this immediate area. We have to stay inconspicuous, you understand," Carlisle explained.

"Of course." Laurent nodded. "We certainly won't encroach on your territory. We just ate outside of Seattle, anyway," he laughed. A shiver ran up my spine.

"We'll show you the way if you'd like to run with us — Emmett and Alice, you can go with Edward and Bella to get the Jeep," he casually added.

Three things seemed to happen simultaneously while Carlisle was speaking. My hair ruffled with the light breeze, Edward stiffened, and the second male, James, suddenly whipped his head around, scrutinizing me, his nostrils flaring.

A swift rigidity fell on all of them as James lurched one step forward into a crouch. Edward bared his teeth, crouching in defense, a feral snarl ripping from his throat.

It was nothing like the playful sounds I'd heard from him this morning; it was the single most menacing thing I had ever heard, and chills ran from the crown of my head to the back of my heels.

"What's this?" Laurent exclaimed in open surprise. Neither James nor Edward relaxed their aggressive poses. James feinted slightly to the side, and Edward shifted in response.

"She's with us." Carlisle's firm rebuff was directed toward James. Laurent seemed to catch my scent less powerfully than James, but awareness now dawned on his face.

"You brought a snack?" he asked, his expression incredulous as he took an involuntary step forward.

Edward snarled even more ferociously, harshly, his lip curling high above his glistening, bared teeth. Laurent stepped back again.

"I said she's with us," Carlisle corrected in a hard voice.

"But she's *human,*" Laurent protested. The words were not at all aggressive, merely astounded.

"Yes." Emmett was very much in evidence at Carlisle's side, his eyes on James. James slowly straightened out of his crouch, but his eyes never left me, his nostrils still wide. Edward stayed tensed like a lion in front of me.

When Laurent spoke, his tone was soothing — trying to defuse the sudden hostility. "It appears we have a lot to learn about each other."

"Indeed." Carlisle's voice was still cool.

"But we'd like to accept your invitation." His eyes flicked toward me and back to Carlisle. "And, of course, we will not harm the human girl. We won't hunt in your range, as I said."

James glanced in disbelief and aggravation at Laurent and exchanged another brief look with Victoria, whose eyes still flickered edgily from face to face.

Carlisle measured Laurent's open expression for a moment before he spoke. "We'll show you the way. Jasper, Rosalie, Esme?" he called. They gathered together, blocking me from view as they converged. Alice was instantly at my side, and Emmett fell back slowly, his eyes locked on James as he backed toward us.

"Let's go, Bella." Edward's voice was low and bleak.

This whole time I'd been rooted in place, terrified into absolute immobility. Edward had to grip my elbow and pull sharply to break my trance. Alice and Emmett were close behind us, hiding me. I stumbled alongside Edward, still stunned with fear. I couldn't hear if the main group had left yet. Edward's impatience was almost tangible as we moved at human speed to the forest edge.

Once we were into the trees, Edward slung me over his back without breaking stride. I gripped as tightly as possible as he took off, the others close on his heels. I kept my head down, but my eyes, wide with fright, wouldn't close. They plunged through the now-black forest like wraiths. The sense of exhilaration that usually seemed to possess Edward as he ran was completely absent, replaced by a fury that consumed him and drove him still faster. Even with me on his back, the others trailed behind.

We reached the Jeep in an impossibly short time, and Edward barely slowed as he flung me in the backseat.

"Strap her in," he ordered Emmett, who slid in beside me.

Alice was already in the front seat, and Edward was starting the engine. It roared to life and we swerved backward, spinning around to face the winding road.

Edward was growling something too fast for me to understand, but it sounded a lot like a string of profanities.

The jolting trip was much worse this time, and the darkness only made it more frightening. Emmett and Alice both glared out the side windows.

We hit the main road, and though our speed increased, I could see much better where we were going. And we were headed south, away from Forks.

"Where are we going?" I asked.

No one answered. No one even looked at me.

"Dammit, Edward! Where are you taking me?"

"We have to get you away from here — far away — now." He didn't look back, his eyes on the road. The speedometer read a hundred and five miles an hour.

"Turn around! You have to take me home!" I shouted. I struggled with the stupid harness, tearing at the straps.

"Emmett," Edward said grimly.

And Emmett secured my hands in his steely grasp.

"No! Edward! No, you can't do this."

"I have to, Bella, now please be quiet."

"I won't! You have to take me back — Charlie will call the FBI! They'll be all over your family — Carlisle and Esme! They'll have to leave, to hide forever!"

"Calm down, Bella." His voice was cold. "We've been there before."

"Not over me, you don't! You're not ruining everything over me!" I struggled violently, with total futility.

Alice spoke for the first time. "Edward, pull over."

He flashed her a hard look, and then sped up.

"Edward, let's just talk this through."

"You don't understand," he roared in frustration. I'd never heard his voice so loud; it was deafening in the confines of the Jeep. The speedometer neared one hundred and fifteen. "He's a tracker, Alice, did you *see* that? He's a tracker!"

I felt Emmett stiffen next to me, and I wondered at his reaction to the word. It meant something more to the three of them than it did to me; I wanted to understand, but there was no opening for me to ask.

"Pull over, Edward." Alice's tone was reasonable, but there was a ring of authority in it I'd never heard before.

The speedometer inched passed one-twenty.

"Do it, Edward."

"Listen to me, Alice. I saw his mind. Tracking is his passion, his obsession — and he wants her, Alice — *her*, specifically. He begins the hunt tonight."

"He doesn't know where —"

He interrupted her. "How long do you think it will take him to cross her scent in town? His plan was already set before the words were out of Laurent's mouth."

I gasped, knowing where my scent would lead. "Charlie! You can't leave him there! You can't leave him!" I thrashed against the harness.

"She's right," Alice said.

The car slowed slightly.

"Let's just look at our options for a minute," Alice coaxed.

The car slowed again, more noticeably, and then suddenly we screeched to a stop on the shoulder of the highway. I flew against the harness, and then slammed back into the seat.

"There are no options," Edward hissed.

"I'm not leaving Charlie!" I yelled.

He ignored me completely.

"We have to take her back," Emmett finally spoke.

"No." Edward was absolute.

"He's no match for us, Edward. He won't be able to touch her."

"He'll wait."

Emmett smiled. "I can wait, too."

"You didn't see — you don't understand. Once he commits to a hunt, he's unshakable. We'd have to kill him."

Emmett didn't seem upset by the idea. "That's an option."

"And the female. She's with him. If it turns into a fight, the leader will go with them, too."

"There are enough of us."

"There's another option," Alice said quietly.

Edward turned on her in fury, his voice a blistering snarl. "There — is — no — other — option!"

Emmett and I both stared at him in shock, but Alice seemed unsurprised. The silence lasted for a long minute as Edward and Alice stared each other down.

I broke it. "Does anyone want to hear my plan?"

"No," Edward growled. Alice glared at him, finally provoked.

"Listen," I pleaded. "You take me back."

"No," he interrupted.

I glared at him and continued. "You take me back. I tell my dad I want to go home to Phoenix. I pack my bags. We wait till this tracker is watching, and then we run. He'll follow us and leave Charlie alone. Charlie won't call the FBI on your family. Then you can take me any damned place you want."

They stared at me, stunned.

"It's not a bad idea, really." Emmett's surprise was definitely an insult.

"It might work — and we simply can't leave her father unprotected. You know that," Alice said.

Everyone looked at Edward.

"It's too dangerous — I don't want him within a hundred miles of her."

Emmett was supremely confident. "Edward, he's not getting through us."

Alice thought for a minute. "I don't see him attacking. He'll try to wait for us to leave her alone."

"It won't take long for him to realize that's not going to happen."

"I *demand* that you take me home." I tried to sound firm.

Edward pressed his fingers to his temples and squeezed his eyes shut.

"Please," I said in a much smaller voice.

He didn't look up. When he spoke, his voice sounded worn.

"You're leaving tonight, whether the tracker sees or not. You tell Charlie that you can't stand another minute in Forks. Tell him whatever story works. Pack the first things your hands touch, and then get in your truck. I don't care what he says to you. You have fifteen minutes. Do you hear me? Fifteen minutes from the time you cross the doorstep."

The Jeep rumbled to life, and he spun us around, the tires squealing. The needle on the speedometer started to race up the dial.

"Emmett?" I asked, looking pointedly at my hands.

"Oh, sorry." He let me loose.

A few minutes passed in silence, other than the roar of the engine. Then Edward spoke again.

"This is how it's going to happen. When we get to the house, if the tracker is not there, I will walk her to the door. Then she has fifteen minutes." He glared at me in the rearview mirror. "Emmett, you take the outside of the house. Alice, you get the truck. I'll be inside as long as she is. After she's out, you two can take the Jeep home and tell Carlisle."

"No way," Emmett broke in. "I'm with you."

"Think it through, Emmett. I don't know how long I'll be gone."

"Until we know how far this is going to go, I'm with you."

Edward sighed. "If the tracker *is* there," he continued grimly, "we keep driving."

"We're going to make it there before him," Alice said confidently.

Edward seemed to accept that. Whatever his problem with Alice was, he didn't doubt her now.

"What are we going to do with the Jeep?" she asked.

His voice had a hard edge. "You're driving it home."

"No, I'm not," she said calmly.

The unintelligible stream of profanities started again.

"We can't all fit in my truck," I whispered.

Edward didn't appear to hear me.

"I think you should let me go alone," I said even more quietly.

He heard that.

"Bella, please just do this my way, just this once," he said between clenched teeth.

"Listen, Charlie's not an imbecile," I protested. "If you're not in town tomorrow, he's going to get suspicious."

"That's irrelevant. We'll make sure he's safe, and that's all that matters."

"Then what about this tracker? He saw the way you acted tonight. He's going to think you're with me, wherever you are."

Emmett looked at me, insultingly surprised again. "Edward, listen to her," he urged. "I think she's right."

"Yes, she is," Alice agreed.

"I can't do that." Edward's voice was icy.

"Emmett should stay, too," I continued. "He definitely got an eyeful of Emmett."

"What?" Emmett turned on me.

"You'll get a better crack at him if you stay," Alice agreed.

Edward stared at her incredulously. "You think I should let her go alone?"

"Of course not," Alice said. "Jasper and I will take her."

"I can't do that," Edward repeated, but this time there was a trace of defeat in his voice. The logic was working on him.

I tried to be persuasive. "Hang out here for a week —" I saw his expression in the mirror and amended "— a few days. Let Charlie see you haven't kidnapped me, and lead this James on a wild-goose chase. Make sure he's completely off my trail. Then come and meet me. Take a roundabout route, of course, and then Jasper and Alice can go home."

I could see him beginning to consider it.

"Meet you where?"

"Phoenix." Of course.

"No. He'll hear that's where you're going," he said impatiently.

"And you'll make it look like that's a ruse, obviously. He'll know that we'll know that he's listening. He'll never believe I'm actually going where I say I am going."

"She's diabolical," Emmett chuckled.

"And if that doesn't work?"

"There are several million people in Phoenix," I in-formed him.

"It's not that hard to find a phone book."

"I won't go home."

"Oh?" he inquired, a dangerous note in his voice.

"I'm quite old enough to get my own place."

"Edward, we'll be with her," Alice reminded him.

"What are *you* going to do in *Phoenix*?" he asked her scathingly.

"Stay indoors."

"I kind of like it." Emmett was thinking about cornering James, no doubt.

"Shut up, Emmett."

"Look, if we try to take him down while she's still around, there's a much better chance that someone will get hurt — she'll get hurt, or you will, trying to protect her. Now, if we get him alone . . ." He trailed off with a slow smile. I was right.

The Jeep was crawling slowly along now as we drove into town. Despite my brave talk, I could feel the hairs on my arms standing up. I thought about Charlie, alone in the house, and tried to be courageous.

"Bella." Edward's voice was very soft. Alice and Emmett looked out their windows. "If you let anything happen to yourself — anything at all — I'm holding you personally responsible. Do you understand that?"

"Yes," I gulped.

He turned to Alice.

"Can Jasper handle this?"

"Give him some credit, Edward. He's been doing very, very well, all things considered."

"Can *you* handle this?" he asked.

And graceful little Alice pulled back her lips in a horrific grimace and let loose with a guttural snarl that had me cowering against the seat in terror.

Edward smiled at her. "But keep your opinions to yourself," he muttered suddenly.

19. GOODBYES

CHARLIE WAS WAITING UP FOR ME. ALL THE HOUSE lights were on. My mind was blank as I tried to think of a way to make him let me go. This wasn't going to be pleasant.

Edward pulled up slowly, staying well back from my truck. All three of them were acutely alert, ramrod straight in their seats, listening to every sound of the wood, looking through every shadow, catching every scent, searching for something out of place. The engine cut off, and I sat, motionless, as they continued to listen.

"He's not here," Edward said tensely. "Let's go."

Emmett reached over to help me get out of the harness.

"Don't worry, Bella," he said in a low but cheerful voice, "we'll take care of things here quickly."

I felt moisture filling up my eyes as I looked at Emmett. I barely knew him, and yet, somehow, not knowing when I would see him again after tonight was anguishing. I knew this was just a faint taste of the goodbyes I would have to survive in the next hour, and the thought made the tears begin to spill.

"Alice, Emmett." Edward's voice was a command. They slithered soundlessly into the darkness, instantly disappearing. Edward opened my door and took my hand, then drew me into the protecting enclosure of his arm. He walked me swiftly toward the house, eyes always roving through the night.

"Fifteen minutes," he warned under his breath.

"I can do this." I sniffled. My tears had given me an inspiration.

I stopped on the porch and took hold of his face in my hands. I looked fiercely into his eyes.

"I love you," I said in a low, intense voice. "I will always love you, no matter what happens now."

"Nothing is going to happen to you, Bella," he said just as fiercely.

"Just follow the plan, okay? Keep Charlie safe for me. He's not going to like me very much after this, and I want to have the chance to apologize later."

"Get inside, Bella. We have to hurry." His voice was urgent.

"One more thing," I whispered passionately. "Don't

listen to another word I say tonight!" He was leaning in, and so all I had to do was stretch up on my toes to kiss his surprised, frozen lips with as much force as I was capable of. Then I turned and kicked the door open.

"Go away, Edward!" I yelled at him, running inside and slamming the door shut in his still-shocked face.

"Bella?" Charlie had been hovering in the living room, and he was already on his feet.

"Leave me alone!" I screamed at him through my tears, which were flowing relentlessly now. I ran up the stairs to my room, throwing the door shut and locking it. I ran to my bed, flinging myself on the floor to retrieve my duffel bag. I reached swiftly between the mattress and box spring to grab the knotted old sock that contained my secret cash hoard.

Charlie was pounding on my door.

"Bella, are you okay? What's going on?" His voice was frightened.

"I'm going *home*," I shouted, my voice breaking in the perfect spot.

"Did he hurt you?" His tone edged toward anger.

"No!" I shrieked a few octaves higher. I turned to my dresser, and Edward was already there, silently yanking out armfuls of random clothes, which he proceeded to throw to me.

"Did he break up with you?" Charlie was perplexed.

"No!" I yelled, slightly more breathless as I shoved everything into the bag. Edward threw another drawer's contents at me. The bag was pretty much full now.

"What happened, Bella?" Charlie shouted through the door, pounding again.

"*I* broke up with *him*!" I shouted back, jerking on the zipper of my bag. Edward's capable hands pushed mine away and zipped it smoothly. He put the strap carefully over my arm.

"I'll be in the truck — go!" he whispered, and pushed me toward the door. He vanished out the window.

I unlocked the door and pushed past Charlie roughly, struggling with my heavy bag as I ran down the stairs.

"What happened?" he yelled. He was right behind me. "I thought you liked him."

He caught my elbow in the kitchen. Though he was still bewildered, his grip was firm.

He spun me around to look at him, and I could see in his face that he had no intention of letting me leave. I could think of only one way to escape, and it involved hurting him so much that I hated myself for even considering it. But I had no time, and I had to keep him safe.

I glared up at my father, fresh tears in my eyes for what I was about to do.

"I *do* like him — that's the problem. I can't do this anymore! I can't put down any more roots here! I don't want to end up trapped in this stupid, boring town like Mom! I'm not going to make the same dumb mistake she did. I hate it — I can't stay here another minute!"

His hand dropped from my arm like I'd electrocuted him. I turned away from his shocked, wounded face and headed for the door.

"Bells, you can't leave now. It's nighttime," he whispered behind me.

I didn't turn around. "I'll sleep in the truck if I get tired."

"Just wait another week," he pled, still shell-shocked. "Renée will be back by then."

This completely derailed me. "What?"

Charlie continued eagerly, almost babbling with relief as I hesitated. "She called while you were out. Things aren't going so well in Florida, and if Phil doesn't get signed by the end of the week, they're going back to Arizona. The assistant coach of the Sidewinders said they might have a spot for another shortstop."

I shook my head, trying to reassemble my now-confused thoughts. Every passing second put Charlie in more danger.

"I have a key," I muttered, turning the knob. He was too close, one hand extended toward me, his face dazed. I couldn't lose any more time arguing with him. I was going to have to hurt him further.

"Just let me go, Charlie." I repeated my mother's last words as she'd walked out this same door so many years ago. I said them as angrily as I could manage, and I threw the door open. "It didn't work out, okay? I really, really *hate* Forks!"

My cruel words did their job — Charlie stayed frozen on the doorstep, stunned, while I ran into the night. I was hideously frightened of the empty yard. I ran wildly for the truck, visualizing a dark shadow behind me. I threw my bag in the bed and wrenched the door open. The key was waiting in the ignition.

"I'll call you tomorrow!" I yelled, wishing more than anything that I could explain everything to him right then, knowing I would never be able to. I gunned the engine and peeled out.

Edward reached for my hand.

"Pull over," he said as the house, and Charlie, disappeared behind us.

"I can drive," I said through the tears pouring down my cheeks.

His long hands unexpectedly gripped my waist, and his foot pushed mine off the gas pedal. He pulled me across his lap, wrenching my hands free of the wheel, and suddenly he was in the driver's seat. The truck didn't swerve an inch.

"You wouldn't be able to find the house," he explained.

Lights flared suddenly behind us. I stared out the back window, eyes wide with horror.

"It's just Alice," he reassured me. He took my hand again.

My mind was filled with the image of Charlie in the doorway. "The tracker?"

"He heard the end of your performance," Edward said grimly.

"Charlie?" I asked in dread.

"The tracker followed us. He's running behind us now."

My body went cold.

"Can we outrun him?"

"No." But he sped up as he spoke. The truck's engine whined in protest.

My plan suddenly didn't feel so brilliant anymore.

I was staring back at Alice's headlights when the truck shuddered and a dark shadow sprung up outside the window.

My bloodcurdling scream lasted a fraction of a second before Edward's hand clamped down on my mouth.

"It's Emmett!"

He released my mouth, and wound his arm around my waist.

"It's okay, Bella," he promised. "You're going to be safe."

We raced through the quiet town toward the north highway.

"I didn't realize you were still so bored with small-town life," he said conversationally, and I knew he was trying to distract me. "It seemed like you were adjusting fairly well — especially recently. Maybe I was just flattering myself that I was making life more interesting for you."

"I wasn't being nice," I confessed, ignoring his attempt at diversion, looking down at my knees. "That was the same thing my mom said when she left him. You could say I was hitting below the belt."

"Don't worry. He'll forgive you." He smiled a little, though it didn't touch his eyes.

I stared at him desperately, and he saw the naked panic in my eyes.

"Bella, it's going to be all right."

"But it won't be all right when I'm not with you," I whispered.

"We'll be together again in a few days," he said, tightening his arm around me. "Don't forget that this was your idea."

"It was the best idea — of course it was mine."

His answering smile was bleak and disappeared immediately.

"Why did this happen?" I asked, my voice catching. "Why me?"

He stared blackly at the road ahead. "It's my fault — I was a fool to expose you like that." The rage in his voice was directed internally.

"That's not what I meant," I insisted. "I was there, big deal. It didn't bother the other two. Why did this James decide to kill *me*? There're people all over the place, why me?"

He hesitated, thinking before he answered.

"I got a good look at his mind tonight," he began in a low voice. "I'm not sure if there's anything I could have done to avoid this, once he saw you. It *is* partially your fault." His voice was wry. "If you didn't smell so appallingly luscious, he might not have bothered. But when I defended you . . . well, that made it a lot worse. He's not used to being thwarted, no matter how insignificant the object. He thinks of himself as a hunter and nothing else. His existence is consumed with tracking, and a challenge is all he asks of life. Suddenly we've presented him with a beautiful challenge — a large clan of strong fighters all bent on protecting the one vulnerable element. You wouldn't believe how euphoric he is now. It's his favorite game, and we've just made it his most exciting game ever." His tone was full of disgust.

He paused a moment.

"But if I had stood by, he would have killed you right then," he said with hopeless frustration.

"I thought . . . I didn't smell the same to the others . . . as I do to you," I said hesitantly.

"You don't. But that doesn't mean that you aren't still a temptation to every one of them. If you *had* appealed to the tracker — or any of them — the same way you appeal to me, it would have meant a fight right there."

I shuddered.

"I don't think I have any choice but to kill him now," he muttered. "Carlisle won't like it."

I could hear the tires cross the bridge, though I couldn't see the river in the dark. I knew we were getting close. I had to ask him now.

"How can you kill a vampire?"

He glanced at me with unreadable eyes and his voice was suddenly harsh. "The only way to be sure is to tear him to shreds, and then burn the pieces."

"And the other two will fight with him?"

"The woman will. I'm not sure about Laurent. They don't have a very strong bond — he's only with them for convenience. He was embarrassed by James in the meadow. . . ."

"But James and the woman — they'll try to kill you?" I asked, my voice raw.

"Bella, don't you *dare* waste time worrying about me. Your only concern is keeping yourself safe and — please, please — *trying* not to be reckless."

"Is he still following?"

"Yes. He won't attack the house, though. Not tonight."

He turned off onto the invisible drive, with Alice following behind.

We drove right up to the house. The lights inside were bright, but they did little to alleviate the blackness of the encroaching forest. Emmett had my door open before the truck was stopped; he pulled me out of the seat, tucked me like a football into his vast chest, and ran me through the door.

We burst into the large white room, Edward and Alice at our sides. All of them were there; they were already on their feet at the sound of our approach. Laurent stood in their midst. I could hear low growls rumble deep in Emmett's throat as he set me down next to Edward.

"He's tracking us," Edward announced, glaring balefully at Laurent.

Laurent's face was unhappy. "I was afraid of that."

Alice danced to Jasper's side and whispered in his ear; her lips quivered with the speed of her silent speech. They flew up the stairs together. Rosalie watched them, and then moved quickly to Emmett's side. Her beautiful eyes were intense and — when they flickered unwillingly to my face — furious.

"What will he do?" Carlisle asked Laurent in chilling tones.

"I'm sorry," he answered. "I was afraid, when your boy there defended her, that it would set him off."

"Can you stop him?"

Laurent shook his head. "Nothing stops James when he gets started."

"We'll stop him," Emmett promised. There was no doubt what he meant.

"You can't bring him down. I've never seen anything like him in my three hundred years. He's absolutely lethal. That's why I joined his coven."

His coven, I thought, of course. The show of leadership in the clearing was merely that, a show.

Laurent was shaking his head. He glanced at me, perplexed, and back to Carlisle. "Are you sure it's worth it?"

Edward's enraged roar filled the room; Laurent cringed back.

Carlisle looked gravely at Laurent. "I'm afraid you're going to have to make a choice."

Laurent understood. He deliberated for a moment. His eyes took in every face, and finally swept the bright room.

"I'm intrigued by the life you've created here. But I won't get in the middle of this. I bear none of you any enmity, but I won't go up against James. I think I will head north — to that clan in Denali." He hesitated. "Don't underestimate James. He's got a brilliant mind and unparalleled senses. He's every bit as comfortable in the human world as you seem to be, and he won't come at you head on. . . . I'm sorry for what's been unleashed here. Truly sorry." He bowed his head, but I saw him flicker another puzzled look at me.

"Go in peace," was Carlisle's formal answer.

Laurent took another long look around himself, and then he hurried out the door.

The silence lasted less than a second.

"How close?" Carlisle looked to Edward.

Esme was already moving; her hand touched an inconspicuous keypad on the wall, and with a groan, huge metal shutters began sealing up the glass wall. I gaped.

"About three miles out past the river; he's circling around to meet up with the female."

"What's the plan?"

"We'll lead him off, and then Jasper and Alice will run her south."

"And then?"

Edward's tone was deadly. "As soon as Bella is clear, we hunt him."

"I guess there's no other choice," Carlisle agreed, his face grim.

Edward turned to Rosalie.

"Get her upstairs and trade clothes," Edward commanded. She stared back at him with livid disbelief.

"Why should I?" she hissed. "What is she to me? Except a menace — a danger you've chosen to inflict on all of us."

I flinched back from the venom in her voice.

"Rose . . . ," Emmett murmured, putting one hand on her shoulder. She shook it off.

But I was watching Edward carefully, knowing his temper, worried about his reaction.

He surprised me. He looked away from Rosalie as if she hadn't spoken, as if she didn't exist.

"Esme?" he asked calmly.

"Of course," Esme murmured.

Esme was at my side in half a heartbeat, swinging me up easily into her arms, and dashing up the stairs before I could gasp in shock.

"What are we doing?" I asked breathlessly as she set me down in a dark room somewhere off the second-story hall.

"Trying to confuse the smell. It won't work for long, but it might help get you out." I could hear her clothes falling to the floor.

"I don't think I'll fit . . ." I hesitated, but her hands were abruptly pulling my shirt over my head. I quickly stripped my jeans off myself. She handed me something, it felt like a shirt. I struggled to get my arms through the right holes. As soon as I was done she handed me her slacks. I yanked them on, but I couldn't get my feet out; they were too long. She deftly rolled the hems a few times so I could stand. Somehow she was already in my clothes. She pulled me back to the stairs, where Alice stood, a small leather bag in one hand. They each grabbed one of my elbows and half-carried me as they flew down the stairs.

It appeared that everything had been settled downstairs in our absence. Edward and Emmett were ready to leave, Emmett carrying a heavy-looking backpack over his shoulder. Carlisle was handing something small to Esme. He turned and handed Alice the same thing — it was a tiny silver cell phone.

"Esme and Rosalie will be taking your truck, Bella," he told me as he passed. I nodded, glancing warily at Rosalie. She was glowering at Carlisle with a resentful expression.

"Alice, Jasper — take the Mercedes. You'll need the dark tint in the south."

They nodded as well.

"We're taking the Jeep."

I was surprised to see that Carlisle intended to go with Edward. I realized suddenly, with a stab of fear, that they made up the hunting party.

"Alice," Carlisle asked, "will they take the bait?"

Everyone watched Alice as she closed her eyes and became incredibly still.

Finally her eyes opened. "He'll track you. The woman will follow the truck. We should be able to leave after that." Her voice was certain.

"Let's go." Carlisle began to walk toward the kitchen.

But Edward was at my side at once. He caught me up in his iron grip, crushing me to him. He seemed unaware of his watching family as he pulled my face to his, lifting my feet off the floor. For the shortest second, his lips were icy and hard against mine. Then it was over. He set me down, still holding my face, his glorious eyes burning into mine.

His eyes went blank, curiously dead, as he turned away.

And they were gone.

We stood there, the others looking away from me as the tears streaked noiselessly down my face.

The silent moment dragged on, and then Esme's phone vibrated in her hand. It flashed to her ear.

"Now," she said. Rosalie stalked out the front door without another glance in my direction, but Esme touched my cheek as she passed.

"Be safe." Her whisper lingered behind them as they slipped out the door. I heard my truck start thunderously, and then fade away.

Jasper and Alice waited. Alice's phone seemed to be at her ear before it buzzed.

"Edward says the woman is on Esme's trail. I'll get the car." She vanished into the shadows the way Edward had gone.

Jasper and I looked at each other. He stood across the length of the entryway from me . . . being careful.

"You're wrong, you know," he said quietly.

"What?" I gasped.

"I can feel what you're feeling now — and you *are* worth it."

"I'm not," I mumbled. "If anything happens to them, it will be for nothing."

"You're wrong," he repeated, smiling kindly at me.

I heard nothing, but then Alice stepped through the front door and came toward me with her arms held out.

"May I?" she asked.

"You're the first one to ask permission." I smiled wryly.

She lifted me in her slender arms as easily as Emmett had, shielding me protectively, and then we flew out the door, leaving the lights bright behind us.

20. IMPATIENCE

WHEN I WOKE UP I WAS CONFUSED. MY THOUGHTS were hazy, still twisted up in dreams and nightmares; it took me longer than it should have to realize where I was.

This room was too bland to belong anywhere but in a hotel. The bedside lamps, bolted to the tables, were a dead giveaway, as were the long drapes made from the same fabric as the bedspread, and the generic watercolor prints on the walls.

I tried to remember how I got here, but nothing came at first.

I did remember the sleek black car, the glass in the windows darker than that on a limousine. The engine was almost silent, though we'd raced across the black freeways at more than twice the legal speed.

And I remembered Alice sitting with me on the dark leather backseat. Somehow, during the long night, my head had ended up against her granite neck. My closeness didn't seem to bother her at all, and her cool, hard skin was oddly comforting to me. The front of her thin cotton shirt was cold, damp with the tears that streamed from my eyes until, red and sore, they ran dry.

Sleep had evaded me; my aching eyes strained open even though the night finally ended and dawn broke over a low peak somewhere in California. The gray light, streaking across the cloudless sky, stung my eyes. But I couldn't close them; when I did, the images that flashed all too vividly, like still slides behind my lids, were unbearable. Charlie's broken expression — Edward's brutal snarl, teeth bared — Rosalie's resentful glare — the keen-eyed scrutiny of the tracker — the dead look in Edward's eyes after he kissed me the last time . . . I couldn't stand to see them. So I fought against my weariness and the sun rose higher.

I was still awake when we came through a shallow mountain pass and the sun, behind us now, reflected off the tiled rooftops of the Valley of the Sun. I didn't have enough emotion left to be surprised that we'd made a three-day journey in one. I stared blankly at the wide, flat expanse laid out in front of me. Phoenix — the palm trees, the scrubby creosote, the haphazard lines of the intersecting freeways, the green swaths of golf courses and turquoise splotches of swimming pools, all submerged in a thin smog and embraced by the short, rocky ridges that weren't really big enough to be called mountains.

The shadows of the palm trees slanted across the freeway — defined, sharper than I remembered, paler than they should be. Nothing could hide in these shadows. The bright, open freeway seemed benign enough. But I felt no relief, no sense of homecoming.

"Which way to the airport, Bella?" Jasper had asked, and I flinched, though his voice was quite soft and un-alarming. It was the first sound, besides the purr of the car, to break the long night's silence.

"Stay on the I-ten," I'd answered automatically. "We'll pass right by it."

My brain had worked slowly through the fog of sleep deprivation.

"Are we flying somewhere?" I'd asked Alice.

"No, but it's better to be close, just in case."

I remembered beginning the loop around Sky Harbor International . . . but not ending it. I suppose that must have been when I'd fallen asleep.

Though, now that I'd chased the memories down, I did have a vague impression of leaving the car — the sun was just falling behind the horizon — my arm draped over Alice's shoulder and her arm firm around my waist, dragging me along as I stumbled through the warm, dry shadows.

I had no memory of this room.

I looked at the digital clock on the nightstand. The red numbers claimed it was three o'clock, but they gave no indication if it was night or day. No edge of light escaped the thick curtains, but the room was bright with the light from the lamps.

I rose stiffly and staggered to the window, pulling back the drapes.

It was dark outside. Three in the morning, then. My room looked out on a deserted section of the freeway and the new long-term parking garage for the airport. It was slightly comforting to be able to pinpoint time and place.

I looked down at myself. I was still wearing Esme's clothes, and they didn't fit very well at all. I looked around the room, glad when I discovered my duffel bag on top of the low dresser.

I was on my way to find new clothes when a light tap on the door made me jump.

"Can I come in?" Alice asked.

I took a deep breath. "Sure."

She walked in, and looked me over cautiously. "You look like you could sleep longer," she said.

I just shook my head.

She drifted silently to the curtains and closed them securely before turning back to me.

"We'll need to stay inside," she told me.

"Okay." My voice was hoarse; it cracked.

"Thirsty?" she asked.

I shrugged. "I'm okay. How about you?"

"Nothing unmanageable." She smiled. "I ordered some food for you, it's in the front room. Edward reminded me that you have to eat a lot more frequently than we do."

I was instantly more alert. "He called?"

"No," she said, and watched as my face fell. "It was before we left."

She took my hand carefully and led me through the door into the living room of the hotel suite. I could hear a low buzz of voices coming from the TV. Jasper sat motionlessly at the desk in the corner, his eyes watching the news with no glimmer of interest.

I sat on the floor next to the coffee table, where a tray of food waited, and began picking at it without noticing what I was eating.

Alice perched on the arm of the sofa and stared blankly at the TV like Jasper.

I ate slowly, watching her, turning now and then to glance quickly at Jasper. It began to dawn on me that they were too still. They never looked away from the screen, though commercials were playing now. I pushed the tray away, my stomach abruptly uneasy. Alice looked down at me.

"What's wrong, Alice?" I asked.

"Nothing's wrong." Her eyes were wide, honest . . . and I didn't trust them.

"What do we do now?"

"We wait for Carlisle to call."

"And should he have called by now?" I could see that I was near the mark. Alice's eyes flitted from mine to the phone on top of her leather bag and back.

"What does that mean?" My voice quavered, and I fought to control it. "That he hasn't called yet?"

"It just means that they don't have anything to tell us."

But her voice was too even, and the air was harder to breathe.

Jasper was suddenly beside Alice, closer to me than usual.

"Bella," he said in a suspiciously soothing voice. "You have nothing to worry about. You are completely safe here."

"I know that."

"Then why are you frightened?" he asked, confused. He might feel the tenor of my emotions, but he couldn't read the reasons behind them.

"You heard what Laurent said." My voice was just a whisper, but I was sure they could hear me. "He said James was lethal. What if something goes wrong, and they get separated? If something happens to any of them, Carlisle, Emmett . . . Edward . . ." I gulped. "If that wild female hurts Esme . . ." My voice had grown higher, a note of hysteria beginning to rise in it. "How could I live with myself when it's my fault? None of you should be risking yourselves for me —"

"Bella, Bella, stop," he interrupted me, his words pouring out so quickly they were hard to understand. "You're worrying about all the wrong things, Bella. Trust me on this — none of us are in jeopardy. You are under too much strain as it is; don't add to it with wholly unnecessary worries. Listen to me!" he ordered, for I had looked away. "Our family is strong. Our only fear is losing you."

"But why should you —"

Alice interrupted this time, touching my cheek with her cold fingers. "It's been almost a century that Edward's been alone. Now he's found you. You can't see the changes that we see, we who have been with him for so long. Do you think any of us want to look into his eyes for the next hundred years if he loses you?"

My guilt slowly subsided as I looked into her dark eyes. But, even as the calm spread over me, I knew I couldn't trust my feelings with Jasper there.

It was a very long day.

We stayed in the room. Alice called down to the front desk and asked them to ignore our maid service for now. The windows stayed shut, the TV on, though no one watched it. At regular intervals, food was delivered for me. The silver phone resting on Alice's bag seemed to grow bigger as the hours passed.

My babysitters handled the suspense better than I did. As I fidgeted and paced, they simply grew more still, two statues whose eyes followed me imperceptibly as I moved. I occupied myself with memorizing the room; the striped pattern of the couches, tan, peach, cream, dull gold, and tan again. Sometimes I stared at the abstract prints, randomly finding pictures in the shapes, like I'd found pictures in the clouds as a child. I traced a blue hand, a woman combing her hair, a cat stretching. But when the pale red circle became a staring eye, I looked away.

As the afternoon wore on, I went back to bed, simply for something to do. I hoped that by myself in the dark, I could give in to the terrible fears that hovered on the edge of my consciousness, unable to break through under Jasper's careful supervision.

But Alice followed me casually, as if by some coincidence she had grown tired of the front room at the same time. I was beginning to wonder exactly what sort of instructions Edward had given her. I lay across the bed, and she sat, legs folded, next to me. I ignored her at first, suddenly tired enough to sleep. But after a few minutes, the panic that had held off in Jasper's presence began to make itself known. I gave up on the idea of sleep quickly then, curling up into a small ball, wrapping my arms around my legs.

"Alice?" I asked.

"Yes?"

I kept my voice very calm. "What do you think they're doing?"

"Carlisle wanted to lead the tracker as far north as possible, wait for him to get close, and then turn and ambush him. Esme and Rosalie were supposed to head west as long as they could keep the female behind them. If she turned around, they were to head back to Forks and keep an eye on your dad. So I imagine things are going well if they can't call. It means the tracker is close enough that they don't want him to overhear."

"And Esme?"

"I think she must be back in Forks. She won't call if there's any chance the female will overhear. I expect they're all just being very careful."

"Do you think they're safe, really?"

"Bella, how many times do we have to tell you that there's no danger to us?"

"Would you tell me the truth, though?"

"Yes. I will always tell you the truth." Her voice was earnest.

I deliberated for a moment, and decided she meant it.

"Tell me then . . . how do you become a vampire?"

My question caught her off guard. She was quiet. I rolled over to look at her, and her expression seemed ambivalent.

"Edward doesn't want me to tell you that," she said firmly, but I sensed she didn't agree.

"That's not fair. I think I have a right to know."

"I know."

I looked at her, waiting.

She sighed. "He'll be *extremely* angry."

"It's none of his business. This is between you and me. Alice, as a friend, I'm begging you." And we were friends now, somehow — as she must have known we would be all along.

She looked at me with her splendid, wise eyes . . . choosing.

"I'll tell you the mechanics of it," she said finally, "but I don't remember it myself, and I've never done it or seen it done, so keep in mind that I can only tell you the theory."

I waited.

"As predators, we have a glut of weapons in our physical arsenal — much, much more than really necessary. The strength, the speed, the acute senses, not to mention those of us like Edward, Jasper, and I, who have extra senses as well. And then, like a carnivorous flower, we are physically attractive to our prey."

I was very still, remembering how pointedly Edward had demonstrated the same concept for me in the meadow.

She smiled a wide, ominous smile. "We have another fairly superfluous weapon. We're also venomous," she said, her teeth glistening. "The venom doesn't kill — it's merely incapacitating. It works slowly, spreading through the bloodstream, so that, once bitten, our prey is in too much physical pain to escape us. Mostly superfluous, as I said. If we're that close, the prey doesn't escape. Of course, there are always exceptions. Carlisle, for example."

"So . . . if the venom is left to spread . . . ," I murmured.

"It takes a few days for the transformation to be complete, depending on how much venom is in the bloodstream, how close the venom enters to the heart. As long as the heart keeps beating, the poison spreads, healing, changing the body as it moves through it. Eventually the heart stops, and the conversion is finished. But all that time, every minute of it, a victim would be wishing for death."

I shivered.

"It's not pleasant, you see."

"Edward said that it was very hard to do . . . I don't quite understand," I said.

"We're also like sharks in a way. Once we taste the blood, or even smell it for that matter, it becomes very hard to keep from feeding. Sometimes impossible. So you see, to actually bite someone, to taste the blood, it would begin the frenzy. It's difficult on both sides — the blood-lust on the one hand, the awful pain on the other."

"Why do you think you don't remember?"

"I don't know. For everyone else, the pain of transformation is the sharpest memory they have of their human life. I remember nothing of being human." Her voice was wistful.

We lay silently, wrapped in our individual meditations.

The seconds ticked by, and I had almost forgotten her presence, I was so enveloped in my thoughts.

Then, without any warning, Alice leaped from the bed, landing lightly on her feet. My head jerked up as I stared at her, startled.

"Something's changed." Her voice was urgent, and she wasn't talking to me anymore.

She reached the door at the same time Jasper did. He had obviously heard our conversation and her sudden exclamation. He put his hands on her shoulders and guided her back to the bed, sitting her on the edge.

"What do you see?" he asked intently, staring into her eyes. Her eyes were focused on something very far away. I sat close to her, leaning in to catch her low, quick voice.

"I see a room. It's long, and there are mirrors everywhere. The floor is wooden. He's in the room, and he's waiting. There's gold . . . a gold stripe across the mirrors."

"Where is the room?"

"I don't know. Something is missing — another decision hasn't been made yet."

"How much time?"

"It's soon. He'll be in the mirror room today, or maybe tomorrow. It all depends. He's waiting for something. And he's in the dark now."

Jasper's voice was calm, methodical, as he questioned her in a practiced way. "What is he doing?"

"He's watching TV . . . no, he's running a VCR, in the dark, in another place."

"Can you see where he is?"

"No, it's too dark."

"And the mirror room, what else is there?"

"Just the mirrors, and the gold. It's a band, around the room. And there's a black table with a big stereo, and a TV. He's touching the VCR there, but he doesn't watch the way he does in the dark room. This is the room where he waits." Her eyes drifted, then focused on Jasper's face.

"There's nothing else?"

She shook her head. They looked at each other, motionless.

"What does it mean?" I asked.

Neither of them answered for a moment, then Jasper looked at me.

"It means the tracker's plans have changed. He's made a decision that will lead him to the mirror room, and the dark room."

"But we don't know where those rooms are?"

"No."

"But we do know that he won't be in the mountains north of Washington, being hunted. He'll elude them." Alice's voice was bleak.

"Should we call?" I asked. They traded a serious look, undecided.

And the phone rang.

Alice was across the room before I could lift my head to look at it.

She pushed a button and held the phone to her ear, but she didn't speak first.

"Carlisle," she breathed. She didn't seem surprised or relieved, the way I felt.

"Yes," she said, glancing at me. She listened for a long moment.

"I just saw him." She described again the vision she'd seen. "Whatever made him get on that plane . . . it was leading him to those rooms." She paused. "Yes," Alice said into the phone, and then she spoke to me. "Bella?"

She held the phone out toward me. I ran to it.

"Hello?" I breathed.

"Bella," Edward said.

"Oh, Edward! I was so worried."

"Bella," he sighed in frustration, "I told you not to worry about anything but yourself." It was so unbelievably good to hear his voice. I felt the hovering cloud of despair lighten and drift back as he spoke.

"Where are you?"

"We're outside of Vancouver. Bella, I'm sorry — we lost him. He seems suspicious of us — he's careful to stay just far enough away that I can't hear what he's thinking. But he's gone now — it looks like he got on a plane. We think he's heading back to Forks to start over." I could hear Alice filling in Jasper behind me, her quick words blurring together into a humming noise.

"I know. Alice saw that he got away."

"You don't have to worry, though. He won't find anything to lead him to you. You just have to stay there and wait till we find him again."

"I'll be fine. Is Esme with Charlie?"

"Yes — the female has been in town. She went to the house, but while Charlie was at work. She hasn't gone near him, so don't be afraid. He's safe with Esme and Rosalie watching."

"What is she doing?"

"Probably trying to pick up the trail. She's been all through the town during the night. Rosalie traced her through the airport, all the roads around town, the school . . . she's digging, Bella, but there's nothing to find."

"And you're sure Charlie's safe?"

"Yes, Esme won't let him out of her sight. And we'll be there soon. If the tracker gets anywhere near Forks, we'll have him."

"I miss you," I whispered.

"I know, Bella. Believe me, I know. It's like you've taken half my self away with you."

"Come and get it, then," I challenged.

"Soon, as soon as I possibly can. I *will* make you safe first." His voice was hard.

"I love you," I reminded him.

"Could you believe that, despite everything I've put you through, I love you, too?"

"Yes, I can, actually."

"I'll come for you soon."

"I'll be waiting."

As soon as the phone went dead, the cloud of depression began to creep over me again.

I turned to give the phone back to Alice and found her and Jasper bent over the table, where Alice was sketching on a piece of hotel stationery. I leaned on the back of the couch, looking over her shoulder.

She drew a room: long, rectangular, with a thinner, square section at the back. The wooden planks that made up the floor stretched lengthwise across the room. Down the walls were lines denoting the breaks in the mirrors. And then, wrapping around the walls, waist high, a long band. The band Alice said was gold.

"It's a ballet studio," I said, suddenly recognizing the familiar shapes.

They looked at me, surprised.

"Do you know this room?" Jasper's voice sounded calm, but there was an undercurrent of something I couldn't identify. Alice bent her head to her work, her hand flying across the page now, the shape of an emergency exit taking shape against the back wall, the stereo and TV on a low table by the front right corner.

"It looks like a place I used to go for dance lessons — when I was eight or nine. It was shaped just the same." I touched the page where the square section jutted out, narrowing the back part of the room. "That's where the bathrooms were — the doors were through the other dance floor. But the stereo was here" — I pointed to the left corner — "it was older, and there wasn't a TV. There was a window in the waiting room — you would see the room from this perspective if you looked through it."

Alice and Jasper were staring at me.

"Are you sure it's the same room?" Jasper asked, still calm.

"No, not at all — I suppose most dance studios would look the same — the mirrors, the bar." I traced my finger along the ballet bar set against the mirrors. "It's just the shape that looked familiar." I touched the door, set in exactly the same place as the one I remembered.

"Would you have any reason to go there now?" Alice asked, breaking my reverie.

"No, I haven't been there in almost ten years. I was a terrible dancer — they always put me in the back for recitals," I admitted.

"So there's no way it could be connected with you?" Alice asked intently.

"No, I don't even think the same person owns it. I'm sure it's just another dance studio, somewhere."

"Where was the studio you went to?" Jasper asked in a casual voice.

"It was just around the corner from my mom's house. I used to walk there after school . . . ," I said, my voice trailing off. I didn't miss the look they exchanged.

"Here in Phoenix, then?" His voice was still casual.

"Yes," I whispered. "Fifty-eighth Street and Cactus."

We all sat in silence, staring at the drawing.

"Alice, is that phone safe?"

"Yes," she reassured me. "The number would just trace back to Washington."

"Then I can use it to call my mom."

"I thought she was in Florida."

"She is — but she's coming home soon, and she can't come back to that house while . . ." My voice trembled. I was thinking about something Edward had said, about the red-haired female at Charlie's house, at the school, where my records would be.

"How will you reach her?"

"They don't have a permanent number except at the house — she's supposed to check her messages regularly."

"Jasper?" Alice asked.

He thought about it. "I don't think there's any way it could hurt — be sure you don't say where you are, of course."

I reached eagerly for the phone and dialed the familiar number. It rang four times, and then I heard my mom's breezy voice telling me to leave a message.

"Mom," I said after the beep, "it's me. Listen, I need you to do something. It's important. As soon as you get this message, call me at this number." Alice was already at my side, writing the number for me on the bottom of her picture. I read it carefully, twice. "Please don't go anywhere until you talk to me. Don't worry, I'm okay, but I have to talk to you right away, no matter how late you get this call, all right? I love you, Mom. Bye." I closed my eyes and prayed with all my might that no unforeseen change of plans would bring her home before she got my message.

I settled into the sofa, nibbling on a plate of leftover fruit, anticipating a long evening. I thought about calling Charlie, but I wasn't sure if I should be home by now or not. I concentrated on the news, watching out for stories about Florida, or about spring training — strikes or hurricanes or terrorist attacks — anything that might send them home early.

Immortality must grant endless patience. Neither Jasper nor Alice seemed to feel the need to do anything at all. For a while, Alice sketched the vague outline of the dark room from her vision, as much as she could see in the light from the TV. But when she was done, she simply sat, looking at the blank walls with her timeless eyes. Jasper, too, seemed to have no urge to pace, or peek through the curtains, or run screaming out the door, the way I did.

I must have fallen asleep on the couch, waiting for the phone to ring again. The touch of Alice's cold hands woke me briefly as she carried me to the bed, but I was unconscious again before my head hit the pillow.

21. PHONE CALL

I COULD FEEL IT WAS TOO EARLY AGAIN WHEN I WOKE, and I knew I was getting the schedule of my days and nights slowly reversed. I lay in my bed and listened to the quiet voices of Alice and Jasper in the other room. That they were loud enough for me to hear at all was strange. I rolled till my feet touched the floor and then staggered to the living room.

The clock on the TV said it was just after two in the morning. Alice and Jasper were sitting together on the sofa, Alice sketching again while Jasper looked over her shoulder. They didn't look up when I entered, too engrossed in Alice's work.

I crept to Jasper's side to peek.

"Did she see something more?" I asked him quietly.

"Yes. Something's brought him back to the room with the VCR, but it's light now."

I watched as Alice drew a square room with dark beams across its low ceiling. The walls were paneled in wood, a little too dark, out of date. The floor had a dark carpet with a pattern in it. There was a large window against the south wall, and an opening through the west wall led to the living room. One side of that entrance was stone — a large tan stone fireplace that was open to both rooms. The focus of the room from this perspective, the TV and VCR, balanced on a too-small wooden stand, were in the southwest corner of the room. An aged sectional sofa curved around in front of the TV, a round coffee table in front of it.

"The phone goes there," I whispered, pointing.

Two pairs of eternal eyes stared at me.

"That's my mother's house."

Alice was already off the couch, phone in hand, dialing. I stared at the precise rendering of my mother's family room. Uncharacteristically, Jasper slid closer to me. He lightly touched his hand to my shoulder, and the physical contact seemed to make his calming influence stronger. The panic stayed dull, unfocused.

Alice's lips were trembling with the speed of her words, the low buzzing impossible to decipher. I couldn't concentrate.

"Bella," Alice said. I looked at her numbly.

"Bella, Edward is coming to get you. He and Emmett and Carlisle are going to take you somewhere, to hide you for a while."

"Edward is coming?" The words were like a life vest, holding my head above the flood.

"Yes, he's catching the first flight out of Seattle. We'll meet him at the airport, and you'll leave with him."

"But, my mother . . . he came here for my mother, Alice!" Despite Jasper, the hysteria bubbled up in my voice.

"Jasper and I will stay till she's safe."

"I can't win, Alice. You can't guard everyone I know forever. Don't you see what he's doing? He's not tracking me at all. He'll find someone, he'll hurt someone I love. . . . Alice, I can't —"

"We'll catch him, Bella," she assured me.

"And what if you get hurt, Alice? Do you think that's okay with me? Do you think it's only my human family he can hurt me with?"

Alice looked meaningfully at Jasper. A deep, heavy fog of lethargy washed over me, and my eyes closed without my permission. My mind struggled against the fog, realizing what was happening. I forced my eyes open and stood up, stepping away from Jasper's hand.

"I don't want to go back to sleep," I snapped.

I walked to my room and shut the door, slammed it really, so I could be free to go to pieces privately. This time Alice didn't follow me. For three and a half hours I stared at the wall, curled in a ball, rocking. My mind went around in circles, trying to come up with some way out of this nightmare. There was no escape, no reprieve. I could see only one possible end looming darkly in my future. The only question was how many other people would be hurt before I reached it.

The only solace, the only hope I had left, was knowing that I would see Edward soon. Maybe, if I could just see his face again, I would also be able to see the solution that eluded me now.

When the phone rang, I returned to the front room, a little ashamed of my behavior. I hoped I hadn't offended either of them, that they would know how grateful I was for the sacrifices they were making on my account.

Alice was talking as rapidly as ever, but what caught my attention was that, for the first time, Jasper was not in the room. I looked at the clock — it was five-thirty in the morning.

"They're just boarding their plane," Alice told me. "They'll land at nine-forty-five." Just a few more hours to keep breathing till he was here.

"Where's Jasper?"

"He went to check out."

"You aren't staying here?"

"No, we're relocating closer to your mother's house."

My stomach twisted uneasily at her words.

But the phone rang again, distracting me. She looked surprised, but I was already walking forward, reaching hopefully for the phone.

"Hello?" Alice asked. "No, she's right here." She held the phone out to me. Your mother, she mouthed.

"Hello?"

"Bella? Bella?" It was my mother's voice, in a familiar tone I had heard a thousand times in my childhood, anytime I'd gotten too close to the edge of the sidewalk or strayed out of her sight in a crowded place. It was the sound of panic.

I sighed. I'd been expecting this, though I'd tried to make my message as unalarming as possible without lessening the urgency of it.

"Calm down, Mom," I said in my most soothing voice, walking slowly away from Alice. I wasn't sure if I could lie as convincingly with her eyes on me. "Everything is fine, okay? Just give me a minute and I'll explain everything, I promise."

I paused, surprised that she hadn't interrupted me yet. "Mom?"

"Be very careful not to say anything until I tell you to." The voice I heard now was as unfamiliar as it was unexpected. It was a man's tenor voice, a very pleasant, generic voice — the kind of voice that you heard in the background of luxury car commercials. He spoke very quickly.

"Now, I don't need to hurt your mother, so please do exactly as I say, and she'll be fine." He paused for a minute while I listened in mute horror. "That's very good," he congratulated. "Now repeat after me, and do try to sound natural. Please say, 'No, Mom, stay where you are.'"

"No, Mom, stay where you are." My voice was barely more than a whisper.

"I can see this is going to be difficult." The voice was amused, still light and friendly. "Why don't you walk into another room now so your face doesn't ruin everything? There's no reason for your mother to suffer. As you're walking, please say, 'Mom, please listen to me.' Say it now."

"Mom, please listen to me," my voice pleaded. I walked very slowly to the bedroom, feeling Alice's worried stare on my back. I shut the door behind me, trying to think clearly through the terror that gripped my brain.

"There now, are you alone? Just answer yes or no."

"Yes."

"But they can still hear you, I'm sure."

"Yes."

"All right, then," the agreeable voice continued, "say, 'Mom, trust me.'"

"Mom, trust me."

"This worked out rather better than I expected. I was prepared to wait, but your mother arrived ahead of schedule. It's easier this way, isn't it? Less suspense, less anxiety for you."

I waited.

"Now I want you to listen very carefully. I'm going to need you to get away from your friends; do you think you can do that? Answer yes or no."

"No."

"I'm sorry to hear that. I was hoping you would be a little more creative than that. Do you think you could get away from them if your mother's life depended on it? Answer yes or no."

Somehow, there had to be a way. I remembered that we were going to the airport. Sky Harbor International Airport: crowded, confusingly laid out . . .

"Yes."

"That's better. I'm sure it won't be easy, but if I get the slightest hint that you have any company, well, that would be very bad for your mother," the friendly voice promised. "You must know enough about us by now to realize how quickly I would know if you tried to bring anyone along with you. And how little time I would need to deal with your mother if that was the case. Do you understand? Answer yes or no."

"Yes." My voice broke.

"Very good, Bella. Now this is what you have to do. I want you to go to your mother's house. Next to the phone there will be a number. Call it, and I'll tell you where to go from there." I already knew where I would go, and where this would end. But I would follow his instructions exactly. "Can you do that? Answer yes or no."

"Yes."

"Before noon, please, Bella. I haven't got all day," he said politely.

"Where's Phil?" I asked tersely.

"Ah, be careful now, Bella. Wait until I ask you to speak, please."

I waited.

"It's important, now, that you don't make your friends suspicious when you go back to them. Tell them that your mother called, and that you talked her out of coming home for the time being. Now repeat after me, 'Thank you, Mom.' Say it now."

"Thank you, Mom." The tears were coming. I tried to fight them back.

"Say, 'I love you, Mom, I'll see you soon.' Say it now."

"I love you, Mom." My voice was thick. "I'll see you soon," I promised.

"Goodbye, Bella. I look forward to seeing you again."
He hung up.

I held the phone to my ear. My joints were frozen with terror — I couldn't unbend my fingers to drop it.

I knew I had to think, but my head was filled with the sound of my mother's panic. Seconds ticked by while I fought for control.

Slowly, slowly, my thoughts started to break past that brick wall of pain. To plan. For I had no choices now but one: to go to the mirrored room and die. I had no guarantees, nothing to give to keep my mother alive. I could only hope that James would be satisfied with winning the game, that beating Edward would be enough. Despair gripped me; there was no way to bargain, nothing I could offer or withhold that could influence him. But I still had no choice. I had to try.

I pushed the terror back as well as I could. My decision was made. It did no good to waste time agonizing over the outcome. I had to think clearly, because Alice and Jasper were waiting for me, and evading them was absolutely essential, and absolutely impossible.

I was suddenly grateful that Jasper was gone. If he had been here to feel my anguish in the last five minutes, how could I have kept them from being suspicious? I choked back the dread, the anxiety, tried to stifle it. I couldn't afford it now. I didn't know when he would return.

I concentrated on my escape. I had to hope that my familiarity with the airport would turn the odds in my favor. Somehow, I had to keep Alice away. . . .

I knew Alice was in the other room waiting for me,

curious. But I had to deal with one more thing in private, before Jasper was back.

I had to accept that I wouldn't see Edward again, not even one last glimpse of his face to carry with me to the mirror room. I was going to hurt him, and I couldn't say goodbye. I let the waves of torture wash over me, have their way for a time. Then I pushed them back, too, and went to face Alice.

The only expression I could manage was a dull, dead look. I saw her alarm and I didn't wait for her to ask. I had just one script and I'd never manage improvisation now.

"My mom was worried, she wanted to come home. But it's okay, I convinced her to stay away." My voice was lifeless.

"We'll make sure she's fine, Bella, don't worry."

I turned away; I couldn't let her see my face.

My eye fell on a blank page of the hotel stationery on the desk. I went to it slowly, a plan forming. There was an envelope there, too. That was good.

"Alice," I asked slowly, without turning, keeping my voice level. "If I write a letter for my mother, would you give it to her? Leave it at the house, I mean."

"Sure, Bella." Her voice was careful. She could see me coming apart at the seams. I *had* to keep my emotions under better control.

I went into the bedroom again, and knelt next to the little bedside table to write.

"Edward," I wrote. My hand was shaking, the letters were hardly legible.

I love you. I am so sorry. He has my mom, and I have to try. I know it may not work. I am so very, very sorry.

Don't be angry with Alice and Jasper. If I get away from them it will be a miracle. Tell them thank you for me. Alice especially, please.

And please, please don't come after him. That's what he wants, I think. I can't bear it if anyone has to be hurt because of me, especially you. Please, this is the only thing I can ask you now. For me.

I love you. Forgive me.
Bella.

I folded the letter carefully, and sealed it in the envelope. Eventually he would find it. I only hoped he would understand, and listen to me just this once.

And then I carefully sealed away my heart.

22. HIDE-AND-SEEK

IT HAD TAKEN MUCH LESS TIME THAN I'D THOUGHT — all the terror, the despair, the shattering of my heart. The minutes were ticking by more slowly than usual. Jasper still hadn't come back when I returned to Alice. I was afraid to be in the same room with her, afraid that she would guess . . . and afraid to hide from her for the same reason.

I would have thought I was far beyond the ability to be surprised, my thoughts tortured and unstable, but I *was* surprised when I saw Alice bent over the desk, gripping the edge with two hands.

"Alice?"

She didn't react when I called her name, but her head was slowly rocking side to side, and I saw her face. Her eyes were blank, dazed. . . . My thoughts flew to my mother. Was I already too late?

I hurried to her side, reaching out automatically to touch her hand.

"Alice!" Jasper's voice whipped, and then he was right behind her, his hands curling over hers, loosening them from their grip on the table. Across the room, the door swung shut with a low click.

"What is it?" he demanded.

She turned her face away from me, into his chest. "Bella," she said.

"I'm right here," I replied.

Her head twisted around, her eyes locking on mine, their expression still strangely blank. I realized at once that she hadn't been speaking to me, she'd been answering Jasper's question.

"What did you see?" I said — and there was no question in my flat, uncaring voice.

Jasper looked at me sharply. I kept my expression vacant and waited. His eyes were confused as they flickered swiftly between Alice's face and mine, feeling the chaos . . . for I could guess what Alice had seen now.

I felt a tranquil atmosphere settle around me. I welcomed it, using it to keep my emotions disciplined, under control.

Alice, too, recovered herself.

"Nothing, really," she answered finally, her voice remarkably calm and convincing. "Just the same room as before."

She finally looked at me, her expression smooth and withdrawn. "Did you want breakfast?"

"No, I'll eat at the airport." I was very calm, too. I went to the bathroom to shower. Almost as if I were borrowing Jasper's strange extra sense, I could feel Alice's wild — though well-concealed — desperation to have me out of the room, to be alone with Jasper. So she could tell him that they were doing something wrong, that they were going to fail. . . .

I got ready methodically, concentrating on each little task. I left my hair down, swirling around me, covering my face. The peaceful mood Jasper created worked its way through me and helped me think clearly. Helped me plan. I dug through my bag until I found my sock full of money. I emptied it into my pocket.

I was anxious to get to the airport, and glad when we left by seven. I sat alone this time in the back of the dark car. Alice leaned against the door, her face toward Jasper but, behind her sunglasses, shooting glances in my direction every few seconds.

"Alice?" I asked indifferently.

She was wary. "Yes?"

"How does it work? The things that you see?" I stared out the side window, and my voice sounded bored. "Edward said it wasn't definite . . . that things change?" It was harder than I would have thought to say his name. That must have been what alerted Jasper, why a fresh wave of serenity filled the car.

"Yes, things change . . . ," she murmured — hopefully, I thought. "Some things are more certain than others . . . like the weather. People are harder. I only see the course they're on while they're on it. Once they change their minds — make a new decision, no matter how small — the whole future shifts."

I nodded thoughtfully. "So you couldn't see James in Phoenix until he decided to come here."

"Yes," she agreed, wary again.

And she hadn't seen me in the mirror room with James until I'd made the decision to meet him there. I tried not to think about what else she might have seen. I didn't want my panic to make Jasper more suspicious. They would be watching me twice as carefully now, anyway, after Alice's vision. This was going to be impossible.

We got to the airport. Luck was with me, or maybe it was just good odds. Edward's plane was landing in terminal four, the largest terminal, where most flights landed — so it wasn't surprising that his was. But it was the terminal I needed: the biggest, the most confusing. And there was a door on level three that might be the only chance.

We parked on the fourth floor of the huge garage. I led the way, for once more knowledgeable about my surroundings than they were. We took the elevator down to level three, where the passengers unloaded. Alice and Jasper spent a long time looking at the departing flights board. I could hear them discussing the pros and cons of New York, Atlanta, Chicago. Places I'd never seen. And would never see.

I waited for my opportunity, impatient, unable to stop my toe from tapping. We sat in the long rows of chairs by the metal detectors, Jasper and Alice pretending to people-watch but really watching me. Every inch I shifted in my seat was followed by a quick glance out of the corner of their eyes. It was hopeless. Should I run? Would they dare to stop me physically in this public place? Or would they simply follow?

I pulled the unmarked envelope out of my pocket and set it on top of Alice's black leather bag. She looked at me.

"My letter," I said. She nodded, tucking it under the top flap. He would find it soon enough.

The minutes passed and Edward's arrival grew closer. It was amazing how every cell in my body seemed to know he was coming, to long for his coming. That made it very hard. I found myself trying to think of excuses to stay, to see him first and then make my escape. But I knew that was impossible if I was going to have any chance to get away.

Several times Alice offered to go get breakfast with me. Later, I told her, not yet.

I stared at the arrival board, watching as flight after flight arrived on time. The flight from Seattle crept closer to the top of the board.

And then, when I had only thirty minutes to make my escape, the numbers changed. His plane was ten minutes early. I had no more time.

"I think I'll eat now," I said quickly.

Alice stood. "I'll come with you."

"Do you mind if Jasper comes instead?" I asked. "I'm feeling a little . . ." I didn't finish the sentence. My eyes were wild enough to convey what I didn't say.

Jasper stood up. Alice's eyes were confused, but — I saw to my relief — not suspicious. She must be attributing the change in her vision to some maneuver of the tracker's rather than a betrayal by me.

Jasper walked silently beside me, his hand on the small of my back, as if he were guiding me. I pretended a lack of interest in the first few airport cafés, my head scanning for what I really wanted. And there it was, around the corner, out of Alice's sharp sight: the level-three ladies' room.

"Do you mind?" I asked Jasper as we passed. "I'll just be a moment."

"I'll be right here," he said.

As soon as the door shut behind me, I was running. I remembered the time I had gotten lost from this bathroom, because it had two exits.

Outside the far door it was only a short sprint to the elevators, and if Jasper stayed where he said he would, I'd never be in his line of sight. I didn't look behind me as I ran. This was my only chance, and even if he saw me, I had to keep going. People stared, but I ignored them. Around the corner the elevators were waiting, and I dashed forward, throwing my hand between the closing doors of a full elevator headed down. I squeezed in beside the irritated passengers, and checked to make sure that the button for level one had been pushed. It was already lit, and the doors closed.

As soon as the door opened I was off again, to the sound of annoyed murmurs behind me. I slowed myself as I passed the security guards by the luggage carousels, only to break into a run again as the exit doors came into view. I had no way of knowing if Jasper was looking for me yet.

I would have only seconds if he was following my scent. I jumped out the automatic doors, nearly smacking into the glass when they opened too slowly.

Along the crowded curb there wasn't a cab in sight.

I had no time. Alice and Jasper were either about to realize I was gone, or they already had. They would find me in a heartbeat.

A shuttle to the Hyatt was just closing its doors a few feet behind me.

"Wait!" I called, running, waving at the driver.

"This is the shuttle to the Hyatt," the driver said in confusion as he opened the doors.

"Yes," I huffed, "that's where I'm going." I hurried up the steps.

He looked askance at my luggage-less state, but then shrugged, not caring enough to ask.

Most of the seats were empty. I sat as far from the other travelers as possible, and watched out the window as first the sidewalk, and then the airport, drifted away. I couldn't help imagining Edward, where he would stand at the edge of the road when he found the end of my trail. I couldn't cry yet, I told myself. I still had a long way to go.

My luck held. In front of the Hyatt, a tired-looking couple was getting their last suitcase out of the trunk of a cab. I jumped out of the shuttle and ran to the cab, sliding into the seat behind the driver. The tired couple and the shuttle driver stared at me.

I told the surprised cabbie my mother's address. "I need to get there as soon as possible."

"That's in Scottsdale," he complained.

I threw four twenties over the seat.

"Will that be enough?"

"Sure, kid, no problem."

I sat back against the seat, folding my arms across my lap. The familiar city began to rush around me, but I didn't look out the windows. I exerted myself to maintain control. I was determined not to lose myself at this point, now that my plan was successfully completed. There was no point in indulging in more terror, more anxiety. My path was set. I just had to follow it now.

So, instead of panicking, I closed my eyes and spent the twenty minutes' drive with Edward.

I imagined that I had stayed at the airport to meet Edward. I visualized how I would stand on my toes, the sooner to see his face. How quickly, how gracefully he would move through the crowds of people separating us. And then I would run to close those last few feet between us — reckless as always — and I would be in his marble arms, finally safe.

I wondered where we would have gone. North somewhere, so he could be outside in the day. Or maybe somewhere very remote, so we could lay in the sun together again. I imagined him by the shore, his skin sparkling like the sea. It wouldn't matter how long we had to hide. To be trapped in a hotel room with him would be a kind of heaven. So many questions I still had for him. I could talk to him forever, never sleeping, never leaving his side.

I could see his face so clearly now . . . almost hear his

voice. And, despite all the horror and hopelessness, I was fleetingly happy. So involved was I in my escapist day-dreams, I lost all track of the seconds racing by.

"Hey, what was the number?"

The cabbie's question punctured my fantasy, letting all the colors run out of my lovely delusions. Fear, bleak and hard, was waiting to fill the empty space they left behind.

"Fifty-eight twenty-one." My voice sounded strangled. The cabbie looked at me, nervous that I was having an episode or something.

"Here we are, then." He was anxious to get me out of his car, probably hoping I wouldn't ask for my change.

"Thank you," I whispered. There was no need to be afraid, I reminded myself. The house was empty. I had to hurry; my mom was waiting for me, frightened, depending on me.

I ran to the door, reaching up automatically to grab the key under the eave. I unlocked the door. It was dark in-side, empty, normal. I ran to the phone, turning on the kitchen light on my way. There, on the whiteboard, was a ten-digit number written in a small, neat hand. My fin-gers stumbled over the keypad, making mistakes. I had to hang up and start again. I concentrated only on the but-tons this time, carefully pressing each one in turn. I was successful. I held the phone to my ear with a shaking hand. It rang only once.

"Hello, Bella," that easy voice answered. "That was very quick. I'm impressed."

"Is my mom all right?"

"She's perfectly fine. Don't worry, Bella, I have no quarrel with her. Unless you didn't come alone, of course." Light, amused.

"I'm alone." I'd never been more alone in my entire life.

"Very good. Now, do you know the ballet studio just around the corner from your home?"

"Yes. I know how to get there."

"Well, then, I'll see you very soon."

I hung up.

I ran from the room, through the door, out into the baking heat.

There was no time to look back at my house, and I didn't want to see it as it was now — empty, a symbol of fear instead of sanctuary. The last person to walk through those familiar rooms was my enemy.

From the corner of my eye, I could almost see my mother standing in the shade of the big eucalyptus tree where I'd played as a child. Or kneeling by the little plot of dirt around the mailbox, the cemetery of all the flowers she'd tried to grow. The memories were better than any reality I would see today. But I raced away from them, toward the corner, leaving everything behind me.

I felt so slow, like I was running through wet sand — I couldn't seem to get enough purchase from the concrete. I tripped several times, once falling, catching myself with my hands, scraping them on the sidewalk, and then lurching up to plunge forward again. But at last I made it to the corner. Just another street now; I ran, sweat pouring down my face, gasping. The sun was hot on my skin, too bright as it bounced off the white concrete and blinded me. I felt dangerously exposed. More fiercely than I would have dreamed I was capable of, I wished for the green, protective forests of Forks . . . of home.

When I rounded the last corner, onto Cactus, I could see the studio, looking just as I remembered it. The parking lot in front was empty, the vertical blinds in all the windows drawn. I couldn't run anymore — I couldn't breathe; exertion and fear had gotten the best of me. I thought of my mother to keep my feet moving, one in front of the other.

As I got closer, I could see the sign inside the door. It was handwritten on hot pink paper; it said the dance studio was closed for spring break. I touched the handle, tugged on it cautiously. It was unlocked. I fought to catch my breath, and opened the door.

The lobby was dark and empty, cool, the air conditioner thrumming. The plastic molded chairs were stacked along the walls, and the carpet smelled like shampoo. The west dance floor was dark, I could see through the open viewing window. The east dance floor, the bigger room, was lit. But the blinds were closed on the window.

Terror seized me so strongly that I was literally trapped by it. I couldn't make my feet move forward.

And then my mother's voice called.

"Bella? Bella?" That same tone of hysterical panic. I sprinted to the door, to the sound of her voice.

"Bella, you scared me! Don't you ever do that to me again!" Her voice continued as I ran into the long, high-ceilinged room.

I stared around me, trying to find where her voice

was coming from. I heard her laugh, and I whirled to the sound.

There she was, on the TV screen, tousling my hair in relief. It was Thanksgiving, and I was twelve. We'd gone to see my grandmother in California, the last year before she died. We went to the beach one day, and I'd leaned too far over the edge of the pier. She'd seen my feet flailing, trying to reclaim my balance. "Bella? Bella?" she'd called to me in fear.

And then the TV screen was blue.

I turned slowly. He was standing very still by the back exit, so still I hadn't noticed him at first. In his hand was a remote control. We stared at each other for a long moment, and then he smiled.

He walked toward me, quite close, and then passed me to put the remote down next to the VCR. I turned carefully to watch him.

"Sorry about that, Bella, but isn't it better that your mother didn't really have to be involved in all this?" His voice was courteous, kind.

And suddenly it hit me. My mother was safe. She was still in Florida. She'd never gotten my message. She'd never been terrified by the dark red eyes in the abnormally pale face before me. She was safe.

"Yes," I answered, my voice saturated with relief.

"You don't sound angry that I tricked you."

"I'm not." My sudden high made me brave. What did it matter now? It would soon be over. Charlie and Mom would never be harmed, would never have to fear. I felt almost giddy. Some analytical part of my mind warned me that I was dangerously close to snapping from the stress.

"How odd. You really mean it." His dark eyes assessed me with interest. The irises were nearly black, just a hint of ruby around the edges. Thirsty. "I will give your strange coven this much, you humans can be quite interesting. I guess I can see the draw of observing you. It's amazing — some of you seem to have no sense of your own self-interest at all."

He was standing a few feet away from me, arms folded, looking at me curiously. There was no menace in his face or stance. He was so very average-looking, nothing re-markable about his face or body at all. Just the white skin, the circled eyes I'd grown so used to. He wore a pale blue, long-sleeved shirt and faded blue jeans.

"I suppose you're going to tell me that your boyfriend will avenge you?" he asked, hopefully it seemed to me.

"No, I don't think so. At least, I asked him not to."

"And what was his reply to that?"

"I don't know." It was strangely easy to converse with this genteel hunter. "I left him a letter."

"How romantic, a last letter. And do you think he will honor it?" His voice was just a little harder now, a hint of sarcasm marring his polite tone.

"I hope so."

"Hmmm. Well, our hopes differ then. You see, this was all just a little too easy, too quick. To be quite honest, I'm disappointed. I expected a much greater challenge. And, after all, I only needed a little luck."

I waited in silence.

"When Victoria couldn't get to your father, I had her find out more about you. There was no sense in running all over the planet chasing you down when I could comfortably wait for you in a place of my choosing. So, after I talked to Victoria, I decided to come to Phoenix to pay your mother a visit. I'd heard you say you were going home. At first, I never dreamed you meant it. But then I wondered. Humans can be very predictable; they like to be somewhere familiar, somewhere safe. And wouldn't it be the perfect ploy, to go to the last place you should be when you're hiding — the place that you said you'd be.

"But of course I wasn't sure, it was just a hunch. I usually get a feeling about the prey that I'm hunting, a sixth sense, if you will. I listened to your message when I got to your mother's house, but of course I couldn't be sure where you'd called from. It was very useful to have your number, but you could have been in Antarctica for all I knew, and the game wouldn't work unless you were close by.

"Then your boyfriend got on a plane to Phoenix. Victoria was monitoring them for me, naturally; in a game with this many players, I couldn't be working alone. And so they told me what I'd hoped, that you were here after all. I was prepared; I'd already been through your charming home movies. And then it was simply a matter of the bluff.

"Very easy, you know, not really up to my standards. So, you see, I'm hoping you're wrong about your boyfriend. Edward, isn't it?"

I didn't answer. The bravado was wearing off. I sensed that he was coming to the end of his gloat. It wasn't meant for me anyway. There was no glory in beating me, a weak human.

"Would you mind, very much, if I left a little letter of my own for your Edward?"

He took a step back and touched a palm-sized digital video camera balanced carefully on top of the stereo. A small red light indicated that it was already running. He adjusted it a few times, widened the frame. I stared at him in horror.

"I'm sorry, but I just don't think he'll be able to resist hunting me after he watches this. And I wouldn't want him to miss anything. It was all for him, of course. You're simply a human, who unfortunately was in the wrong place, at the wrong time, and indisputably running with the wrong crowd, I might add."

He stepped toward me, smiling. "Before we begin . . ."

I felt a curl of nausea in the pit of my stomach as he spoke. This was something I had not anticipated.

"I would just like to rub it in, just a little bit. The answer was there all along, and I was so afraid Edward would see that and ruin my fun. It happened once, oh, ages ago. The one and only time my prey escaped me.

"You see, the vampire who was so stupidly fond of this little victim made the choice that your Edward was too weak to make. When the old one knew I was after his little friend, he stole her from the asylum where he worked — I *never* will understand the obsession some vampires seem to form with you humans — and as soon as he freed her he made her safe. She didn't even seem to notice the pain, poor little creature. She'd been stuck in that black hole of a cell for so long. A hundred years earlier and she would have been burned at the stake for her visions. In the nineteen-twenties it was the asylum and the shock treatments. When she opened her eyes, strong with her fresh youth, it was like she'd never seen the sun before. The old vampire made her a strong new vampire, and there was no reason for me to touch her then." He sighed. "I destroyed the old one in vengeance."

"Alice," I breathed, astonished.

"Yes, your little friend. I *was* surprised to see her in the clearing. So I guess her coven ought to be able to derive some comfort from this experience. I get you, but they get her. The one victim who escaped me, quite an honor, actually.

"And she did smell so delicious. I still regret that I never got to taste . . . She smelled even better than you do. Sorry — I don't mean to be offensive. You have a very nice smell. Floral, somehow . . ."

He took another step toward me, till he was just inches away. He lifted a lock of my hair and sniffed at it delicately. Then he gently patted the strand back into place, and I felt his cool fingertips against my throat. He reached up to stroke my cheek once quickly with his thumb, his face curious. I wanted so badly to run, but I was frozen. I couldn't even flinch away.

"No," he murmured to himself as he dropped his hand, "I don't understand." He sighed. "Well, I suppose we should get on with it. And then I can call your friends and tell them where to find you, and my little message."

I was definitely sick now. There was pain coming, I could see it in his eyes. It wouldn't be enough for him to win, to feed and go. There would be no quick end like I'd been counting on. My knees began to shake, and I was afraid I was going to fall.

He stepped back, and began to circle, casually, as if he were trying to get a better view of a statue in a museum. His face was still open and friendly as he decided where to start.

Then he slumped forward, into a crouch I recognized, and his pleasant smile slowly widened, grew, till it wasn't a smile at all but a contortion of teeth, exposed and glistening.

I couldn't help myself — I tried to run. As useless as I knew it would be, as weak as my knees already were, panic took over and I bolted for the emergency door.

He was in front of me in a flash. I didn't see if he used his hand or his foot, it was too fast. A crushing blow struck my chest — I felt myself flying backward, and then heard the crunch as my head bashed into the mirrors. The glass buckled, some of the pieces shattering and splintering on the floor beside me.

I was too stunned to feel the pain. I couldn't breathe yet.

He walked toward me slowly.

"That's a very nice effect," he said, examining the mess of glass, his voice friendly again. "I thought this room would be visually dramatic for my little film. That's why I picked this place to meet you. It's perfect, isn't it?"

I ignored him, scrambling on my hands and knees, crawling toward the other door.

He was over me at once, his foot stepping down hard on my leg. I heard the sickening snap before I felt it. But then I *did* feel it, and I couldn't hold back my scream of agony. I twisted up to reach for my leg, and he was standing over me, smiling.

"Would you like to rethink your last request?" he asked pleasantly. His toe nudged my broken leg and I heard a piercing scream. With a shock, I realized it was mine.

"Wouldn't you rather have Edward try to find me?" he prompted.

"No!" I croaked. "No, Edward, don't —" And then something smashed into my face, throwing me back into the broken mirrors.

Over the pain of my leg, I felt the sharp rip across my scalp where the glass cut into it. And then the warm wetness began to spread through my hair with alarming speed. I could feel it soaking the shoulder of my shirt, hear it dripping on the wood below. The smell of it twisted my stomach.

Through the nausea and dizziness I saw something that gave me a sudden, final shred of hope. His eyes, merely intent before, now burned with an uncontrollable need. The blood — spreading crimson across my white shirt, pooling rapidly on the floor — was driving him mad with thirst. No matter his original intentions, he couldn't draw this out much longer.

Let it be quick now, was all I could hope as the flow of blood from my head sucked my consciousness away with it. My eyes were closing.

I heard, as if from underwater, the final growl of the hunter. I could see, through the long tunnels my eyes had become, his dark shape coming toward me. With my last effort, my hand instinctively raised to protect my face. My eyes closed, and I drifted.

23. THE ANGEL

As I drifted, I dreamed.

Where I floated, under the dark water, I heard the happiest sound my mind could conjure up — as beautiful, as uplifting, as it was ghastly. It was another snarl; a deeper, wilder roar that rang with fury.

I was brought back, almost to the surface, by a sharp pain slashing my upraised hand, but I couldn't find my way back far enough to open my eyes.

And then I knew I was dead.

Because, through the heavy water, I heard the sound of an angel calling my name, calling me to the only heaven I wanted.

"Oh no, Bella, no!" the angel's voice cried in horror.

Behind that longed-for sound was another noise — an awful tumult that my mind shied away from. A vicious bass growling, a shocking snapping sound, and a high keening, suddenly breaking off . . .

I tried to concentrate on the angel's voice instead.

"Bella, please! Bella, listen to me, please, please, Bella, please!" he begged.

Yes, I wanted to say. Anything. But I couldn't find my lips.

"Carlisle!" the angel called, agony in his perfect voice. "Bella, Bella, no, oh please, no, no!" And the angel was sobbing tearless, broken sobs.

The angel shouldn't weep, it was wrong. I tried to find him, to tell him everything was fine, but the water was so deep, it was pressing on me, and I couldn't breathe.

There was a point of pressure against my head. It hurt. Then, as that pain broke through the darkness to me, other pains came, stronger pains. I cried out, gasping, breaking through the dark pool.

"Bella!" the angel cried.

"She's lost some blood, but the head wound isn't deep," a calm voice informed me. "Watch out for her leg, it's broken."

A howl of rage strangled on the angel's lips.

I felt a sharp stab in my side. This couldn't be heaven, could it? There was too much pain for that.

"Some ribs, too, I think," the methodical voice continued.

But the sharp pains were fading. There was a new pain, a scalding pain in my hand that was overshadowing everything else.

Someone was burning me.

"Edward." I tried to tell him, but my voice was so heavy and slow. I couldn't understand myself.

"Bella, you're going to be fine. Can you hear me, Bella? I love you."

"Edward," I tried again. My voice was a little clearer.

"Yes, I'm here."

"It hurts," I whimpered.

"I know, Bella, I know" — and then, away from me, anguished — "can't you do anything?"

"My bag, please. . . . Hold your breath, Alice, it will help," Carlisle promised.

"Alice?" I groaned.

"She's here, she knew where to find you."

"My hand hurts," I tried to tell him.

"I know, Bella. Carlisle will give you something, it will stop."

"My hand is burning!" I screamed, finally breaking through the last of the darkness, my eyes fluttering open. I couldn't see his face, something dark and warm was clouding my eyes. Why couldn't they see the fire and put it out?

His voice was frightened. "Bella?"

"The fire! Someone stop the fire!" I screamed as it burned me.

"Carlisle! Her hand!"

"He bit her." Carlisle's voice was no longer calm, it was appalled.

I heard Edward catch his breath in horror.

"Edward, you have to do it." It was Alice's voice, close by my head. Cool fingers brushed at the wetness in my eyes.

"No!" he bellowed.

"Alice," I moaned.

"There may be a chance," Carlisle said.

"What?" Edward begged.

"See if you can suck the venom back out. The wound is fairly clean." As Carlisle spoke, I could feel more pressure on my head, something poking and pulling at my scalp. The pain of it was lost in the pain of the fire.

"Will that work?" Alice's voice was strained.

"I don't know," Carlisle said. "But we have to hurry."

"Carlisle, I . . ." Edward hesitated. "I don't know if I can do that." There was agony in his beautiful voice again.

"It's your decision, Edward, either way. I can't help you. I have to get this bleeding stopped here if you're going to be taking blood from her hand."

I writhed in the grip of the fiery torture, the movement making the pain in my leg flare sickeningly.

"Edward!" I screamed. I realized my eyes were closed again. I opened them, desperate to find his face. And I found him. Finally, I could see his perfect face, staring at me, twisted into a mask of indecision and pain.

"Alice, get me something to brace her leg!" Carlisle was bent over me, working on my head. "Edward, you must do it now, or it will be too late."

Edward's face was drawn. I watched his eyes as the doubt was suddenly replaced with a blazing determination. His jaw tightened. I felt his cool, strong fingers on my burning hand, locking it in place. Then his head bent over it, and his cold lips pressed against my skin.

At first the pain was worse. I screamed and thrashed against the cool hands that held me back. I heard Alice's voice, trying to calm me. Something heavy held my leg to the floor, and Carlisle had my head locked in the vise of his stone arms.

Then, slowly, my writhing calmed as my hand grew more and more numb. The fire was dulling, focusing into an ever-smaller point.

I felt my consciousness slipping as the pain subsided. I was afraid to fall into the black waters again, afraid I would lose him in the darkness.

"Edward," I tried to say, but I couldn't hear my voice. They could hear me.

"He's right here, Bella."

"Stay, Edward, stay with me. . . ."

"I will." His voice was strained, but somehow triumphant.

I sighed contentedly. The fire was gone, the other pains dulled by a sleepiness seeping through my body.

"Is it all out?" Carlisle asked from somewhere far away.

"Her blood tastes clean," Edward said quietly. "I can taste the morphine."

"Bella?" Carlisle called to me.

I tried to answer. "Mmmmm?"

"Is the fire gone?"

"Yes," I sighed. "Thank you, Edward."

"I love you," he answered.

"I know," I breathed, so tired.

I heard my favorite sound in the world: Edward's quiet laugh, weak with relief.

"Bella?" Carlisle asked again.

I frowned; I wanted to sleep. "What?"

"Where is your mother?"

"In Florida," I sighed. "He tricked me, Edward. He watched our videos." The outrage in my voice was pitifully frail.

But that reminded me.

"Alice." I tried to open my eyes. "Alice, the video — he knew you, Alice, he knew where you came from." I meant to speak urgently, but my voice was feeble. "I smell gasoline," I added, surprised through the haze in my brain.

"It's time to move her," Carlisle said.

"No, I want to sleep," I complained.

"You can sleep, sweetheart, I'll carry you," Edward soothed me.

And I was in his arms, cradled against his chest — floating, all the pain gone.

"Sleep now, Bella" were the last words I heard.

24. AN IMPASSE

My eyes opened to a bright, white light. I was in an unfamiliar room, a white room. The wall beside me was covered in long vertical blinds; over my head, the glaring lights blinded me. I was propped up on a hard, uneven bed — a bed with rails. The pillows were flat and lumpy. There was an annoying beeping sound somewhere close by. I hoped that meant I was still alive. Death shouldn't be this uncomfortable.

My hands were all twisted up with clear tubes, and something was taped across my face, under my nose. I lifted my hand to rip it off.

"No, you don't." And cool fingers caught my hand.

"Edward?" I turned my head slightly, and his exquisite face was just inches from mine, his chin resting on the edge of my pillow. I realized again that I was alive, this time with gratitude and elation. "Oh, Edward, I'm so sorry!"

"Shhhh," he shushed me. "Everything's all right now."

"What happened?" I couldn't remember clearly, and my mind rebelled against me as I tried to recall.

"I was almost too late. I could have been too late," he whispered, his voice tormented.

"I was so stupid, Edward. I thought he had my mom."

"He tricked us all."

"I need to call Charlie and my mom," I realized through the haze.

"Alice called them. Renée is here — well, here in the hospital. She's getting something to eat right now."

"She's here?" I tried to sit up, but the spinning in my head accelerated, and his hand pushed me gently down onto the pillows.

"She'll be back soon," he promised. "And you need to stay still."

"But what did you tell her?" I panicked. I had no interest in being soothed. My mom was here and *I* was recovering from a vampire attack. "Why did you tell her I'm here?"

"You fell down two flights of stairs and through a window." He paused. "You have to admit, it could happen."

I sighed, and it hurt. I stared down at my body under the sheet, the huge lump that was my leg.

"How bad am I?" I asked.

"You have a broken leg, four broken ribs, some cracks in your skull, bruises covering every inch of your skin, and you've lost a lot of blood. They gave you a few transfusions. I didn't like it — it made you smell all wrong for a while."

"That must have been a nice change for you."

"No, I like how *you* smell."

"How did you do it?" I asked quietly. He knew what I meant at once.

"I'm not sure." He looked away from my wondering eyes, lifting my gauze-wrapped hand from the bed and holding it gently in his, careful not to disrupt the wire connecting me to one of the monitors.

I waited patiently for the rest.

He sighed without returning my gaze. "It was impossible . . . to stop," he whispered. "Impossible. But I did." He looked up finally, with half a smile. "I *must* love you."

"Don't I taste as good as I smell?" I smiled in response. That hurt my face.

"Even better — better than I'd imagined."

"I'm sorry," I apologized.

He raised his eyes to the ceiling. "Of all the things to apologize for."

"What *should* I apologize for?"

"For very nearly taking yourself away from me forever."

"I'm sorry," I apologized again.

"I know why you did it." His voice was comforting. "It was still irrational, of course. You should have waited for me, you should have told me."

"You wouldn't have let me go."

"No," he agreed in a grim tone, "I wouldn't."

Some very unpleasant memories were beginning to come back to me. I shuddered, and then winced.

He was instantly anxious. "Bella, what's wrong?"

"What happened to James?"

"After I pulled him off you, Emmett and Jasper took care of him." There was a fierce note of regret in his voice.

This confused me. "I didn't see Emmett and Jasper there."

"They had to leave the room . . . there was a lot of blood."

"But you stayed."

"Yes, I stayed."

"And Alice, and Carlisle . . . ," I said in wonder.

"They love you, too, you know."

A flash of painful images from the last time I'd seen Alice reminded me of something. "Did Alice see the tape?" I asked anxiously.

"Yes." A new sound darkened his voice, a tone of sheer hatred.

"She was always in the dark, that's why she didn't remember."

"I know. She understands now." His voice was even, but his face was black with fury.

I tried to reach his face with my free hand, but something stopped me. I glanced down to see the IV pulling at my hand.

"Ugh." I winced.

"What is it?" he asked anxiously — distracted, but not enough. The bleakness did not entirely leave his eyes.

"Needles," I explained, looking away from the one in my hand. I concentrated on a warped ceiling tile and tried to breathe deeply despite the ache in my ribs.

"Afraid of a needle," he muttered to himself under his breath, shaking his head. "Oh, a sadistic vampire, intent on torturing her to death, sure, no problem, she runs off to meet him. An *IV*, on the other hand . . ."

I rolled my eyes. I was pleased to discover that this reaction, at least, was pain-free. I decided to change the subject.

"Why are *you* here?" I asked.

He stared at me, first confusion and then hurt touching his eyes. His brows pulled together as he frowned. "Do you want me to leave?"

"No!" I protested, horrified by the thought. "No, I meant, why does my mother think you're here? I need to have my story straight before she gets back."

"Oh," he said, and his forehead smoothed back into marble. "I came to Phoenix to talk some sense into you, to convince you to come back to Forks." His wide eyes were so earnest and sincere, I almost believed him myself. "You agreed to see me, and you drove out to the hotel where I was staying with Carlisle and Alice — of course I was here with parental supervision," he inserted virtuously, "but you tripped on the stairs on the way to my room and . . . well, you know the rest. You don't need to remember any details, though; you have a good excuse to be a little muddled about the finer points."

I thought about it for a moment. "There are a few flaws with that story. Like no broken windows."

"Not really," he said. "Alice had a little bit too much fun fabricating evidence. It's all been taken care of very convincingly — you could probably sue the hotel if you wanted to. You have nothing to worry about," he promised, stroking my cheek with the lightest of touches. "Your only job now is to heal."

I wasn't so lost to the soreness or the fog of medication that I didn't respond to his touch. The beeping of the monitor jumped around erratically — now he wasn't the only one who could hear my heart misbehave.

"That's going to be embarrassing," I muttered to myself.

He chuckled, and a speculative look came into his eye. "Hmm, I wonder . . ."

He leaned in slowly; the beeping noise accelerated wildly before his lips even touched me. But when they did, though with the most gentle of pressure, the beeping stopped altogether.

He pulled back abruptly, his anxious expression turning to relief as the monitor reported the restarting of my heart.

"It seems that I'm going to have to be even more careful with you than usual." He frowned.

"I was not finished kissing you," I complained. "Don't make me come over there."

He grinned, and bent to press his lips lightly to mine. The monitor went wild.

But then his lips were taut. He pulled away.

"I think I hear your mother," he said, grinning again.

"Don't leave me," I cried, an irrational surge of panic flooding through me. I couldn't let him go — he might disappear from me again.

He read the terror in my eyes for a short second. "I won't," he promised solemnly, and then he smiled. "I'll take a nap."

He moved from the hard plastic chair by my side to the turquoise faux-leather recliner at the foot of my bed, leaning it all the way back, and closing his eyes. He was perfectly still.

"Don't forget to breathe," I whispered sarcastically. He took a deep breath, his eyes still closed.

I could hear my mother now. She was talking to someone, maybe a nurse, and she sounded tired and upset. I wanted to jump out of the bed and run to her, to calm her, promise that everything was fine. But I wasn't in any sort of shape for jumping, so I waited impatiently.

The door opened a crack, and she peeked through.

"Mom!" I whispered, my voice full of love and relief.

She took in Edward's still form on the recliner, and tiptoed to my bedside.

"He never leaves, does he?" she mumbled to herself.

"Mom, I'm so glad to see you!"

She bent down to hug me gently, and I felt warm tears falling on my cheeks.

"Bella, I was so upset!"

"I'm sorry, Mom. But everything's fine now, it's okay," I comforted her.

"I'm just glad to finally see your eyes open." She sat on the edge of my bed.

I suddenly realized I didn't have any idea *when* it was. "How long have they been closed?"

"It's Friday, hon, you've been out for a while."

"Friday?" I was shocked. I tried to remember what day it had been when . . . but I didn't want to think about that.

"They had to keep you sedated for a while, honey — you've got a lot of injuries."

"I know." I could feel them.

"You're lucky Dr. Cullen was there. He's such a nice man . . . very young, though. And he looks more like a model than a doctor. . . ."

"You met Carlisle?"

"And Edward's sister Alice. She's a lovely girl."

"She is," I agreed wholeheartedly.

She glanced over her shoulder at Edward, lying with his eyes closed in the chair. "You didn't tell me you had such good friends in Forks."

I cringed, and then moaned.

"What hurts?" she demanded anxiously, turning back to me. Edward's eyes flashed to my face.

"It's fine," I assured them. "I just have to remember not to move." He lapsed back into his phony slumber.

I took advantage of my mother's momentary distraction to keep the subject from returning to my less-than-candid behavior. "Where's Phil?" I asked quickly.

"Florida — oh, Bella! You'll never guess! Just when we were about to leave, the best news!"

"Phil got signed?" I guessed.

"Yes! How did you guess! The Suns, can you believe it?"

"That's great, Mom," I said as enthusiastically as I could manage, though I had little idea what that meant.

"And you'll like Jacksonville so much," she gushed while I stared at her vacantly. "I was a little bit worried when Phil started talking about Akron, what with the snow and everything, because you know how I hate the cold, but now Jacksonville! It's always sunny, and the humidity really isn't *that* bad. We found the cutest house, yellow, with white trim, and a porch just like in an old movie, and this huge oak tree, and it's just a few minutes from the ocean, and you'll have your own bathroom —"

"Wait, Mom!" I interrupted. Edward still had his eyes closed, but he looked too tense to pass as asleep. "What are you talking about? I'm not going to Florida. I live in Forks."

"But you don't have to anymore, silly," she laughed. "Phil will be able to be around so much more now . . . we've talked about it a lot, and what I'm going to do is trade off on the away games, half the time with you, half the time with him."

"Mom." I hesitated, wondering how best to be diplomatic about this. "I *want* to live in Forks. I'm already settled in at school, and I have a couple of girlfriends" — she glanced toward Edward again when I reminded her of friends, so I tried another direction — "and Charlie needs me. He's just all alone up there, and he can't cook *at all.*"

"You want to stay in Forks?" she asked, bewildered. The idea was inconceivable to her. And then her eyes flickered back toward Edward. "Why?"

"I told you — school, Charlie — ouch!" I'd shrugged. Not a good idea.

Her hands fluttered helplessly over me, trying to find a safe place to pat. She made do with my forehead; it was unbandaged.

"Bella, honey, you hate Forks," she reminded me.

"It's not so bad."

She frowned and looked back and forth between Edward and me, this time very deliberately.

"Is it this boy?" she whispered.

I opened my mouth to lie, but her eyes were scrutinizing my face, and I knew she would see through that.

"He's part of it," I admitted. No need to confess how big a part. "So, have you had a chance to talk with Edward?" I asked.

"Yes." She hesitated, looking at his perfectly still form. "And I want to talk to you about that."

Uh-oh. "What about?" I asked.

"I think that boy is in love with you," she accused, keeping her voice low.

"I think so, too," I confided.

"And how do you feel about him?" She only poorly concealed the raging curiosity in her voice.

I sighed, looking away. As much as I loved my mom, this was not a conversation I wanted to have with her. "I'm pretty crazy about him." There — that sounded like something a teenager with her first boyfriend might say.

"Well, he *seems* very nice, and, my goodness, he's incredibly good-looking, but you're so young, Bella . . ." Her voice was unsure; as far as I could remember, this was the first time since I was eight that she'd come close to trying to sound like a parental authority. I recognized the reasonable-but-firm tone of voice from talks I'd had with her about men.

"I know that, Mom. Don't worry about it. It's just a crush," I soothed her.

"That's right," she agreed, easily pleased.

Then she sighed and glanced guiltily over her shoulder at the big, round clock on the wall.

"Do you need to go?"

She bit her lip. "Phil's supposed to call in a little while . . . I didn't know you were going to wake up. . . ."

"No problem, Mom." I tried to tone down the relief so she wouldn't get her feelings hurt. "I won't be alone."

"I'll be back soon. I've been sleeping here, you know," she announced, proud of herself.

"Oh, Mom, you don't have to do that! You can sleep at home — I'll never notice." The swirl of painkillers in my brain was making it hard to concentrate even now, though, apparently, I'd been sleeping for days.

"I was too nervous," she admitted sheepishly. "There's been some crime in the neighborhood, and I don't like being there alone."

"Crime?" I asked in alarm.

"Someone broke into that dance studio around the corner from the house and burned it to the ground — there's nothing left at all! And they left a stolen car right out front. Do you remember when you used to dance there, honey?"

"I remember." I shivered, and winced.

"I can stay, baby, if you need me."

"No, Mom, I'll be fine. Edward will be with me."

She looked like that might be why she wanted to stay. "I'll be back tonight." It sounded as much like a warning as it sounded like a promise, and she glanced at Edward again as she said it.

"I love you, Mom."

"I love you, too, Bella. Try to be more careful when you walk, honey, I don't want to lose you."

Edward's eyes stayed closed, but a wide grin flashed across his face.

A nurse came bustling in then to check all my tubes and wires. My mother kissed my forehead, patted my gauze-wrapped hand, and left.

The nurse was checking the paper readout on my heart monitor.

"Are you feeling anxious, honey? Your heart rate got a little high there."

"I'm fine," I assured her.

"I'll tell your RN that you're awake. She'll be in to see you in a minute."

As soon as she closed the door, Edward was at my side.

"You stole a car?" I raised my eyebrows.

He smiled, unrepentant. "It was a good car, very fast."

"How was your nap?" I asked.

"Interesting." His eyes narrowed.

"What?"

He looked down while he answered. "I'm surprised. I thought Florida . . . and your mother . . . well, I thought that's what you would want."

I stared at him uncomprehendingly. "But you'd be stuck inside all day in Florida. You'd only be able to come out at night, just like a real vampire."

He almost smiled, but not quite. And then his face was grave. "I would stay in Forks, Bella. Or somewhere like it," he explained. "Someplace where I couldn't hurt you anymore."

It didn't sink in at first. I continued to stare at him blankly as the words one by one clicked into place in my head like a ghastly puzzle. I was barely conscious of the sound of my heart accelerating, though, as my breathing became hyperventilation, I *was* aware of the sharp aching in my protesting ribs.

He didn't say anything; he watched my face warily as the pain that had nothing to do with broken bones, pain that was infinitely worse, threatened to crush me.

And then another nurse walked purposefully into the room. Edward sat still as stone as she took in my expression with a practiced eye before turning to the monitors.

"Time for more pain meds, sweetheart?" she asked kindly, tapping the IV feed.

"No, no," I mumbled, trying to keep the agony out of

my voice. "I don't need anything." I couldn't afford to close my eyes now.

"No need to be brave, honey. It's better if you don't get too stressed out; you need to rest." She waited, but I just shook my head.

"Okay," she sighed. "Hit the call button when you're ready."

She gave Edward a stern look, and threw one more anxious glance at the machinery, before leaving.

His cool hands were on my face; I stared at him with wild eyes.

"Shhh, Bella, calm down."

"Don't leave me," I begged in a broken voice.

"I won't," he promised. "Now relax before I call the nurse back to sedate you."

But my heart couldn't slow.

"Bella." He stroked my face anxiously. "I'm not going anywhere. I'll be right here as long as you need me."

"Do you swear you won't leave me?" I whispered. I tried to control the gasping, at least. My ribs were throbbing.

He put his hands on either side of my face and brought his face close to mine. His eyes were wide and serious. "I swear."

The smell of his breath was soothing. It seemed to ease the ache of my breathing. He continued to hold my gaze while my body slowly relaxed and the beeping returned to a normal pace. His eyes were dark, closer to black than gold today.

"Better?" he asked.

"Yes," I said cautiously.

He shook his head and muttered something unintelligible. I thought I picked out the word "overreaction."

"Why did you say that?" I whispered, trying to keep my voice from shaking. "Are you tired of having to save me all the time? Do you *want* me to go away?"

"No, I don't want to be without you, Bella, of course not. Be rational. And I have no problem with saving you, either — if it weren't for the fact that I was the one putting you in danger . . . that I'm the reason that you're here."

"Yes, you are the reason." I frowned. "The reason I'm here — *alive.*"

"Barely." His voice was just a whisper. "Covered in gauze and plaster and hardly able to move."

"I wasn't referring to my most recent near-death experience," I said, growing irritated. "I was thinking of the others — you can take your pick. If it weren't for you, I would be rotting away in the Forks cemetery."

He winced at my words, but the haunted look didn't leave his eyes.

"That's not the worst part, though," he continued to whisper. He acted as if I hadn't spoken. "Not seeing you there on the floor . . . crumpled and broken." His voice was choked. "Not thinking I was too late. Not even hearing you scream in pain — all those unbearable memories that I'll carry with me for the rest of eternity. No, the very worst was feeling . . . knowing that I couldn't stop. Believing that I was going to kill you myself."

"But you didn't."

"I could have. So easily."

I knew I needed to stay calm . . . but he was trying to talk himself into leaving me, and the panic fluttered in my lungs, trying to get out.

"Promise me," I whispered.

"What?"

"You know what." I was starting to get angry now. He was so stubbornly determined to dwell on the negative.

He heard the change in my tone. His eyes tightened. "I don't seem to be strong enough to stay away from you, so I suppose that you'll get your way . . . whether it kills you or not," he added roughly.

"Good." He hadn't promised, though — a fact that I had not missed. The panic was only barely contained; I had no strength left to control the anger. "You told me how you stopped . . . now I want to know why," I demanded.

"Why?" he repeated warily.

"*Why* you did it. Why didn't you just let the venom spread? By now I would be just like you."

Edward's eyes seemed to turn flat black, and I remembered that this was something he'd never intended me to know. Alice must have been preoccupied by the things she'd learned about herself . . . or she'd been very careful with her thoughts around him — clearly, he'd had no idea that she'd filled me in on the mechanics of vampire conversions. He was surprised, and infuriated. His nostrils flared, his mouth looked as if it was chiseled from stone.

He wasn't going to answer, that much was clear.

"I'll be the first to admit that I have no experience with relationships," I said. "But it just seems logical . . . a man and woman have to be somewhat equal . . . as in, one of them can't always be swooping in and saving the other one. They have to save each other *equally*."

He folded his arms on the side of my bed and rested his chin on his arms. His expression was smooth, the anger reined in. Evidently he'd decided he wasn't angry with *me*. I hoped I'd get a chance to warn Alice before he caught up with her.

"You *have* saved me," he said quietly.

"I can't always be Lois Lane," I insisted. "I want to be Superman, too."

"You don't know what you're asking." His voice was soft; he stared intently at the edge of the pillowcase.

"I think I do."

"Bella, you *don't* know. I've had almost ninety years to think about this, and I'm still not sure."

"Do you wish that Carlisle hadn't saved you?"

"No, I don't wish that." He paused before continuing. "But my life was over. I wasn't giving anything up."

"You *are* my life. You're the only thing it would hurt me to lose." I was getting better at this. It was easy to admit how much I needed him.

He was very calm, though. Decided.

"I can't do it, Bella. I won't do that to you."

"Why not?" My throat rasped and the words weren't as loud as I'd meant them to be. "Don't tell me it's too hard! After today, or I guess it was a few days ago . . . anyway, after *that,* it should be nothing."

He glared at me.

"And the pain?" he asked.

I blanched. I couldn't help it. But I tried to keep my expression from showing how clearly I remembered the feeling . . . the fire in my veins.

"That's my problem," I said. "I can handle it."

"It's possible to take bravery to the point where it becomes insanity."

"It's not an issue. Three days. Big deal."

Edward grimaced again as my words reminded him that I was more informed than he had ever intended me to be. I watched him repress the anger, watched as his eyes grew speculative.

"Charlie?" he asked curtly. "Renée?"

Minutes passed in silence as I struggled to answer his question. I opened my mouth, but no sound came out. I closed it again. He waited, and his expression became triumphant because he knew I had no true answer.

"Look, that's not an issue either," I finally muttered; my voice was as unconvincing as it always was when I lied. "Renée has always made the choices that work for her — she'd want me to do the same. And Charlie's resilient, he's used to being on his own. I can't take care of them forever. I have my own life to live."

"Exactly," he snapped. "And I won't end it for you."

"If you're waiting for me to be on my deathbed, I've got news for you! I was just there!"

"You're going to recover," he reminded me.

I took a deep breath to calm myself, ignoring the spasm of pain it triggered. I stared at him, and he stared back. There was no compromise in his face.

"No," I said slowly. "I'm not."

His forehead creased. "Of course you are. You may have a scar or two. . . ."

"You're wrong," I insisted. "I'm going to die."

"Really, Bella." He was anxious now. "You'll be out of here in a few days. Two weeks at most."

I glared at him. "I may not die now . . . but I'm going to die sometime. Every minute of the day, I get closer. And I'm going to get *old*."

He frowned as what I was saying sunk in, pressing his long fingers to his temples and closing his eyes. "That's how it's supposed to happen. How it should happen. How it would have happened if I didn't exist — and I *shouldn't exist*."

I snorted. He opened his eyes in surprise. "That's stupid. That's like going to someone who's just won the lottery, taking their money, and saying, 'Look, let's just go back to how things should be. It's better that way.' And I'm not buying it."

"I'm hardly a lottery prize," he growled.

"That's right. You're much better."

He rolled his eyes and set his lips. "Bella, we're not having this discussion anymore. I refuse to damn you to an eternity of night and that's the end of it."

"If you think that's the end, then you don't know me very well," I warned him. "You're not the only vampire I know."

His eyes went black again. "Alice wouldn't dare."

And for a moment he looked so frightening that I

couldn't help but believe it — I couldn't imagine someone brave enough to cross him.

"Alice already saw it, didn't she?" I guessed. "That's
why the things she says upset you. She knows I'm going to
be like you . . . someday."

"She's wrong. She also saw you dead, but that didn't
happen, either."

"You'll never catch *me* betting against Alice."

We stared at each other for a very long time. It was
quiet except for the whirring of the machines, the beeping, the dripping, the ticking of the big clock on the wall.
Finally, his expression softened.

"So where does that leave us?" I wondered.

He chuckled humorlessly. "I believe it's called an
impasse."

I sighed. "Ouch," I muttered.

"How are you feeling?" he asked, eyeing the button for
the nurse.

"I'm fine," I lied.

"I don't believe you," he said gently.

"I'm not going back to sleep."

"You need rest. All this arguing isn't good for you."

"So give in," I hinted.

"Nice try." He reached for the button.

"No!"

He ignored me.

"Yes?" the speaker on the wall squawked.

"I think we're ready for more pain medication," he said
calmly, ignoring my furious expression.

"I'll send in the nurse." The voice sounded very bored.

"I won't take it," I promised.

He looked toward the sack of fluids hanging beside my bed. "I don't think they're going to ask you to swallow anything."

My heart rate started to climb. He read the fear in my eyes, and sighed in frustration.

"Bella, you're in pain. You need to relax so you can heal. Why are you being so difficult? They're not going to put any more needles in you now."

"I'm not afraid of the needles," I mumbled. "I'm afraid to close my eyes."

Then he smiled his crooked smile, and took my face between his hands. "I told you I'm not going anywhere. Don't be afraid. As long as it makes you happy, I'll be here."

I smiled back, ignoring the ache in my cheeks. "You're talking about forever, you know."

"Oh, you'll get over it — it's just a crush."

I shook my head in disbelief — it made me dizzy. "I was shocked when Renée swallowed that one. I know *you* know better."

"That's the beautiful thing about being human," he told me. "Things change."

My eyes narrowed. "Don't hold your breath."

He was laughing when the nurse came in, brandishing a syringe.

"Excuse me," she said brusquely to Edward.

He got up and crossed to the end of the small room,

leaning against the wall. He folded his arms and waited. I kept my eyes on him, still apprehensive. He met my gaze calmly.

"Here you go, honey." The nurse smiled as she injected the medicine into my tube. "You'll feel better now."

"Thanks," I mumbled, unenthusiastic. It didn't take long. I could feel the drowsiness trickling through my bloodstream almost immediately.

"That ought to do it," she muttered as my eyelids drooped.

She must have left the room, because something cold and smooth touched my face.

"Stay." The word was slurred.

"I will," he promised. His voice was beautiful, like a lullaby. "Like I said, as long as it makes you happy . . . as long as it's what's best for you."

I tried to shake my head, but it was too heavy. "'S not the same thing," I mumbled.

He laughed. "Don't worry about that now, Bella. You can argue with me when you wake up."

I think I smiled. "'Kay."

I could feel his lips at my ear.

"I love you," he whispered.

"Me, too."

"I know," he laughed quietly.

I turned my head slightly . . . searching. He knew what I was after. His lips touched mine gently.

"Thanks," I sighed.

"Anytime."

I wasn't really there at all anymore. But I fought against the stupor weakly. There was just one more thing I wanted to tell him.

"Edward?" I struggled to pronounce his name clearly.

"Yes?"

"I'm betting on Alice," I mumbled.

And then the night closed over me.

EPILOGUE:
AN OCCASION

EDWARD HELPED ME INTO HIS CAR, BEING VERY CAREFUL of the wisps of silk and chiffon, the flowers he'd just pinned into my elaborately styled curls, and my bulky walking cast. He ignored the angry set of my mouth.

When he had me settled, he got in the driver's seat and headed back out the long, narrow drive.

"At what point exactly are you going to tell me what's going on?" I asked grumpily. I really hated surprises. And he knew that.

"I'm shocked that you haven't figured it out yet." He threw a mocking smile in my direction, and my breath caught in my throat. Would I ever get used to his perfection?

"I did mention that you looked very nice, didn't I?" I verified.

"Yes." He grinned again. I'd never seen him dress in black before, and, with the contrast against his pale skin, his beauty was absolutely surreal. That much I couldn't deny, even if the fact that he was wearing a tuxedo made me very nervous.

Not quite as nervous as the dress. Or the shoe. Only one shoe, as my other foot was still securely encased in plaster. But the stiletto heel, held on only by satin ribbons, certainly wasn't going to help me as I tried to hobble around.

"I'm not coming over anymore if Alice is going to treat me like Guinea Pig Barbie when I do," I griped. I'd spent the better part of the day in Alice's staggeringly vast bathroom, a helpless victim as she played hairdresser and cosmetician. Whenever I fidgeted or complained, she reminded me that she didn't have any memories of being human, and asked me not to ruin her vicarious fun. Then she'd dressed me in the most ridiculous dress — deep blue, frilly and off the shoulders, with French tags I couldn't read — a dress more suitable for a runway than Forks. Nothing good could come of our formal attire, of that I was sure. Unless . . . but I was afraid to put my suspicions into words, even in my own head.

I was distracted then by the sound of a phone ringing. Edward pulled his cell phone from a pocket inside his jacket, looking briefly at the caller ID before answering.

"Hello, Charlie," he said warily.

"Charlie?" I frowned.

Charlie had been . . . difficult since my return to Forks. He had compartmentalized my bad experience into two defined reactions. Toward Carlisle he was almost worshipfully grateful. On the other hand, he was stubbornly convinced that Edward was at fault — because, if not for him, I wouldn't have left home in the first place. And Edward was far from disagreeing with him. These days I had rules that hadn't existed before: curfews . . . visiting hours.

Something Charlie was saying made Edward's eyes widen in disbelief, and then a grin spread across his face.

"You're kidding!" He laughed.

"What is it?" I demanded.

He ignored me. "Why don't you let me talk to him?" Edward suggested with evident pleasure. He waited for a few seconds.

"Hello, Tyler, this is Edward Cullen." His voice was very friendly, on the surface. I knew it well enough to catch the soft edge of menace. What was Tyler doing at my house? The awful truth began to dawn on me. I looked again at the inappropriate dress Alice had forced me into.

"I'm sorry if there's been some kind of miscommunication, but Bella is unavailable tonight." Edward's tone changed, and the threat in his voice was suddenly much more evident as he continued. "To be perfectly honest, she'll be unavailable every night, as far as anyone besides myself is concerned. No offense. And I'm sorry about your evening." He didn't sound sorry at all. And then he snapped the phone shut, a huge smirk on his face.

My face and neck flushed crimson with anger. I could feel the rage-induced tears starting to fill my eyes.

He looked at me in surprise. "Was that last part a bit too much? I didn't mean to offend you."

I ignored that.

"You're taking me to *the prom*!" I yelled.

It was embarrassingly obvious now. If I'd been paying any attention at all, I'm sure I would have noticed the date on the posters that decorated the school buildings. But I'd never dreamed he was thinking of subjecting me to this. Didn't he know me at all?

He wasn't expecting the force of my reaction, that was clear. He pressed his lips together and his eyes narrowed. "Don't be difficult, Bella."

My eyes flashed to the window; we were halfway to the school already.

"Why are you doing this to me?" I demanded in horror.

He gestured to his tuxedo. "Honestly, Bella, what did you think we were doing?"

I was mortified. First, because I'd missed the obvious. And also because the vague suspicions — expectations, really — that I'd been forming all day, as Alice tried to transform me into a beauty queen, were so far wide of the mark. My half-fearful hopes seemed very silly now.

I'd guessed there was some kind of occasion brewing. But *prom*! That was the furthest thing from my mind.

The angry tears rolled over my cheeks. I remembered with dismay that I was very uncharacteristically wearing mascara. I wiped quickly under my eyes to prevent any smudges. My hand was unblackened when I pulled it away; maybe Alice had known I would need waterproof makeup.

"This is completely ridiculous. Why are you crying?" he demanded in frustration.

"Because I'm *mad*!"

"Bella." He turned the full force of his scorching golden eyes on me.

"What?" I muttered, distracted.

"Humor me," he insisted.

His eyes were melting all my fury. It was impossible to fight with him when he cheated like that. I gave in with poor grace.

"Fine," I pouted, unable to glare as effectively as I would have liked. "I'll go quietly. But you'll see. I'm way overdue for more bad luck. I'll probably break my other leg. Look at this shoe! It's a death trap!" I held out my good leg as evidence.

"Hmmm." He stared at my leg longer than was necessary. "Remind me to thank Alice for that tonight."

"Alice is going to be there?" That comforted me slightly.

"With Jasper, and Emmett . . . and Rosalie," he admitted.

The feeling of comfort disappeared. There had been no progress with Rosalie, though I was on quite good terms with her sometimes-husband. Emmett enjoyed having me around — he thought my bizarre human reactions were hilarious . . . or maybe it was just the fact that I fell down a lot that he found so funny. Rosalie acted as if I didn't exist. While I shook my head to dispel the direction my thoughts had taken, I thought of something else.

"Is Charlie in on this?" I asked, suddenly suspicious.

"Of course." He grinned, and then chuckled. "Apparently Tyler wasn't, though."

I gritted my teeth. How Tyler could be so delusional, I couldn't imagine. At school, where Charlie couldn't interfere, Edward and I were inseparable — except for those rare sunny days.

We were at the school now; Rosalie's red convertible was conspicuous in the parking lot. The clouds were thin today, a few streaks of sunlight escaping through far away in the west.

He got out and walked around the car to open my door. He held out his hand.

I sat stubbornly in my seat, arms folded, feeling a secret twinge of smugness. The lot was crowded with people in formal dress: witnesses. He couldn't remove me forcibly from the car as he might have if we'd been alone.

He sighed. "When someone wants to kill you, you're brave as a lion — and then when someone mentions dancing . . ." He shook his head.

I gulped. Dancing.

"Bella, I won't let anything hurt you — not even yourself. I won't let go of you once, I promise."

I thought about that and suddenly felt much better. He could see that in my face.

"There, now," he said gently, "it won't be so bad." He leaned down and wrapped one arm around my waist. I took his other hand and let him lift me from the car.

He kept his arm tightly around me, supporting me as I limped toward the school.

In Phoenix, they held proms in hotel ballrooms. This dance was in the gym, of course. It was probably the only room in town big enough for a dance. When we got inside, I giggled. There were actual balloon arches and twisted garlands of pastel crepe paper festooning the walls.

"This looks like a horror movie waiting to happen," I snickered.

"Well," he muttered as we slowly approached the ticket table — he was carrying most of my weight, but I still had to shuffle and wobble my feet forward — "there are *more* than enough vampires present."

I looked at the dance floor; a wide gap had formed in the center of the floor, where two couples whirled gracefully. The other dancers pressed to the sides of the room to give them space — no one wanted to stand in contrast with such radiance. Emmett and Jasper were intimidating and flawless in classic tuxedos. Alice was striking in a black satin dress with geometric cutouts that bared large triangles of her snowy white skin. And Rosalie was . . . well, Rosalie. She was beyond belief. Her vivid scarlet dress was backless, tight to her calves where it flared into a wide ruffled train, with a neckline that plunged to her waist. I pitied every girl in the room, myself included.

"Do you want me to bolt the doors so you can massacre the unsuspecting townsfolk?" I whispered conspiratorially.

"And where do you fit into that scheme?" He glared.

"Oh, I'm with the vampires, of course."

He smiled reluctantly. "Anything to get out of dancing."

"Anything."

He bought our tickets, then turned me toward the dance floor. I cringed against his arm and dragged my feet.

"I've got all night," he warned.

Eventually he towed me out to where his family was twirling elegantly — if in a style totally unsuitable to the present time and music. I watched in horror.

"Edward." My throat was so dry I could only manage a whisper. "I *honestly* can't dance!" I could feel the panic bubbling up inside my chest.

"Don't worry, silly," he whispered back. "I *can*." He put my arms around his neck and lifted me to slide his feet under mine.

And then we were whirling, too.

"I feel like I'm five years old," I laughed after a few minutes of effortless waltzing.

"You don't look five," he murmured, pulling me closer for a second, so that my feet were briefly a foot from the ground.

Alice caught my eye on a turn and smiled in encouragement — I smiled back. I was surprised to realize that I was actually enjoying myself . . . a little.

"Okay, this isn't half bad," I admitted.

But Edward was staring toward the doors, and his face was angry.

"What is it?" I wondered aloud. I followed his gaze, disoriented by the spinning, but finally I could see what was bothering him. Jacob Black, not in a tux, but in a long-sleeved white shirt and tie, his hair smoothed back into his usual ponytail, was crossing the floor toward us.

After the first shock of recognition, I couldn't help but feel bad for Jacob. He was clearly uncomfortable — excruciatingly so. His face was apologetic as his eyes met mine.

Edward snarled very quietly.

"Be*have*!" I hissed.

Edward's voice was scathing. "He wants to chat with you."

Jacob reached us then, the embarrassment and apology even more evident on his face.

"Hey, Bella, I was hoping you would be here." Jacob sounded like he'd been hoping the exact opposite. But his smile was just as warm as ever.

"Hi, Jacob." I smiled back. "What's up?"

"Can I cut in?" he asked tentatively, glancing at Edward for the first time. I was shocked to notice that Jacob didn't have to look up. He must have grown half a foot since the first time I'd seen him.

Edward's face was composed, his expression blank. His only answer was to set me carefully on my feet, and take a step back.

"Thanks," Jacob said amiably.

Edward just nodded, looking at me intently before he turned to walk away.

Jacob put his hands on my waist, and I reached up to put my hands on his shoulders.

"Wow, Jake, how tall are you now?"

He was smug. "Six-two."

We weren't really dancing — my leg made that impossible. Instead we swayed awkwardly from side to side without moving our feet. It was just as well; the recent growth spurt had left him looking gangly and uncoordinated, he was probably no better a dancer than I was.

"So, how did you end up here tonight?" I asked without true curiosity. Considering Edward's reaction, I could guess.

"Can you believe my dad paid me twenty bucks to come to your prom?" he admitted, slightly ashamed.

"Yes, I can," I muttered. "Well, I hope you're enjoying yourself, at least. Seen anything you like?" I teased, nodding toward a group of girls lined up against the wall like pastel confections.

"Yeah," he sighed. "But she's taken."

He glanced down to meet my curious gaze for just a second — then we both looked away, embarrassed.

"You look really pretty, by the way," he added shyly.

"Um, thanks. So why did Billy pay you to come here?" I asked quickly, though I knew the answer.

Jacob didn't seem grateful for the subject change; he looked away, uncomfortable again. "He said it was a 'safe' place to talk to you. I swear the old man is losing his mind."

I joined in his laughter weakly.

"Anyway, he said that if I told you something, he would get me that master cylinder I need," he confessed with a sheepish grin.

"Tell me, then. I want you to get your car finished." I grinned back. At least Jacob didn't believe any of this. It made the situation a bit easier. Against the wall, Edward was watching my face, his own face expressionless. I saw a

sophomore in a pink dress eyeing him with timid speculation, but he didn't seem to be aware of her.

Jacob looked away again, ashamed. "Don't get mad,
okay?"

"There's no way I'll be mad at you, Jacob," I assured him.
"I won't even be mad at Billy. Just say what you have to."

"Well — this is so stupid, I'm sorry, Bella — he wants
you to break up with your boyfriend. He asked me to tell
you 'please.'" He shook his head in disgust.

"He's still superstitious, eh?"

"Yeah. He was . . . kind of over the top when you got
hurt down in Phoenix. He didn't believe . . ." Jacob trailed
off self-consciously.

My eyes narrowed. "I fell."

"I know that," Jacob said quickly.

"He thinks Edward had something to do with me getting hurt." It wasn't a question, and despite my promise, I
was angry.

Jacob wouldn't meet my eyes. We weren't even bothering to sway to the music, though his hands were still on
my waist, and mine around his neck.

"Look, Jacob, I know Billy probably won't believe this,
but just so you know" — he looked at me now, responding
to the new earnestness in my voice — "Edward really did
save my life. If it weren't for Edward and his father, I'd be
dead."

"I know," he claimed, but he sounded like my sincere
words had affected him some. Maybe he'd be able to convince Billy of this much, at least.

"Hey, I'm sorry you had to come do this, Jacob," I apologized. "At any rate, you get your parts, right?"

"Yeah," he muttered. He was still looking awkward . . . upset.

"There's more?" I asked in disbelief.

"Forget it," he mumbled, "I'll get a job and save the money myself."

I glared at him until he met my gaze. "Just spit it out, Jacob."

"It's so bad."

"I don't care. Tell me," I insisted.

"Okay . . . but, geez, this sounds bad." He shook his head. "He said to tell you, no, to *warn* you, that — and this is his plural, not mine" — he lifted one hand from my waist and made little quotations marks in the air — "'We'll be watching.'" He watched warily for my reaction.

It sounded like something from a mafia movie. I laughed out loud.

"Sorry you had to do this, Jake," I snickered.

"I don't mind *that* much." He grinned in relief. His eyes were appraising as they raked quickly over my dress. "So, should I tell him you said to butt the hell out?" he asked hopefully.

"No," I sighed. "Tell him I said thanks. I know he means well."

The song ended, and I dropped my arms.

His hands hesitated at my waist, and he glanced at my bum leg. "Do you want to dance again? Or can I help you get somewhere?"

Edward answered for me. "That's all right, Jacob. I'll take it from here."

Jacob flinched, and stared wide-eyed at Edward, who stood just beside us.

"Hey, I didn't see you there," he mumbled. "I guess I'll see you around, Bella." He stepped back, waving half-heartedly.

I smiled. "Yeah, I'll see you later."

"Sorry," he said again before he turned for the door.

Edward's arms wound around me as the next song started. It was a little up-tempo for slow dancing, but that didn't seem to concern him. I leaned my head against his chest, content.

"Feeling better?" I teased.

"Not really," he said tersely.

"Don't be mad at Billy," I sighed. "He just worries about me for Charlie's sake. It's nothing personal."

"I'm not mad at Billy," he corrected in a clipped voice. "But his son is irritating me."

I pulled back to look at him. His face was very serious. "Why?"

"First of all, he made me break my promise."

I stared at him in confusion.

He half-smiled. "I promised I wouldn't let go of you tonight," he explained.

"Oh. Well, I forgive you."

"Thanks. But there's something else." Edward frowned. I waited patiently.

"He called you *pretty,*" he finally continued, his frown

deepening. "That's practically an insult, the way you look right now. You're much more than beautiful."

I laughed. "You might be a little biased."

"I don't think that's it. Besides, I have excellent eyesight."

We were twirling again, my feet on his as he held me close.

"So are you going to explain the reason for all of this?" I wondered.

He looked down at me, confused, and I glared meaningfully at the crepe paper.

He considered for a moment, and then changed direction, spinning me through the crowd to the back door of the gym. I caught a glimpse of Jessica and Mike dancing, staring at me curiously. Jessica waved, and I smiled back quickly. Angela was there, too, looking blissfully happy in the arms of little Ben Cheney; she didn't look up from his eyes, a head lower than hers. Lee and Samantha, Lauren, glaring toward us, with Conner; I could name every face that spiraled past me. And then we were outdoors, in the cool, dim light of a fading sunset.

As soon as we were alone, he swung me up into his arms, and carried me across the dark grounds till he reached the bench beneath the shadow of the madrone trees. He sat there, keeping me cradled against his chest. The moon was already up, visible through the gauzy clouds, and his face glowed pale in the white light. His mouth was hard, his eyes troubled.

"The point?" I prompted softly.

He ignored me, staring up at the moon.

"Twilight, again," he murmured. "Another ending. No matter how perfect the day is, it always has to end."

"Some things don't have to end," I muttered through my teeth, instantly tense.

He sighed.

"I brought you to the prom," he said slowly, finally answering my question, "because I don't want you to miss anything. I don't want my presence to take anything away from you, if I can help it. I want you to be *human*. I want your life to continue as it would have if I'd died in nineteen-eighteen like I should have."

I shuddered at his words, and then shook my head angrily. "In what strange parallel dimension would I *ever* have gone to prom of my own free will? If you weren't a thousand times stronger than me, I would never have let you get away with this."

He smiled briefly, but it didn't touch his eyes. "It wasn't so bad, you said so yourself."

"That's because I was with you."

We were quiet for a minute; he stared at the moon and I stared at him. I wished there was some way to explain how very uninterested I was in a normal human life.

"Will you tell me something?" he asked, glancing down at me with a slight smile.

"Don't I always?"

"Just promise you'll tell me," he insisted, grinning.

I knew I was going to regret this almost instantly. "Fine."

"You seemed honestly surprised when you figured out that I was taking you here," he began.

"I *was,*" I interjected.

"Exactly," he agreed. "But you must have had some other theory . . . I'm curious — what did you *think* I was dressing you up for?"

Yes, instant regret. I pursed my lips, hesitating. "I don't want to tell you."

"You promised," he objected.

"I know."

"What's the problem?"

I knew he thought it was mere embarrassment holding me back. "I think it will make you mad — or sad."

His brows pulled together over his eyes as he thought that through. "I still want to know. Please?"

I sighed. He waited.

"Well . . . I assumed it was some kind of . . . occasion. But I didn't think it would be some trite human thing . . . prom!" I scoffed.

"Human?" he asked flatly. He'd picked up on the key word.

I looked down at my dress, fidgeting with a stray piece of chiffon. He waited in silence.

"Okay," I confessed in a rush. "So I was hoping that you might have changed your mind . . . that you were going to change *me*, after all."

A dozen emotions played across his face. Some I recognized: anger . . . pain . . . and then he seemed to collect himself and his expression became amused.

"You thought that would be a black tie occasion, did you?" he teased, touching the lapel of his tuxedo jacket.

I scowled to hide my embarrassment. "I don't know how these things work. To me, at least, it seems more rational than prom does." He was still grinning. "It's not funny," I said.

"No, you're right, it's not," he agreed, his smile fading. "I'd rather treat it like a joke, though, than believe you're serious."

"But I am serious."

He sighed deeply. "I know. And you're really that willing?"

The pain was back in his eyes. I bit my lip and nodded.

"So ready for this to be the end," he murmured, almost to himself, "for this to be the twilight of your life, though your life has barely started. You're ready to give up everything."

"It's not the end, it's the beginning," I disagreed under my breath.

"I'm not worth it," he said sadly.

"Do you remember when you told me that I didn't see myself very clearly?" I asked, raising my eyebrows. "You obviously have the same blindness."

"I know what I am."

I sighed.

But his mercurial mood shifted on me. He pursed his lips, and his eyes were probing. He examined my face for a long moment.

"You're ready now, then?" he asked.

"Um." I gulped. "Yes?"

He smiled, and inclined his head slowly until his cold lips brushed against the skin just under the corner of my jaw.

"Right now?" he whispered, his breath blowing cool on my neck. I shivered involuntarily.

"Yes," I whispered, so my voice wouldn't have a chance to break. If he thought I was bluffing, he was going to be disappointed. I'd already made this decision, and I was sure. It didn't matter that my body was rigid as a plank, my hands balled into fists, my breathing erratic . . .

He chuckled darkly, and leaned away. His face did look disappointed.

"You can't really believe that I would give in so easily," he said with a sour edge to his mocking tone.

"A girl can dream."

His eyebrows rose. "Is that what you dream about? Being a monster?"

"Not exactly," I said, frowning at his word choice. Monster, indeed. "Mostly I dream about being with you forever."

His expression changed, softened and saddened by the subtle ache in my voice.

"Bella." His fingers lightly traced the shape of my lips. "I *will* stay with you — isn't that enough?"

I smiled under his fingertips. "Enough for now."

He frowned at my tenacity. No one was going to surrender tonight. He exhaled, and the sound was practically a growl.

I touched his face. "Look," I said. "I love you more than everything else in the world combined. Isn't that enough?"

"Yes, it is enough," he answered, smiling. "Enough for forever."

And he leaned down to press his cold lips once more to my throat.

Acknowledgments

A huge thank you to:
my parents, Steve and Candy,
for a lifetime of love and support,
for reading great books to me when I was young,
and for still holding my hand through the
things that make me nervous;
my husband, Pancho, and my sons, Gabe, Seth, and Eli,
for sharing me so often with my imaginary friends;
my friends at Writers House,
Genevieve Gagne-Hawes, for giving me that first chance,
and my agent Jodi Reamer, for turning the most
unlikely dreams into realities;
my editor Megan Tingley, for all her help in
making *Twilight* better than it started out;
my brothers, Paul and Jacob, for their expert advice on all
my automotive questions; and my online family,
the talented staff and writers at fansofrealitytv.com,
particularly Kimberly "Shazzer," and Collin "Mantenna"
for the encouragement, advice,
and inspiration.

Here's a sneak peek at

NEW MOON,

the irresistible sequel to *Twilight*.

PREFACE

I FELT LIKE I WAS TRAPPED IN ONE OF THOSE TERRIFYING nightmares, the one where you have to run, run till your lungs burst, but you can't make your body move fast enough. My legs seemed to move slower and slower as I fought my way through the callous crowd, but the hands on the huge clock tower didn't slow. With relentless, uncaring force, they turned inexorably toward the end—the end of everything.

But this was no dream, and, unlike the nightmare, I wasn't running for *my* life; I was racing to save something infinitely more precious. My own life meant little to me today.

Alice had said there was a good chance we would both

die here. Perhaps the outcome would be different if she weren't trapped by the brilliant sunlight; only I was free to run across this bright, crowded square.

And I couldn't run fast enough.

So it didn't matter to me that we were surrounded by our extraordinarily dangerous enemies. As the clock began to toll out the hour, vibrating under the soles of my sluggish feet, I knew I was too late—and I was glad something bloodthirsty waited in the wings. For in failing at this, I forfeited any desire to live.

The clock tolled again, and the sun beat down from the exact center point of the sky.

1. PARTY

I WAS NINETY-NINE POINT NINE PERCENT SURE I WAS
dreaming.

The reasons I was so certain were that, first, I was
standing in a bright shaft of sunlight—the kind of blinding clear sun that never shone on my drizzly new hometown in Forks, Washington—and second, I was looking at
my Grandma Marie. Gran had been dead for six years now,
so that was solid evidence toward the dream theory.

Gran hadn't changed much; her face looked just the
same as I remembered it. The skin was soft and withered,
bent into a thousand tiny creases that clung gently to the
bone underneath. Like a dried apricot, but with a puff of
thick white hair standing out in a cloud around it.

Our mouths—hers a wizened pucker—spread into the same surprised half-smile at just the same time. Apparently, she hadn't been expecting to see me, either.

I was about to ask her a question; I had so many—What was she doing here in my dream? What had she been up to in the past six years? Was Pop okay, and had they found each other, wherever they were?—but she opened her mouth when I did, so I stopped to let her go first. She paused, too, and then we both smiled at the little awkwardness.

"Bella?"

It wasn't Gran who called my name, and we both turned to see the addition to our small reunion. I didn't have to look to know who it was; this was a voice I would know anywhere—know, and respond to, whether I was awake or asleep . . . or even dead, I'd bet. The voice I'd walk through fire for—or, less dramatically, slosh every day through the cold and endless rain for.

Edward.

Even though I was always thrilled to see him—conscious or otherwise—and even though I was *almost* positive that I was dreaming, I panicked as Edward walked toward us through the glaring sunlight.

I panicked because Gran didn't know that I was in love with a vampire—nobody knew that—so how was I supposed to explain the fact that the brilliant sunbeams were shattering off his skin into a thousand rainbow shards like he was made of crystal or diamond?

Well, Gran, you might have noticed that my boyfriend glitters. It's just something he does in the sun. Don't worry about it. . . .

What was he *doing?* The whole reason he lived in Forks, the rainiest place in the world, was so that he could be outside in the daytime without exposing his family's secret. Yet here he was, strolling gracefully toward me— with the most beautiful smile on his angel's face—as if I were the only one here.

In that second, I wished that I was not the one exception to his mysterious talent; I usually felt grateful that I was the only person whose thoughts he couldn't hear just as clearly as if they were spoken aloud. But now I wished he could hear me, too, so that he could hear the warning I was screaming in my head.

I shot a panicked glance back at Gran, and saw that it was too late. She was just turning to stare back at me, her eyes as alarmed as mine.

Edward—still smiling so beautifully that my heart felt like it was going to swell up and burst through my chest—put his arm around my shoulder and turned to face my grandmother.

Gran's expression surprised me. Instead of looking horrified, she was staring at me sheepishly, as if waiting for a scolding. And she was standing in such a strange position— one arm held awkwardly away from her body, stretched out and then curled around the air. Like she had her arm around someone I couldn't see, someone invisible . . .

Only then, as I looked at the bigger picture, did I notice the huge gilt frame that enclosed my grandmother's form. Uncomprehending, I raised the hand that wasn't wrapped around Edward's waist and reached out to touch her. She mimicked the movement exactly, mirrored it. But where our fingers should have met, there was nothing but cold glass . . .

With a dizzying jolt, my dream abruptly became a nightmare.

There was no Gran.

That was *me*. Me in a mirror. Me—ancient, creased, and withered.

Edward stood beside me, casting no reflection, excruciatingly lovely and forever seventeen.

He pressed his icy, perfect lips against my wasted cheek.

"Happy birthday," he whispered.

I woke with a start—my eyelids popping open wide—and gasped. Dull gray light, the familiar light of an overcast morning, took the place of the blinding sun in my dream.

Just a dream, I told myself. *It was only a dream.* I took a deep breath, and then jumped again when my alarm went off. The little calendar in the corner of the clock's display informed me that today was September thirteenth.

Only a dream, but prophetic enough in one way, at least. Today was my birthday. I was officially eighteen years old.

I'd been dreading this day for months.

All through the perfect summer—the happiest summer I had ever had, the happiest summer *anyone anywhere* had ever had, and the rainiest summer in the history of the Olympic Peninsula—this bleak date had lurked in ambush, waiting to spring.

And now that it had hit, it was even worse than I'd feared it would be. I could feel it—I was older. Every day

I got older, but this was different, worse, quantifiable. I was eighteen.

And Edward never would be.

When I went to brush my teeth, I was almost surprised that the face in the mirror hadn't changed. I stared at myself, looking for some sign of impending wrinkles in my ivory skin. The only creases were the ones on my forehead, though, and I knew that if I could manage to relax, they would disappear. I couldn't. My eyebrows stayed lodged in a worried line over my anxious brown eyes.

It was just a dream, I reminded myself again. Just a dream . . . but also my worst nightmare.

I skipped breakfast, in a hurry to get out of the house as quickly as possible. I wasn't entirely able to avoid my dad, and so I had to spend a few minutes acting cheerful. I honestly tried to be excited about the gifts I'd asked him not to get me, but every time I had to smile, it felt like I might start crying.

I struggled to get a grip on myself as I drove to school. The vision of Gran—I would *not* think of it as me—was hard to get out of my head. I couldn't feel anything but despair until I pulled into the familiar parking lot behind Forks High School and spotted Edward leaning motionlessly against his polished silver Volvo, like a marble tribute to some forgotten pagan god of beauty. The dream had not done him justice. And he was waiting there for *me,* just the same as every other day.

Despair momentarily vanished; wonder took its place. Even after half a year with him, I still couldn't believe that I deserved this degree of good fortune.

His sister Alice was standing by his side, waiting for me, too.

Of course Edward and Alice weren't really related (in Forks the story was that all the Cullen siblings were adopted by Dr. Carlisle Cullen and his wife, Esme, both plainly too young to have teenage children), but their skin was precisely the same pale shade, their eyes had the same strange golden tint, with the same deep, bruise-like shadows beneath them. Her face, like his, was also startlingly beautiful. To someone in the know—someone like me—these similarities marked them for what they were.

The sight of Alice waiting there—her tawny eyes brilliant with excitement, and a small silver-wrapped square in her hands—made me frown. I'd told Alice I didn't want anything, *anything,* not gifts or even attention, for my birthday. Obviously, my wishes were being ignored.

I slammed the door of my '53 Chevy truck—a shower of rust specks fluttered down to the wet blacktop—and walked slowly toward where they waited. Alice skipped forward to meet me, her pixie face glowing under her spiky black hair.

"Happy birthday, Bella!"

"Shh!" I hissed, glancing around the lot to make sure no one had heard her. The last thing I wanted was some kind of celebration of the black event.

She ignored me. "Do you want to open your present now or later?" she asked eagerly as we made our way to where Edward still waited.

"No presents," I protested in a mumble.

She finally seemed to process my mood. "Okay . . .

later, then. Did you like the scrapbook your mom sent you? And the camera from Charlie?"

I sighed. Of course she would know what my birthday presents were. Edward wasn't the only member of his family with unusual skills. Alice would have "seen" what my parents were planning as soon as they'd decided that themselves.

"Yeah. They're great."

"*I* think it's a nice idea. You're only a senior once. Might as well document the experience."

"How many times have *you* been a senior?"

"That's different."

We reached Edward then, and he held out his hand for mine. I took it eagerly, forgetting, for a moment, my glum mood. His skin was, as always, smooth, hard, and very cold. He gave my fingers a gentle squeeze. I looked into his liquid topaz eyes, and my heart gave a not-quite-so-gentle squeeze of its own. Hearing the stutter in my heartbeats, he smiled again.

He lifted his free hand and traced one cool fingertip around the outside of my lips as he spoke. "So, as discussed, I am not allowed to wish you a happy birthday, is that correct?"

"Yes. That is correct." I could never quite mimic the flow of his perfect, formal articulation. It was something that could only be picked up in an earlier century.

"Just checking." He ran his hand through his tousled bronze hair. "You *might* have changed your mind. Most people seem to enjoy things like birthdays and gifts."

Alice laughed, and the sound was all silver, a wind

chime. "Of course you'll enjoy it. Everyone is supposed to be nice to you today and give you your way, Bella. What's the worst that could happen?" She meant it as a rhetorical question.

"Getting older," I answered anyway, and my voice was not as steady as I wanted it to be.

Beside me, Edward's smile tightened into a hard line.

"Eighteen isn't very old," Alice said. "Don't women usually wait till they're twenty-nine to get upset over birthdays?"

"It's older than Edward," I mumbled.

He sighed.

"Technically," she said, keeping her tone light. "Just by one little year, though."

And I supposed . . . if I could be *sure* of the future I wanted, sure that I would get to spend forever with Edward, and Alice and the rest of the Cullens (preferably not as a wrinkled little old lady) . . . then a year or two one direction or the other wouldn't matter to me so much. But Edward was dead set against any future that changed me. Any future that made me like him—that made me immortal, too.

An impasse, he called it.

I couldn't really see Edward's point, to be honest. What was so great about mortality? Being a vampire didn't look like such a terrible thing—not the way the Cullens did it, anyway.

"What time will you be at the house?" Alice continued, changing the subject. From her expression, she was up to exactly the kind of thing I'd been hoping to avoid.

"I didn't know I had plans to be there."

"Oh, be fair, Bella!" she complained. "You aren't going to ruin all our fun like that, are you?"

"I thought my birthday was about what *I* want."

"I'll get her from Charlie's right after school," Edward told her, ignoring me altogether.

"I have to work," I protested.

"You don't, actually," Alice told me smugly. "I already spoke to Mrs. Newton about it. She's trading your shifts. She said to tell you 'Happy Birthday.'"

"I—I still can't come over," I stammered, scrambling for an excuse. "I, well, I haven't watched *Romeo and Juliet* yet for English."

Alice snorted. "You have *Romeo and Juliet* memorized."

"But Mr. Berty said we needed to see it performed to fully appreciate it—that's how Shakespeare intended it to be presented."

Edward rolled his eyes.

"You've already seen the movie," Alice accused.

"But not the nineteen-sixties version. Mr. Berty said it was the best."

Finally, Alice lost the smug smile and glared at me. "This can be easy, or this can be hard, Bella, but one way or the other—"

Edward interrupted her threat. "Relax, Alice. If Bella wants to watch a movie, then she can. It's her birthday."

"So there," I added.

"I'll bring her over around seven," he continued. "That will give you more time to set up."

Alice's laughter chimed again. "Sounds good. See you tonight, Bella! It'll be fun, you'll see." She grinned—the wide smile exposed all her perfect, glistening teeth—then pecked me on the cheek and danced off toward her first class before I could respond.

"Edward, please—" I started to beg, but he pressed one cool finger to my lips.

"Let's discuss it later. We're going to be late for class."

No one bothered to stare at us as we took our usual seats in the back of the classroom (we had almost every class together now—it was amazing the favors Edward could get the female administrators to do for him). Edward and I had been together too long now to be an object of gossip anymore. Even Mike Newton didn't bother to give me the glum stare that used to make me feel a little guilty. He smiled now instead, and I was glad he seemed to have accepted that we could only be friends. Mike had changed over the summer— his face had lost some of the roundness, making his cheekbones more prominent, and he was wearing his pale blond hair a new way; instead of bristly, it was longer and gelled into a carefully casual disarray. It was easy to see where his inspiration came from—but Edward's look wasn't something that could be achieved through imitation.

As the day progressed, I considered ways to get out of whatever was going down at the Cullen house tonight. It would be bad enough to have to celebrate when I was in the mood to mourn. But, worse than that, this was sure to involve attention and gifts.

Attention is never a good thing, as any other accident-prone klutz would agree. No one wants a spotlight when they're likely to fall on their face.

And I'd very pointedly asked—well, ordered really—

that no one give me any presents this year. It looked like Charlie and Renée weren't the only ones who had decided to overlook that.

I'd never had much money, and that had never bothered me. Renée had raised me on a kindergarten teacher's salary. Charlie wasn't getting rich at his job, either—he was the police chief here in the tiny town of Forks. My only personal income came from the three days a week I worked at the local sporting goods store. In a town this small, I was lucky to have a job. Every penny I made went into my microscopic college fund. (College was Plan B. I was still hoping for Plan A, but Edward was just so stubborn about leaving me human. . . .)

Edward had a *lot* of money—I didn't even want to think about how much. Money meant next to nothing to Edward or the rest of the Cullens. It was just something that accumulated when you had unlimited time on your hands and a sister who had an uncanny ability to predict trends in the stock market. Edward didn't seem to understand why I objected to him spending money on me— why it made me uncomfortable if he took me to an expensive restaurant in Seattle, why he wasn't allowed to buy me a car that could reach speeds over fifty-five miles an hour, or why I wouldn't let him pay my college tuition (he was ridiculously enthusiastic about Plan B). Edward thought I was being unnecessarily difficult.

But how could I let him give me things when I had nothing to reciprocate with? He, for some unfathomable reason, wanted to be with me. Anything he gave me on top of that just threw us more out of balance.

As the day went on, neither Edward nor Alice brought my birthday up again, and I began to relax a little.

We sat at our usual table for lunch.

A strange kind of truce existed at that table. The three of us—Edward, Alice, and I—sat on the extreme southern end of the table. Now that the "older" and somewhat scarier (in Emmett's case, certainly) Cullen siblings had graduated, Alice and Edward did not seem quite so intimidating, and we did not sit here alone. My other friends, Mike and Jessica (who were in the awkward post-breakup friendship phase), Angela and Ben (whose relationship had survived the summer), Eric, Conner, Tyler, and Lauren (though that last one didn't really count in the friend category) all sat at the same table, on the other side of an invisible line. That line dissolved on sunny days when Edward and Alice always skipped school, and then the conversation would swell out effortlessly to include me.

Edward and Alice didn't find this minor ostracism odd or hurtful the way I would have. They barely noticed it. People always felt strangely ill at ease with the Cullens, almost afraid for some reason they couldn't explain to themselves. I was a rare exception to that rule. Sometimes it bothered Edward how very comfortable I was with being close to him. He thought he was hazardous to my health— an opinion I rejected vehemently whenever he voiced it.

The afternoon passed quickly. School ended, and Edward walked me to my truck as he usually did. But this time, he held the passenger door open for me. Alice must have been taking his car home so that he could keep me from making a run for it.

I folded my arms and made no move to get out of the rain. "It's my birthday, don't I get to drive?"

"I'm pretending it's not your birthday, just as you wished."

"If it's not my birthday, then I don't have to go to your house tonight . . ."

"All right." He shut the passenger door and walked past me to open the driver's side. "Happy birthday."

"Shh," I shushed him halfheartedly. I climbed in the opened door, wishing he'd taken the other offer.

Edward played with the radio while I drove, shaking his head in disapproval.

"Your radio has horrible reception."

I frowned. I didn't like it when he picked on my truck. The truck was great—it had personality.

"You want a nice stereo? Drive your own car." I was so nervous about Alice's plans, on top of my already gloomy mood, that the words came out sharper than I'd meant them. I was hardly ever bad-tempered with Edward, and my tone made him press his lips together to keep from smiling.

When I parked in front of Charlie's house, he reached over to take my face in his hands. He handled me very carefully, pressing just the tips of his fingers softly against my temples, my cheekbones, my jawline. Like I was especially breakable. Which was exactly the case—compared with him, at least.

"You should be in a good mood, today of all days," he whispered. His sweet breath fanned across my face.

"And if I don't want to be in a good mood?" I asked, my breathing uneven.

His golden eyes smoldered. "Too bad."

My head was already spinning by the time he leaned closer and pressed his icy lips against mine. As he intended, no doubt, I forgot all about my worries, and concentrated on remembering how to inhale and exhale.

His mouth lingered on mine, cold and smooth and gentle, until I wrapped my arms around his neck and threw myself into the kiss with a little too much enthusiasm. I could feel his lips curve upward as he let go of my face and reached back to unlock my grip on him.

Edward had drawn many careful lines for our physical relationship, with the intent being to keep me alive. Though I respected the need for maintaining a safe distance between my skin and his razor-sharp, venom-coated teeth, I tended to forget about trivial things like that when he was kissing me.

"Be good, please," he breathed against my cheek. He pressed his lips gently to mine one more time and then pulled away, folding my arms across my stomach.

My pulse was thudding in my ears. I put one hand over my heart. It drummed hyperactively under my palm.

"Do you think I'll ever get better at this?" I wondered, mostly to myself. "That my heart might someday stop trying to jump out of my chest whenever you touch me?"

"I really hope not," he said, a bit smug.

I rolled my eyes. "Let's go watch the Capulets and Montagues hack each other up, all right?"

"Your wish, my command."

Edward sprawled across the couch while I started the movie, fast-forwarding through the opening credits.

When I perched on the edge of the sofa in front of him, he wrapped his arms around my waist and pulled me against his chest. It wasn't exactly as comfortable as a sofa cushion would be, what with his chest being hard and cold—and perfect—as an ice sculpture, but it was definitely preferable. He pulled the old afghan off the back of the couch and draped it over me so I wouldn't freeze beside his body.

"You know, I've never had much patience with Romeo," he commented as the movie started.

"What's wrong with Romeo?" I asked, a little offended. Romeo was one of my favorite fictional characters. Until I'd met Edward, I'd sort of had a thing for him.

"Well, first of all, he's in love with this Rosaline— don't you think it makes him seem a little fickle? And then, a few minutes after their wedding, he kills Juliet's cousin. That's not very brilliant. Mistake after mistake. Could he have destroyed his own happiness any more thoroughly?"

I sighed. "Do you want me to watch this alone?"

"No, I'll mostly be watching you, anyway." His fingers traced patterns across the skin of my arm, raising goose bumps. "Will you cry?"

"Probably," I admitted, "if I'm paying attention."

"I won't distract you then." But I felt his lips on my hair, and it was very distracting.

The movie eventually captured my interest, thanks in large part to Edward whispering Romeo's lines in my ear— his irresistible, velvet voice made the actor's voice sound weak and coarse by comparison. And I did cry, to his amusement, when Juliet woke and found her new husband dead.

"I'll admit, I do sort of envy him here," Edward said, drying the tears with a lock of my hair.

"She's very pretty."

He made a disgusted sound. "I don't envy him the *girl*—just the ease of the suicide," he clarified in a teasing tone. "You humans have it so easy! All you have to do is throw down one tiny vial of plant extracts. . . ."

"What?" I gasped.

"It's something I had to think about once, and I knew from Carlisle's experience that it wouldn't be simple. I'm not even sure how many ways Carlisle tried to kill himself in the beginning . . . after he realized what he'd become. . . ." His voice, which had grown serious, turned light again. "And he's clearly still in excellent health."

I twisted around so that I could read his face. "What are you talking about?" I demanded. "What do you mean, this something you had to think about once?"

"Last spring, when you were . . . nearly killed . . ." He paused to take a deep breath, struggling to return to his teasing tone. "Of course I was trying to focus on finding you alive, but part of my mind was making contingency plans. Like I said, it's not as easy for me as it is for a human."

For one second, the memory of my last trip to Phoenix washed through my head and made me feel dizzy. I could see it all so clearly—the blinding sun, the heat waves coming off the concrete as I ran with desperate haste to find the sadistic vampire who wanted to torture me to death. James, waiting in the mirrored room with my mother as his hostage—or so I'd thought. I hadn't known it was all a ruse. Just as James hadn't known that Edward was racing to save me; Edward made it in time, but it had been a close one. Unthinkingly, my fingers traced the crescent-shaped scar on my hand that was always just a few degrees cooler than the rest of my skin.

I shook my head—as if I could shake away the bad memories—and tried to grasp what Edward meant. My stomach plunged uncomfortably. "Contingency plans?" I repeated.

"Well, I wasn't going to live without you." He rolled his eyes as if that fact were childishly obvious. "But I wasn't sure how to *do* it—I knew Emmett and Jasper would never help . . . so I was thinking maybe I would go to Italy and do something to provoke the Volturi."

I didn't want to believe he was serious, but his golden eyes were brooding, focused on something far away in the distance as he contemplated ways to end his own life. Abruptly, I was furious.

"What is a *Volturi?*" I demanded.

"The Volturi are a family," he explained, his eyes still remote. "A very old, very powerful family of our kind. They are the closest thing our world has to a royal family, I suppose. Carlisle lived with them briefly in his early years, in Italy, before he settled in America—do you remember the story?"

"Of course I remember."

I would never forget the first time I'd gone to his home, the huge white mansion buried deep in the forest beside the river, or the room where Carlisle—Edward's father in so many real ways—kept a wall of paintings that illustrated his personal history. The most vivid, most wildly colorful canvas there, the largest, was from Carlisle's time in Italy. Of course I remembered the calm quartet of men, each with the exquisite face of a seraph, painted into the highest balcony overlooking the swirling mayhem of color. Though the painting was centuries old, Carlisle—the blond angel—remained unchanged. And I remembered the three others, Carlisle's early acquaintances. Edward had never used the name *Volturi* for the beautiful trio, two black-haired, one snow white. He'd called them Aro, Caius, and Marcus, nighttime patrons of the arts. . . .

"Anyway, you don't irritate the Volturi," Edward went on, interrupting my reverie. "Not unless you want to die—or whatever it is we do." His voice was so calm, it made him sound almost bored by the prospect.

My anger turned to horror. I took his marble face between my hands and held it very tightly.

"You must never, never, never think of anything like that again!" I said. "No matter what might ever happen to me, you are *not allowed* to hurt yourself!"

"I'll never put you in danger again, so it's a moot point."

"*Put* me in danger! I thought we'd established that all the bad luck is my fault?" I was getting angrier. "How dare you even think like that?" The idea of Edward ceasing to exist, even if I were dead, was impossibly painful.

"What would you do, if the situation were reversed?" he asked.

"That's not the same thing."

He didn't seem to understand the difference. He chuckled.

"What if something did happen to you?" I blanched at the thought. "Would you want me to go *off* myself?"

A trace of pain touched his perfect features.

"I guess I see your point . . . a little," he admitted. "But what would I do without you?"

"Whatever you were doing before I came along and complicated your existence."

He sighed. "You make that sound so easy."

"It should be. I'm not really that interesting."

He was about to argue, but then he let it go. "Moot point," he reminded me. Abruptly, he pulled himself up into a more formal posture, shifting me to the side so that we were no longer touching.

"Charlie?" I guessed.

Edward smiled. After a moment, I heard the sound of the police cruiser pulling into the driveway. I reached out and took his hand firmly. My dad could deal with that much.

Charlie came in with a pizza box in his hands.

"Hey, kids." He grinned at me. "I thought you'd like a break from cooking and washing dishes for your birthday. Hungry?"

"Sure. Thanks, Dad."

Charlie didn't comment on Edward's apparent lack of appetite. He was used to Edward passing on dinner.

"Do you mind if I borrow Bella for the evening?" Edward asked when Charlie and I were done.

I looked at Charlie hopefully. Maybe he had some concept of birthdays as stay-at-home, family affairs—this was my first birthday with him, the first birthday since my mom, Renée, had remarried and gone to live in Florida, so I didn't know what he would expect.

"That's fine—the Mariners are playing the Sox tonight," Charlie explained, and my hope disappeared. "So I won't be any kind of company. . . . Here." He scooped up the camera he'd gotten me on Renée's suggestion (because I would need pictures to fill up my scrapbook), and threw it to me.

He ought to know better than that—I'd always been coordinationally challenged. The camera glanced off the tip of my finger, and tumbled toward the floor. Edward snagged it before it could crash onto the linoleum.

"Nice save," Charlie noted. "If they're doing something fun at the Cullens' tonight, Bella, you should take some pictures. You know how your mother gets—she'll be wanting to see the pictures faster than you can take them."

"Good idea, Charlie," Edward said, handing me the camera.

I turned the camera on Edward, and snapped the first picture. "It works."

"That's good. Hey, say hi to Alice for me. She hasn't been over in a while." Charlie's mouth pulled down at one corner.

"It's been three days, Dad," I reminded him. Charlie was crazy about Alice. He'd become attached last spring when she'd helped me through my awkward convalescence; Charlie would be forever grateful to her for saving him from the horror of an almost-adult daughter who needed help showering. "I'll tell her."

"Okay. You kids have fun tonight." It was clearly a dismissal. Charlie was already edging toward the living room and the TV.

Edward smiled, triumphant, and took my hand to pull me from the kitchen.

When we got to the truck, he opened the passenger door for me again, and this time I didn't argue. I still had a hard time finding the obscure turnoff to his house in the dark.

Edward drove north through Forks, visibly chafing at the speed limit enforced by my prehistoric Chevy. The engine groaned even louder than usual as he pushed it over fifty.

"Take it easy," I warned him.

"You know what you would love? A nice little Audi coupe. Very quiet, lots of power . . ."

"There's nothing wrong with my truck. And speaking of expensive nonessentials, if you know what's good for you, you didn't spend any money on birthday presents."

"Not a dime," he said virtuously.

"Good."

"Can you do me a favor?"

"That depends on what it is."

He sighed, his lovely face serious. "Bella, the last real birthday any of us had was Emmett in 1935. Cut us a little slack, and don't be too difficult tonight. They're all very excited."

It always startled me a little when he brought up things like that. "Fine, I'll behave."

"I probably should warn you . . ."

"Please do."

"When I say they're all excited . . . I do mean *all* of them."

"Everyone?" I choked. "I thought Emmett and Rosalie were in Africa." The rest of Forks was under the impression that the older Cullens had gone off to college this year, to Dartmouth, but I knew better.

"Emmett wanted to be here."

"But . . . Rosalie?"

"I know, Bella. Don't worry, she'll be on her best behavior."

I didn't answer. Like I could just *not* worry, that easy. Unlike Alice, Edward's other "adopted" sister, the golden blond and exquisite Rosalie, didn't like me much. Actually, the feeling was a little bit stronger than just dislike. As far as Rosalie was concerned, I was an unwelcome intruder into her family's secret life.

I felt horribly guilty about the present situation, guessing that Rosalie and Emmett's prolonged absence was my fault, even as I furtively enjoyed not having to see her. Emmett, Edward's playful bear of a brother, I *did* miss. He was in many ways just like the big brother I'd always wanted . . . only much, much more terrifying.

Edward decided to change the subject. "So, if you won't let me get you the Audi, isn't there anything that you'd like for your birthday?"

The words came out in a whisper. "You know what I want."

A deep frown carved creases into his marble forehead. He obviously wished he'd stuck to the subject of Rosalie.

It felt like we'd had this argument a lot today.

"Not tonight, Bella. Please."

"Well, maybe Alice will give me what I want."

Edward growled—a deep, menacing sound. "This isn't going to be your last birthday, Bella," he vowed.

"That's not fair!"

I thought I heard his teeth clench together.

We were pulling up to the house now. Bright light shined from every window on the first two floors. A long line of glowing Japanese lanterns hung from the porch eaves, reflecting a soft radiance on the huge cedars that surrounded the house. Big bowls of flowers—pink roses—lined the wide stairs up to the front doors.

I moaned.

Edward took a few deep breaths to calm himself. "This is a party," he reminded me. "Try to be a good sport."

"Sure," I muttered.

He came around to get my door, and offered me his hand.

"I have a question."

He waited warily.

"If I develop this film," I said, toying with the camera in my hands, "will you show up in the picture?"

Edward started laughing. He helped me out of the car, pulled me up the stairs, and was still laughing as he opened the door for me.

They were all waiting in the huge white living room; when I walked through the door, they greeted me with a loud chorus of "Happy birthday, Bella!" while I blushed and looked down. Alice, I assumed, had covered every flat surface with pink candles and dozens of crystal bowls filled with hundreds of roses. There was a table with a white cloth draped over it next to Edward's grand piano, holding a pink birthday cake, more roses, a stack of glass plates, and a small pile of silver-wrapped presents.

It was a hundred times worse than I'd imagined.

Edward, sensing my distress, wrapped an encouraging arm around my waist and kissed the top of my head.

Edward's parents, Carlisle and Esme—impossibly youthful and lovely as ever—were the closest to the door. Esme hugged me carefully, her soft, caramel-colored hair brushing against my cheek as she kissed my forehead, and then Carlisle put his arm around my shoulders.

"Sorry about this, Bella," he stage-whispered. "We couldn't rein Alice in."

Rosalie and Emmett stood behind them. Rosalie didn't smile, but at least she didn't glare. Emmett's face was stretched into a huge grin. It had been months since I'd seen them; I'd forgotten how gloriously beautiful Rosalie was—it almost hurt to look at her. And had Emmett always been so . . . *big?*

"You haven't changed at all," Emmett said with mock disappointment. "I expected a perceptible difference, but here you are, red-faced just like always."

"Thanks a lot, Emmett," I said, blushing deeper.

He laughed, "I have to step out for a second"—he paused to wink conspicuously at Alice—"Don't do anything funny while I'm gone."

"I'll try."

Alice let go of Jasper's hand and skipped forward, all her teeth sparkling in the bright light. Jasper smiled, too, but kept his distance. He leaned, long and blond, against the post at the foot of the stairs. During the days we'd had to spend cooped up together in Phoenix, I'd thought he'd gotten over his aversion to me. But he'd gone back to exactly how he'd acted before—avoiding me as much as possible—

the moment he was free from that temporary obligation to protect me. I knew it wasn't personal, just a precaution, and I tried not to be overly sensitive about it. Jasper had more trouble sticking to the Cullens' diet than the rest of them; the scent of human blood was much harder for him to resist than the others—he hadn't been trying as long.

"Time to open presents," Alice declared. She put her cool hand under my elbow and towed me to the table with the cake and the shiny packages.

I put on my best martyr face. "Alice, I know I told you I didn't want anything—"

"But I didn't listen," she interrupted, smug. "Open it." She took the camera from my hands and replaced it with a big, square silver box.

The box was so light that it felt empty. The tag on top said that it was from Emmett, Rosalie, and Jasper. Self-consciously, I tore the paper off and then stared at the box it concealed.

It was something electrical, with lots of numbers in the name. I opened the box, hoping for further illumination. But the box *was* empty.

"Um . . . thanks."

Rosalie actually cracked a smile. Jasper laughed. "It's a stereo for your truck," he explained. "Emmett's installing it right now so that you can't return it."

Alice was always one step ahead of me.

"Thanks, Jasper, Rosalie," I told them, grinning as I remembered Edward's complaints about my radio this afternoon—all a setup, apparently. "Thanks, Emmett!" I called more loudly.

I heard his booming laugh from my truck, and I couldn't help laughing, too.

"Open mine and Edward's next," Alice said, so excited her voice was a high-pitched trill. She held a small, flat square in her hand.

I turned to give Edward a basilisk glare. "You promised."

Before he could answer, Emmett bounded through the door. "Just in time!" he crowed. He pushed in behind Jasper, who had also drifted closer than usual to get a good look.

"I didn't spend a dime," Edward assured me. He brushed a strand of hair from my face, leaving my skin tingling from his touch.

I inhaled deeply and turned to Alice. "Give it to me," I sighed.

Emmett chuckled with delight.

I took the little package, rolling my eyes at Edward while I stuck my finger under the edge of the paper and jerked it under the tape.

"Shoot," I muttered when the paper sliced my finger; I pulled it out to examine the damage. A single drop of blood oozed from the tiny cut.

It all happened very quickly then.

"No!" Edward roared.

He threw himself at me, flinging me back across the table. It fell, as I did, scattering the cake and the presents, the flowers and the plates. I landed in the mess of shattered crystal.

Jasper slammed into Edward, and the sound was like the crash of boulders in a rock slide.

There was another noise, a grisly snarling that seemed to be coming from deep in Jasper's chest. Jasper tried to shove past Edward, snapping his teeth just inches from Edward's face.

Emmett grabbed Jasper from behind in the next second, locking him into his massive steel grip, but Jasper struggled on, his wild, empty eyes focused only on me.

Beyond the shock, there was also pain. I'd tumbled down to the floor by the piano, with my arms thrown out instinctively to catch my fall, into the jagged shards of glass. Only now did I feel the searing, stinging pain that ran from my wrist to the crease inside my elbow.

Dazed and disoriented, I looked up from the bright red blood pulsing out of my arm—into the fevered eyes of the six suddenly ravenous vampires.

Twilight Discussion Questions

1. Is the fact that Edward can't read Bella's thoughts more important than it seems? Do you think it will it serve a larger purpose?

2. Bella faints at the smell of blood. If she were to become a vampire, how might this serve as a hindrance? How might it be an asset?

3. Is Edward selfishly putting Bella in danger, or is Bella being too stubborn for her own good? Is it a little bit of both? What are the threatening factors facing Bella and are there ways to avoid them?

4. Temptation is a major theme in Twilight—more accurately, resisting one's temptations. Discuss the subplot of Carlisle's job as a doctor in relation to this major theme. How well does he handle temptation? What do you feel would be the most difficult part for him in his role? Why does he remain working as a doctor when the Cullens don't seem to need his income?

5. The Cullens live, act, and care for one another as a family. How much of their ability to do so is dependant on Carlisle's rule that they live in a manner that contradicts their nature—hunting animals instead of humans? Do you think that they would be able to maintain their bond if they weren't all committed to his plan?

6. Edward saves Bella on more than one occasion. Discuss the different instances and how Bella reacts before she knows what he is and after. Also discuss how Edward reacts after each instance both before and after she learns he is a vampire.

7. Alice explains to Bella the theory of how vampires come to exist. She mentions that most have some memories of the transition and their life prior to it. How does what we learn from James about Alice's past explain her lack of memory?

8. Once Edward has tasted Bella's blood, do you think it will make it harder to resist Bella—specifically her blood? Will the fact that he is able to control himself make Bella want to be changed into a vampire? Do you think that it is fair of her to ask that of him? Do you think it is fair of him to refuse?

9. Jacob Black tells Bella a story about his tribe and the "cold ones." He doesn't believe any of it but says his father clearly dislikes the Cullens. If Jacob's father believes the Cullens are dangerous, why doesn't he warn Bella or Jacob? Is he hiding a secret of his own?

10. Stephenie Meyer has noted that each of the novels in the Twilight Saga pays homage to other literary classics. For *Twilight*, she has said *Pride and Prejudice* was the key inspiration. *Pride and Prejudice* is often described as a "romantic comedy." What parts of *Twilight* are romantic? What parts are comic? Describe the similarities between Elizabeth Bennet and Bella Swan, Fitzwilliam Darcy and Edward Cullen. What role would Bella's friends play in a "remake" of Jane Austen's classic story?

Are You Thirsty for More?

twilight:
the complete illustrated movie companion

This lavishly illustrated edition is an exclusive behind-the-scenes guide featuring full-color photos of the cast, locations and sets, as well as storyboards, interviews, and more.

Available November 2008

the twilight saga: the official guide

You may think you already know everything there is to know about the Twilight Saga, but this essential edition will put your knowledge to the test! With character profiles, genealogical charts, maps, extensive cross-references, never-before-read scenes deleted from the original books, and much more, this comprehensive handbook is a must-have.

Available December 30, 2008